FROM NO WHERE

ALSO BY JEWEL E. ANN

The Wildfire Series

From Air

FROM NO WHERE

JEWEL E. ANN

This is a work of fiction. Names, characters, organizations, places, events, and incidents are either products of the author's imagination or are used fictitiously. Otherwise, any resemblance to actual persons, living or dead, is purely coincidental.

Published by Montlake, Seattle

www.apub.com

ISBN-13: 9781662523663 (paperback)
ISBN-13: 9781662523656 (digital)

Cover design by Hang Le
Cover photography © Regina Wamba
Cover image: © Rexjaymes / Shutterstock; © Landscape Hero / Shutterstock

Printed in the United States of America

For my dad, the hardest-working man I will ever know

Chapter One

OZZY

"If you want to have sex again before you die, I'm okay with it."

I nearly fall off my bike.

Lola is ten going on twenty. Sex shouldn't be in my daughter's vocabulary.

She stands so her skinny legs can pump the pedals to get in front of me, curly blond hair flowing in the breeze over her worn coral-and-blue Patagonia backpack. It belonged to her mom, just like everything else about our daughter. She's Brynn's mini-me: expressive blue eyes, ornery dimpled cheeks, beaming smile, and infectious laugh that I feel in my chest.

"What do you know about sex? Never mind. Let me rephrase that. What made you say that to me? Did Nana or Pa mention something?" I ride alongside her when the cracked sidewalk widens as we bike through an affluent neighborhood. We might hit record-high temperatures again today, with no breeze and a cloudless sky. Spring in Missoula feels like summer this year, and we need rain.

"Yum. Smell that?" Lola inhales. "Doughnuts. Can we stop?" She's changing the subject, but I'm okay with not talking about my sex life.

"No. You had breakfast. You'll be late to school, and I'll be late to work."

"I'll eat it on the way."

"You can't eat while riding your bike."

Lola stretches her arms out like an eagle, riding with no hands.

Show-off.

Then she takes a right into the parking lot as if it's a foregone conclusion that I will say yes. *Dang it!* I smell it, too: sweet cinnamon-apple fritters. She's right; we're buying doughnuts.

"I'm getting glazed chocolate." She hangs her neon-pink helmet from the handlebar and skips into the shop.

I'm in over my head with this girl. By the time I grumble my grievances over losing control of my child, she's at the counter ordering for us.

The wiry-haired brunette shoots me a half grin while smacking her gum. "That'll be seven dollars."

I dig out my wallet and deposit a ten on the counter beside some crumbs.

"Are you married?" Lola asks the lady.

"No. Why?" She hands Lola the change, and my generous daughter stuffs all three bills into the tip jar.

"You should go on a date with my dad."

This isn't happening. Very few things embarrass me, but this sends flames to my cheeks.

"Sorry. My daughter hit her head yesterday." I yank Lola by her backpack away from the counter while offering a stiff smile to the employee bagging our doughnuts. Given the permanent scars on Lola's forehead and right cheek, I'm sure this lady doesn't get my head-injury humor. Still, after a beat, she blushes as well.

Does Lola know this is the last time we will visit her favorite doughnut joint? Because it is.

Lola wriggles out of my hold and turns toward me with a crinkled nose, which makes the horizontal scar below her eye disappear. "I didn't hit my head," she says.

"Oh dear. You don't even remember," I say. "I think we'll have to get it checked out. I hope your memory loss isn't permanent." I nab the white paper bag from the counter and give the much-younger woman a final glance.

She bites her lower lip and bats her creepy tarantula eyelashes. We are *for sure* never coming back here.

The second we step outside, I retrieve my apple fritter and shove part of it into my mouth, holding it with my teeth before tossing the bag into the garbage.

"Dad, my doughnut was in there!"

I fasten my helmet and take the fritter from my mouth. "This afternoon, when you get home from school, and I ask you what you learned today, I expect you to say: 'If I embarrass my dad in public, I will not get a doughnut.'"

Her jaw drops. "You are the worst father in the world."

"I love you too. Let's get to school so you won't be late *and* hankering for a doughnut."

I inhale all but one bite of my fritter, and just as we begin to ride out of the parking lot, I offer her the last morsel.

She frowns despite steering her bike closer to take my peace offering.

"Lola, I don't need your help finding a date."

"Dakota said his sister said their mom said she's surprised you haven't started dating."

When we stop at the light, holding our breaths from the bus exhaust, I replay her statement for comprehension—Dakota, his sister, and their mom.

Dakota's mom is on her third husband. I can see why she'd be surprised.

It's hard to date when I can't drive a car. And it's hard to explain this to Lola when Victoria, her therapist, said I should never say anything that might make my daughter feel bad about "the situation."

"Have you discussed this with Victoria?" I ask. Thankfully, the bus turns right, and we can breathe again.

"No. Why?"

"I think you should," I say, just as we pass the congested line of cars along the street in front of the school.

"Fine. I will next week."

"Great," I say.

"Dad, that's far enough." Lola glances over her shoulder, eyeing me before I roll past an invisible line.

I stop at the crosswalk. Heaven forbid Lola's friends see her dad escorting her to school.

"Have a great day," I say.

"How am I supposed to do that when I'm starving?" Without another glance at me, she walks her bike through the intersection with the crossing guard.

The gray-haired lady holding up the stop sign in the middle of the street eyes me with disapproval.

"She had a breakfast burrito."

While I finish my coffee, Taylor, the maintenance manager at Cielo Aviation, gives me the rundown on the plane engine I need to rebuild. And before donning my coveralls, I use the men's room. After I flush the urinal, someone in the stall clears their throat.

"Excuse me," *she* says.

I quickly zip my pants as if I'm in the wrong restroom. "Yeah?" I say slowly.

"Could you find me a roll of toilet paper?"

There's only one stall, so I glance around the floor-to-ceiling tiled room for toilet paper while washing my hands.

Nothing.

"Uh, give me a minute," I say.

"I'll be here," she singsongs, followed by a tiny laugh as I leave the men's room.

Near the door to the hangar, Taylor stares at his phone's screen.

"Where's the toilet paper?" I ask.

He glances up at me, removes his hat, and scratches his head of sparse gray-and-brown hair. "Why?"

"Because there's someone in the stall who needs toilet paper."

He grunts. "Is it Miles? Let him figure it out."

"No. It's . . ." I clear my throat. "A woman."

Taylor squints. "In the men's room?" He peers over my shoulder and frowns at the **Out of Order** sign on the women's restroom door. Then he grumbles and leads me toward the main office. On the opposite side of the corridor, he unlocks a supply closet. "Don't be weird about it. I don't want any sexual harassment allegations," he says, handing me a roll of cheap one-ply bathroom tissue wrapped in white paper.

"How would I be weird about it?"

"Don't linger. Don't ask questions. Deliver the roll and get out of there."

"So I'm not allowed to wipe her ass for her?"

"Christ, Ozzy. That's what I'm talking about."

I laugh while returning to the men's room.

"Here you go." I set it on the floor and slide it under the stall with the toe of my black boot.

"Thanks. I owe you one."

I open my mouth to respond, but that might count as lingering, so I turn.

"One more favor?"

"Uh . . ." I stop, turning toward the sound of something scraping along the floor. It's a quarter.

"The women's restroom is closed because of plumbing issues," she says. "But the tampon dispenser should work. Are you man enough to help a gal out?"

I focus on the quarter. It's heads up. Is it someone's lucky day? I don't think so. I step on George Washington's head and slide it several feet away from the stall before picking it up. *Man enough?* What's that supposed to mean?

"Thanks. You're the best," she chirps.

"Sure," I murmur in a *manly* tone.

After glancing in both directions, I hustle across the hall to the women's restroom, insert the quarter, and turn the knob.

Nothing.

I shake it, bang on it, and dig change out of my pocket to try it again. Either it's empty or broken. "Shit," I mumble. Again, I head into the hallway, making a beeline for the front office and crossing my fingers that Hillary is at her desk.

"Good morning, Ozzy." She bats her brown hair away from her green-framed glasses and sips her coffee.

"Hey! I need a tampon." I spew the words like the building is on fire.

Her nose crinkles as she returns her "cat lady" coffee mug to the desk. "Excuse me?"

"The women's room is empty, and someone in the men's room needs one."

She gawks at me, lips parted.

I sigh. "It's a woman."

Hillary nods slowly. "Oh. Well, let me see." She retrieves her red leather purse from under the desk. "I have a pad. Will that work?"

"I'm going to say yes. But I have no clue." I dig into my pocket and pull out a quarter.

"Are you serious?" She laughs when I set it on her desk in exchange for the pad.

"Is it not enough?"

"Ozzy, take your money. Don't make this awkward." Hillary tosses her purse beneath her desk.

Too late. Everything about this is awkward.

"Thanks." I shut the door and jog to the men's room. "Sorry, the machine is broken or empty. I found a pad." I tear off a paper towel, set the pad on it, and slide it under the stall with my boot.

"Does everyone in the building know I was unprepared to start my period?" she asks.

"No."

"Well, that's a relief. Thanks."

"Sure," I reply, already halfway out the door before bolting to the hangar, donning my coveralls, and praying the woman on her period is not a Cielo Aviation employee.

Just as I get into a groove, Taylor says my name. "Have you met Ozzy?"

I fumble my wrench and smack my head on the hunk of metal above me.

"Yo, Ozzy?" Taylor calls.

I rub my head and step around the engine. "Yeah?"

"This is Maren Bernabe. She's been flying with us for seven fire seasons. A real talent. Montana's lucky to have her."

Maren casually slides her long, wavy blond ponytail through one hand while sipping her mug of coffee with the other. A blush fills her cheeks as she rolls her blue eyes at how Taylor's gushing about her.

"Maren, this is Ozzy. He's been here four, five months?"

"Almost five," I say, wiping my hands on a rag.

Her eyes widen, lips pressed together until they start to turn white.

"Maren, this guy is saving the earth. He rides his bicycle to work, even in the snow. And—" Taylor glances at his phone. "Oh, excuse me for a second. I have to answer this." He takes a few steps away from us, holding his phone to his ear.

She's an impressive tanker pilot, and I ride a bicycle. I feel two feet tall as I inhale to pull back my shoulders and fake more confidence than Taylor has bestowed upon me this morning.

Too late.

Maren smells like flowers while I emit the appealing scents of kerosene, oil, and solvents—just a few of the daily odors that permeate my clothes and skin.

"Nice to meet you," I say.

She cringes while whispering "You're the guy who got me toilet paper and a pad."

I try not to smile, but only half-succeed. "I don't know what you're talking about."

Maren's smile is confident, with just the right amount of vulnerability, like she knows how to laugh at herself. "You do. But thank you for playing it so cool. My day's not off to a great start. I just stopped by to update some paperwork before my first shift next week, and it's gone downhill from there."

A few seconds later, I lift my gaze to hers, realizing she hasn't missed me eyeing her long legs in tight jeans or that coffee stain by her boob. I swear I was only looking at the stain.

Her eyes narrow a fraction. Yeah, she thinks I'm a perv. Now I have to shit on her day to save myself.

"Maybe you should head home, get in bed, and climb out on the opposite side." I nod to her shirt.

Glancing down, she runs her hand over the stain and mumbles, "Are you kidding me? God, I make the worst first impressions."

"You're a beautiful mess."

What. The. Hell?

Why did I say that? It just came out of nowhere.

Maren lifts her head. "Thank you, but you're too kind."

Kind? Perhaps.

An idiot? Definitely.

"So, bicycling in the snow?" Maren furrows her brow.

"It's a fat-tire bike. And honestly, when we had that heavy snow in January, I walked."

"Wow. You must live close."

"Four miles." *Six from Lola's school.*

Her head draws back. "You walked four miles to work? In the snow?"

"Guilty." I lift a shoulder.

"That's . . ."

"Manly. And complicated." I playfully puff out my chest.

With a slow nod, she echoes, "Complicated, indeed." Then she smirks when my *manly* reference registers. "I was stressed out. I get snarky when I'm stressed. Sorry."

I brush it off with a tiny headshake.

"Are you new to Missoula?" she asks.

"No." I leave it short and sweet while tucking the rag into the pocket of my coveralls.

"Oh? Where were you previously employed?"

Behind me, Miles turns on the angle grinder, making it hard to hear, so I smile until he's done. "It's a long story. I've been at home caring for my daughter. Her mom died in a car accident two years ago, right after I was offered a position here," I say. "And luckily, another position became available when I was ready to work again."

Maren frowns. "I'm so sorry."

Her mom. I called my wife "her mom," and I did it because I'm attracted to this woman. And it's the first time the thought of another woman has crossed my mind in two years. I don't know if I should celebrate this moment or berate myself for needing to avoid the word *wife*. My thoughts are far from idle. They dig up that seemingly innocent statement from Lola this morning.

If you want to have sex again before you die, I'm okay with it.

"Thank you," I say, rubbing my neck. "It's been a rough road, but it's good to be working again. Normalcy is refreshing." I don't know if Maren buys it. But I keep telling myself this while riding my bike to work, the grocery store, the bank—everywhere. That's not normal.

"My brother, Brandon, died three years ago," she says with an empathetic smile. "So I feel you."

"Oh, no. I'm sorry," I say.

Maren nods several times. "Thanks. I'll, uh"—she jerks her chin toward the engine—"let you get back to work. Again, thanks for your help earlier. If the stars align and we never see each other again, my pride will have a chance to recover."

I shrug. "I don't know. Your idea of the stars aligning is a lot different than mine." I can't look at her. She'll see right through my stupid schoolboy crush. So I think of Lola and the car I no longer drive or the date I will never ask Maren to go on with me. And with that sobering reminder, I lift my gaze from the floor to her one last time and offer a platonic, non-schoolboy-crush smile. "See ya around."

Maren smiles until tiny crinkles form at the corners of her blue eyes. "Maybe."

She's flirting with me or busting my balls; either one is fine with me.

Chapter Two

"Where's Tia and Lola?" I ask my father-in-law while unzipping my hoodie. It's just past five thirty, and my kitchen smells like garlic. The Weber grill is pulled away from the edge of the deck, and I bet Amos's famous dry-rubbed rib eyes are sizzling to perfection.

He retrieves a bottle of ranch dressing from the fridge. After Brynn died, I remodeled the four-bedroom ranch house. Lola wanted white cabinets and blue retro appliances, so I caved and gave my grieving daughter what she wanted: a beach-blue metal fridge with chrome trim and a pivoting handle. I struggled with retro "updates." It seemed like an oxymoron.

However, Lola still gushes over the blue appliances and the two-person round chrome pedestal table with sparkly red vinyl chairs. So the decor has grown on me because her enthusiasm is contagious.

"Lola had to stay for detention," Amos says. "But Tia didn't find out until Lola failed to come outside after school. They should be home any minute."

I check my phone for missed messages. Sure enough, there's a call from the school that I didn't see. "Why did Lola get detention?" I ask, but it's not her first offense, so I have trouble mustering a shocked response.

"Dunno," Amos mumbles. "Want to make a little wager before they get home?" He eyes me with a half grin as he drizzles the dressing over the bowls of mixed greens.

"Ten bucks. Someone said something about her bike, and she kicked them in the shin," I say, because it's a statistically good guess.

Amos runs a hand over his spiky gray hair before scratching his saggy turkey neck. "Twenty bucks, some little punk pulled her hair, and she throat punched them."

"You think she's graduated to the throat punch?" My eyes widen.

He carries two salad bowls to the dining room table, next to a Palladian window overlooking the backyard filled with trees and bird feeders. "Ozzy, she's halfway through fourth grade. I can see her testing out some new tactics."

We're dancing around the truth because it's less painful than the likely reality that someone said something about the scars on her face. By now, every kid in her school should be used to them, but kids can be relentless little assholes.

I follow Amos, carrying the other two bowls. "That girl has my temper. I should be the one in detention."

Amos pulls four plates from the oak buffet. "Don't beat yourself up. You've been a saint with that girl since Brynn died. Ground her, ignore her tantrum, and let her learn things the hard way. She's coddled enough."

I coddle her. He won't directly point a finger at me, but it's implied by his tone and reinforced when he doesn't look at me.

Last year, after Thanksgiving, Amos and Tia sold their ranch in Yellowstone and moved to Missoula so I could go back to work. Since they're giving up or postponing their planned retirement in Ocala, Florida, to help me raise Lola, I must accept a little scrutiny.

A jab here and there. They walk the line without making pointed comments about my dad because he's a hard limit for me.

The back door creaks, followed by Lola's dramatic huff. "We're home. Don't be mad. It wasn't my fault."

Amos and I force straight faces while we meet Tia and Lola in the kitchen.

Tia inspects me with squinted blue eyes, her dark-gray, chin-length hair matted from her bike helmet. She's daring me to let Lola off easy. Tia helped brand and castrate cows until the day they sold the ranch. She has the energy of someone half her age and believes kids should be raised with a loving hand and stern voice. Brynn was the same way.

Lola's always been a daddy's girl, and watching her heal from the car accident and grieve the loss of her mother has only made me softer.

"I'm listening," I say, taking Lola's backpack before she fills a glass with water from the filter pitcher in the fridge.

Tia surgically washes her hands and dark, leathery forearms while eyeing my daughter. I don't know if Lola feels an ounce of fear, but I still have a healthy respect for Tia's challenging scowl. The first time I met her, she sized me up and told me I'd better plan on marrying her daughter if I was sticking my dick in her.

My balls instantly shriveled into raisins.

"At recess, Bailey said I have a crush on Miss Obermeier. I said that's stupid. So Bailey called me a name, but it's not one I'm allowed to use, so I won't say it. But then she shoved me, so I shoved her back, and she tripped and hurt her wrist. So I got sent to the principal's office while Bailey went to the nurse for an ice pack. I know she was faking it just to get attention." Lola makes the most dramatic eye roll before gulping down her glass of water.

"Why does Bailey think you have a crush on Miss Obermeier?" I ask, unzipping her bag and removing the lunch box filled with a half-eaten chicken sandwich. Her carrots are untouched in the Ziploc, but the chocolate chip cookie Tia made is gone.

"Because she heard me asking Miss Obermeier if she has a husband or boyfriend."

"That's weird," I mumble, handing her the backpack.

"Lola, tell your dad why you asked Miss Obermeier if she's married or has a boyfriend," Tia prods, pulling the garlic bread from the oven while Amos retrieves the steaks from the grill.

Eyeing my frizzy-haired girl, I cross my arms and widen my stance.

Lola mirrors me. She's a little shit. I love her, but she's all attitude. "Since you didn't like the lady at Dolly's Doughnuts this morning, I asked Miss Obermeier. She's really pretty, and she likes kids."

"Lola's trying to find you a date, Ozzy. Why is that?" Tia shoots me that ball-shriveling look while transferring the garlic bread to a basket.

"How should I know?"

Lola pleads her case. "You're sad and lonely. That's what Dakota's mom said. And I don't want you to be sad and lonely. I know Mom is gone forever."

Dakota's mom can suck my dick. Scratch that thought. She'd probably do it.

"Lola." I cup her face in my hands, forcing her to look at me. "I miss your mom. I'll miss her every day for the rest of my life. But that doesn't mean I'm lonely and sad. I have you, and you're all I need."

She frowns. "But—"

"No buts. Put your bag in your room and wash your hands for dinner."

"Fine," she grumbles, sulking toward the basement stairs.

When Amos and Tia came to stay with us, Lola and I moved to the basement so they could have the two main-level bedrooms. They don't sleep together, because Amos snores, and Tia gets restless legs syndrome in the middle of the night.

When Lola's not in earshot, Tia grumbles about the "hideous" retro vibe of the remodel. That also makes me love Lola's groovy yellow swivel chair and my black Eames lounger a little more. The only furniture we didn't replace is Brynn's cream glider, which she used to sit in to rock Lola to sleep.

"We moved here to help with Lola, not so you could date," Tia says just as Amos brings the steaks into the house. She partially blames me for the car accident, so my happiness is not on her list of priorities.

"Tia, this is all Lola. I'm not sad and lonely. I'm not looking for anyone. But . . ." I pause for a moment.

"But what?" she asks.

"Nothing. Let's eat." I take the bread basket from her and carry it to the dining room.

"It hasn't been long enough," Tia says as she and Amos follow me.

"Long enough for what?" Lola asks, reaching the top of the stairs. My daughter never misses anything unless I need her to listen; then, she magically hears nothing.

Brynn would have said the same thing about me and my selective hearing.

"Lola, I don't want you trying to find someone for your dad," Tia says, sitting beside my snoopy daughter and nodding toward the napkin. According to Tia, I've been a little lax in teaching Lola "proper manners," like protecting her lap when she eats and doing chores without an allowance.

"Why not?" Lola sets her folded napkin on her lap.

Tia leans toward Lola, unfolding it and spreading it over her legs. "That's a silly question, since you landed in detention today from an incident that started because you thought your dad needed a date."

Amos uses tongs to set a rib eye on his plate before passing the steaks to me. I can't read his expression, but I think he's conflicted. He, too, partially blames me for the accident, but I don't sense his need to see me repent for eternity, imprisoned in a life of solitude beyond my daughter.

Lola deflates while I cut her steak. If I let her cut it, she'll give up after one failed attempt and pick up the whole slab of meat, tearing off a chunk with her teeth like a wild animal. It's not coddling; it's encouraging manners.

"Did you know I met your mom without anyone's help?"

She lifts her head.

"It's true. I met her at a concert. I was behind her in line for a . . ."

Beer.

I smile. "A snack. When she reached into her purse, her wallet was missing. She freaked out, so I paid for her food and helped her find her wallet, which took forever. By the time we found it, the concert was half-over. She felt terrible that I missed the show but grateful we retrieved her wallet."

"Where was it?" Lola asks.

"Under her car. It must have fallen out when she opened the door."

"Then what happened?" Lola can't help her smile and the sparkle of curiosity in her eyes.

"She offered to buy me dinner instead of watching the rest of the concert." I take a bite of steak and smirk while chewing it. "Your mom fell in love with me pretty quickly."

Lola whips her head in the direction of Amos and Tia. "Is that true?"

They share a knowing glance and a rare smile. Most of the time, talking about Brynn only reignites their anger toward me—mainly Tia's.

"It's true," Tia concedes. "Your mom called me late that night to tell me she met the man she was going to marry."

Lola's eyes bug out. "Really?"

Tia shrugs and stabs her fork into her salad. "Really. Of course, I thought she was out of her mind."

There it is, the little jab.

"So you need to go to a concert, Dad."

We laugh.

"We'll see. I'm working now. I don't have a lot of extra time to go to concerts. When I get off work, I only want to be with you."

It's like Lola stopped listening the second she made her concert comment. That look on her face says she's already scheming. I don't understand the sudden change. How did she go from asking me every day if I missed her mom to matchmaking with any available woman in Missoula?

Chapter Three

MAREN

"Reagan wants your phone number. Can I give it to him?" Will, my roommate, asks while I sit at the counter and tear into my Chinese takeout.

"Remind me who Reagan is?"

Will turns off the faucet after the sink is half-filled with soapy dishwater. "The new guy across the street who owns chickens."

I pause the chopsticks at my lips, lo mein noodles dangling from them while the mixed aroma of garlic and oyster sauce wafts up my nose. "Isn't he my dad's age?"

"No. He's forty-seven. He just hasn't aged well. What are you? Forty? Forty-one?"

I'm thirty-three, and he knows it. "When I'm done eating, I'm going to shove these chopsticks up your ass, William Landry."

With his chin down, he smirks and scrubs the frying pan. Will is the stereotypical male firefighter centerfold, tall with thick sandy-blond hair, countable abs, and a strong jaw. Like an ornery child, he has a sparkle in his blue eyes. It's punctuated with a tiny mole below his left eye. However, he's hell bent on keeping that '80s mustache, and he takes tai chi (which our other roommate calls ballet). So he's sexy with a few footnotes.

"He's a lot younger than Professor Gray Balls," Will says, rinsing the pan while shooting me a glance, eyebrows waggling.

Ted Gracey is my dad's best friend. He owns a lot of the farmland around my parents' property. Ted's a semiretired professor of environmental physics. He travels all over the world to conferences. He's brilliant, sought after, and almost eighty-four. When it's not fire season, I transport him in his private jet to conferences. He doesn't have a wife or kids, and his sister died six months ago, so Will and our other roommate, Fitz, think I'm going to inherit everything when he dies.

I'm not.

"You know what would be funny?" I point my chopsticks at Will. "If he did leave me everything, I could afford to buy you a woman. Everyone knows the only way someone will stay with you is if it's their job."

He scoffs. "That's harsh. How can you say that?"

"Because no woman wants to be with a guy who would rather play video games than have sex."

"I have plenty of sex." He flicks water and suds at me.

I cringe with a scrunched nose while inspecting my food for soap bubbles. "Masturbating to female avatars doesn't count."

"When you shit all over my chosen bachelor's life, do you ever stop to look in the mirror or at your left hand? Where's your wedding ring? Who keeps you warm at night? Nobody. But I know a guy who owns four chickens who'd love to spoon you until his rooster crows in the morning. Shit!" He smacks his forehead with his fist. "I just flubbed the perfect cock joke."

"I'm going to kill that *cock*," I grumble.

Will drains the sink. "That makes two of us. It's a loud son of a bitch."

"Actually, if you want to know a little secret, I think a mechanic at work is interested in me."

"Oh? Did he ask you out?"

"No."

"Did he check out your boobs?"

"Yes, but . . ." I point to my shirt.

Will squints before laughing. "Coffee?"

I nod. "I thought he was staring at my boobs, but then he gestured to my shirt. Did I mention this happened after the women's bathroom was closed, so I had to use the men's? There was no toilet paper, *and* I started my period. So Ozzy, this mechanic, fetched me toilet paper and a pad. Nothing embarrassing about that."

Will shakes with silent laughter, hand fisted at his mouth. "Christ, Maren. How do you get yourself into these situations?"

I roll my eyes.

"And I guarantee he was looking at your boobs. You could have 'Don't look at my boobs' written in blood across your chest, and men would not see anything in their pursuit of finding your nipple outlines."

"You're a man. Does that mean you're always looking for my nips?"

"I found them years ago. I no longer have to look."

"You're *so* funny."

"So let's be real for a minute," he says. "What if this mechanic wasn't searching for the cherry pebbles? What if it was the coffee stain? And you think he's interested in you, but maybe he finds you interesting, but only in the way that one cannot turn away from a train wreck."

"Flame," I say.

"What?"

"He looked at me like someone who can't turn away from a fire, watching the flames. I'm hot."

"Indeed. Nothing gets a guy horny quite like fetching toilet paper and a maxi pad for a stranger in the men's bathroom." Will puts his clean dishes away.

"Why must you rain on my parade? Can't you just lie to me like a real friend?"

Will chuckles. "Sure. This Ozzy guy's probably at home right now, jerking off to the vision of your jeans wadded up at your ankles in the men's bathroom stall while you beg him for a maxi pad."

I snort, covering my mouth. "You're right. Did you say my future husband's name is Reagan?"

Will winks and clicks his tongue twice. "Attagirl. Once you lower your standards, the world is your oyster."

◆ ◆ ◆

On my way to the airport to fly Ted to Chicago (my last flight with him until the end of this upcoming fire season), I pass a guy on a bike. But not just any guy. It's Ozzy in the rain. I pull my RAV4 to the side of the road and step out when it's safe.

He stops his fat-tire bike a few feet from the back of my dirty black RAV.

"Get in," I say, holding the hood of my rain jacket to keep it from blowing off my head. "I'll collapse my back seats so your bike can go in the back."

"I'm good, but thanks." He squints against the rain.

I chuckle. "It's no big deal. Really, get in."

"I can't." He licks the water from his lips.

"Why not?"

"I made a promise."

"Like a fitness goal? Or a promise to the environment?" I shake my head. "Don't answer that. It's none of my business. Just be careful. It's dangerous when the roads are wet, and drivers can't see you."

"I appreciate the offer." Ozzy smiles with rivulets of water sticking to his short-trimmed beard, a few shades darker than his chestnut hair, which was a thick, chaotic mess the day I met him. He probably can't wear a helmet *and* give a shit about his hair.

After a final nod and smile, I hop back into my vehicle and continue along the road. Cielo Aviation is next to the airport, so I pull into the parking lot and wait.

Ten minutes later, Ozzy arrives. Since I'm pulled right next to the back entrance, I know he sees me, so I climb out of my RAV and run under the red awning, catching him right before he scans his ID card to enter the building.

"Hey," I say with a smile, immediately losing my nerve. I want to ask him out. "How old is your daughter?"

Ozzy lights up, white teeth peeking through his full lips. "Lola's ten."

"Lola is a great name." I squint when the wind blows rain in our direction.

Ozzy glances around. "You coming inside?"

"No, I'm headed to the airport. I'm flying someone to Chicago today. It's my offseason job that's coming to an end after this trip."

Ozzy nods slowly while eyeing me with an unreadable expression. "Did you just want to know my daughter's age?"

Flirting is my thing. I know how to do it and get men to ask me out, except with this man. With Ozzy, I'm a word-fumbling fool. "I was also going to ask what grade she's in."

His lips bend into a smirk. "Fourth. Too smart for her own good."

I nod several times. "My brother, Brandon, was smart like that. He never had to study. When our mom would make him help me with my schoolwork, all he did was sigh heavily because he didn't understand why I didn't get everything the first time. He would have been an awful teacher." I scrape my teeth along my bottom lip several times. "I rarely talk about my brother, but it felt good to tell you that."

Again, Ozzy surveys our rainy surroundings with his deep-brown eyes just as another employee runs under the awning. He gives Ozzy a quick "Hey" and swipes his ID card to enter the building.

Ozzy grabs the door to keep it from shutting and props it open with his back while unzipping his jacket.

I stare at his fitted black T-shirt and admire his broad, defined chest. "How would you feel about going out sometime?" My heart races. Did I really just ask him out while ogling him?

Ozzy's lips twist. "Can I get back to you on that?"

What am I supposed to say? No. He needs to give me an answer right now.

"Sure." I smile. "No pressure. It's okay to say no. Maybe you're not dating yet." I narrow my eyes. "Or you might not want to go out with me. I'm clearly a hot mess. And by hot, I don't mean I think I'm hot. I mean . . ." I press my lips together and close my eyes. "I'm going to shut up now. Just forget I asked. I should get to the airport."

By the time I open my eyes, his grin has doubled.

"I'll get back to you after I consider your offer and decide if you are, in fact, too hot for me. Which, I can already say, you are," he says.

Oh my god. He's flirting with me. Will was wrong. I didn't blow things with what will forever be called The Period Fiasco.

Ozzy fishes his phone out of the inside pocket of his rain jacket. "What's your number?"

"Five. One. Nine . . ." I spew my number without sounding too desperate.

He slides his phone back into his pocket. "Have a safe flight."

"Thanks," I say with no control over my grin. "I hope you call me."

For the record, I have never said those five words aloud.

Ozzy's smile is all kinds of sexy. "I hope so too."

I chuckle, shaking my head and returning to my vehicle while butterflies swirl in my tummy. By the time I fasten my seat belt, Ozzy is inside the building. Before I start the engine, my phone pings with a text.

Ozzy: Cedar's at seven this Friday?

"Now you're just toying with me," I mumble with a laugh.

Chapter Four

OZZY

Friday morning, I broach the topic while I pack lunch for Lola and myself. Tia and Amos have already eaten their eggs and sausage. Now they're sipping coffee and staring out the dining room window at the bird feeders.

"I have plans tonight. I can ask the sitter to watch Lola if you have plans too. Otherwise—"

"Are you going to Diego's? Lola would love to play with Kai," Tia says without looking in my direction.

"No. I'm going to dinner with some people from work." I don't want to lie, but I don't have time to argue this morning, and the truth would spark an unnecessary fight.

My date could be a one-and-done, so why start something now?

"Will you be drinking?" Tia asks.

I don't drink around my in-laws, but that doesn't mean I pass up an occasional beer when I don't have to worry about people judging me. "Just water."

"What time will you be home?" Tia prods.

"By ten." I slide my lunch sack into my backpack just as Lola runs up the stairs.

"Teeth brushed. Bag packed. Let's go, Dad."

I grab her shoulders and kiss her head. "Here's your lunch."

She wrinkles her nose. "It's not chicken again, is it?" She jams it into her backpack.

"Nope. It's leftover pasta."

"Yes!" She skips to the back door and shoves her feet into her red sneakers without untying them.

"We'll be home. You don't have to ask the neighbor to watch Lola." Tia carries her coffee mug to the kitchen sink.

"Thanks," I say before shutting the back door behind us.

I escort Lola to school, clock in my eight hours at work, and make it home in time to discover my wardrobe is stale and a decade out of style. I didn't think this through. Brynn picked out my clothes whenever we had someplace to go that required more than jeans and a T-shirt. I own two ties and one suit. Is this a suit date? I don't know. All four of my button-down shirts are faded and worn or missing buttons.

"Where are you going?" Lola jumps onto my bed and crosses her legs.

"Out with friends from work." I pull a pilled-and-dated sweater from my dresser drawer. Who am I kidding? Despite the temps dipping into the forties tonight, I'll sweat through this thing before I get to the restaurant.

"Are any of your friends girls?"

I keep my back to her. "Maybe. Why?"

"No reason."

"That's what I figured." I smirk, daring her to say more after Tia scolded us. "What should I wear? One of these button-down shirts?" I hold up the two shirts that aren't missing buttons.

Lola wrinkles her nose. "Wear your shirt that Aunt Jenny gave you."

It's a black T-shirt that says *That's what I do. I fix stuff. And I know things.* I don't think I've ever worn it, so it's not faded.

"Lola, it's not very dressy."

"Why do you have to wear something dressy to go out with friends?"

She's right. I'm riding my bike to dinner. A suit wouldn't fit with my mode of transportation.

"The T-shirt it is." I pull it on, and it looks pretty good with my dark jeans and boots. "Should I trim my scruff?" I rub my chin in the full-length mirror.

"I like it prickly." She smiles.

"You do, huh?" I turn, resting my hands on the bed and nuzzling my *prickly* face into her neck.

She giggles and squirms. "Stop!"

I fix my hair in the mirror, shifting my gaze to Lola, my wife's mini-me. Will the day ever come that I see Lola as Lola and not Brynn's reflection?

"Okay. I have to get going. Be good for Nana and Pa, okay?"

"Will you be home before I go to bed?"

"Probably not. So give me a hug and kiss."

She stands on the bed and throws herself into my arms. "Look for a pretty woman who likes kids," she whispers.

I chuckle, lifting her off the bed and onto her feet. "You don't give up, do ya? Good night, pumpkin."

When I reach the main floor, Tia ignores me while reading her book in Brynn's cream glider.

"Have a good time," Amos says, turning down the volume on the television.

"Thanks." I zip my jacket and grab my helmet.

I hope Maren has a thing for guys with helmet hair.

Chapter Five

MAREN

I arrive at the restaurant fifteen minutes early, just before the clouds open into a downpour. There was no rain in the forecast, and the sun's still partially shining beyond that one angry cloud.

The young hostess with a full head of beautiful black hair and a warm smile seats me by the front window so I can watch for Ozzy. After a glass of wine, the rain begins to let up, and a drenched man parks his bike by the lamppost.

"Oh god," I whisper. It's Ozzy.

Is he this much of a tree hugger?

As he turns, we make eye contact. His shoulders lift for a second before slinking into a heavy shrug. I hold up a finger, leave cash on the table for the wine, and step out the front door.

"I'm sorry," he says, with water dripping down his face. His soaked jeans sag from the weight of it.

I try not to laugh, but it's hard, so I cover my mouth and shake my head.

"I'm an idiot. I didn't know it was going to rain."

"No." I drop my hand and clear my throat. "I think it was a pop-up shower. Can I take you home to change?"

"No." He rubs his eyes and exhales. "If I go home, the date's over. But maybe that's for the best."

"Why does it have to be over? Because your daughter is at home? Or are you allergic to rain?"

"Are you always a smart-ass?"

I smile. "Yes."

He rubs his fingers over his lips to hide his smirk.

"No one's at my place tonight. Why don't we go there, and you can dry your clothes in my dryer?"

He squints. "How far is that?"

"A mile or so."

He nods. "What's the address?"

"Ozzy. I'll give you a ride."

"I'll get your vehicle wet. Besides, riding might help me dry out. Except . . ." He unzips his jacket and pulls out yellow wildflowers that are droopy and a little squished. "I had them in my hand, but when it started to rain, I had to shove them into my jacket, which, in hindsight, is stupid because flowers can get wet." He hands them to me.

"You brought me flowers?" I reach for them. "No one's ever . . ." I pause, suddenly feeling vulnerable. "Given me flowers. Except when my brother died."

Ozzy frowns. "Are you serious?"

Giving him a sheepish grin, I nod.

After a beat, he pulls a folded-up piece of paper from his pocket, but it's stuck together. When he opens it, there's nothing more than giant blotches of blue ink. "Uh, well, it was a note about the flowers. But I'll just tell you, even though you probably already know." He lifts his gaze. "They're glacier lilies. After the snow melts, they are one of the first to bloom. And they are edible. But you don't have to eat them."

Flying gives me butterflies, the really good kind. No man has given me flowers or butterflies—until now.

"Oh!" He holds up a finger and smiles. "And I picked six for you because six is the smallest perfect number. The next perfect number is twenty-eight, but I stuck to a more manageable number and ethical harvesting."

I'm speechless.

"So"—he clasps his hands behind his back—"I'll follow you home?"

I shake it off, this surreal feeling. "Um, I'll text it to you so you have it in case I don't drive slow enough and I lose you." I send him my address.

"What about dinner?" he asks.

"Pizza delivery?" I suggest.

Ozzy nods. "I'll order it. What do you want on it?"

"I'll eat anything."

"Every man's favorite line," he says.

I dig my key fob from my purse and pause when his words register.

A shit-eating grin spreads across his face. "Sorry. Too soon?"

I roll my eyes. "See you in a bit. Try to keep up."

"Don't worry about that," he says with a wink while bringing his phone to his ear.

I chuckle, walking toward my RAV.

After parking in the driveway, I run into the house, deposit the flowers in a mason jar (since I don't own a vase), and ensure everything is picked up in my room. Will he be in my room? I don't know, but a girl should be prepared.

While I'm shoving the last of my dirty clothes into the white wicker hamper, there's a knock at the door. "Coming!" I steal sweatpants and a T-shirt from Will's room and jog down the stairs to open the door.

Ozzy's bent over, untying his black boots on the porch. "Do you want me to strip?"

"Uh . . ." My tongue swipes along my lower lip.

Yes. I absolutely want you to strip for me.

Loosening the laces to his other boot, he glances up at me. "*Should* I strip? God, you're such a perv."

"Stop!" I cup a hand over my mouth and laugh. "You're obnoxious. Just go." I point to the right of the stairs toward the back of the house.

"It's all hard surfaces from here to the laundry room. That way and to the left. Here's something to wear while your things are drying."

He stares at them. "Your husband's?"

"Yes. He's with his mistress tonight, so he won't mind."

"Well, he's an idiot for not minding because I'm a messy eater."

"*So* obnoxious." I roll my eyes. "In case you are wondering, I have two roommates who are guys. Will's an engine chief, he owns the house, and Fitz is a smoke jumper."

Ozzy accepts the clothes with a smirk and treks to the laundry room. "Those lucky bastards."

Ozzy has game.

"Did you order the pizza?" I holler.

"I did," he says with the door closed.

This is weird. I don't bring guys here, probably because I live with two. And I'm nervous because I like Ozzy despite all the questions he evokes.

"Can I get you something to drink?" I ask with my head in the fridge when the laundry-room door opens.

"Anything is fine."

"Water? Wine? Beer?" I glance over my shoulder. Ozzy wears those gray sweats and that white T-shirt better than Will, or maybe I refuse to look at Will like I'm gawking at Ozzy's muscular body.

"Beer," he says.

I steal the last bottle and shut the door.

"Thanks." Ozzy takes it and twists off the cap.

We stare at each other and smile at the same time, like we're sharing a private joke, but I don't know what it is other than I really like this man.

"Stop. You make it impossible to be serious." Heat fills my cheeks.

"What?" He shrugs before taking a swig of his beer. After he licks his lips, he tries to give me a solemn expression. "Sorry. Ask me a serious question."

"Who's watching Lola tonight?" I pour myself a glass of wine.

"Her grandparents."

"Oh, your parents live in Missoula?"

"No. Yes. Well, my mom lives here, but she's legally blind, so Lola can't stay with her. She's with my in-laws. Ex-in-laws." His gaze slides to the side, and he hums. "Lola's grandparents." He scrubs a hand over his face, then drops it to his side with a heavy sigh. "I haven't mastered this postdeath terminology. I also haven't been on a date since my wife died, so it's never been a big deal."

I'm his first date since his wife died? It takes a moment for that to sink in. I prefer our flirty banter. Death is a heavy subject for a first date. "I'll lower the bar for you since this is your first date."

"I cleared that bar by a mile when I persevered after the torrential downpour, nearly drowning, yet still able to go forward with the night."

I laugh.

His face sobers. "Sorry. I don't know how to talk about my wife with a woman who I'm trying to flirt with." Ozzy shifts his weight to his other leg and drops his gaze to his beer. "I'm off to a winning start on this date."

I snort. "You're the best worst date I've ever had."

"That makes no sense, and you know it." He gives me the hairy eyeball.

"It makes perfect sense. It makes as much sense as going on a date with someone I met on the toilet in the men's room." I nod toward the sofa and adjacent leather recliner.

Ozzy follows me so closely I feel the warmth from his body and catch the faint scent of his cologne or bodywash—bourbon and oak.

After his proximity knocks me off kilter, I clear my throat and sit on the far end of the sofa. "Listen, I don't expect you to pretend that you didn't lose your wife or that you don't have a daughter. In fact, if you need someone to talk to, I'm your person. I might even throw in some memories of my brother."

He sits on the opposite end of the sofa. "My wife's name was Brynn."

I sip my wine before nodding. He's right. It's a difficult first-date topic. I want to ask him how they met and what she was like, but I don't. Not yet. "Tell me about Lola. What's she like, if you don't mind me asking? I don't know the protocol for dating a guy with a child. Maybe you'd prefer other questions, like what do you enjoy doing in your free time?"

Ozzy chuckles. It's genuine and soothing, like someone squeezing my hand. He makes me nervous in a good way. I know virtually nothing about him, but I want to know everything. I've had that vibe since our first encounter. Public-bathroom chivalry will do that. I couldn't stop thinking about him when I was in Chicago.

"In my free time, I like hanging out with Lola," he says.

Of course he does. Have I been missing out on an untapped segment of Missoula's eligible men, the secret society of nice guys, a.k.a. single dads?

"And I like watching her play softball, chase fireflies and butterflies, build snowmen, and hearing her gossip with her friends about boys at school when she doesn't know I'm listening."

I'm in over my head with this guy. One date and my heart already recognizes something that feels so different from anyone before him.

"And you enjoy riding your bike." I smile.

After a beat, his brows pull together with a slow nod. "*Enjoy* might be a strong word. Lola was in the car accident with her mom. She was injured pretty badly. Her face will carry the scars forever despite several surgeries. But she's alive, and that's all that matters. However, she equates all vehicles to death traps. She refuses to get into a car and doesn't want me driving or riding in one, either, because, in her words, I'm all she has."

Jesus, that's heartbreaking.

"So you haven't been in a car since the accident?" I ask, trying not to sound so shocked, but it is unbelievable.

There's no way. How would he function?

Ozzy shakes his head, risking a glance at me as if to gauge my reaction. I'm not sure I have one, just lots of questions.

"No taxis or Ubers?"

Again, he shakes his head.

"Buses?"

"Nope."

"Has she talked to anyone about her fear? Like a therapist? And just tell me to shut up. She's not my child. I'm not a therapist. And I'm not judging you. I promise."

Ozzy eyes me, which makes me squirm. I've overstepped.

"Judge me," he says. "Out of ten, what would you give me? An eight for sure, right? I mean, I was a little late to the date, but I brought flowers. So . . ."

I tap the rim of my wineglass on my lower lip. "You use humor as a coping mechanism."

"Pfft." He inspects his beer bottle like he's reading it. "Everyone uses humor as a coping mechanism because it's the best medicine. Right?"

I nod slowly.

He angles his body toward me and stretches an arm across the back of the sofa. "You can ask me whatever you want. Yes, Lola sees a therapist. The goal is to get her back in a car, but she's young, and it's hard to reason with her. I don't want to force her to walk before she can crawl. And right now, we're still learning to crawl."

I think about his words—his life—even after he's no longer speaking. "You're a good father. A good person, Ozzy . . ." I laugh. "I don't know your last name."

"Laster."

"Ozzy Laster." I nod. "Is Ozzy short for anything?"

"I'm named after my mom's father, Oswald. Everyone called him Grandpa Waldo, but my parents didn't want my nickname to be Waldo."

"Well"—I pull my knee toward my chest and take another sip of wine—"it's a great name."

Ozzy belly laughs while tipping his head back. "Thank you. I don't know if I agree, but you're the first person to say it, so today is the first day I like my name."

I start to speak, but the doorbell rings.

"Let me." Ozzy stands and heads to the entry. "I assume it's the pizza." He opens the door. "Hey, Mike, thanks. Have a great evening."

I finish the last of my wine while padding toward the kitchen to retrieve plates. "You know the delivery guy?"

Ozzy sets the box on the table and grabs his phone from the counter, probably tipping delivery-guy *Mike*. "People who don't drive tend to be on a first-name basis with all the delivery drivers."

"That makes sense. What about groceries? Do you have those delivered too?" I set the plates on the table.

He waits for me to sit before he does. Seriously, single dads are gold.

"It depends. If I need a lot, I have it delivered. If I need only a handful of things, I pick them up. And Brynn's parents pick stuff up. Lola's okay with them driving. Her fear is over losing me."

I give him a sad smile and a slow nod before focusing on the pizza.

"Tell me, how did you end up living with two guys?" he asks. "Is it a financial situation or a kink?"

I pick a mushroom off my pizza and flick it at him.

"You're such a child." He laughs, peeling the mushroom off his neck.

"I'm not the child. I'm trying to have a serious conversation about your daughter."

"And I'm trying to have a serious conversation about your living arrangements." He takes a bite of pizza, but his smile still reaches his eyes, even while he's chewing.

"Brandon, my brother, was friends with Fitz. He moved in when a room opened up. And when they built a she shed in the backyard, I moved into it. I'd been living with a friend who returned to Nebraska, so I chose to live here instead of looking for another roommate. When

Brandon died, I eventually moved upstairs to his old room. It was hard at first, but now it's a comforting space for me."

"And when will your roommates be home? How long do I have to make my move?"

I laughed. "Will's on shift until tomorrow morning, and Fitz is visiting his grandma in California until his fiancée, Jamie, returns, which should be soon. She's a travel nurse. They met when she rented the she shed."

Three knocks at the door pull our gazes in that direction. Ozzy gives me a questioning glance.

I shrug while sliding my chair back. "Probably someone selling something."

When I reach the door and open it, my prematurely aging neighbor smiles through his full, dark beard. "Maren, what a pleasant surprise. How are you?" Reagan removes his straw cowboy hat and smooths his hand over his thick, messy, salt-and-pepper hair. His jeans and ratty T-shirt are as weathered as his loose, wrinkly skin.

"I'm well. What's up?"

"You haven't seen Kentucky and Slim by any chance, have you?"

My eyes narrow. "Uh, I've been to Kentucky. But I'm not sure what you mean by Slim."

He chuckles. "You're funny. I love your sense of humor."

"Thanks, but I'm not trying to be funny."

"Oh, Kentucky and Slim are two of my chickens." He named his chickens after chicken restaurants. That's a little messed up but kind of funny.

"Sorry, I haven't. I take it they're missing?"

He scratches his throat. "Yeah. But they must be close by. They don't wander far from the roost. I need to find them before it gets dark. Ya never know what might get a hold of one of 'em. You don't by any chance have a few extra minutes to help me look, do ya?"

"Actually, I'm in the middle of a—"

"We'd love to help," Ozzy says, stepping next to me and opening the door a little wider. "I'm Ozzy."

"A new roommate?" Reagan asks.

"A friend." Ozzy shoves his feet into his black boots and ties them.

"I'm Reagan, and I'd really appreciate all the help I can get. Here." He reaches into the pocket of his baggy jeans and holds out his fist. "Take a little crumble with you in case you find 'em."

Ozzy opens his hand, accepting the chicken feed, while I slip on my white sneakers and step onto the porch.

"Here ya go, Maren." Reagan punches his fist in my direction. I take the rest of the crumble. "Kentucky is a buff gold-and-orange mix, and Slim is chestnut. If you see one, hold out the feed to attract her. When she's about done pecking the treat from your hand, pick her up by holding both wings snug to her body so she doesn't flap, and then hug her close to you. Feel free to pet her. They love it when you pet 'em."

"Where should we start looking?" Ozzy asks with a straight face while I curl my lips together to keep from laughing.

This isn't happening.

"You go that way; I'll head in the opposite direction," Reagan says. "You might have to take a peek in some backyards. I wouldn't go more than a few houses down. Like I said, they can't be too far away."

"Got it." Ozzy returns a resolute nod.

When Reagan heads down the driveway, Ozzy winks. "I was hoping we'd get to look for chickens tonight."

I snort. "Stop. I'm so sorry. You didn't have to offer—"

"I did. This is my first chicken hunt. How could I say no?"

We turn right at the end of the driveway.

"Speaking of hunting, what if we find them dead?" I ask. "Several neighbors have hunting dogs. And nobody cares for Reagan's rooster, which wakes us up so early. Someone might kill one of the hens just to send a message."

"Let's be positive." He playfully nudges my arm.

I don't look at him, but I smile.

We scour the block, sneaking between houses to peek into neighbors' backyards. Just when we're about to give up because the sun has set and there's minimal illumination from the streetlights, I spy something out of the corner of my eye.

"There!" I point.

"Good job," Ozzy whispers, stealthily approaching the two hens pecking in the grass.

They start to bolt in the opposite direction, but Ozzy makes a funny clicking sound and squats with his hand open, spilling feed onto the ground. Both chickens strut toward him, so I slowly crouch down and open my hand to them.

The buff one pecks at the feed, and I jump with a giggle as it tickles my hand.

Ozzy's grin swells to the most handsome proportions. It feels tangible.

"The food's almost gone. We'd better pick them up," I say.

"You're right." Ozzy doesn't hesitate. He's the original chicken wrangler—hands pressed to Slim's wings while tucking her close to him.

"Eek!" I squeal when I don't get Kentucky's wings pressed to her body the first time, and they flap in my face.

"Got it?" Ozzy asks.

After a quick adjustment, I nod. "Yeah."

As we make our way back to Reagan's, Ozzy says, "Don't forget to pet Kentucky." He strokes Slim's back.

"I'm too afraid to loosen my hold. Poor Kentucky will just have to settle for an emotionless rescue. Besides, should we reward them for running away?"

"You're a real hard-ass." Ozzy laughs.

"I'm decisive and firm. That's what my boss says about me."

"Well, my boss says you're a badass."

I glance up at him. "Taylor said that?"

"He sure did."

I bite the inside of my cheek to keep from overflowing pride. It's always gratifying to hear men compliment women in jobs that have been dominated by men forever.

"You found my little rascals! I was about to give up. Thank you so much." Reagan opens the door to the pen.

"You're welcome," Ozzy says while we set them on the ground. "Maren spotted them. She's got a great eye."

I roll my *great* eyes. It was luck. "Good night," I say to Reagan.

"I owe ya, neighbor."

"You don't," I say while pivoting and leading Ozzy back to my house.

"I wondered what dating would be like after all these years," Ozzy says. "It's a lot different than I remember."

I giggle, kicking off my sneakers and heading to the kitchen to wash my hands while he follows me. "Our pizza is cold."

"Who cares? I'd eat anything. Wrangling chickens works up an appetite."

I pass him the dish towel, and his hand touches mine. For a few seconds we stand idle, both holding the towel, skin on skin. It's simple and innocent, yet electrifying. Attraction is addictive. It's a slow dance to a favorite chorus, one note—one heartbeat—at a time.

Before my blush hits the boiling point, I turn and sit at the table.

He joins me. "I have to leave soon," he says before eating his pizza.

I glance at my watch. It's nine fifteen.

"I said I'd be home by ten." He corkscrews his lips.

"Well, your clothes should be dry."

He nods. "We should do this again."

"Minus the chickens?"

"If being with you involves chickens, then I'll deal with chickens."

Tipping my chin to hide my smile, I murmur, "For someone who hasn't been on a date in years, you're pretty good at it."

"I'm not."

"You are." I lift my gaze. "It's effortless. You say all the right things, not because you're trying. It's just"—I shrug—"kind people say nice things, and you're a genuinely kind person, Ozzy Laster."

He adjusts in his chair, an uncomfortable squirm. "Whatever you think I'm saying that's so right and effortless, it's dumb luck." When his eyes meet mine, we hold each other's gaze for a few seconds of silence.

"Well." I break it first, picking at the toppings on my half-eaten slice of pizza. "Luck is on your side."

"And yours."

I laugh. "How do you figure?"

"I had your back in the men's room."

I flick a black olive at him, and he jerks to the side so it lands on the floor behind him. "I thought we weren't ever going to talk about it again."

"You're the only one talking about it." He slides out of his chair and picks the olive off the floor. "I just *mentioned* it. There's a difference. Anyhow, I have to go. Thank your roommate for loaning me clothes." Ozzy disappears into the laundry room.

Minutes later, he emerges in dry clothes, except for his wet jacket, which is still on the porch. I get a good look at his shirt for the first time and laugh.

"You fix things. Good to know. I hope you fix them well, since my life sort of depends on it."

He steps onto the porch with me right behind him. "Your safety is my number one priority. It was before we ever met. And now that I've met you, I'm going to drive every other mechanic crazy with my constant need to check and recheck everyone's work. In return, you have to prioritize your safety too. You have to do your part." He finishes tying his boots and scrunches his nose while threading his arms through his wet coat.

To keep from touching him, because I fear I wouldn't be able to stop, I busy my hands with his zipper, working it up his torso like dressing a child. "Thanks for the flowers." Our proximity hits me when

I meet his gaze, stealing my breath. I let go of his zipper and take a step back.

"They're just flowers." He shrugs. "I didn't buy them. I just picked them."

Biting my lower lip, I shake my head. "You *just* picked them," I whisper with a soft chuckle.

"Maren?"

"Hmm?"

He flicks his gaze over my shoulder. "If I weren't riding off into the proverbial sunset on a bicycle, I'd kiss you. But my life is complicated, so I have to take it slow."

More slow dancing.

"That's my line when I fly off into the literal sunset. Slow works for me," I say.

Ozzy shakes his head. "And you thought I was the one saying all the right things." His lips twitch. "Good night."

"Night."

When he passes me, the back of his hand slowly grazes mine.

"Now you're just teasing me." I glance over my shoulder just as he peeks over his and winks.

I'm a goner. Single dads who say all the right things, pick the perfect number of wildflowers, *and* have the perfect hand brush before riding off into the sunset on a bicycle are officially my new favorite drug.

Chapter Six

OZZY

The following morning, the foot of my bed dips, rousing me from a good dream about flying. Three weeks before the car accident, I got my pilot's license. And now I may never use it.

"It's Saturday, pumpkin. Do you want to crawl into bed and go back to sleep with me?" I mumble, rolling to my side and pulling the covers over my shoulders.

"Not really," Amos says.

I quickly lift onto my elbows, blinking hard to see in the dark.

He stands, then opens my room-darkening shades, and I squint as the light burns my retinas.

"We have to talk," he mumbles, but it sounds more like a grumble.

I reach for my watch on the nightstand. It's not quite seven. So much for sleeping in this morning. With a deep sigh, I swing my legs off the side of the bed and stretch before twisting my back from side to side. "What do we need to talk about?"

"Have you had the talk with Lola?"

"The talk?" I stand and stretch some more.

"The sex talk."

I step into a pair of jeans and wait for something real to wake me up. There's no way Amos is in my room, this early on a Saturday, asking me about the sex talk.

"If not, today might be a good time to bring it up," he says.

Shit. I'm not waking up. This must be real. It's the 2.0 version of "What are your intentions with my daughter?" Men joke and brag about sex; we don't *talk* about it.

"Not gonna lie, Amos. I was planning on doing yard work today. So, sadly, I'll need you to elaborate on why I should talk about sex with Lola." I give him my dead eyes after pulling on a T-shirt.

Amos adjusts his Texas-size belt buckle. He's always in Wrangler jeans with a big-ass belt buckle and a western button-down. "There was an incident last night," he says. "Lola forgot to take a glass of water to sit by her bed. So she woke up a little after midnight and came upstairs."

I don't like where this is going.

He glances behind him and closes the door. "I was watching TV."

"Porn?"

He clears his throat. "Sexually explicit."

"Porn?"

Amos frowns and nods several times. "I'm not sure she saw much. She was rubbing her eyes when she stepped into the living room and said, 'Hi, Pa.' I immediately turned off the TV." Again, he adjusts his belt buckle and sniffs, as if throwing back his shoulders and acting all manly will make this less awkward.

Staring at the gray carpet, I pinch the bridge of my nose. "Were you just watching it? Or were you *participating*?"

"I was under a blanket."

He was participating. *Fuck my life.*

"I asked her what she needed, and she said a glass of water. So she got it and headed back downstairs with nothing more than a good night. I don't think she saw anything. But in case she did, I thought I should mention it."

My hand falls to my side as my whole body deflates. "This is yours, Amos. Your actions. Yours to clean up. I don't have an issue talking to her about sex," I say, even though that's not entirely true. "But pornography is not a conversation I'm ready to have with my ten-year-old daughter."

"What am I supposed to say to her?" he asks, narrowing his eyes until every line on his old face collapses into a deep wrinkle.

I hold my hands out to the side. "I don't know. This is your lesson to learn, not mine. As a rule, we shouldn't do things in this house that we're unwilling to explain to the resident child. There's a reason bedrooms and bathrooms have locks on the doors. I guess you can start with the sex talk that usually involves two people falling in love. Now, how you get from that to an old man on the sofa jerking off under a blanket to two strangers on television having sex . . . well, that's a complicated bridge to build."

Before opening the door, I slap a hand on his shoulder, giving him a firm squeeze (which I have never done nor ever imagined having the upper hand to do). "Good luck." I stop short of saying "buddy" because Amos has a locked gun chest in his bedroom. I only have a crossbow because Brynn never wanted guns in the house with a child, despite her father having an armory on the property where she grew up.

"Tia doesn't know. And if Lola doesn't say anything, I won't broach the subject. I just wanted to give you a heads-up in case she mentions it to you," Amos says with a dismissive headshake while following me upstairs.

I pause midway for a moment. "Thanks. I guess."

"How was your evening?" Tia asks the second I step into the kitchen, which smells of burnt toast. "Did you get caught in the rain?" She takes her toast to the kitchen table.

"I did," I say, reaching for the coffeepot.

"I heard you come in a little before ten, so I assumed you spent the evening in wet clothes."

"I did." I face her, leaning against the counter while sipping my coffee.

Amos slides around the corner and heads to his bedroom. Coward.

Tia scrutinizes me over her jeweled reading glasses while scraping the butter knife along her toast. "You wouldn't have to ride your bike everywhere if you'd show that girl a little tough love."

I pause the mug at my lips. "You mean restrain her and make her ride in a car? We've talked about this ad nauseam. It has a high chance of backfiring."

"It's ridiculous that she's okay with riding her bike near streets filled with cars, but she won't get into a car. Have you explained that to her?"

"No. Because if she refuses to ride a bike or let me ride one, I'm screwed."

Tia scoffs, removing her readers and letting them dangle from the chain around her neck. "Do you hear yourself? Since when do parents need permission from their children to do things?"

"Do you hear *yourself*? Did you raise a child who lost a parent in a horrific car accident? Did you raise a child who spent a month in the hospital recovering from near-fatal injuries? Did you raise a child who looked in the mirror and cried when they saw their face because they didn't think they'd ever be pretty? Did you raise a child who had panic attacks just at the sight of a car in the garage? I need you to stop judging me for how I'm navigating this journey that you have never taken. I know I'm not going to do everything right, but I'm heeding the advice of experts who have experience with childhood trauma. It's the best I can do. And I believe it's what Brynn would want me to do for Lola."

Tia bites into her toast, squinting at me while she slowly chews. This is where she expects me to apologize for challenging her, but I won't do it today. As grateful as I am for her help with Lola, I won't sell my soul and bow down to her reign.

"How long?" she asks.

"For what?"

"How long will you ride a bike and let her fears dictate your lives?"

"I don't know. When she gets into a vehicle, I'll check my calendar and let you know how long it took."

"You sold your car. Don't you think it's time to buy a new one? At least take that first step. Don't you find it odd that she'll let me and Amos drive?"

"Don't take this too personally, but I don't think she feels like you're her whole world."

Tia frowns.

"And I didn't sell my car. Diego took it to his place."

Her expression softens. "Well, it's good to hear you didn't completely give up on her recovery."

"Dad? The toilet won't stop running," Lola calls.

I glance at the microwave clock. She's up earlier than usual for a Saturday. "I love her more than life, so I'll never give up on her," I say before leaving Tia (and her high horse) to check out the plumbing situation downstairs.

When I turn the corner into the bathroom at the bottom of the stairs, the toilet is not running or clogged, and there's no toilet paper in it. "Lola?"

"Psst! In here," she calls from her room, head poking out the cracked open door.

"What are you doing?"

"Shh!" She presses a finger to her pursed lips.

When I close her bedroom door behind me, she jumps onto her bed, pulling her knees into her chest so that her purple nightshirt covers her whole body.

"I needed water in the middle of the night," she says before popping her lips several times.

Shit. Here we go.

"So I went upstairs, and Pa was watching TV." Her lips corkscrew, and she averts her gaze for a few seconds. "Dad." She presses her hand to her chest like a drama queen. "There were two girls and a guy naked on television, then Pa quickly turned it off. But I know what I saw."

Two girls and a guy. He couldn't stick to vanilla porn. How am I supposed to have a talk about the birds and the bees with a bee and *two* birds?

"Before I talk about sex with you, maybe I should ask how much you already know."

"I know about sex." She rolls her eyes.

Do I quiz her to make sure? Do I ask where she learned it?

With a slow nod, I map out this conversation when I should be punting it to Amos. "Well, sex is how babies are made—"

"Dad! Duh."

"You didn't let me finish." I cross my arms over my chest. "People—adults—*married* adults sometimes have sex because they love each other, and it's a way to bond." I uncross my arms and lace my fingers behind my head. This is not what I had planned for today. "And it can feel good," I continue. "However, some people also enjoy watching it, like how I used to play football, but now I just watch it."

Dear god. Did I just make sex a spectator sport in my daughter's eyes?

"What I mean is—"

"So Pa doesn't have sex anymore, he just watches it?"

Make it stop!

"Sometimes. Not very often. And only when he's alone and needs to"—I rub my forehead—"relax."

When this train wreck of a conversation ends, I need to clear shelf space for my Worst Dad of the Year trophy. She's ten. I'm sure there are books on this, but what should I say? *I'll get back to you.*

"Okay," Lola says with a shrug.

Okay? That's it? We're done?

"Are you going to help me do yard work today?" I ask, grasping for any change in subject.

"Do I have to?"

"Yes."

She frowns.

"Do you want me to heat a breakfast burrito for you?"

"Dad, I think doughnuts go with yard work."

"Nice try. What if pizza for dinner goes with yard work?"

"Cinnamon breadsticks for dessert?"

"That can be arranged."

"Fine. I'll help."

"Attagirl." I shut her door and head upstairs to kill Amos.

Chapter Seven

MAREN

"We need to clean the house," Calvin "Fitz" Fitzgerald says the second I open my bedroom door in the morning. With the bucket of supplies in his hand, he rounds the corner into his and Will's bathroom. He's my grumpy roommate, but he's marrying a sunshine, so he'll even out.

"This means my BFF is coming home!" I clap my hands several times before propping myself against the doorframe.

Fitz eyes me over his shoulder while squeezing cleaner into the toilet bowl. Over six feet tall, with thick brown hair, blue eyes, and a sexy scowl, Fitz could be a centerfold for a firefighter calendar, just like Will. But his personality isn't as sexy. He's a smoke jumper who would rather read a book than socialize.

"I think she's *my* BFF," he mumbles.

"She's your fiancée."

"Can't she be both?"

"No." I smirk. "When will she be here?"

"Any minute."

I laugh. "Thanks for the short notice. She's going to have to deal with my messy bathroom mirror. Is Will awake?"

"He didn't come home last night." Fitz scrubs the hell out of the toilet. His fiancée, Jamie, loves a clean house. When she lived here full time, she was the cleaning drill sergeant.

"Are we worried that he's been in a car accident, or are we happy he got laid?" I ask.

"Nah, we would have heard about an accident by now. He probably stayed at the firehouse to make us think he got laid."

I giggle. "You're so mean."

The front door creaks open.

"She's here," I whisper, eyes wide.

Fitz stands, drops the toilet brush into the bucket of supplies, and quickly washes his hands. "Why don't you make yourself scarce for an hour or two?"

"Why?"

He glances up at my reflection in the mirror and smirks. "It's about to get loud."

I roll my eyes. "Why don't you have your loud sex in the shed?"

"My bed is bigger."

The creaky stairs alert us to Jamie's proximity.

"There's my BFF!" I meet her at the top of the stairs with a bear hug. Jamie's a travel nurse, enjoying the rest of her twenties and the opportunity to explore new places before marrying Fitz and starting a family. They spend most of the winter together; then she takes assignments when it's fire season. But she agreed to a six-week position at a psych hospital in Seattle before the start of fire season because the pay was too good to pass up.

And because I like to make my friends squirm, I keep a firm hold on Jamie, knowing she's dying to be in Fitz's arms and his bed after six weeks apart.

Fitz pries her from my hold.

Jamie giggles. "Missed you, too, Maren. How have—"

Fitz smashes his mouth to hers, hands tangled in her long black hair, a few inches longer than when I met her.

She moans, and he walks her backward into his bedroom and kicks the door shut. Then the door makes a *thunk* sound like something hit it.

She did. He's going to screw her against the door before they make it to the bed.

I don't plan on standing this close to the bedroom, listening to their loud sex, but I take a few seconds to envy that kind of passion. No one thought Fitz would ever marry or attempt a committed relationship. The firefighter profession, in general, doesn't have a great track record with long-lasting relationships.

"Oh god, Fitz . . ." Jamie moans.

Suppressing a grin, I jog down the stairs to grab a coffee.

When I'm half-caffeinated and under a blanket on the sofa, I text Ozzy since he hasn't texted me. Not that he needed to, but it's nice to get a follow-up after a date if it was a good one.

I know scavenging for chickens wasn't the dream date, but I hope he gave me points for originality.

Maren: G-morning

I start to vomit a long message about how much fun I had last night despite Reagan and his chickens, but I delete everything except the basic good morning.

Ozzy: Who's this?

Maren: Lol it's Maren. You should flesh out my contact information

Ozzy: Maren who?

I laugh. It's funny—I think.

Maren: The chicken lady. Am I that forgettable?

Ozzy: You have chickens?

Maren: Cute. What are you doing?

Ozzy: Yard work

Maren: Sounds like fun

Ozzy: It's not

Ozzy: My daughter is helping me. She's the best daughter in the world. When we are done I'm buying her pizza and dessert breadsticks

Maren: You're a nice dad

Ozzy: I'm an okay dad. I should let my daughter ride her bike to school by herself

Maren: How far is the school?

Ozzy: 2 miles

Maren: I'm sure that's a hard decision

Ozzy: It's not. I don't know why I haven't let her do it

Maren: I don't want to keep you from yard work. Thank you for the pizza. I hope you're getting a different kind tonight

Ozzy: When did I have pizza?

I stare at the message. He needs to use emojis. Is this his idea of texting humor?

Maren: Last night. Did you fall off your bike on the way home and hit your head?

Ozzy: I don't think so

Ozzy: Did I meet you at the bar?

I set my phone on the coffee table like it's too hot to hold. *What's going on?*

OZZY

"Dad?"

"Huh?" I cut another wad of dried ornamental grass and shove it in the lawn bag. "Lola, you're supposed to be helping me. What are you doing?"

"Who's Maren?" she asks.

I freeze for a second before slowly glancing over my shoulder and squinting at her sitting on the bottom deck step, staring at my phone screen. "Why are you messing with my phone?"

"I wasn't, but then it vibrated with a message from someone named Maren. And she called herself the chicken lady when I asked who she was."

"Lola, you're not supposed to mess with my phone," I say before grumbling a few expletives beneath my breath as I trek toward her, peeling off my leather gloves.

"I'm helping you by being your secretary." She gives me a toothy grin and bats her eyelashes while I pluck my phone from her hands.

Based on Maren's responses, she thought she was talking to me, and why wouldn't she? Except Lola's responses make me sound like a dumbass.

Ozzy: It's me. My daughter took my phone and was responding for me. So sorry

"Who's Maren? You had pizza last night? Does she like you? Why is she texting you? Does she have chickens? We should get chickens. Ellie has chickens. They eat the eggs."

"You're not riding to school on your own." I glare at her.

"But Dad—"

"And you're not getting dessert breadsticks tonight because you snooped in my phone and pretended to be me. And you haven't helped me do anything outside yet."

Lola narrows her eyes and parks her hands on her hips. "You. Are. A. Big. Meanie." She spins on her heel and stomps up the deck stairs.

Instead of responding to Maren's cringe emoji, I call her.

"I am so sorry," she answers without a hello.

"That's my line." I laugh, inspecting the tulips blooming along the back fence. "It's fine. She won't let it go, but I'll keep her grounded in her room until she promises never to mention your name again."

"You know how to make a girl feel special," Maren says.

I scratch the back of my head. "That came out all wrong. It's not you; it's Lola's recent obsession with my dating life." *And my sex life.*

"I don't blame her," Maren says. "I'm curious about your dating life too. Have you had any recent dates? Been caught in the rain? Wrangled any chickens?"

My smile grows exponentially. "What are you up to today?"

"Oh, I thought you'd never ask. I'm finishing my coffee while my roommate and his fiancée have loud sex upstairs. I should probably make them a snack. They'll be famished when they're done, at the rate they're going. I bet you're jealous that you don't get to enjoy my level of fun."

I kick at the clump of mulch under the tree. "No. I get a different kind of *fun* in the form of having to explain pornography to a ten-year-old."

"Oh my god, what?"

"She woke up after midnight and needed a drink of water, and she found her grandfather in the living room watching porn."

"Nooooo . . ." Maren laughs. "I'm sorry. I know it's not funny, but—"

"It's fine. If it weren't my life, it would be hilarious."

"You win, Ozzy. No one has to explain to me what my roommates are doing upstairs. I can't imagine what it's like to be a parent, let alone a single parent—a single parent of a daughter who experienced something incredibly traumatic. Well, not counting the porn incident."

"There's no cake for surviving this parenting gig. There should be cake," I say.

"Mmm, cake. What kind of cake should there be?"

I chuckle. "Carrot, of course."

"Stop. You did not just say my favorite cake."

"Seriously?"

"Yes," she says. "But it has to have pineapple in it. That's the secret ingredient. Crushed pineapple makes it so moist. And the frosting has to be cream cheese."

"Keep talking," I say, gobbling up every ounce of her cheeriness.

Maren giggles. "I'd better not. I think my metabolism took a nosedive just dreaming about it. Besides, you have work to do, and my offseason client is taking me to lunch. I just wanted to tell you that I had a great time. In case you were wondering."

I cringe. "I should have called earlier. That's probably proper dating etiquette, huh?"

"I'm not sure," Maren says. "I've never dated anyone who's taken the time to consider proper dating etiquette. I'm sure my eagerness to message you seems a little desperate."

"I rode my bike in the rain just to spend time with you. Who's the desperate one?"

She doesn't respond right away. There's a pause, and then she hums like she's eating something good, like carrot cake. "Ozzy." I swear she purrs my name. "You're not desperate, but thank you for making me feel better. I hope you get things worked out with Lola. And I'm sorry if I caused any tension between you."

"Don't sweat it. Can I ask about your offseason client?"

"He's a professor and a friend of my dad's. I fly his private jet in the offseason, and he has another pilot friend who only likes to fly during the summer, so it works out perfectly."

"Always in the air," I murmur, feeling a pang of envy.

She hums again. God, I love her hums. "Yes. It's the best place to be."

I like living vicariously through her. "I'm sure. Is your first shift Monday?"

"Wednesday," she says. "My shifts are ten days on, five off."

"Oh, Maren, Maren, Maren . . ."

She chuckles. "What is it, Oswald?"

I gaze at the mostly sunny sky just as a plane leaves a vapor trail. "You're my idol."

Chapter Eight

MAREN

"Hey." Jamie peeks into my bedroom while I hang my laundry before heading out. "Where are you off to?"

"Ted is taking me to lunch."

She sits on the end of my bed, cheeks red from three hours of sex that I assume were broken up with a few catnaps.

"How long are you home?" I ask, threading the hanger into the sleeves of my white button-down.

"I'm not sure. I haven't taken another job yet."

"That's awesome. Lots of time to catch up."

"You can help Fitz and me look for a house."

I close my closet door and open my shades. "You have a house."

Jamie chuckles. "Will has a house. We have a room, a shared kitchen, and a living room."

Leaning my backside against the oak dresser, I cross my arms. "You want to have sex in other rooms of the house?"

Jamie curls her hair behind her ears, lips tucked between her teeth.

"You two are going to guilt me into moving out," I grumble.

"Not at all. I think Will would be heartbroken if he lost all of us. Do you *want* to move out?" She tucks her legs into her gray, oversize sweatshirt, which I think belongs to Fitz.

Do I want to move out? No. Do I want to have a three-hour sexcapade with a man who adores me beyond words and who makes me want my (our) own place?

"What's that look?" Jamie's head slants to the side.

"What look?"

"You have a dreamy look on your face. Are you imagining your own place?"

"I met someone."

She parts her lips, eyebrows sliding up her forehead. "Someone is not anyone. Do tell."

"He's a new mechanic at Cielo. We had the most embarrassing first encounter. Remind me to tell you all about it when I get back home. His name is Ozzy. He lost his wife in a car accident two years ago, and he has a ten-year-old daughter named Lola."

"A single dad? Wow."

I frown. "I know. I'm conflicted about it. Single parents are a package deal. And I really like him, but I don't want to lead him on if I'm uncomfortable with the idea of someone else's child being part of my life, ya know? It feels like a lot of responsibility."

Jamie nods slowly.

"And there's one other thing about him."

"What's that?" She narrows her eyes.

"He rides a bike."

"And?" Jamie chuckles.

"No, you don't understand. He rides a bicycle because his daughter won't ride in a car, and she doesn't want *him* riding in one or driving one either. So he walks or rides his bike everywhere—rain, snow, or shine."

"Oof. That's complicated. I've dealt with patients like her. It's a heartbreaking and debilitating fear. Is she getting help?"

"Yes. I don't know a lot. I haven't wanted to pry. We've only had one date. But I really like him."

Jamie hops off the bed and steps toward me. "I can see it from your face. You're glowing. He looks good on you."

I smirk. "He hasn't been on me yet."

"Well, that's a shame," she says knowingly.

"It really is. He wants to take it slow. *And* he picked those six yellow glacier lilies that are in the mason jar downstairs. Six because it's the smallest perfect number, and he wrote a note about the flowers, but it got wet."

"Maren." Jamie grabs my shoulders. "Marry him."

We giggle together.

"Seriously," she says, "if you like him, don't back down. He's worth the wait, so give him time."

"I listened to you and Fitz for three hours. I know you think Fitz was worth the wait." I follow her out of the bedroom and down the stairs.

"How did I sound?" she asks. "Was it sexy like a lion roaring, or was it a moan like I was giving birth?"

"You sounded like a sinner who found Jesus." I laugh, dropping my handbag at the door before making my way through the living room to the kitchen, where Fitz is cutting an onion. "Your special chili?"

"Yep," he says while Jamie wraps her arms around his waist and presses her cheek to his back.

I think I want what they have; at least, I feel this when I'm around them, but when I'm flying, I don't want to ever feel like my wings have been clipped. How is it possible to want to soar *and* feel grounded?

"Maren's thinking of getting her own place, too, so she can entertain her new boyfriend and his daughter."

Fitz glances over at me while I fill my bottle with water from the fridge.

"That's oversimplified. Jamie's still in a sex fog. You literally screwed her brains out."

"Maren's filthy rich. She should move out," Fitz says, scraping the onion off the cutting board and putting it into the pot while Jamie opens the cans of tomatoes.

I shake my head. It's no secret that I make way more money than Fitz and Will, and I do it in a matter of five to six months. Then there's the money I make from flying Ted everywhere in the offseason, which is more than I make as a tanker pilot. And I've saved most of my money or invested it. But I like having roommates, and even though Brandon is no longer alive, I feel him in this house. Leaving would resurrect the grief.

"Why would I move out if you two are moving? Then I can have your room, since it's bigger than mine."

"Or you could pay cash for your own house and get ten cats," Fitz says.

"Fitz!" Jamie punches his arm, and he laughs. "I just said she met someone."

"That's right. Sorry. Do I need to vet him? Brandon would have wanted me to do that." Fitz narrows his eyes.

"When are you getting your vasectomy reversed?" I ask to wiggle my way out of the hot seat.

He buckles at the waist with a sour expression. "Not talking about it."

"At the end of fire season." Jamie pinches his butt. "And then we're planning a wedding."

"Well"—I screw the lid onto my water bottle—"I'll clear my schedule to help you two find a house so you can get married. And maybe I'll find one, too, so I can . . ." I press my lips together because I don't know where I'm going with this.

"So you can what?" Jamie gawks. "Get married?" Excitement explodes across her face.

I roll my eyes. Oswald Laster is messing with my mind.

OZZY

"You have to tell me." Lola bursts after keeping her mouth shut all day and through half of dinner at the restaurant. "Who's Maren?"

"A friend." I slide another slice of pizza onto my plate.

"A girlfriend?"

"She *is* a girl."

"Dad."

"Lola." I smirk while chewing.

"Is she married?"

"No."

"Kids?"

"No."

"Is she pretty?"

I shrug. *She's beautiful.*

"Do you want to have sex with her?"

I almost choke before I can swallow. Fisting my hand at my mouth, I shake my head. "Enough with the sex talk."

"Well, Dakota said you're too young to stop having sex."

"You're grounded from seeing Dakota."

She rolls her dramatic eyes. "He's in my class. Duh. I have to see him."

"Well, you don't have to talk to him."

"Are you going to go on a date?"

"We just discussed this with Nana and Pa. I have you. I'm not lonely or missing anything or anyone in my life."

"I'm not going to live with you forever. I'm going to college."

"Excellent. Your mom would be proud."

"Do you think she'd want you to find a girlfriend?" Lola pulls the cheese off her pizza, recovers the mushrooms and sausage, and puts those back on without the cheese.

I'll end up eating her cheese, so it doesn't go to waste. "Lola, your mom and I didn't talk about that."

That's a lie.

"If you had died instead, would you have wanted her to find a new boyfriend?"

This girl is not ten. She's twenty.

"Sure," I say in defeat.

"Well, then . . ."

"Sweetie, Nana and Pa moved in with us to help out. In return, they want to know I'm focused solely on you. So I think I should respect their wishes for the time being."

"Hogwash."

Again, I choke. She picked that up from Tia. It's what she says to Lola when my darling daughter gets overdramatic, which is all too often.

"Do you even know what that means?" I ask.

"It means BS, but you won't let me say that."

I frown. "Let's talk about you. Where do you plan on going to college?"

"UM, where Mom taught."

I didn't expect her to answer. I don't want her to make plans beyond this slice of pizza on her plate. "I was joking. It's a big world, Lola. And you're ten. However, when the time comes, you may decide to spread your wings and go to school in another state."

She deflates. "I have to go to UM because I can ride my bike there."

Oh, sweet girl.

"Do you wish you could ride in a car without thinking about the accident? Without thinking about Mom dying? If someone could erase the fear and the bad memories from your mind, and you could be like your friends at school who don't fear riding in cars, would you want that?"

Lola presses her fingertip to the parmesan cheese on her plate and then licks it off. "Yeah."

On the inside, I enjoy a sigh of relief.

"Is Victoria going to erase my memories?"

"No. I think she's working to make your memories feel less scary. I'm just happy to hear that you want to have a different life. You have a lot of years before you need to think about college. So why not imagine a day you can ride or even drive in a car?"

She tries to smile, but it falls down her face like her shoulders collapsing inward. I don't push anymore.

"Still have room for dessert breadsticks?" I ask.

She perks up. "I thought you said no."

"I did, but I changed my mind."

Her spine straightens, and that smile I adore returns to her beautiful face. "Maybe you can change your mind about other things, like letting me ride to school by myself," she says.

"I could, but I'm not going to."

Chapter Nine

MAREN

I'm a fraud, and I blame Ozzy Laster.

It's been three days since I talked with him. I start my ten-day shift tomorrow. Could I text him? Sure, but I want him to make the next move so that I know it's not one sided. Yet here I am, driving to Cielo with a plate of homemade cookies. Jamie is an excellent baker and an even better friend. She said popping into a guy's workplace with cookies is always a win.

"Hey, Maren," Hillary says. "What brings you in today?"

"You know, I got to thinking about the form I filled out for the insurance update, and I think I forgot to sign it. So I decided to pop in and check, and I thought I'd bring some cookies to leave in the break room."

"You bake?" Hillary narrows her brown eyes.

No. I don't bake. And I know I signed my insurance-update form. Again, I'm a fraud, and I blame Ozzy.

I shrug. "Sometimes."

"Wow. Well, I'm sure everyone will scarf down those cookies, but there was no need to stop by, because you signed the form. I always check for signatures."

"Phew. Now I feel silly. I should have just called. I'll set these in the break room and finish running errands." I have no errands. Getting Ozzy's attention is my only plan for today.

"Better let me steal one before you take off with them." She winks.

"Of course." I fold back the plastic wrap so she can grab a cookie.

"These smell amazing. I love a classic chocolate chip cookie." She takes a bite, and her eyes roll back in her head. "You *have* to give me your recipe."

"I'll do that."

Hillary narrows her eyes and slowly chews another bite. "There's something extra. It's so good, but I can't quite place the taste. What is it?"

"It's a secret ingredient."

"If you're giving me the recipe, you can just tell me." She chuckles.

That's such a good point.

"It's the vanilla." I smile.

"Really? I think vanilla is standard in chocolate chip cookies."

She could be right. I need to make more things from scratch.

Her eyes widen. "Let me guess. Do you use vanilla straight from the bean instead of an extract?"

Retreating toward the door, I tap the tip of my nose. "Bingo."

"Thanks, Maren."

"You're welcome."

Before reaching the break room, I peek into the hangar to see if I can spot my favorite single dad. When I come up empty, I turn. "Oof!"

Plunk!

Taylor cringes at the eight cookies scattered at our feet. His cringe intensifies when he sees the one stuck to my pink blouse. Finally, he eyes the two still protected by the plastic on one side and the plate on the other. "Shit, Maren. I'm so sorry. I was looking at my phone and—"

"No biggie. I turned too quickly and—"

Ozzy steps around the corner, zipping his coveralls. He smiles at me, but it fades when he sees the mess on my blouse and all over the floor.

Taylor squats and picks up the cookies. "Were these for us? I'm such an oaf, Maren. God. I'm sorry."

"They were for Ozzy's daughter. I think I got her in trouble the other day." I change my story on the fly. Hopefully, no one will ask Hillary to corroborate it.

Ozzy's gaze slides from Taylor's quick cleanup to my shirt. "You made Lola cookies?"

"I did."

"What can I do to make this right?" Taylor stares at the cookies. "I'll put them in the break room. I think there's a three-second rule, right?"

Ozzy smirks at me.

I tear my gaze from him and smile at Taylor. "Go for it. And don't worry about it. I have more at home."

Well, Jamie does, unless Fitz already inhaled them.

"Uh . . ." Taylor nods to my shirt.

I peel the gooey cookie from it. "Really, it will wash off," I assure him.

Taylor shakes his head. "Sorry, Maren," he mumbles, heading toward the break room.

"As a rule, I refuse to have anything go right around you," I say, giving Ozzy a toothy grin.

"Maybe I'm just bad luck." He easily encircles my wrist with his big calloused hand.

With a silent gasp, I part my lips. I've been daydreaming about his touch—conscious, well-thought-out daydreams.

He lifts my hand and takes a bite of the cookie. "Damn, Maren. That's a good cookie. A badass pilot *and* a baker."

I'll correct him later, when I'm not wearing chocolate or burning up from his touch. I open my hand to let him take the rest of the cookie. He releases my wrist and snags it, popping the other half into his mouth.

Lucky cookie.

"I should take off my shirt," I murmur.

He licks the chocolate from his lips, eyes flared.

"What I mean"—I clear my throat—"is I should get home and stain treat this shirt. That sounded like I wanted to flash you."

"Do you?" He lifts a serious eyebrow.

"Flashing feels like a third-date thing. We've only had one date," I say with a nervous laugh.

And you need to ask me for a second date!

"The cookies were a kind gesture. Lola would have loved them, but don't worry about her. I took her for pizza and let her get dessert. And Sunday, she had a softball game in the afternoon, which ended with ice cream."

"Such a good dad."

He smiles. "I was thinking about stopping by your house on my way home, if I got out of here on time. But now you're here, so I don't have to worry about interrupting your evening plans."

I think he's just saying that to be polite since I brought cookies. "You don't have to say that."

"I know." He shrugs. "But it's true."

I nod slowly. "Okay. Sure." I glance down at my shirt. "Well, I'd better sneak into the restroom to clean up a little before I finish my errands."

"I'll see you around," he says, opening the door to the hangar.

"Yeah, see you around." I hide my dashed hopes behind a smile before sulking toward the restroom.

After doing a little damage control to my stained shirt, I head to my car, replaying my conversation with Ozzy. He wasn't going to stop by my house, but the opportunity presented itself to say it and not look like he was ghosting me, so he went for it. I can't blame him.

As I reach for my door handle, something on my windshield catches my eye. Six yellow flowers are attached to it, with the stems tucked behind the wipers, along with a folded note.

I take the note first.

> The arrowleaf balsamroot is part of the sunflower family. The root can be made into a respiratory aid tincture. Hope you love them!
>
> Ozzy x

That part of the note is in blue ink, but there's a PS in black ink.

> PS Thanks for the cookies. What an unexpected surprise. Drive safely.

I glance over my shoulder before turning in a slow circle with the note pressed to my chest. He had to have scribbled a quick PS and run everything out here at record-breaking speed. And while I don't see him anywhere, I can't help but wonder if he's hiding somewhere, watching me.

One by one, I carefully retrieve each flower and scan the area for a final time before climbing into my RAV.

Maren: Be still, my heart

I press send and drive my swooning heart home.

Three days and no fires. I work out at the base, read a thriller book that Fitz recommended, and play cards, idly waiting for the first call.

And when no one's paying attention to me, I text Ozzy.

Maren: What position does Lola play?

Maren: When is her next game?

Maren: What did you tell her about me?

It takes him a while to respond because his job involves steady work.

Ozzy: Pitcher. Tomorrow. Not much.

I chuckle at his thorough reply.

Maren: A man of few words. I respect that level of minimalism

Ozzy: Twiddling your thumbs?

I laugh.

Maren: Boredom is half the job. An existential threat to my profession. Are you on a break?

Ozzy: No. My phone kept vibrating in the pocket of my coveralls, tickling my balls until I felt the need to take a piss.

Covering my mouth, I suppress a snort.

Maren: My apologies

Ozzy: None needed. What's happening to the 2 fires at Flathead?

Maren: Letting them burn

Ozzy: Don't get a thumb cramp. I have to go back to work

Maren: Haha! Bye

That's the last I hear from him for the next week. And maybe it's because he heard that I've been sent to Nevada for two days and back to Missoula for more thumb twiddling until I end my ten-day stint with a fire near Flathead that they don't let burn. I'm grateful for the distraction. Fending off boredom at the bases or playing games on the tarmac leaves too much time to obsess over Ozzy.

On the first of my five days off, I let Will talk me into yard work.

"Spill," Will says while we prune the front yard shrubs on this breezy Saturday morning.

"You'll have to elaborate." I cast a glance in his direction.

"Jamie said you've found a new guy. She baked him cookies—don't get me started on that bait and switch tactic—and I heard he hasn't called."

"Sounds like Jamie spilled everything. What more can I tell you? That about covers it."

"Since when have you gotten so hung up on a guy to the point of pretending you can bake?"

"I can bake," I say in a high-pitched voice while flicking a twig at him.

Will chuckles. "I mean from scratch."

"I can bake from scratch. I just don't do it very often. For your information, there are many things I am very capable of doing that I simply choose not to do, or I choose an easier alternative."

"That's your problem. You must not have shown your full capabilities on the first date, and now he's uninspired by the bar you've set so low for yourself," Will says, as if he wants me to physically hurt him.

"What's that supposed to—" I squint at him. "Is that a sexual reference? You had better not be implying that I was bad in bed, therefore he doesn't want another date. Because I didn't sleep with him. I don't do that on the first date."

Will shoots me the hairy eyeball, but I keep my gaze aimed at the shrub.

"I *rarely* do that on the first date. My point is that even if I would have been willing to do it, he didn't want it to happen because he has a daughter, and he said he wanted to take things slow." I roll my eyes. "Why must you be such a perv, William Landry?"

"I'm just trying to help by figuring out where you went wrong." He nods to the paper yard bag, and I hold it open for him to stuff the trimmings into.

"It's rich that my single roommate is advising me on keeping a guy interested. Maybe I should talk to Fitz when he's done banging Jamie."

Will laughs. "Goddamn. They're always having sex. I'm all for making up for lost time, but I have legitimate concerns that he will snap her in half."

I giggle until I can't hold the bag open anymore. When I've caught my breath, I sigh and mumble, "I want that."

Will eyes me.

"You know what I mean," I say.

After a beat, he nods. "Yeah, it sucks feeling like everyone you know is married and having kids."

I shake the bag to make more room, and when I glance up at Will, he's examining me with a fixed stare. "What?"

"Nothing."

"That look isn't nothing. *Spill.*" I use his word.

"Let's do that thing." He continues to stuff yard waste into the bag.

"What thing?"

"The single-roommates-handshake contract."

"I'm lost, Will."

"If both of us are still single in, say . . . two years, we marry each other."

I scan his face, looking for a hint of amusement. "Are you serious?"

He shrugs. "Sure. Why not? I'm good looking, and you're decent. We understand each other's careers and the risks that come with them.

I mean, before long, it will just be the two of us living here until I find new roommates. It will basically feel like we're married anyway, minus the sex."

I survey the yard, tugging off my gloves. "I've been thinking about getting my own place." When my attention returns to Will, I wrinkle my nose. "We know I haven't been living here out of financial necessity. I just don't like living alone; this place makes me feel close to Brandon. But when I invited Ozzy, the guy who's ghosting me, over to the house, I realized how rare it is to have that opportunity. I have to find a night when my other roommates are gone."

"Go to his place instead," Will says.

"He has a daughter, and his deceased wife's parents live with him."

Will narrows his eyes and tilts his head.

"It's complicated and beside the point. I don't know if I'll have a second date with him, but it got me thinking about my life, age, and financial situation. Then Fitz and Jamie's announcement that they're looking for a house nudged me further into realizing I need to grow up. I'm not a young woman anymore. And this house is paid for. You don't need us here either."

Will rests a hand on his hip and momentarily gazes at the sky. "Without roommates, women will expect me to bring them here, and I can't sneak out of my own house at four in the morning."

I cough a laugh. "You are terrible. And you're going to die a bachelor."

He squints in my direction. "Not if you marry me."

"Yeah, about that . . . it would feel like marrying my brother, if he were still here. The ick factor is too big to overcome."

Will frowns.

Tapping my finger on my chin, I narrow my eyes. "Back before Fitz and Jamie got engaged, wasn't that doctor interested in you?"

Will quickly busies himself with picking up the trimming tools while he mumbles, "I don't know what you're talking about."

"You do. What's her name? She's the prodigy. You know, the one who became a doctor before she could legally drink? And I'm pretty sure she credited you with taking her virginity."

"Everleigh was in *medical school* before she turned eighteen. How the fuck was I supposed to know?"

I cover my mouth and giggle while Will's face reddens with frustration. "*Everleigh.* So you do remember her. That's a great name, by the way. Oh, Reichart. That's her name. Dr. Everleigh Reichart."

"We'll do the backyard tomorrow," he says, changing the subject.

I roll the top of the yard bag. "I wonder if she's still single. I bet Jamie would know. I'll ask her for you."

"Speaking of ick factors." Will inspects me through slitted eyes, but it only makes me laugh harder, so he stomps toward the garage, mumbling a few expletives.

Chapter Ten

OZZY

"Race you to the top!" Lola bolts to the right as we climb the stairs to the M Trail by the university. Brynn used to hike the trail over her lunch break and sit on the edge of the giant hillside M to eat her sandwich with a beautiful view of Missoula. It's a steep hill with many switchbacks, but Lola barely loses her breath, and I don't break a sweat.

Riding our bikes and walking everywhere for two years has whipped us into good shape. Victoria, Lola's therapist, likes to remind me of that when I feel the need to pull her aside and complain about Lola's slow progress and the ridiculousness of biking everywhere, even in the winter.

What do you think people did before they had cars? she said.

It's not that I don't like Victoria. She has a good rapport with Lola but is also annoying at times. Maybe that's just my occasional impatience, which gets exacerbated by Tia constantly yapping in my ear.

"Lola, trail etiquette," I holler as she approaches a couple and their dog headed down the trail. Last year, she accidentally knocked a lady on her ass.

My eager daughter stops, steps off the trail, and glances back at me with an angelic smile that's anything but innocent. According to friends with older kids, she's entrenched in the "I know" phase of adolescence, which I've been assured lasts until she's well into adulthood.

As soon as the couple and their dog pass her, she continues up the trail in a series of hops, skips, and jumps like it's no big deal despite the people catching their breaths on the benches at the switchbacks.

"Wish I had her energy," the guy with the dog says when I pass him.

I grunt and smile. "I wish she had half the energy."

The couple laughs.

I'll take Lola's endless energy as long as that contagious smile and dimpled cheeks always accompany it.

There's not a lot of wiggle room around the M, and it's a little more crowded this afternoon, so when I catch up to my daughter, I have to squeeze past hikers to reach her. She always goes straight to the top.

"Excuse me. Pardon me. Sorry, I'm just squeezing past." I shuffle and wedge my way to the top.

"Ozzy?"

I glance over my shoulder toward the familiar voice from the woman wearing a white floral hair scarf, gray leggings, and a fitted pink tee.

"Maren," I say as if it's ridiculous that she's hiking the same (incredibly popular) trail. Then I swallow the "What are you doing here?" part so I don't sound like an idiot.

I haven't texted or called her since she initiated contact a week ago. Do I tell her all the reasons why?

She has a serious job, and I don't want to interrupt her.

I have a weird living situation.

Transportation is a challenge.

I think I like her too much.

It's a long list.

"And here I thought nobody would be hiking this today." Maren laughs with a sarcastic eye roll.

I survey the gathering of hikers, including my daughter, six feet away, petting someone's yellow lab. "Yeah. I think everyone's out today."

She adjusts her hair scarf and averts her gaze when we make eye contact.

"Listen, I've been meaning to text—"

She waves me off. "You don't need to explain. I've been busy too."

I nod. "Twiddling your thumbs?"

She slaps a grin on her face when our gazes lock.

The grin is too big.

I remember big grins. Brynn used to punch me in the face with an exaggerated one when I was in trouble. It's the deranged look.

I'm joking about the thumb twiddling. She knows I'm kidding, right?

"Regardless"—I attempt to get back in her good graces—"I've been meaning to contact you."

"Dad? Coming?" Lola calls.

Maren cranes her neck past me. "Is that your daughter?" Her grin relaxes into something more genuine, less like a sharp knife dripping blood.

"Yes," I say.

Maren's gaze returns to me. It's expectant. And why wouldn't she anticipate me introducing her to my daughter, who's six feet away? The daughter for whom she made chocolate chip cookies.

Yet introducing her to Lola would be a disaster because my child has no chill.

"Well, it was really good seeing you. Be careful on your way down the trail. More accidents happen on the descent," I say.

You're an idiot! My inner voice speaks the truth.

Maren parts her lips, sliding her eyebrows up her forehead until they're hidden beneath her hair scarf. "Is this separation of church and state?"

I cringe while relinquishing several tiny nods. "Not because of church." I point to her. "It's state"—I jab my thumb over my shoulder at Lola—"who cannot handle this."

"Why am I church?"

I chuckle, scratching my jaw. "I don't know. I'm just saying—"

"Who are you?" Lola chirps behind me.

Too damn late. I press my lips together and cringe.

Maren looks to me for guidance.

I deflate. "Lola, this is a friend of mine. She works at Cielo too."

"Hi, Lola." Maren waves. "I'm Maren."

My cringe deepens while Maren unknowingly digs my grave. There's a reason I called her my friend.

Lola remembers everything.

"You texted my dad."

Maren gives me an apologetic smile, showing that realization happened a little too late on her part.

"You're pretty. Isn't she pretty, Dad?"

"Lola, speaking of pretty, it's pretty crowded up here. We should make our way down so other people can have our spots and enjoy the view."

"My mom died. And my dad's lonely."

For the love of god. Why? Just *why*?

I'm ready to roll her down this hill like a bowling ball.

With a nervous laugh, Maren's gaze ping-pongs between me and my diarrhea-mouthed daughter.

"Maren knows your mom died, and she knows I'm so busy raising you that I have no time to be lonely."

Maren's smile fades.

I can't win. I'm juggling my words to appease both these girls—women—and I'm fumbling and failing most spectacularly.

"I'm going to catch up to that dog." Lola points to the lady with the yellow lab as she descends the trail.

"Well, it was good to see you. Sort of," Maren murmurs, before turning and navigating her way past the M.

I sigh, having no choice but to walk down behind her.

"That came out all wrong," I say.

Maren keeps walking, rocks crunching beneath her trail shoes. "No. I think it came out as intended. No biggie."

When Lola's adequately out of earshot, I make a better case for myself. "It is a biggie. I like you. And I want to go out again, but I don't know how to navigate dating while raising a snoopy ten-year-old who has recently decided she desperately wants me to find someone to date. On top of that, her grandparents, whose help I need, don't want me to have any sort of life outside raising Lola. So I have to lie and sneak around, and I'm not good at it. But—"

Maren stops, and I nearly bump into her. "But what?" She turns to me, crosses her arms over her chest.

Are we having our first fight? After one date?

Maren is beautiful when she's mad. Maybe it's the breeze in her hair or the sun on her face. But her cheeks are red, and her eyes look extra blue today.

I want to kiss her. I've wanted to kiss her since our date.

"But maybe I can get good at it," I say.

She tightens her brow. "Good at what? Sneaking around?"

The more my grin swells, the more her eyes narrow.

"Yeah. Do you want to sneak around with me?"

"I'm not fourteen, Ozzy." She rolls her eyes and pivots, continuing down the trail.

"No. But wasn't fourteen fun? I loved my teen years. Not a real care in the world. Hormones raging out of control. Weekends were two days of nonstop shenanigans with friends. And there was nothing more exhilarating than sneaking around."

Maren chuckles, shakes her head, and alternates her gait between cautious steps and a slow jog while she navigates the dips and bumps of the descent. "That's not real anymore. You actually have *real* cares in the world."

"Not twenty-four seven. I found time to wrangle chickens with you."

"I don't buy it. You were the one who said we should take it slow because your life is complicated. And I was fine with it, but slow shouldn't mean you can't even send me the occasional text."

"I didn't want to lead you on or give you false hope."

She shoots me a quick glance over her shoulder. "But now you want to sneak around? When did you change your mind?"

"Literally the second the words left my mouth," I say while scratching the back of my head and trying not to smile until I'm sure she won't kill me for downplaying my inability to date a woman properly.

"You gave me flowers and notes," she says.

"Is that wrong? Or weird? It probably seems cheap since I'm not buying the flowers. But—"

Maren turns 180 degrees, and I almost run into her. "Wrong? Weird? Cheap?" She narrows her eyes. "Ozzy, I tied twine around the stems, dried them upside down to keep them indefinitely, and attached the note to the bouquet too. Then I waited for you to call or text me."

I smirk. "You liked the flowers."

Maren rolls her eyes and heads the rest of the way down the trail.

I should have called.

By the time we reach the steps at the parking lot, Lola has a kitten in her arms.

"Whose is that?" I ask, catching up to Maren and passing her to deal with Lola and her googly eyes.

"No one's. It's all alone. I found him by that bush, crying."

"What have I told you about touching stray animals?"

"He's a kitten, Dad."

"Lola, put it down. I'm sure its mom will be looking for it."

Maren pets the cat in Lola's arms, not helping my case.

"Dad, I bet his mom is dead, and that's why he's all alone. If we don't take him home, he will die."

Ouch. This girl packs an emotional punch. "It's called life, Lola. And how do you know he's a he?"

"How do *you* know you're a he?" She rolls her eyes.

Maren tries to suppress her laugh.

"We're not taking it home," I say.

"Why not?"

"Because."

"Because why? And don't say because you said so. Remember when you promised to always explain things to me?"

When I look to Maren for help, she curls her lips between her teeth and shrugs. In the next breath, she tries to find an excuse. "Lola, what if your grandparents are allergic to cats?"

I silently commend Maren for trying, but that's not the right defense.

"They aren't," Lola says. "They used to have cats. A lot of them. Right, Dad?"

"Lola. We don't have a car."

"Put him in your backpack," Lola says.

"He'll suffocate."

She frowns, sad eyes on the kitten before gazing at Maren.

"I bet he finds a good home." Maren nods with reassurance.

Lola nestles the cat in the bush and mumbles, "I bet something eats him before tomorrow."

I don't touch this conversation with another word. She's relinquishing the cat, and that's a win, even if I know she'll give me the cold shoulder for the next few days.

"It was nice meeting you, Lola," Maren says, sliding her key fob from her pocket.

Lola manages a lukewarm "You too" before sulking toward our bikes.

I walk down the stairs next to Maren and take several steps with her toward her RAV, keeping my back to Lola. "Can I call you later?"

Maren grunts, unlocking her car. "I don't know, Ozzy. Can you?"

"Let me rephrase. What are you doing later? Want to sneak out with me? Grab a drink at a bar?"

With her chin tucked, she opens her door. "You're all talk, Ozzy. But sure. I'll sneak out with you *if* you call. But I won't wait up for you."

"I'll check in with you at"—I glance at my watch—"nineteen hundred."

She giggles, shakes her head, and slides into the driver's seat.

"Later." I shut her door and tap twice on the window with my flat hand.

She finally glances in my direction, biting her lower lip.

I have no clue what I'm doing or where this is going.

Chapter Eleven

MAREN

Lola has heartbreaking scars on her face. She'll wear those reminders of her mother's death for a long time. Not a single day will pass that she won't look in the mirror and think about the tragedy and the hole in her chest that it has undoubtedly left.

"No." Will sneezes. "Just—" He sneezes again, eyes red, nose running. "No." He tosses his gaming controller aside and makes a dash for the bathroom, returning with a wad of tissue to blow his nose.

"How can you be allergic to cats? Isn't rescuing them from trees your job?"

"Fuck you, Maren. How did—*ACHOO!*" He wipes his eyes. "How did you not know that I'm allergic to cats?"

"I'll keep Bandit in my room."

"Dude. No! I'll be dead by morning. The furnace will disperse that shit all through the house. You have to take him outside now."

"I'll keep him in the shed."

"No. I'm going to rent it out."

"You've been saying that since Jamie moved out. Besides, I told you I will look for my own place."

"Whatever." He plops onto the sofa. "But that thing leaves the house immediately."

"He's a cat, not a thing. And I can't buy a house immediately. I'll keep him in the shed." I head toward the back door with Bandit meowing in my arms.

"Hope he has money. I'm charging him rent," Will hollers.

I stop and huff just before opening the door. Dozens of fighting words rush to the tip of my tongue, but I swallow them. "Fine. I'll pay double the rent so Bandit can stay in the shed until I find my own place." I snatch the key from the hook by the door and take Bandit to his new home.

After I find a box, cut air holes into it, and line the bottom with an old blanket, so Bandit doesn't decide to use the mattress as a litter box, I leave him in the shed to run to the pet store for supplies. And just as I pull back into the driveway, around seven, my phone rings.

"I can't believe you called," I say, slinging my purse over my shoulder and heading toward the backyard with my supplies.

"I'm a man of my word, even if I have very few words."

I laugh, opening the shed door. "What's with the whispering? Are you hiding?"

"No. I'm in my room. Not hiding."

"Then why are you whispering?"

"This is the voice I use when I'm sneaking around," he says.

My face hurts from smiling so much. It's been a long time since a guy has made me feel this giddy. "Are we still meeting for a drink somewhere close to your house, since you'll be walking or biking?"

"How about the Cider Snake at twenty-two hundred hours? They're open until zero hundred hours."

I chuckle. "Will everyone at your house be asleep by then?" I hit speaker on my phone and set it on the bed so I can dump kitty litter into the litter box.

"Yes. What's that sound?" he asks.

"Uh, I just got home from running errands, and I'm putting things away. What happens if someone wakes up and needs you, and you're not there?"

"I have one of those new inventions," Ozzy says. "It's a phone I can take with me so that I can be reached anytime. It's called a mobile or cellular phone."

"Don't be an ass. I was just starting to like you."

"Just? Wow. I thought we had a connection before *just*."

"I thought so, too, but then you ghosted me for days."

"Perhaps it seemed like that, but I was thoroughly thinking about you."

I take the stickers off the water and food bowls. "*Thoroughly* sounds a little invasive."

"Not invasive. Just thorough. I was thinking about all of you in every way. Wait. That sounds creepy."

I'm so glad he can't see my red cheeks. "Ozzy, you're my favorite creep."

"Don't say that. I need a better word."

"Too late. I'm sticking with creep. See you at twenty-two hundred." I end the call before he can continue to plead his I'm Not a Creep case.

"All right, little Bandit." I transfer him from the cardboard box to the litter box. "You do your duties while I wash out your new bowls."

He meows, which I interpret as an "okay." We're off to a great start, as long as Will's not dead from anaphylactic shock.

I arrive at the bar a few minutes early, and to my surprise, Ozzy's already in a booth with a beer, a plate of nachos, and purple flowers. This time, they have a delicate white ribbon around them.

"Breathe," I whisper on my way to the booth. Everything flutters to life from my chest to my tummy when I'm with him. "I don't eat after eight," I say, sliding into the opposite side of the booth, taking in Ozzy's messy but sexy hair and beaming white smile.

He's trimmed his beard since I saw him this afternoon. It's sexy too.

"Are these for me?" I pick up the six-stemmed bouquet of purple flowers. "Do you have all these wildflowers in your yard?"

"I cannot reveal my sources." He winks while I read the note.

> Shooting stars are pollinated by bees using sonication to release pollen from the flower's anthers. Hope you love them!
>
> Ozzy x

"I do love them," I whisper, blushing because he's so sweet and innocent, yet sexy beyond words.

My out-of-control mind imagines kissing him, sliding his white T-shirt over his head, and slowly unbuttoning his dark blue jeans. It's been a hot minute since I've had sex.

"What can I get you to drink?" he asks.

"Pinot noir."

Ozzy nods and makes his way to the bar. I feel like such a guy when he turns just before the counter, catching me staring at his ass. I quickly shift my attention to the nachos and toss a chip into my mouth.

When he returns with my wine, I catch his scent of bourbon and oak.

I'm in trouble.

"Thought you didn't eat after eight," he says.

"I'm not eating. I'm sneaking a few chips." I nod to my glass of wine while shrugging off my jacket. "Thank you."

"You're welcome." As he sips his beer, he narrows his eyes. "What happened?"

I glance down at my blue blouse. Please don't let there be food on it. I just want to be with this man *and* put together at least once. No coffee spills. No cookies stuck to my shirt. No begging for tampons.

Not seeing anything, I glance up at him.

He brushes his hand over his neck and chest by his collarbone. "You have scratch marks."

"Oh." I cover my neck. "They're from my cat."

He nods. "Well, thanks for not telling Lola that you have a cat. I thought for sure that the incident was headed south. I think she held it together because you were there. However, I never heard the end of it this afternoon. Even when I tucked her into bed, she was still hypothesizing about that kitten, guilting me for not bringing it home. Mourning its inevitable death. Calling me a kitten killer." He shakes his head. "I can't win with her."

I trace the foot of my wineglass with my finger. "I'm sure the kitten is fine."

He returns a raised eyebrow while eating another chip. "Or dead."

I shrug. "Or fine."

"I like your optimism." He adjusts his body, and his leg brushes mine; then he stops, leaving his leg touching mine.

I don't move, because I like it when our bodies touch, and from the twitch of his lips, I'd say he does too.

"Where was your cat the night I was at your place?" he asks.

As much as I want to play this out for a while, I'm dying to see his reaction. "I didn't have him. He's new."

Ozzy dips a chip in the cheese sauce, letting it linger while he coats it. His eyes are hyperfocused, like his mind is reeling. "What made you decide to get a cat?" His eyes meet mine while he shoves the chip into his mouth.

"It was an impulse," I say.

"And your roommates are okay with that?"

I sip my wine to hide my grin. "No. I recently discovered Will is highly allergic to them, so Bandit is staying in the she shed."

"Where'd you get him?" Ozzy asks.

This is so hard. I rub my lips together, fighting to hold back my laughter. What if he doesn't find this funny?

"I found him. He got separated from his litter." I resort to chewing on the inside of my cheek while he eyes me with a scrutinizing gaze.

Finally, with a slight chuckle, he rubs the back of his neck. "Uh, where did you find him?"

My fingers drum the table. "On a hiking trail."

Ozzy doesn't move beyond several slow blinks, lips parted. "When?" he murmurs.

"This afternoon."

He squints for a few seconds while we have a silent stare-off. "What color?"

He knows the answer, but I like the game, so I play along. "Gray, black, and white tiger stripes. White chest and paws."

Ozzy scans the bar before taking a long swig of his beer.

"I can't wait for you to see him . . . again."

"Why would you do that?" He pins me with narrowed eyes.

"The kitten needed a home." I shrug.

"Had we not been there, and you found the cat, would you have taken it home?"

"No. I would not have picked up the kitten. But Lola picked him up, and then I petted him. He imprinted on us, so since you wouldn't let her take him home, it felt like my duty."

He brushes some crumbs off the table. "Imprinting, huh? You're going with that?"

"I am," I say, swirling my wine.

"Now you've put me in a predicament."

"How so?" I adjust my leg, and he adjusts his, but he keeps it touching mine.

"We're supposed to be sneaking around. But that cat has partially imprinted on my daughter, so now I feel like she'll deserve visiting rights at some point."

"I love that you've put a positive spin on things, like this kitten and your housing situation. In your shoes, I think I'd have trouble not resenting Lola's grandparents for attaching conditions to the help they're giving you—a grown man."

"What's the positive spin?"

"This. Sneaking around like teenagers past curfew."

Ozzy's grin has its own personality. It's like there's Ozzy, then there's his grin. And I'm starting to read the subtleties of how he bends those full lips.

Flirty.

Innocent.

Sad.

Mischievous.

Vulnerable.

And my favorite—the sexy grin. This one starts with his teeth pressed to his lower lip, then he wets it, and finally, it curls into something that makes my insides melt.

It's that slow dance.

"Lola is the positive spin on my life. And tonight, I'm beginning to feel a little dizzy from the spin you're putting on my life too."

I hum, just short of closing my eyes. Everything feels good when I'm with Ozzy. "Tell me about Brynn."

With a hint of confusion pulling at his brow, he fiddles with the white paper under the remaining nachos. "You want me to talk about my wife on our date?"

"Yes. But only if you're comfortable with it."

"Why?"

"Because you created another life with her. And I think the most beautiful thing about a man is how he loves a woman. I'm giving you a chance to shine after ghosting me."

Ozzy runs a hand through his hair while pulling in a long breath. He tells me how he met his wife at a concert in California, where she lost her wallet.

Love never dies. I see it in his eyes, the glimmer of memories.

"Brynn was older than me. She had two years left of her PhD, and I was working in Arizona. We didn't set out to have a long-distance relationship, but that's where it led, and somehow it worked. Over those two years, I made a dozen trips to California to visit her. We talked on the phone daily, and by the time she donned her cap and gown, I had a ring in my pocket."

With a faraway look in his eyes and a pleasant smile, he continues, "She was so smart, an expert in linguistics. And I was a grease monkey with jumbled thoughts and mumbled words. She was delicate and refined; I was an ox with stained fingernails. But I loved everything about her that was nothing like me, and I think that's what she liked about me too. When we had Lola, it all made sense. Everything we did together was better. You know—the whole is greater than the sum of the parts. That was us."

I smile when that faraway expression subsides, and he's back with me. "How did you end up in Missoula?"

"We'd been living in California. Lola was seven. My parents lived here, and hers lived in Yellowstone, where they owned a ranch. There was a position available at UM, and I knew there was a chance I could eventually get a job here. I sent an application to Cielo and stayed home with Lola for that first year. A job opened up. Things were looking good for us. Lola liked her school. My parents loved having us in Missoula, and we were closer to Brynn's family. Then . . ." Ozzy frowns, gaze cast at the empty beer mug before him.

He doesn't have to finish. I don't need to know the details of the accident or what came next. I've pieced those together pretty well.

"See." I nudge his leg, prompting him to look at me. "You're even better than I thought. Your wife was a smart woman with a PhD, and I do not doubt that the smartest thing she did was marry you."

With his head cocked, he studies me. "Why are you trying to seduce a guy who rides a bike everywhere?"

I laugh. "If you must know, in my dating 'fish stories,' I'll refer to you as a biker."

"You'll tell people I have something bigger between my legs than what's there?" He smirks.

Covering my mouth, I snort. "Stop." I shake my head and drop my hand.

"Come on," he says, sliding out of the booth.

"Where are we going?" I follow him, threading my arms into my jacket while he holds my bouquet and the note.

"Let's take a walk."

"At this time of night?"

"I'll protect you." He holds open the door for me.

We worm through the parking lot to the sidewalk and gaze at the path in front of us.

"I'm sure you get asked this all the time, but what got you into this profession? Were you in the military?" he asks.

"No. I was a crop duster. I had my pilot's license by the time I turned seventeen, and I was spraying fields the summer after I graduated high school. Fast-forward eight years, and I was flying tanker planes for Cielo. I've never wanted to do anything but fly planes. I've been fighting fires for seven years. Four years in the right seat and the past three years on my own."

"And you're good at it."

"I'm okay."

"You're being modest. Taylor said you thread the needle. Impeccable precision with your drops."

I chuckle, tipping my chin and shaking my head. "I'm above average."

He playfully nudges me. "Badass."

We stroll a block without saying much. There's something special about being with someone, feeling comfortable in silence, and holding space.

"What do you do besides hiking and rescuing stray cats on your days off?"

I chuckle. "Depends on the summer, but mostly I'm outdoors, hiking, kayaking, and hanging out with friends. Occasionally dating." I return the playful nudge. "But I'm seriously considering buying a house. If I make that happen, I might spend my days off renovating it."

"So you'd buy an older home?" he asks.

"Probably. I like the older neighborhoods."

"Are you handy?"

"I have handy friends. Same thing, right?" I laugh.

"Those are the best kind. Feel free to add my name to your list. I have a few skills from past lives."

"Do tell."

For the remainder of our short walk, Ozzy gives me a quick rundown of his seemingly infinite home-renovation skills. He follows me to my car when we return to the parking lot.

"Thanks for sneaking around with me," he says.

I nod, fiddling with my key fob while standing at my door, not wanting the night to end. "I was wrong. I'm not too old to sneak around. We should do it again."

"We should." He fiddles with the ribbon on my bouquet.

"You should bring Lola by to visit Bandit." I lift my gaze.

"Hmm, we'll see about that." He lifts a single brow, which matches his crooked grin.

"You do that." I nudge the toe of my white sneaker into his black boot. "Well, thanks for the drink," I say, but I can't bring myself to turn and open the door.

"You're welcome," he says without moving an inch.

This is where he should kiss me. But we're taking it slow, so maybe this is not where he kisses me. It's just where the tiny embers in my chest slowly burn, making it hard to breathe while standing this close to him.

"I'm tripped up right now," he murmurs.

"How so?"

"I feel like I should sneak a kiss, but I also feel like it's unfair to you."

I swallow hard. "Why?"

"*Because* you're going to get in your vehicle and *drive* home, and I'm not. *Because* I unintentionally ghosted you. *Because* I think we should take it slow, but I don't know what's considered slow. Instead, I'm standing here trying to figure it out in real time, and—"

I lift onto my toes, press my palms to his cheeks, and kiss him. It's not long, but it's not short. It's not a hungry kiss, nor is it a peck. It's a first kiss.

The perfect first kiss.

And when it's over, we share the same smile as I lower to my feet in tiny increments, letting my hands linger on his warm face, whiskers tickling my skin. "Sometimes you just have to say fuck it and kiss the girl. We'll figure the rest out later," I murmur.

If torture had an expression, it would be Ozzy's face. I'm the first woman he's kissed since his wife died. Brynn wove threads of her soul into his heart, and any woman who comes after her will get tangled in a mess of abandoned emotions.

Am I willing to be that woman?

I don't know, but I can't stop thinking about him. And I rescued a kitten today because his daughter lost her mom and will forever live with those scars from the accident. I couldn't let the kitten she held in her arms die.

"Say something," I whisper.

"I . . ." He shakes his head. "I don't know what to say."

"You could say good night."

"I'm not ready to do that."

Is vulnerability sexy?

Yes. It absolutely is.

"Do you like cool photos of fires?" I ask.

He narrows his eyes. "Maybe."

I jerk my head toward my RAV. "No driving. I won't even start it. We can sit in my car, and I'll show you some cool wildfire photos."

"You fly and take photos? Seems dangerous."

"Ha! No. I have a friend who's a photojournalist."

Ozzy reaches past me, opening my door. "After you."

We spend more than an hour leaning into each other over the center console, scrolling through photos on my phone. Ozzy eats up every single one. And anything with a plane or helicopter, he zooms in and names the aircraft and everything amazing about it.

"I gotta go," he says, shifting his attention from my phone to me.

I click off my phone screen, and we gaze at each other. Actually, we focus on each other's mouths until our attraction pulls us into another kiss.

His hand gently cups the side of my neck, his fingers grazing my nape, sending a shiver along my spine. The kiss ends too soon. I'm not sure what would constitute a long-enough kiss, but it wasn't that.

Ozzy gets out of the car, leaving me wanting more.

After a final wave, he puts on his helmet, and I pull out of the empty parking lot a little before one in the morning.

Dear god, I'm falling for this guy.

Chapter Twelve

OZZY

"What are you so happy about?" Tia asks, refilling her coffee mug while Lola eats breakfast.

I slide my sandwich into a brown bag and glance to my right, unsure who she's talking to.

"You've had a smirk from the moment you came upstairs. And you had one all day yesterday, even when Lola's team lost their softball game."

I point to myself, eyes wide.

She frowns before nodding—the happiness police.

Yawning, I shake my head. "You've mistaken my grimace for a smirk. I didn't sleep well."

"Why not?"

"Were you up late watching TV with Pa?" Lola asks, milk dripping down her chin after taking a bite of cereal. *That's* a smirk.

"Amos doesn't stay up late watching TV. He's snoring on the sofa by nine," Tia says, eyeing Amos sitting across from Lola at the kitchen table.

Amos keeps his head bowed to his phone. Maybe he's intentionally ignoring us, or perhaps he's not wearing his hearing aids.

"That's not true," Lola says. "One night I—"

"Yes. One night, you thought he was up late, but he was actually asleep," I say, cutting her off before she rats him out.

Lola looks at Amos and then at me.

I give her a tight-lipped grin and jerk my head toward the door. "Brush your teeth, and let's go."

With her signature eye roll, she heads toward the stairs, and I put her bowl and spoon in the dishwasher.

"Are you taking Lola to her shrink appointment, or am I?" Tia asks.

I slide Lola's lunch into her backpack. "I'm taking her to her *therapist*."

"You should get an update. See how close we are to revisiting the car situation."

"Yes. I'll see how close *we* are to that," I mumble.

"Ozzy, you need to—"

"Ready." Lola saves me from a lecture with her perfect timing. There's no way she brushed her teeth for more than five seconds.

"Later," I say without another glance in Tia's direction.

After we get our bikes from the garage and pedal onto the sidewalk, I ride beside Lola. "I really need you to forget about that night you saw Pa watching TV late."

"Dakota said it's called pornography or porn. His mom talked to him about it after his sister and her friends got in trouble for watching it online."

So much for my next request, which was that she never mention it to any of her friends.

What's happening to the world? There's no way I knew anything about porn when I was ten.

"Starting now, I don't want you to say another word about it to anyone. Can you do that?"

"Why? Pa is an adult. Dakota said porn is just for adults."

"True. But do you remember when you first got invited to a sleepover, and I told you not to forget your stuffed bear, and you didn't want your friends to know you still sleep with a stuffed animal?"

"Yeah."

"I told you it's perfectly normal for someone your age to sleep with one, but you still didn't want everyone to know. Well, even though Pa is old enough to watch whatever he wants, he probably doesn't want the world to know he's watching that."

"Like when he smokes out back and tells me not to tell you?"

I mimic her eye roll. I knew the cigarette butts weren't blowing into our yard from the neighbor's. "Yeah," I grumble, "like that."

"I promise not to say anything if you promise to get me a cat, since you let that kitten on the trail die."

"First, you don't know if that kitten died. It's quite possible that some cat lover with a car showed up after us and rescued it. Second, it's not okay to blackmail me into getting you a cat, or anything, for that matter. I asked you not to say another word about the incident with Pa, and that's final. No negotiating. No blackmailing. No ifs, ands, or buts. Got it?"

"Mom would have saved the kitten."

I bite my tongue so hard I taste blood. It's not often that Lola plays the Mom-would-have card, but when it happens, it knocks the air from my lungs and makes me question whether she's right. Would Brynn have taken the cat home?

We don't say another word the rest of the way to school. When I stop at my designated spot across the street, and Lola walks her bike through the crosswalk with the crossing guard, I call, "Love you. Have a good day."

Nothing from her in return.

◆ ◆ ◆

Ozzy: How's your day? What are you doing?

I text Maren while eating my lunch in the break room.

Maren: I'm house shopping with Jamie and Fitz. They're thinking of making an offer on the house I want!

I chuckle.

Ozzy: Outbid them

Maren: It has a tree house in the backyard for Bandit

Ozzy: Maybe don't outbid them

Maren: Because you don't think Bandit deserves a tree house?

Ozzy: I was dragging ass yesterday, but Saturday night was so worth it. When do you want to sneak out again?

Maren: I empathize with Lola. The way you dismiss Bandit is heartbreaking

Ozzy: You should send me pictures of Bandit

She sends me a half dozen pics of the tiger-striped kitten in the next ten seconds.

Ozzy: lol how many are on your phone?

Maren: Let's just say I had to pay for more cloud storage

Ozzy: Lola has therapy after school. We usually go out to dinner on therapy nights. What if you happened to be at Build a Bowl around five-thirty?

Maren: Two chance encounters in a few days?

Ozzy: Too suspicious?

Maren: I'm good at faking it

Ozzy: Noted

Maren: Omg! No! Not that

"Maren? Maren Bernabe?" my nosy coworker asks, disrupting me.

I turn my phone face down on the table as Ira sits beside me with her white take-out bag that smells like fries.

She eyes me with a shit-eating grin while adjusting her black-and-gray-streaked ponytail. Ira's the only female A&P mechanic at this base. She's been here the longest; according to Taylor, she's a genius. So everyone looks over her shoulder to see what she does that's so extraordinary.

Can I complain that she looked over my shoulder just now?

"What's for lunch?" I nod to her bag as she opens it.

"Oswald, are you ignoring my question? Were you texting Maren Bernabe? I don't think that's a good idea." Ira pulls out a chicken sandwich and fries before handing me the sack with stray fries at the bottom.

I don't turn them down. "Hypothetically, if I was texting her, why don't you think it's a good idea?" I'm not conceding that she's a genius. But she has more than ten years of life experience over me, so I'm open to her wisdom.

"Your daughter lost her mother in a car accident. And the effects were so catastrophic that you ride a bicycle everywhere. So you think it's a smart idea to date a woman who flies a plane over wildfires?"

She's one of only a few people here who know why I ride my bike to work. I've found that the women here are more curious and sense the trauma behind my behavior. In contrast, the guys, including my boss, assume I'm a pussy tree hugger obsessed with my carbon footprint.

"I think my wife had one of the least dangerous jobs in the world, yet she died," I say.

Ira stops midchew and glances at me, eyebrows forming two perfect peaks. She has grease on her cheek. "Oh my god," she mumbles with a mouthful, her words muffled. "You really like her."

"It's new. I'm not telling anyone. So, can you keep a secret?"

She swallows, shaking her head. "No. I'm the worst secret keeper. Ask anyone." She sips her drink through the straw. "But I'll try."

"That's not comforting, Ira. But I have faith in you." I scoot my chair back and stand. "I know you can keep this between us. Taylor says you're a genius." I grab my water bottle and lunch bag. "But I know you're more than that. You're a trusted friend." I squeeze her shoulder, and she leans into my touch.

"Aw, Oswald, you think of me as a friend?"

"If you keep my secret," I say, heading toward the door, "you might be my best friend."

Brynn used to say that people will exceed your expectations if you let them know what you expect. If you set failure as an expectation, they can fail miserably, or they can be smashing successes if you set the bar high.

I'm setting the bar high for Ira, *my friend.*

Chapter Thirteen

Ozzy: You're a good kisser

I feel like a giddy kid as I text Maren from the waiting room while Lola has her therapy session.

Maren: I know

Ozzy: Apparently you're confident too

Maren: What are you doing?

Ozzy: Waiting for Lola to finish her therapy session

Maren: I thought men liked confident women

Ozzy: I don't speak for all men. I like real women

Maren: My boobs are real

I softly laugh.

Ozzy: But is your confidence? Is it genuine?

Maren: Depends on the day

Ozzy: That's the right answer

Maren: How so?

Ozzy: Confidence is a state of being

Maren: That's deep. Are you in therapy too?

Ozzy: I married a deep woman who made me a little less shallow

Maren: Haha I love that

Maren: Am I allowed to talk to Lola about Bandit?

Ozzy: Not sure yet. I'm waiting to see her reaction to accidentally running into you again

Maren: Reaction?

Ozzy: I need to know if she can be cool about it or if she's going to embarrass me by asking you personal questions

Maren: She can ask me anything

Ozzy: Don't say that

Maren: Ozzy?

Ozzy: Yes?

Maren: You're a good kisser too

Ozzy: I know

When a young couple comes into the office, I slide my phone into my jacket pocket. A few minutes later, Lola emerges.

"I'm starving," she says while rubbing her tummy.

"Shocking." I smile, helping her thread her arms through her backpack before we head outside.

It's a fifteen-minute ride to Build a Bowl. Before I can lock up our bikes, Lola runs inside, leaving both locks and our helmets with me. When I get everything situated and reach the door, Lola's found Maren at a tall table in the corner.

"Dad! Look who's here."

I smile and nod toward the register. "I assume my daughter ordered for us," I say to the employee behind the counter while retrieving my wallet.

"She did, and the woman over there already paid."

Lola waves me toward the table, where Maren's back is to me.

"What a pleasant surprise," I say. "Here." I lay cash on the table by her water glass.

Maren glances at me while sliding the cash toward me. "The surprise is mine. And I'll pay top dollar for good company." She winks at Lola, who's kneeling on the wooden stool.

"Put your butt on the chair before you fall over, goofy," I say to Lola. She frowns before following my order.

I sit next to Maren because it's conveniently the closest stool.

"Thank you. Now I owe you." I pocket the cash.

"Lola said she's been at her *talk doc*."

I chuckle, angling my body toward Maren until our legs touch like the other night at the bar. Her glossed lips twitch with the recognition that, even now, we're sneaking around. "Yes. Victoria is her *talk doc*."

"Maren," the guy behind the counter calls out.

"I've got it." I get our bowls and set them on the table.

"Thank you for not asking me about my scars," Lola says, giving Maren a shy smile that rips at my chest. My mom told her to say that to anyone she liked because people feel at ease when the obvious is out in the open.

The good news: Lola likes Maren.

The bad news: Maren has tears in her eyes.

Maren swallows hard and nods, averting her gaze to her rice, veggie, and steak bowl.

Lola smiles at me, proud of herself for—in her mind—making a friend. I have a warm, fuzzy feeling for five seconds before Lola goes too far.

"Are you married?" she asks.

Maren shakes her head, chewing slowly.

"Do you like my dad?"

"Lola—"

"I do like your dad."

My thoughts go up in smoke. I've lost control of this conversation. I'm the third wheel.

Lola lights up. I haven't seen her look this happy in a long time. Her wide, unblinking eyes jump to mine.

"You should come to our house and meet my nana and pa."

This girl has no clue what a terrible idea that is. I wait for Maren to squirm in her seat or stutter a nervous reply.

"You should come to *my* house to meet my cat," Maren says.

Yep. It's like I'm not even here. Neither one of them gives a single shit about what I want.

"Yes! Dad, can we go after dinner?"

I shake my head. "The sun's setting, and it's too far for you to ride in the dark."

Lola deflates.

"What if you come tomorrow?" Maren suggests.

"We'd love to," Lola says. I roll my eyes at her, speaking for us like I have no say. "What kind of cat do you have?"

"I'm not sure. It was a stray cat," Maren says.

Lola's lower lip makes its debut. "My dad killed that kitten on the trail."

"I did not."

"You abandoned it. What do you think happened to it? Even Dakota said he probably died."

"I think you and Dakota should take a break from talking to each other."

Lola ignores me. "What's your cat's name?"

"Bandit."

"I like that name. I was going to name my kitten Mouse because Dakota has a fish named Shark. But now the kitten's dead, so it doesn't matter."

Jesus Christ . . .

"Mouse is a great name," Maren says. "Had I thought of it, I would have named my cat Mouse. But he's already used to his name, so I'd better keep it as Bandit."

"His middle name could be Mouse. What's your last name?" Lola asks.

"Bernabe."

"Bandit Mouse Bernabe." Lola shoves food into her mouth, then snorts, spitting a little into the bowl.

I shake my head.

"I . . ." Lola giggles. "I like that name."

"Then that's settled. Bandit's middle name is Mouse." Maren gives Lola a resolute nod.

I think Lola might explode with excitement. She's gripping her fork so hard that her hand is shaking. All this over a middle name. She's going to lose herself when she sees Bandit.

"I have to use the bathroom." Lola hops off the stool. This seems right since she looked ready to wet herself with excitement upon hearing the kitten news.

"Let me check it." I follow her to the single-stall bathroom for a quick peek. "Don't forget to lock the door." I close it behind me and return to the table, where I can still see the door.

Maren starts to say something, but I grab her face and kiss her because I *need* to kiss her.

My daughter already adores her, which makes me like her more than I did Saturday night, which was a hell of a lot.

I smile, releasing her face and sitting on my stool.

She rubs her lips together. "You're killing me, Ozzy."

"How so?" I start eating my food again.

"You're a slow burn."

"In your line of work, isn't a slow burn a good thing?"

"Yes, but I don't fuel the fire. You . . ." She stirs her water with the straw.

"I what?"

"Nothing." Her cheeks redden.

"That look isn't nothing."

Maren's gaze focuses in the direction of the restroom. "You made sure no one was hiding in the restroom."

"I did."

She slowly nods, shifting her attention to me. "You're fueling my fire," she whispers. "Every text. Every word. Every glance. Every touch."

"Should I do something to extinguish you?" I smirk.

Again, she watches for Lola. "You should burn with me."

Fuck me . . .

My mind reels, plotting, planning, desperately searching for a solution. I have to take Lola home and wait for her to go to bed. Then I can ride my bike to Maren's. That's another twenty-five minutes. Will her roommates be there?

Then it hits me. This is what she's talking about. Right now, this desperate need to touch, kiss, and feel every inch of her *is* burning with her.

Misery loves company.

"Do you have hand sanitizer, Dad? The bathroom was out of soap," Lola announces, returning to the table.

I shake my head. "Sorry, it's in my backpack, but I didn't bring it."

"I've got you." Maren digs a small bottle from her purse and sprays it in Lola's cupped hands.

I was all talk at work with Ira because I don't like borrowing trouble. But she wasn't wrong. Maren has a high-risk job. Is it fair to bring someone into Lola's life who could be ripped away from her like Brynn was? Could my heart handle falling for another woman only to lose her?

"Are you a mechanic like my dad?"

"No. I'm a pilot—a firefighter. I help control wildfires by dumping a special retardant onto them from a plane. Your dad keeps my plane in tip-top shape." Maren winks at me.

I so badly want to kiss her again.

"That's a cool job."

Maren nods. "It is."

"Is it scary?"

"I'd say it's more exciting than scary. I get to feel like a bird in the sky."

"Have you ever crashed?" Lola asks.

Jesus.

"I have not." Maren doesn't miss a beat.

Lola picks at her food, her face tense, like she's formulating her next question.

"Why don't you finish up, Lola? We need to get you home. Tomorrow is a school day."

"I am. I am. I am. Besides, it's almost summer break."

Maren snickers, wiping her mouth, and I rest my hand on her leg, knowing that Lola can't see it. She slides her hand over mine, interlacing our fingers and moving my hand a few inches higher and toward her inner thigh.

I clear my throat, adjusting in my seat because I'm getting an erection. It's been a long time since I've had this sort of intimate contact with a woman.

My old friend has impeccable timing—three feet from my daughter, minutes before I have to climb onto a bicycle and ride home.

"I'm full," Lola says, prompting Maren to release my hand.

I gulp down the rest of my water and think about Tia's permanent scowl, roadkill, and the stench of vomit, just a few things that make my dick go limp.

"Thanks for dinner," Lola says, hopping off her stool.

I stand, eyeing her until she smirks. My ten-year-old thanked Maren for dinner without a fatherly "What do you say?" prompt.

It's a modern-day miracle. Is my little girl all grown up? Did Amos's late-night porn and Dakota's nosy opinions catapult her into adulthood? God, I hope not.

It has to be Maren; she must bring out the best version of Lola.

"What do you say, Dad?"

Damn! Now she's making me look bad.

I chuckle. "Sorry, your sudden mastery of manners has left me speechless. Thank you, Maren. I'm so glad we happened to be eating at the same place tonight."

Maren threads one arm into her thin pink hoodie, and I hold it so she can easily thread the other arm. That's when I notice Lola eyeing my every move with a huge grin.

"Thank you," Maren murmurs, eyes flitting between Lola and me like she's a little nervous.

Lola leads the way to the door, and I nod for Maren to follow her so I can discreetly rest my hand on her lower back.

So her breath hitches.

So my pulse quickens.

So my fucking erection tries to return.

I remove my hand when we reach the door, just as Lola skips toward our bikes by the lamppost.

As soon as we're outside, I step in front of Maren, keeping Lola at my back. "My head is messed up," I say, hushed. "I'm ten feet from my daughter, yet I'm having very detailed thoughts about you."

Maren's gaze finds my mouth. And since God likes to torture me, she wets her lips. "I need to know more about your *detailed* thoughts."

Humans are pretty because our minds are so filthy.

Amos is a perv for watching porn, but over the past twenty-four hours, I've painted a naked picture of Maren in my mind that no one else can see, and therefore, I'm a perfect gentleman.

Right?

I've imagined the shape and texture of her nipples against my tongue; her warm, minty breath quickening over my mouth while my middle fingers slide between her legs; and the slow moan vibrating her chest when I fill her.

"Where are you?" Maren asks, bringing everything back into focus.

With a soft chuckle and a headshake, I glance back at Lola, who has our bikes unlocked. "Uh, I was just thinking about how I missed church last week. I need to do better."

"Church?" Maren lifts her brow a fraction.

"Yes." I clear my throat. "Only pure thoughts."

She returns a slow, suspicious nod before stepping closer and whispering, "I'm going home to take a bath and do things I don't think Jesus would do. Lord, I'm so sorry." She brushes past me, hand grazing mine. "Good night, Lola. See you tomorrow."

By the time we get home, I have a text from her.

Maren: Omg. When did you put this note in my purse?!

I pulled the note from my pocket and slipped it into her purse when we exited the restaurant. Since flowers would have sent Lola into a tizzy, I had to sketch six flowers on the note.

> Bitterroot is Montana's state flower. I couldn't harvest any because you need permission from a Native American elder. Hope you love them!
>
> Ozzy x

Chapter Fourteen

I'll hand it to Lola; my ten-year-old kept the secret for the rest of the night and the first five minutes of breakfast this morning. That's an entire week for an adult.

It's not that I want my daughter to lie. I didn't make that request. On the way home from Build a Bowl, I asked her not to mention seeing Maren because I wasn't in the mood to answer Tia's questions. I know it's controversial, but when it suits me, I stand on the side of the omission of truth not being an actual lie. Will I support the other side of that argument when Lola's a teenager? Absolutely.

Parenting is the art of hypocrisy.

"We're going to see a cat after Dad gets home from work," Lola announces between bites of her cheese-and-mushroom omelet.

Tia and Amos eye her before looking to me for further explanation while I chew my toast.

"A friend from work has a new cat." I shrug like it's no big deal.

Like I haven't been texting Maren all week.

Like I'm not dying to sneak around with her again.

"Does this friend live close by?" Tia asks diplomatically, but I know she already has her back up at just the mention of me having a friend.

In Tia's mind, I'm not allowed to have anything or anyone outside Lola. And she's right; Lola is enough. But who lives life confined to merely enough?

"She's twenty-five minutes away," Lola replies.

"She?"

"Yes. Her name is Maren. She's a pilot who fights fires. Dad fixes her plane. And she has a cat named Bandit. I said the cat's middle name should be Mouse because I'd name it Mouse if I had a cat. And guess what?" Lola widens her eyes in irresistible animation. "Maren said Bandit's middle name can be Mouse!"

Amos chuckles. "That's nice of her."

"When did you talk with this Maren person?" Tia pulls out her dick, which is twice the size of Amos's, and pisses all over the conversation. Only Lola doesn't see that. She doesn't understand why I didn't want her to say anything about Maren.

Lola's eyes bug out. I call it her oh-shit-I'm-in-trouble face. Well, I don't tell her that's what I call it, but it's one of her signature expressions. With this one expression, Tia knows I told her not to say anything. Now I'm guilty of telling my daughter to keep secrets (a.k.a. lie), and I'm guilty of having a female friend.

"When we went to Build a Bowl after Lola's appointment with Victoria, we saw Maren there."

Tia twists her dry, wrinkled lips and hums. "Well, isn't that a coincidence?"

We have no alcohol in the house, but I sure could use a drink. No wonder Amos gets his rocks off to late-night porn. This woman is an anti-erection. The original ballbuster.

I bet if they have sex, she ties him to the bed and gags him.

"What's that look?" Tia asks.

"Huh?" I narrow my eyes.

"You winced," she says.

I thought of you having sex, Tia. It's pretty fucking cringeworthy.

"Nothing. Does anyone want the rest of the orange juice?" I hold up the small glass pitcher with a few ounces left.

No one answers, so I pour the rest into my glass and carry it, along with my plate, to the kitchen.

"Don't let her guilt you, son." Amos sets his plate on the counter and opens the dishwasher.

"I haven't done anything to feel guilty about. Am I not allowed to have acquaintances?"

He chuckles while I hand him the dirty dishes. "Some days, Tia resents the air you breathe. So anything more than that feels extravagant to her. She just misses Brynn."

"Well, I miss her too. But I don't know what more I can say or do. I don't know what level of misery I must endure to satisfy Tia's need to see me suffer."

"What are you two talking about?" Tia asks as she and Lola haul more dishes into the kitchen.

"I was just asking Ozzy if he's recently had his prostate checked. But now that I think about it, he's still young."

Tia frowns, sizing up her lying husband.

"Dad, I need help with homework," Lola says.

"You two go do that. Tia and I will clean this up." Amos shoos us toward the stairs.

"Lola, we have to leave for school in ten minutes. Why didn't you mention your homework last night?" I ask.

When we reach the basement, I follow Lola to her bedroom. She pivots at the door and lowers her voice. "I don't have homework."

She's ten.

I think it a lot, but this girl is too astute and clever to be only ten. Brynn would be proud of her. She always knew Lola was intelligent beyond her years.

"You know this will come back to haunt you when you try the homework excuse on me in the future," I say.

"I do need you to sign the permission form for track-and-field day. So it's not a whole lie. It's not technically homework, so it's half a lie. See how good I am at math?"

I grab her head and kiss the top of it. "Get the form, and let's go."

"Can we get ice cream from Swirls on the way to Maren's after school?"

I stop at my bedroom door. "Swirls isn't on our way. You need to work on geography."

"Remember, asking too many personal questions is not polite." I do a final prep with Lola after school when we're a block from Maren's house.

"You mean it's not polite to embarrass you?"

Yes.

"No. That's not what I mean, but that's a good rule too."

"I hope Bandit likes me."

"I hope so, too, but cats can be finicky."

The driveway is full of vehicles when we arrive. I'm meeting her roommates with my daughter. Fantastic.

What could go wrong?

Maren steps outside in an oversize gray T-shirt and white leggings, hair pulled into a ponytail. "Hey!"

We park our bikes on the walkway, just past the vehicles, and remove our helmets.

"Where's Bandit?" Lola asks.

"Let's start with hello." I stand behind Lola, resting my hands on her shoulders.

"Hello. Where's Bandit?"

Maren laughs. "He's in the shed out back. Follow me." Her gaze lingers on me while she walks past us. It's mischievous and sexy.

"Oh! Dad, get the gift out," Lola says, spinning toward me.

I nod several times, retrieving six stalks of rhubarb from the pack attached to my bike. They're tied with hemp string.

Lola hands them to Maren. "My dad said it's polite to bring a gift when you visit someone's house for the first time."

Maren's gaze shoots to me. "Thank you. Your dad is something else."

I wink, and Maren leads us to the backyard.

"Looks like you have a full house tonight," I say.

"Yeah. Will starts his next shift in the morning. He'll be leaving for his tai chi class soon. And Fitz and Jamie are eating an early dinner before checking out a few houses. But I just know they will make an offer on *my* house."

"The one with the cat tree house?"

"Yes." She unlocks the shed door and opens it.

"It's a bedroom!" Lola covers her mouth.

"Yes. It's called a she shed. I used to sleep out here, and then my friend Jamie stayed out here; now it's Bandit's room."

We step inside, and Lola's world explodes with glitter, rainbows, and butterflies.

"That's the kitten, that's the kitten, that's the kitten!" Lola scoops the kitten off the bed, kissing his head. "You saved my kitten!"

Maren tears up, as she did at the restaurant when Lola mentioned the scars on her face. I'm not entirely immune to this moment, either, but I won't cry. It's just a cat.

"I saved your kitten, but my roommate is allergic to cats, so that's why Bandit must live in the shed, which is obviously just a really cool bedroom. And I spend lots of time in here with him, so he never feels abandoned."

"It's a cool shed." Lola nods.

"Do you want to come meet my roommates before they leave?" Maren asks.

"Can I bring Bandit?"

"Lola, she just said Bandit can't be in the house," I remind her with my own exaggerated eye roll.

Lola doesn't even look up from the cat. "If I go inside and meet them, do I have to stay for *adult talk*? Or can I come back out here with Bandit?"

I close my eyes and shake my head.

Maren laughs. "You can absolutely come back out here. Adult talk is pretty boring."

"Fine," Lola says with an exasperated sigh, following us to the house.

A dark-haired woman jumps away from the window, hand tangled in the window blind's lift cord.

"Were you spying on me?" Maren asks as we step into the house.

The woman blushes, her gaze ping-ponging between Maren, Lola, and me as she backs into the kitchen. "No. I was just . . ."

"Yes. She's been watching the whole time," a guy in jeans and a Missoula Smoke Jumper hoodie says, leaning against the counter while eating a piece of what looks like old pizza.

"Snitch," the dark-haired woman says, turning and stealing a bite of his pizza.

He smirks at her, wiping her mouth with the pad of his thumb. She teasingly nibbles it.

I need to get laid.

"These are two of my roommates, Jamie and Fitz. Well, *Calvin*, but we call him Fitz. And this is Ozzy and his daughter, Lola," Maren says, setting the rhubarb on the counter.

"Hi. It's nice to meet you." Jamie offers her hand to me and then to Lola. "Did you meet Bandit?"

Lola nods with wide eyes.

Fitz gives us a quick smile with a "Hey."

"Oh, the house thieves?" I ask.

Jamie narrows her eyes at Maren. "You don't need a three-bedroom house."

"Neither do you." Maren retrieves a container from the freezer and peels off the lid. "Lola, do you want a cookie–ice cream sandwich?"

"Yes, please," Lola says with wide eyes, taking one when Maren holds out the container.

She offers one to me too.

"I'm good. Thanks. Did you make those with the leftover cookies you baked?"

Maren's gaze shoots to Jamie and Fitz, and Jamie smiles, while Fitz narrows his eyes.

"Um, yeah. No. I mean, Jamie made them into ice cream sandwiches," Maren says, fidgeting with the hem of her T-shirt.

"Are you a real smoke jumper?" Lola asks Fitz before licking the side of the ice cream sandwich.

He wipes his mouth with the back of his hand and clears his throat after swallowing. "I am."

"My class took a tour of the museum." She frowns. "But I didn't get to go because I don't ride in buses. My friends said it was super cool."

"Get your dad to bring you sometime. If I'm there, you can have a private tour," Fitz says.

"Tomorrow?" Lola looks at me.

I shake my head. "You have school. When school is out, we can do it." I nod toward the door. "Why don't you take that out back, so you don't drip onto the floor? But make sure your hands aren't sticky when you return to the shed with the cat."

"His name is Bandit," Lola says, pivoting toward the door as I open it for her.

"Are you stealing my house tonight or waiting?" Maren asks Jamie and Fitz, returning the container to the freezer.

Jamie shakes her head. "The house we're seeing tonight is going to be better anyway. So you and your cat can have the tree house." She pulls back her shoulders with confidence.

"Unless it's not. Then we're making an offer," Fitz says, stealing Jamie's can of strawberry-basil Aura Bora sparkling water from her hand.

Maren sticks her tongue out at Fitz and then quickly composes herself. "Can I get you something to drink?" She opens the fridge to survey what she has to offer me.

"I'm good. Thanks."

She uncorks a bottle of wine and pours a half glass.

"We have to get going," Jamie says. "I hope we can spend more time with you, Ozzy."

I smile, and Fitz pulls her toward the door. "Me too," I say. "See ya."

As the door clicks shut behind them, Maren faces me, taking a sip of wine before setting the glass on the counter and resting her hands on the edge of it. "Something weird happened when I worked my last shift. The unfamiliarity shook me."

"What's that?" I ask, sliding my hands into my back pockets.

"I missed a guy."

"Lucky guy."

"Right?" She bites her bottom lip.

"I bet he missed you too."

Her head cocks to the side. "You think?"

"Definitely."

Maren makes me feel alive with every flirty glance and restrained smile.

"Will's upstairs."

I nod. "Lola's outside."

The tension is palpable. God, my hands itch to touch her.

Maren covers her face and makes a noise that sounds like the marriage between a laugh and a groan. "Sorry. I'm struggling. I don't know how to navigate this." She drops her hands and sighs.

"Navigate what?"

"These feelings combined with our living situations." She tucks her chin. "This is embarrassing. I'm a grown woman. What is wrong with me?"

I glance out the back window before closing the space between us. "Tell me about your feelings."

She laughs, shaking her head. "They're not emotional feelings. I don't need therapy. They're . . ." Lifting her gaze to mine, she wrinkles her nose. "Physical."

"Physical? Like this?" I feather my knuckles along her cheek.

"Kind of," she murmurs.

"Or this?" My fingers ghost down her neck.

"Kind of," she whispers before wetting her lips.

I slide my hand down her arm to her waist and pause for a second, taking another glance out the back window just as Lola licks her fingers before opening the door to the shed. Then I snake my hand up the inside of Maren's T-shirt, teasing the skin along her ribs until I reach her bra.

Again, I pause.

She doesn't move, doesn't blink.

I cup her breast over her bra, and my heart channels all the blood in my body straight to my dick. My thumb traces the outline of her hard nipple beneath the thin material. "Like this?" I whisper.

Her eyelids blink heavily. "Yes."

This is nice. Too nice.

I'm out of my mind in the best possible way.

I pull my hand from her shirt and turn, scratching my head a half dozen times while cringing. "Nope. No, no, no. I'm torturing myself. This is a bad idea. Or a good idea at the worst time. What am I doing?" I take several steps away from Maren and then pivot back toward her. "I'm sorry." I exhale a harsh breath and lace my fingers behind my head.

A slow smile blooms along her face. "Ozzy, I like our slow dance. I hate it, too, but mostly I like it. I feel like you've blindfolded me and tied me up. And every time we see each other, you feed me a morsel of something irresistible, leaving me a little satisfied but always wanting more."

I blurt my confession. "I haven't had sex in over two years."

Real smooth. Idiot!

Maren lifts her eyebrows. "I'm . . ." She purses her lips and slowly shakes her head. "Well, I'm not surprised. But it's pretty much how I'm sure you remember. All the parts connect like they did two years ago."

I laugh, arms flopping to my sides. "That's, uh, good to hear. Are there no new trends I should know about?"

She keeps a straight face—all business. "It's still the preferred method of procreation and recreation. It's still good." She lights up. "I recommend it."

"But are you good at it?"

"I'm the best you've never had," she says with a sexy confidence.

I rest a hand on my hip and drop my head with a laugh. "I don't doubt that."

"Ozzy?"

When I lift my gaze, her expression softens. It's honest and genuine.

"I don't expect anything from you. Lola is and should be your priority. Every second I get to steal is bliss, but it's just extra in my life. I don't need you like she does. So if I've ever made you feel bad about not calling or texting, please forgive me."

"Don't do that. Don't feel bad for me. Don't settle for anything less than being with someone who makes you feel special and needed. *I* think you're very special. And maybe *I'm* the one who needs you. Have you considered that?"

Her lips part, and she begins to say something but stops. Instead, she steps in front of me and takes my hand, sliding it back up her shirt.

I grin.

She does too. Then she lifts onto her toes. I meet her halfway and press my lips to hers in a slow kiss, slipping my hand into the cup of her bra, eliciting a soft moan. She jumps away from me, quickly fixing her bra.

In the next breath, a guy strolls into the kitchen. Maren either has Spidey sense, or she heard a floor creak that I did not.

He smiles before yawning, covering his mouth with a fist.

Maren clears her throat. "Hey, Will, this is Ozzy. Ozzy, Will. He owns the house."

"Nice to meet you," I say.

He fills a water bottle from the fridge spigot. "You too. Are you the mechanic?"

"Are there others?" I tuck my hands in my front pockets, discreetly adjusting my dying erection. "I'm the mechanic. Is there a chef? A teacher? A doctor?"

"There's a Professor Gray Balls—"

"William, shut it," Maren says.

"No others. You're the only one willing to put up with her. I don't know if I should say congratulations or condolences." He meets Maren's scowl and offers her a smirk. "I'll just say good luck, buddy."

I laugh, and it earns me a scowl, too, so I jab my thumb over my shoulder. "I should check on Lola."

"Wait, are you the period guy?" Will narrows his eyes.

"We definitely should check on Lola," Maren says, grabbing my arms and trying to turn and push me toward the door.

"Bathroom attendant, but I get what you're asking. Yes, I'm him," I say to Will while submitting to Maren's forceful attempt to escort me from the kitchen.

"You've told your roommates about me," I say as she shuts the back door behind us. "I'm flattered. Good ears, by the way. I didn't hear him coming down the stairs."

Maren faces me when we reach the shed. "I've caught all of my roommates in much more compromising positions. Part of me wanted him to see us because I don't think they believe me when I say a guy is interested in me. I jumped away so you wouldn't feel embarrassed meeting Will with your hand up my shirt and your tongue in my mouth."

I cock my head to the side. "Why wouldn't they believe I'm interested in you?"

"He asked if you were the period guy. Isn't it obvious that I'm a hot mess?"

Before I can answer, she opens the shed door. Lola is cuddled on the bed with the kitten, and he's purring while she pets him. "Can we take him home?"

"He's Maren's," I say.

"Just for one night? Like a sleepover."

Maren sits on the edge of the bed. "Maybe you can watch him for me if I have to go out of town for a few days. If it's okay with your dad?"

Lola's big eyes find me. Doesn't Maren know never to suggest something directly to a child under the premise of "if it's okay with your dad?"

How can I say no at this point?

"We'll see." It's my go-to answer that buys me time but very little peace. Lola will fixate on this until I make a promise in blood. "We should head home, Lola."

"I need to go to the bathroom first." She cups her hands around her lips and mouths *Poop* to me.

"Here. I'll show you the restroom." Maren stands, setting the kitten on the floor.

"I'll wait here," I say.

Maren takes Lola to the house and returns a minute later. "Should I have waited inside the house with her?" She pauses just inside the door.

"She'll be a while," I say. "There's nothing quick about her using the bathroom. Even when she's done, she'll spend five minutes washing her hands and talking to herself in the mirror."

"I love that," Maren says, closing the door. "I used to talk to myself in the mirror when I was her age."

I sit at the end of the bed and pick up Bandit, but he squirms out of my hands and hides under the bed.

"He knows you tried to let him die." Maren crosses her arms over her chest. I stare at her. After a few seconds, she narrows her eyes. "What? Why are you looking at me like that?"

"I'm just imagining things."

"What things?"

I shrug. "They're a little inappropriate, so I'd rather not say."

Her face flushes, and she fiddles with her ponytail. "Stop."

"I'm tired of stopping. Aren't you?" I stand.

She retreats a step, and her back hits the door.

"Don't look at me like that when your daughter will be back any minute."

"She'll be a while." I duck my head and kiss her soft lips.

Maren breaks the kiss and grips my shirt. "Is this a good idea?" she whispers before kissing my neck.

Two. Fucking. Years.

She's killing me.

I wrap her ponytail around my hand and gently tug until her neck stretches, giving me full access to her mouth again.

We kiss harder than we have thus far; an urgency burns between us. My other hand dips down the front of her leggings and into her underwear.

She moans, tightening her grip on my shirt.

This is the wrong time. Wrong place. Hell, it's probably the wrong life.

But I can't bring myself to care. Clarity is never punctual.

I like to flesh out my résumé for Father of the Year. Only a man with my elite set of skills, including morally sound decisions and impeccable timing, would attempt to get a woman off while his daughter uses the restroom.

The mind is an unsupervised playground, and mine has Maren naked. It's not my hand between her legs; it's my mouth. That one thought sends my tongue deep into her throat.

She releases my shirt and grips my hair instead. Then she looks for something else to hold as she squirms, breaking our kiss. Labored breaths fall from her lips while her hands smack the door, and I release her hair. Her head lolls side to side, pupils dilated, face tense.

I rest my free hand on the door just above her head, and we point our gazes to my other hand in her pants, her hips jerking against my touch.

"Oh god," she whispers while her fingernails scrape the wood, and her chest heaves over and over. "Don't stop, Ozzy. Don't . . . stop . . ."

She's wet and warm around my fingers as I move them in and out of her, as her soft flesh pulses and grips me with her release.

If I sneeze or even clear my throat, I'll come because watching her orgasm is mind blowing. So I hold my breath while slowly withdrawing my hand from her pants. Maren breathlessly slides down the door to her butt, hugging her knees to her chest.

I rest my forearms on the door and close my eyes, ruining the moment out of necessity with visions of Tia's scowl and roadkill—anything to quickly alleviate *the situation* and compose myself before Lola returns.

"Thank you," Maren says with her blue eyes pointed up at me when I open mine.

I'm speechless. Sometimes, I shock myself with this level of self-torture. Instead of words, I return a slight "Mm-hm" and offer her my hand.

She straightens her leggings when she's on her feet again. I pull a card from my pocket and hand it to her.

Maren's face explodes into a blinding smile as she takes it.

> Rhubarb is a vegetable, not a fruit. And you can hear it grow. Hope you love them!
>
> Ozzy x

"Ozzy," she starts to say just as the door handle turns.

Jesus, that was close.

Maren jumps away from the door like it might bite her ass. And I'd be jealous because, in my NSFW thoughts, I want to bite her ass.

"Can we come back tomorrow?" Lola asks.

I point for her to head toward the front of the house. "You're being greedy."

Halfway around the house, I glance back at Maren. She's fixing her ponytail, and it makes me smirk.

"Don't look so smug," she murmurs before narrowing her eyes.

Smug isn't the right word. I'm going with *lucky bastard.* I have a nice reel to replay in my head when I'm in the shower, catching a few minutes of me-time. Maren's pinched eyes and parted, full lips nearly brought me to my knees when she orgasmed.

I shrug, palms up.

When we reach the bikes, Maren stays laser focused on me as if the slightest shift in facial expression will signal I'm gloating.

I'm not. Really.

If anything, I'm trying to avoid all eye contact so that my dick stays limp for a more comfortable journey home. "Well." I close one eye and scratch my eyelid before rubbing my forehead, gazing at the ground. "Thanks for letting Lola meet Bandit."

Thanks for the kiss.

Thanks for letting me get to second base in the kitchen.

Thanks for letting me explore third base in the shed.

You have terrific bases.

"Anytime. It was my pleasure," Maren says.

"Clearly," I mutter under my breath.

She teed it up. How could I not take a swing?

"Did you say something, Ozzy?" Maren crosses her arms, flipping out her hip.

I cave, giving her the quickest of glances, tongue poking into my cheek to disguise my lucky-bastard (smug) grin.

"Bye, Maren." Lola walks her bike past the Bronco in the driveway.

"Later, Lola."

I don't wait for a farewell because I don't think Maren's offering one to me. I love that she's on the defensive over an orgasm. A little bit of guilt never hurt anyone. I follow Lola instead of telling Maren that I'm headed home for a cold shower while she changes her underwear.

Chapter Fifteen

MAREN

The following day, I wake too early to a text.

Ozzy: Good morning

Maren: Morning. What's up?

Ozzy: Just saying good morning

I smile at my phone screen as I descend the stairs. The heavenly aroma of coffee and banana bread makes me drool.

"Will said you were getting felt up yesterday after we left," Jamie says. She's sitting on Fitz's lap at the kitchen table. They have two coffees and one plate of buttered banana bread. I'll miss this level of sweetness when they move out, but I'll miss Jamie's baking more.

"Will saw nothing." I yawn, going straight for the coffee. "What are you still doing here, Fitz?"

Fitz doesn't look at me but smirks while staying focused on his phone. "I'm at the bottom of the jump list, so I let Jamie talk me into staying for breakfast."

I'm sure her idea of talking him into staying for breakfast involved very little talking.

"Will said it was all over your face." Jamie slides out of Fitz's hold and rests her forearms on the island. "What if his daughter had caught you?" she asks, as if it would have been an exciting event.

"It wouldn't have been as bad as her catching us in the shed after she came in the house to use the bathroom."

"I'm out of here." Fitz stands and kisses Jamie on the back of her neck, on her tattoo. "Love you." He pockets his phone and carries his YETI and banana bread to the door.

Jamie giggles, glancing over her shoulder. "Love you, too, babe." When Fitz shuts the door, she returns her attention to me. "Okay. Spill. What happened in the shed? Surely you didn't have sex while his daughter took a bathroom break."

I can't look at her, so I focus on cutting a slice of banana bread. "No. Of course not."

"Then what happened? You don't have to tell me. It's your business. But seriously, what happened?"

I chuckle before taking a bite of bread. "I like him so much, and I like his daughter. But navigating our living situations, his transportation limitations, and his daughter is *a lot*. So we get these stolen moments, but they're never the right moments to go . . ." I slowly shake my head without finishing.

"The distance?" Jamie asks.

"Yeah."

Again, my phone vibrates with a text.

Ozzy: I have a busy day at work

Ozzy: So please don't send me too many inappropriate texts

Ozzy: Keep it to 5 or less

"I'll leave you two alone," Jamie says.

"Who?" I glance up from my phone.

"That grin on your face can only be from one guy. Plan a sex date." Jamie heads upstairs. "I'm going back to bed. Getting up early enough to make Fitz breakfast *and* convincing him to stay for it was exhausting."

I laugh while calling Ozzy.

"Good morning," he answers.

I open my mouth to ask him when and where we can have sex, just not in those exact words, but then I choke.

"Maren?"

"Yeah, I'm here. I'm not sending you inappropriate texts. That would require inappropriate thoughts. And I'm not having any of those."

"I bet you'll be heading south later this week. They're dealing with new fires every day. And I know you're thinking about the shed."

"You could be right about the fires. But not the shed. If I'm in town Friday, I could drop Bandit off at your house to stay. I think Lola's itching to keep him for a few days."

"She'll be thrilled."

"Bandit will be too," I say.

He chuckles.

"What are you doing?" I take one more sip of my coffee before heading upstairs.

"I worked out and just got out of the shower. I need to wake Lola. Did I pass the test with your roommates?"

I laugh. "I should ask you if they passed."

"They passed."

"Listen, I need you to know that I don't let every guy I date do what you did to me."

"Okay, then. We're changing the subject. I like this subject change. I knew you were thinking about it. And it's good to know, I guess"—he laughs—"that you don't let *every* guy do that to you."

I squeeze toothpaste onto my toothbrush. "I don't want you to think I'm a bad influence on Lola."

Ozzy laughs. "I'm not sure how to respond. I hope what happened between us yesterday isn't revealed to my daughter in any way that could be influential. On the other hand, I must remind you that I said no to the stray cat, and then you took it home. And now I'm hosting it at my place when you're out of town this summer."

"You're upset," I mumble over my toothbrush.

"I'm not upset."

"You're frustrated with me."

"Before you called, I was looking for any excuse to run an errand so I could swing by your place later today. I'd call that desperation, not frustration."

The right guy can make any woman feel like a girl—a giddy, emotional, bursting-with-excitement girl. I spit out the suds and press a towel to my mouth to hold in my squeal.

I know I'm a talented pilot.

I'm a leader.

I can be fearless.

And sometimes even a little badass.

But with Ozzy, I'm just a girl who doesn't have to prove herself.

"Maren?"

I blow out a slow, silent breath before clearing my throat. "What if, in the future, I were to be in your neighborhood some evening—late at night? After you put Lola to bed. Could you sneak me inside?"

"Sneak you inside my house with Lola *and* her grandparents?" He chuckles. "I don't know. That's—"

"You're not a real sneaker. When I was in high school, my boyfriend squeezed his big body through a daylight window in the basement, nearly getting stuck on more than one occasion, just to make out with me for a few minutes before he missed his curfew. That's dedication. You're not dedicated to making this thing between us work." I'm glad he can't see the massive smile on my face as I grab my bag and start toward the shed to check Bandit's food and water.

Am I shaming a single dad for not acting like a teenager? Yes. Yes, I am.

I'm ruthless because he's awakened my need for sex.

"Uh . . ." A nervous laugh accompanies his drawn-out pause.

"I'm kidding."

I'm *so* not kidding, but I'm thirty-three, and my conscience is getting the best of me.

"Lola's in bed by eight on school nights. Realistically, she's not asleep until closer to nine. My window is on the south side, and it's a full-size window."

I bite my thumbnail. Anything to keep from losing my composure. "Really, Ozzy, I was kidding. We're grown adults. Sneaking around like this is silly. Right?"

"It's probably unusual for two people in their thirties," he says.

"Exactly."

"It was your idea," he says.

I nod to myself. "A joke. Clearly." Bandit's food and water are fine, so I give him a long stroke down his back and head to my RAV.

"Clearly," he echoes.

A long pause settles between us.

"So you'll drop the cat off Friday night?"

I'm not thinking of Bandit, because I'm too busy wondering what Ozzy's room looks like, the size of his bed, and the thickness of his walls.

"Maren?"

"Yeah." I fasten my seat belt. "Friday it is, unless I'm not in town."

"Great. I can't wait to see . . ."

"Me?"

He chuckles. "Never mind."

"What do you mean, never mind?"

"I was going to make a joke, but it's inappropriate, and I'm a dad, so never mind."

"Now you have to tell me." I start my RAV.

Again he laughs. "It was nothing. Just, uh, a cat joke. I was going to say I can't wait to see your cat."

I chuckle because he's laughing. The joke is not that funny. In fact, I don't get it.

"Except I was going to use a different word for cat, and that's when I realized I would sound like an immature boy, so never mind."

"What word for . . ." I shift into reverse. "Oh my god. Pussy?"

He snorts.

"Now who's the perv?"

I try to suppress my laughter. He's right. It's a childish joke. So why am I so tempted to tell him my pussy can't wait to be seen?

Chapter Sixteen

OZZY

Maren leaves town Thursday, so Lola doesn't cat-sit. It would have worked out if I could have driven to Maren's house to pick him up. Instead, she talks Jamie into keeping an eye on Bandit.

By Sunday, Maren's scheduled to head home, with six more days until she has a break. And all I can think about is her sneaking into my bedroom.

Why did I try to talk her out of it?

Idiot!

Who am I kidding? I'm not prepared for this. I have an ex-mother-in-law who'd be happy to see me die a lonely man, and my ten-year-old daughter sleeps thirty feet from my bedroom.

And I don't have condoms.

That is the one thing I can solve because, at some point, I want to be in the position to need a condom.

After breakfast on Sunday, I shower, slide on a hoodie, and head upstairs, where Lola's giggling about something. She and Amos shift their attention to me, a half-empty box of doughnuts on the kitchen table between them.

"Where's Tia?" I ask.

"Showering," Amos says.

"Well, I'm running to the store for a few things."

"I'm coming." Lola hops out of her chair, wiping the back of her hand over her mouth.

"It's Sunday. Why do you want to go to the store with me?" I fetch a glass of water.

"Because I like going places with you."

This girl. "Maybe we can go hiking later."

"I want to go with you now."

Amos eyes me like he doesn't understand why I'm pushing back, so I press my lips into a firm line and nod. "Do you need to use the bathroom?"

She shakes her head, shoving her feet into her dirty red sneakers without untying them.

"We'll be back." I offer Amos a tight smile.

He nods, closing the lid of the box of doughnuts.

When we get to the store, Lola skips ahead of me and grabs a basket. "What are we getting?"

"Apples."

"Nana just got apples."

"I meant oranges."

"How many?" She finds the oranges.

"Three."

We meander around the store, grabbing a handful of miscellaneous items we probably don't need.

"Now I know why you wanted to come with me."

Lola smirks while scanning the items through the self-checkout, her favorite pastime. "Maybe I'll get a job here. I'm good at scanning things."

I tap my credit card and arrange the items in the bag, except for her natural soda. "I forgot something. Why don't you take your soda out front and wait for me by the bikes?"

Her eyes widen. "By myself?"

I think it over for a few seconds before nodding. "I'll be really quick. Don't talk to anyone, and stay where lots of people can see you."

"Does this mean I can ride my bike to school alone?"

"No." I take the bag and hand her the soda.

She frowns.

"Meet you out front." I ignore her displeasure and make a beeline for the personal-care aisle.

"Jesus . . . ," I whisper, surveying the condoms.

Her Pleasure.

His Pleasure.

Extended Pleasure.

Double Ecstasy.

BareSkin.

Fire & Ice.

Is there such a thing as "classic"? A basic one-size-fits-all that will prevent pregnancy and STDs? I think I can figure out the pleasure and ecstasy parts on my own. Fire & Ice sounds risky. BareSkin sounds less effective.

I grab one and head toward the checkout.

"Your bike blew over," Lola says.

I jump out of my fucking skin at the sound of her voice, dropping the condom box into the paid bag of groceries.

She sips her soda.

"You can't drink that in here," I say with the urgency of her carrying a loaded gun.

She wrinkles her nose. "Why not? You paid for it."

"Just meet me out front. Don't worry about my bike." I rest my hand on her back, ushering her toward the exit.

"Excuse me, sir."

I turn toward the man's voice. He's wearing a baseball hat with the store's logo, a green apron, and a scowl. "I need to check your bag."

Fuck.

I pinch the bridge of my nose. "Can we do this in private? And is there somewhere my daughter can stay that's safe?" I grit through my teeth.

He narrows his bushy eyebrows at her and then nods at me.

"Come on, Lola. Follow me."

"Where are we going?" She stays right behind me.

"I'm taking a survey for the store. It will only take a few minutes," I say.

The guy stops at the door across from the restrooms. "The glass is one-way. You'll be able to see her."

I point to a spot on the floor. "Stand right here. Don't move."

She rolls her eyes. "Is blinking moving?"

I don't answer with more than a frown before following the man into the office.

"One of our employees said they saw you put something in your bag without paying for it." He nods to the bag. "I need to see your bag and your receipt."

I set the bag on the desk. "The receipt is in the bag. But I can tell you right now there is a box of condoms in the bag that won't be on the receipt."

He retrieves the receipt and unloads the groceries.

I keep my mouth shut until he finishes and makes eye contact.

"Listen." I sigh. "I don't know if you have kids, but I'm a single dad, and—"

"Sir, if money is an issue, there are places you can get free contraceptives. I really should report—"

"No." I shake my head a half dozen times. "I know what this must have looked like, but can I tell you what actually happened?"

He glances at his watch as if he may or may not have time to listen to my explanation.

"It wasn't my plan to bring my daughter with me, but I had no choice."

That's not entirely true, but I don't think he has time to hear how Lola's sad eyes have brought me to my knees since her mother died.

"I bought all of those groceries, sent her out to wait by our bikes, and then I was trying to buy a box of condoms without her knowing. But she came back inside, and I panicked and tossed them into the bag so she wouldn't see them. Then I was ushering her toward the door to have her wait outside for me while I paid for them, but you stopped me before I had the chance to do that."

He removes his hat, exposing his bald head, and scratches above his ear while eyeing me with suspicion.

I pull out my wallet and set a fifty on the desk. "You can keep the change if I can walk out of this store without the police being called."

"Are you trying to bribe me?"

I deflate, hand on my hip, head bowed. "I'm trying to thank you for understanding my situation. I'm trying to thank you for not making a big deal out of this, since the last thing my daughter needs, after surviving a car accident that killed her mom, is for her dad to be arrested for shoplifting a box of condoms."

I hate myself. This is the lowest. I never imagined the day would come when I'd use Brynn's death and Lola's trauma to elicit sympathy.

The guy clears his throat and pockets the fifty. I'm not the only one in this room struggling with morality. He repacks the groceries, putting the box of condoms at the bottom of the bag.

"I'm sorry about your wife." He hands me the bag of groceries.

I take them with more force than necessary and turn toward the door. "Yeah, I can tell you're really sorry."

Lola licks her lips after taking a sip of the soda. "What's a survey?"

"Come on. I'll tell you later."

Chapter Seventeen

MAREN

"This is stupid." I stare at Ozzy's house from across the street. It's nine fifteen on Sunday night, and the main level of his house is dark. With a shallow breath of courage and a lapse in common sense, I climb out of my RAV and sneak around to the south side of the house, loose rocks along the hill threatening my footing. There are two windows, but one is small, like a bathroom window, so I choose the bigger window, with light behind the drawn shades. Before I tap on it, I play it safe and text Ozzy.

Maren: Hey

Ozzy: Hey! U back in Missoula?

Maren: Yes. What are you doing?

Ozzy: Staring at the TV

Maren: Want to stare at me instead?

My phone vibrates with a FaceTime from Ozzy. I bite my lower lip and shake my head while answering it.

He squints at the screen. "Where are you? I can barely see you."

"Sorry. I'm outside."

"What are you doing outside at this time of night?"

"I think I'm on a booty call of sorts that's not going as planned," I say.

He blinks several times before he stands up from his bed. "Are you . . ." He opens his blinds, and I wave.

The etched confusion on his face softens, and his lips curl into a killer smile. He ends the call and opens the window.

"Is this okay?"

He helps me inside. "It's definitely okay."

I glance around his room while unzipping my hoodie. My curiosity about his space takes a back seat to his bare chest.

Ozzy's lips twitch when I tear my gaze away from his chest and focus on his face.

I blush with a slight laugh. "Sorry. I, uh . . ." I cross my arms.

Uncross them.

Look for back pockets that I don't have with these lounge pants.

Finally, I manage to shove my hands into the pockets of my hoodie.

"You, uh what?" He cocks his head to the side.

Ozzy has abs. I don't know why I expected a dad bod beneath his shirt, but I did. He also has tool tattoos below his right ribs.

"I wanted to see you," I murmur.

He nods slowly, wetting his lips. "It's nice to be seen."

I wet my lips. "I underestimated things."

"Oh?"

Again, I make a slow inspection of his bare chest. "Yeah. I, uh, didn't know you had all of this."

"All of what?"

I nod toward him. "Muscles and tattoos." I clear my throat, meeting his gaze. "I would have worn something sexier."

He chuckles. "Maren, you don't have to try to be sexy. You just are." He steps past me and locks his bedroom door.

My heart takes off, rattling my nerves.

"So, how was your day?" I step toward his black desk in the corner. Beside his laptop, there's a silver-framed picture of Lola and a blond woman I assume is Brynn.

"Today hasn't been the best day, but now that you've crawled through my window, I believe the anguish was worth it." He rests his hands on my hips and kisses my neck.

I turn toward him because I can't let him touch me with his wife watching. I think every woman should set that minimum standard, whether said wife is dead or alive.

"Sounds cryptic," I whisper.

He slides my unzipped hoodie off my shoulders until it releases from my arms and falls to the floor.

"Parenting is challenging." His fingers weave into my hair, and an ambush of nerves tingles my skin.

I visibly shiver.

Ozzy's dark eyes narrow. "Cold?"

"Nervous," I whisper with an equally shaky laugh.

"I've touched you before." His mischievous expression doesn't help my situation.

"I was high on adrenaline."

"Then let's wait for your nerves to trigger a little adrenaline." He takes a step backward and sits on the edge of his bed.

My gaze flits to the television. He's watching something with Jason Statham.

"Take off your clothes," he says.

My attention jerks back to him. He rests his hands behind him.

My god, he's sexy.

"Wh-what?" I shift my weight from one foot to the other, unsure what to do with my hands.

"Strip for me."

My nervous laugh returns, and I decide it's best to watch Jason Statham instead of Ozzy. "For the record"—I risk a glance at Ozzy, and he wets his lips just to torture me a little more—"I'm not usually this nervous. But your ex-in-laws are upstairs, and I assume your daughter is not far from this room. And I'm afraid I might be too . . ." I twist my lips, rethinking the wisdom of confessing my fear.

This was a terrible idea. Grown-ass adults don't sneak around like this. I meet a guy at a bar, and we do it at his place. No sneaking. No awkward moments like this.

"Too what?" Ozzy prods.

"Are they sound sleepers?" I chew the corner of my lower lip.

"Who?"

"Everyone else in the house."

He lifts his eyebrows. "Are you a screamer, Maren?"

I don't know what I am other than every shade of red imaginable, pitting out profusely.

"I'll stop before you scream."

I cough a laugh, refocusing on him. "That sounds like an excuse not to"—I shake my head several times—"satisfy me." The words come out like a croak as my bravery disintegrates.

"Well, it *is* my turn." Ozzy's head angles to the side while he sizes me up like prey.

I cross my arms over my chest, but it feels unnatural. I thought it would feel more confident, but Ozzy has claimed all the confidence in this room tonight, and I'm grasping for something short of a puddle at his feet. "You have other responsibilities. I shouldn't be here."

He chuckles, which flexes his abs even tighter. "Now you sound like Brynn's mom."

"How so?"

"I'm pretty sure she thinks I don't deserve any pleasure."

"Why?"

His expression falls off his face, replaced with regret, while he averts his gaze. "It's a long story."

"I have time."

Ozzy eyes me. "You specifically said booty call."

"My booty can wait."

"I really need you to take off your clothes." Tension fills his brow.

I only make him wait a few seconds before removing my shirt and tossing it aside, along with my nerves. Realization smacks me upside the head. It's his confidence. I need the upper hand. I'm a competitor. Confident Ozzy makes me weak in the knees and jittery as hell, but somber Ozzy makes me want to give him pleasure.

I discard my shoes and pants, standing idle momentarily while his gaze roves along my body. It stops at my breasts when I reach behind me to unhook my bra.

I pause for a second to feel the high.

My adrenaline surges, feeding off the fact that he's waiting for me to show him the parts of my body that he's touched but never seen. And suddenly, I don't want to strip anymore. I want to be a poster he pins to his ceiling.

I want those rich brown eyes on me forever.

I want to drown in this warm anticipation until it kills me.

My hands drop to my sides, bra still in place.

Ozzy drags his gaze to mine. "What's wrong?"

"Nothing," I whisper, taking a step closer to him.

He sits up straight, pulling me to stand between his spread legs. My breath hitches from the heat of his hands on my hips.

I swallow hard. "I like the way you look at me."

He kisses the swell of my breast. "How do I look at you?"

My eyes drift shut, hands threading through his hair. "Like the sun after forty days and forty nights of rain."

"Sounds about right," he murmurs before skating his mouth to my other breast, kissing only the exposed flesh. "So why are you making me wait?"

I curl my fingers into his hair, tipping his head back to brush my lips against his. "Because the sun rises slowly."

"No." Ozzy pulls my hands from his hair, planting them at my sides, and he smiles, stealing my control. "That's just an illusion." He unhooks my bra. "The sun doesn't move."

I bite back my moan when he cups my breast and sucks my nipple into his mouth.

Lola can hear. Lola can hear . . .

My black bra lands at my feet as Ozzy's other hand slides into the back of my matching hipster underwear, squeezing my flesh while his teeth tease my nipple.

I can't get enough of his strong, calloused hands on my body. And while I've loved our slow dance, it's been brutal.

"D-do . . . you . . ." I might wake Lola up just from breathing so hard. I couldn't possibly sound more aroused and desperate.

"Do I want to do this?" He guides my legs to straddle his lap. "Yes." His jeans feel like an extension of his rough hands, teasing my sensitive skin. "I've been patiently waiting to see your *cat*."

I laugh as he lies back, my hair brushing his face when I gaze down at him with my hands on either side of his head. My lips descend to his, and he unbuttons his jeans while we kiss.

Lifting my head, I rub my lips together. "Do you have a condom?"

He narrows his eyes a fraction, and the corner of his mouth twitches into a devilish smirk. "Yeah, I've got a whole fucking box."

His words, tone, and facial expression nag at my curiosity. Why did he say it like that?

Is he mad that I want him to wear one?

Before I can ask, he cups my face and kisses me. My hips sink until his erection slides between my legs, two layers of cotton gatekeeping until he gets into his *whole fucking box* of condoms.

He rolls us to our sides, hiking my leg over his hip without breaking the kiss. I moan as he skates his fingers along the back of my leg until they reach the edge of my underwear and slide beneath the material.

I rock my pelvis into his familiar touch.

Tiny noises work their way up my throat, and Ozzy kisses me harder, swallowing each one. It's no longer just my hips moving. Every time I hum into the kiss, he thrusts his pelvis, and his restrained cock fights to share space with his fingers between my legs.

Then, despite my silent chants to God, thanking Him for this moment, He demonstrates His absolute power by allowing three tiny knocks at the bedroom door.

I help save lives. That's my job.

I rescued an abandoned kitten.

I volunteer in my spare time.

What more does a girl have to do to get laid?

We freeze, waiting as if the knocks didn't happen.

"Dad? Why is your door locked?"

I fly. That's my specialty. I fly fast. But never have I flown as fast as I am now, out of bed and gathering my clothes. Of course, my shirt is inside out, and I'm a fumble-finger trying to hook my bra.

Ozzy has it easy. He stands, buttons and zips his jeans.

"Dad? I'm going to be sick."

Ozzy's eyes widen, shooting me a panicked look while jerking his head toward the closet and opening the bifold doors. With my clothes and shoes hugged to my chest, I wedge into the corner of his closet. A pair of his boots dig into my ass when I squat to keep from knocking clothes off hangers.

I'm sorry, he mouths just before closing the doors.

I'm rethinking my decision to come here tonight.

"I didn't make it," Lola says and sniffles past a tiny sob.

"It's okay, baby. I'll clean it up. Let's get you in the bathroom."

It only takes a few seconds before the sour stench of vomit makes its way to me.

Don't puke! I pinch my nose and breathe through my mouth.

Minutes later, Ozzy opens the closet doors. "She's in the shower. I hate to do this but—"

"Don't apologize." I stumble, getting past the minefield of shoes, and he grabs my arms to help me. I take one look at the vomit outside his open bedroom door, and I cover my mouth and turn away.

"You don't do vomit?" He chuckles.

I quickly shake my head while he hooks my bra, rights my shirt, and helps me put it over my head. Then he holds my pants while I step into them. Ozzy completely dresses me, including tying my shoes.

He's a good man—the best.

"I'll make this right. I promise." He cups my face and kisses me, keeping my back to the doorway. Then he opens the window.

I stare at it for a second, shaking my head. "This is so messed up."

He laces his hands behind his head and sighs. "I'm really sorry. And I have no flowers or notes for you."

I grab the edge of the window and hike myself up while he grabs my hips to support me. "I think a messy life is a good one." When I'm outside, I slide on my hoodie and zip it. "And the fact that not having flowers and a note for me bums you out, well, that puts you in an untouchable class of your own, Ozzy Laster." I blow him a kiss. "Hope Lola feels better."

"I'll call you tomorrow," he says in defeat.

"Yep." I can't hide my chuckle or my headshake. "Good night." I take a few steps and glance back as he shuts the window.

Anguish paints his face in sad lines.

I don't know what we're doing, where we're going, or if there's a real chance for us. But damn! I hope we can figure it out.

Chapter Eighteen

As promised, Ozzy texts me. More like he spams my phone with a slew of profusely apologetic messages and GIFs of wildflowers while I drink my coffee the following day.

Ozzy: If this is too much, I understand

Maren: It's not

Ozzy: Lola's feeling better and she wants to watch Bandit

Maren: Tonight?

Ozzy: You're amazing

Maren: I know

Ozzy: God hates me

Maren: Lol he doesn't

And then there's my favorite:

Ozzy: I nearly got arrested for shoplifting condoms. It's a long story. Just want you to know my level of dedication

I send him shocked-faced emojis.

Maren: I'm off to work. CU 2night

After a full day at the base and a quick burrito for dinner, I pack up Bandit and his supplies and head to Ozzy's. Entering through the front door is a nice change.

Before it even opens, Lola's squeals sound in the distance, along with the thumping of feet nearing the door. "He's here!" She throws open the door.

I can't help but laugh.

"You must be Ozzy's coworker." A woman with short graying hair and pursed lips inspects me with beady eyes.

Coworker is a stretch.

"Hi. Yes. I'm Maren." I hand Bandit to Lola and set the bag of supplies on the entry floor before offering her my hand.

She stares at it and returns a forced smile instead. "I'm Tia. Brynn's mother."

Okay. She's going the don't-forget-my-daughter route instead of opting for *Lola's grandma*.

"Well, it's nice to meet you, Tia." Where's Ozzy? Why am I being ambushed alone?

"Bandit's going to sleep with me," Lola says, kissing his head.

Tia gives her granddaughter a more genuine smile, but the second her gaze returns to me, it morphs into an untrusting scowl. Now I know why Ozzy insists we sneak around.

"Hey! Sorry, I wanted to grab a quick shower," Ozzy says, reaching the top of the stairs in a white T-shirt and black jeans, with wet hair.

Pure torture.

"I'm a few minutes early," I say.

He eyes Tia. "This is Maren. She's—"

"We already made introductions." She crosses her arms over her chest.

Ozzy gives her a stiff smile. "Great. Well . . ." His face softens as he focuses on me again. "Let's take Bandit's stuff downstairs, and you can give Lola any specific instructions."

I grab the bag again. "Sounds good." When I pass Tia, her glare bores into the side of my head, but I keep a friendly grin.

"Sorry," Ozzy says as soon as we reach the bottom of the stairs. "I hope Tia wasn't too intense with you."

"I peed my pants a little, but it's fine."

He cringes, but I laugh and hand him the bag. "You can set up the litter box wherever you want, just as long as Bandit can always get to it."

"Hear that, Lola? You have to ensure that Bandit can always get to his litter box."

"I heard," she mumbles, toting Bandit into her bedroom.

Ozzy shakes his head at her and tucks his hands into his back pockets. "About last night . . . ," he says, lowering his voice.

"Please don't apologize any more. I regret nothing."

He gives me a sexy smile. "I used to be better than this."

I laugh, eating up his rare vulnerability. "What do you mean?"

Ozzy glances into Lola's room before focusing on me. "I had game. Good game. Great game, really."

Pressing my teeth into my lower lip, I nod several times. "I think you still have game." I check on Lola's vicinity and lower my voice. "In fact, I like your game *a lot*."

"Don't say that. I can do so much better."

I don't speak. Ozzy just planted a new garden of possibilities, and with so many inappropriate images in my head, I can't think of words.

"I want to kiss you," he whispers.

Heat crawls up my neck. "You're being cruel because you can't deliver, and now I can't stop thinking about it."

"Good," he whispers. "I don't want you to stop thinking about it."

I step closer, again checking on Lola. "I didn't even make it home last night," I murmur so only Ozzy can hear me. "I went straight to my car and touched myself."

Ozzy blinks several times. Then his gaze inspects the stairway followed by Lola's room. His lips twist, eyes narrowed, and he steps past me to her doorway. "Lola, it's time for you to take a bath."

"No! Bandit just got here." She plucks the kitten from the pile of stuffed animals on her bed and hugs him.

"Fifteen minutes," Ozzy says.

"Dad! It's not even seven thirty."

Ozzy sighs. "Fine. I'll give you twenty minutes."

"Thirty," she counters.

"Twenty-five."

"Fine," she grumbles.

Ozzy turns, jerking his head to his left. I hesitate for a second before following him. He opens the door to a windowless room with a mirror on one wall and exercise equipment lining the other three walls.

"I already exercised," I say.

He shuts the door after I step into the room. "Lola won't leave that room until I drag her out. And her grandparents won't come downstairs until nine to tell her good night. So we have time."

"To exerci—"

Ozzy cups my face and kisses me. He pulls back and grins. "To kiss," he whispers, sliding his lips from my mouth to my ear. "To touch." He laces his fingers with mine and kisses my neck. "To dream."

I smile, eyes closed. "Tell me about the dream."

"I get you to myself. No disruptions. No curfews. For a whole night."

Releasing his hands, I rest mine on his chest as he lifts his head. "How do we make that happen?" I ask.

His brow tightens. "I don't know."

"Tia seems . . ."

"Bitter. Harsh. Unbendable."

I nod several times. "But why? Was Brynn's death your fault?"

"No. It's guilt by association." His fingertips ghost along my jaw as he bends to brush his lips over mine. "But I don't want to talk about her when we don't have much time."

I nip at his lower lip. "Then what do you want to talk about?"

"I don't think we should talk at all. Someone could hear us." He kisses me again, flicking his tongue against mine.

"He pooped!" Lola yells. "Good job, Bandit!"

Ozzy sighs, resting his forehead against mine. "I'm never going to have sex again."

I shake with suppressed laughter.

"But *you* should," he says. "You deserve a guy who has a future beyond vomit, poop, and penance for his past."

My hands frame his stubble-covered face. "Ask her if she's ready to take a bath."

He squints at me.

"Just do it."

Ozzy cracks open the door. "Lola, are you ready for your bath?"

"No! It hasn't been that long. You said twenty-five minutes!" She slams her door shut.

Ozzy closes the door to the exercise room. Then I push his chest until his back hits it.

He lifts a single brow. "What are you—"

"Sit."

"On the floor?"

I nod.

He slides down the door, and it makes me giggle because it's *so* slow. When his butt touches the floor, he stretches out his legs, and I straddle them and sit on his lap.

"You make me feel sixteen," I say wrapping my arms around his neck. "Nervous. Shaky. Shivers down my spine. And don't even get me started on butterflies."

Ozzy wets his lips, rubbing them together. "We're adults hiding from a ten-year-old. You left through my window after said ten-year-old puked. *That* gives you butterflies?"

I smile, brushing my nose against his. "What's the next flower? Or vegetable? It's asparagus season."

"I've created a monster." He chuckles. "What if there are no more flowers? No more cards? Will the butterflies die?" He pecks at my lips.

I lean in for more than a peck, prolonging our tiny stolen moment. Ozzy's hand cups the back of my neck while his tongue teases mine. He weaves his fingers into my hair.

As a young girl, I dreamed of flying in the clouds more than I thought about boys' kisses, love notes, and flowers. Either my heart is bigger than I ever imagined, or Ozzy Laster is stealing it from my first love.

He ghosts his lips from my mouth to my ear. "I'm so unprepared for you," he whispers.

I sigh while settling into him.

"My neighbor has them in his yard," Ozzy says.

"Has what?" I sit up.

He leans to the side just enough to pull a piece of paper from his pocket—a folded note.

My heart can't take this level of romance as he offers it to me with a single-shoulder shrug.

I open it.

> Yarrow is a medicinal herb with delicate clusters of flowers that attract bees and butterflies. Hope you love them!
>
> Ozzy x

I keep my gaze on the note. "Oswald, the problem with men like you is that you make it impossible for the average Joe to stand a chance. There are so many Joes out there buying clearance bouquets tied with rubber bands and packets of flower food. Do you see what you're doing to me?" I stand and fold the note, sliding it into my back pocket because I'm keeping everything he gives me. "You're ruining me. You've set the bar impossibly high."

He lumbers to his feet, studying me. The hint of a grin touches his lips as he gathers my hair and pulls it over one shoulder so he can kiss my bare neck. "In that case, I've never wanted to ruin someone so much in my life."

"How much time do we have before Lola looks for us?" I ask.

"A while. Why?"

I hold a finger to my lips. "Shh."

He tracks my hands as I unbutton his jeans and pull at his zipper.

I smirk, eyeing his intense expression while I slide his jeans partway down his muscly thighs.

"Maren," he says in exhalation before wetting his lips.

When I free him from his briefs, his eyes leaden. I drop to my knees and tease him with my tongue.

"Fuck . . . Maren . . ." He blinks heavily, grabbing the base of his cock and guiding it past my lips.

Ozzy's abs tighten, and I focus on his tattoos. I thought they were random tools, but they're in the shape of Lola's name. For some reason, his love for her only turns me on more.

He buries his fingers in my hair, breaths gaining momentum, each one ripping from his chest a little harsher than the previous one. When our gazes meet, I feel an odd jolt of emotion. My body does its own thing while my thoughts wrap around the sadness on his face, like he feels undeserving of this.

Of intimacy.

Of an escape.

Of life.

Is it the sacrificial burden that seems to come naturally to parents? Or is it about Brynn? Will every intimate moment remind him of her?

These questions swirl in my head while he closes his eyes and tips his head back. Is he thinking of her?

His body curls inward, abs rock hard, and he drops his chin, lips parted to release each shallow breath. As hard as he tries to stifle every sound, a few grunts and groans slide past his throat. They feed my desire. A desire that will not be satisfied tonight, and that's okay.

Tonight, it's about him.

I take his warm release and swallow it.

Ozzy's expression softens into pure gratitude. He relaxes as I continue to slide my tongue along his length.

He feathers his knuckles across my cheek, and when I completely release him, the pad of his thumb traces my bottom lip. "Is this the wrong time to tell you how beautiful you are?"

I stand, pulling up his jeans as he tucks himself back into his briefs. "A good orgasm makes everything look better," I say, zipping and buttoning his jeans the way he dressed me the previous night.

"Good? That was beyond good." He claims my face.

I press my lips together for a beat before he tries to kiss me. "It wouldn't be wrong of you to let me use your bathroom and tell me where you keep your mouthwash."

Ozzy chuckles before releasing me.

I think he might be blushing, and I love it.

Chapter Nineteen

OZZY

"It's us, Grandma," Lola says when we step into my mom's light-green house with a white door and weed-infested yard. I need to spend a day here giving it some TLC.

"Sweetheart, come here." Mom stands from her rocking chair and slides on her thick glasses. She's lost most of her vision, which explains why her chin-length brown-and-gray hair is always ratted in the back and her button-down blouse is usually off by one or two buttons. She's not the put-together Gina "Perfectionist" Laster she used to be.

Lola hugs her.

"How is school?"

"Almost over," Lola says.

"Where's Ruth?" I ask about her sister, who moved in to help my mom after my dad died.

"She had a hair appointment." Mom holds out her arms to me, and I embrace her.

"I have a kitten," Lola says with her eyes alight. "Well, he's not really mine, but I found him, and sometimes I get to watch him. His name is Bandit Mouse Bernabe."

Mom eases back into her chair and turns down the volume on the TV. "That's a nice name."

"Where's Paxton?" Lola pokes her head into the kitchen, searching for Aunt Ruth's parrot.

"He's in the bedroom," Mom says.

Lola skips down the small hallway to the bedroom.

"How's she doing?" Mom asks.

I sit on the faded green-and-white striped sofa. "She's good. Great, actually, now that she gets to have a part-time pet."

"And therapy?"

"The same."

"How are you? How's work?"

"I'm good. Work's good," I say, leaning back and craning my neck to look for any sign of Lola. "I've met someone."

Mom straightens in her chair. "Oswald, that's great. Tell me about her."

"She's a breath of fresh air. Unexpected. And I can't stop grinning when I'm with her. Her humor is refreshing. When she laughs, I feel it deep in my chest. And she seems to adore Lola."

Mom presses her hand to her chest. "Do you hear yourself?" she says, with thick emotion.

"Hear myself?"

"You didn't tell me her name. You didn't tell me what she looks like. And you didn't tell me what she does for a living. I hope this woman knows how lucky she is to have you. A man who really sees the parts of her that matter."

I laugh. "You might be a little biased."

"Perhaps. But you're a hundred times the man your father was. God rest his soul. I loved him, but he wasn't, well, you know." She folds her wrinkly hands and nervously wrings them. It's what she does whenever she or anyone else mentions my father. I feel indifferent about him. It's the only way I can reconcile the way he died and everything he stole in the process. Anger and regret are a waste of time.

But I don't want to talk about him. "Well"—I act like she didn't mention my father—"just to give you a few of those details, her name is Maren. She is beautiful inside and out. She's a firefighter—a tanker pilot. And she's never been married."

"See how boring all of that is compared to you feeling her laughter in your chest?"

I hum. "True. Also, Lola thinks we're just friends."

"Why? Don't you think she's old enough to handle the truth?"

"She's old enough to handle the truth but not old enough to keep a secret."

"A secret from who?"

"Tia and Amos. Well, mainly Tia."

Mom frowns. "Is she still holding a grudge?"

"An eternal one."

"Oswald, you can't let her tell you how to live your life."

"I need their help. That puts me at their mercy."

"They love Lola. They're not going to abandon her because you want to move on with your life," she says.

"No. But I don't want Lola living in a house where the adults are at each other's throats. And I don't want Tia bringing up the accident more than she already does. They love Lola, but they show their love differently than you show your love. Tia has always been tough on me, and she was tough on Brynn too. She's never been a coddler. So she didn't approve of every choice we made raising Lola. As is, she's frustrated that Lola's therapist hasn't miraculously cured her or forced her to get into a car.

"If I push her by stepping out of line, she and Amos will pack up and leave. It won't be about Lola. She'll blame it on me. She'll let Lola know that it's all because of me."

"I could help with Lola," Mom says.

I don't say anything.

"She's ten, not two." Mom blows out an exasperated breath because she's offered to help with Lola before now. I haven't felt comfortable leaving Lola with someone who is legally blind.

Mom continues to make her case. "And Ruth can help."

"Ruth is already helping by staying with you," I say, swiping my hand along the cobwebs inside the shade of her standing lamp.

"Oswald, Ruth does very little to help me. Ask her, if you don't believe me."

"You can't drive."

"What does that matter when Lola won't get in a car?"

She's not wrong.

"Now, what can I do? Would you like Lola to stay with me while you take your new lady friend on a date?"

A date.

We've done that.

I want a night.

Can I tell my mom that? Or is that basically saying I need her to watch Lola so I can get laid?

I don't push my luck. "What if Lola spent a Friday or Saturday evening with you?"

"A sleepover?"

I rub the back of my neck. "It wouldn't have to be."

"What if you don't want your date to end with dinner?" Mom smirks.

"Grandma, can I take Paxton out of his cage?" Lola yells from the bedroom.

"Come here, Lola," Mom says.

"Please don't say anything," I beg.

Lola pokes her head around the corner. "What?"

"I think Aunt Ruth should be here if you take Paxton out of his cage. But since she's not here right now, I think you should return and spend the night sometime."

Lola slides her wide-eyed gaze to me. "Really?"

Not once has Lola spent the night with my mom, or even with both my parents when my father was alive, even though she's begged to do it. But she's not a baby anymore, and Aunt Ruth is trustworthy. Still, it will spur a conversation with Tia and Amos that I don't want to have.

But the question is: Am I willing to have it for the chance to spend a whole night with Maren?

"Really," I say, not just because thinking of Maren gives me a semi-erection.

It's time to expand Lola's world. Even Victoria is encouraging Lola to try new experiences since her refusal to get into a car has made everything smaller.

"That would be amazing." Lola inflates with enthusiasm, and I can't help but smile.

◆ ◆ ◆

Once again, Lola proves that secret-keeping isn't her forte. I haven't even mentioned it to Maren yet because I want to surprise her. However, Lola spills the beans.

"Where will I sleep?" Lola asks during our late dinner following her softball practice.

As Tia and Amos lift their gazes from their dinner plates, Lola cringes with her signature "oops" look.

"What are you talking about?" Tia asks Lola while peering at me.

I press my napkin to my mouth and clear my throat. "Lola's going to spend the night with my mom and Ruth sometime."

Tia and Amos exchange a look.

"Lola wants to play with Paxton. And she's old enough that she won't require much from Ruth or my mom."

"What about that cat?" Tia scrutinizes Lola.

It's ridiculous.

"Bandit will be back with Maren. This is a chance for Lola to try something new, expand her world, and build confidence." I spew Victoria's words, but they've also been Tia's. She can't have it both ways. If she doesn't want me to "coddle" Lola, she can't do it either.

"We could visit Leroy," Amos suggests.

Tia regards him with narrowed eyes for a second. Leroy is their son, who lives in Arkansas.

I drop my gaze to my plate when Tia inspects me. I need to play it cool, but it's hard because this is the best-case scenario. Not only will Lola be at my mom's for the night, but if Tia and Amos are gone, I won't have to explain why I'm not here. More than that, I can be here, and Maren can stay the night.

As I imagine this, I start to feel like a lovestruck dummy getting giddy over seeing a girl.

"Ozzy, let me know when you're thinking so I can check airfare," Tia says.

I must restrain myself from voicing my enthusiasm or punching the air excitedly.

My grin is dying to spread across my face, and my heart is racing. Still, I manage to contain my reaction and offer nothing more than a few easy nods.

◆ ◆ ◆

After Lola is in bed, I call Maren.

"Still in Missoula?" I ask.

"I am, but I'm tired. No sneaking out tonight. Sorry."

"That's fine. That's not why I'm calling."

"You sound chipper. What's up?" she asks.

"I'm hopeful," I say. "Because I have just moved Heaven and Earth to be with you. When do you have time off again?"

"I'm off Sunday to Wednesday," she says. "Heaven *and* Earth? Ozzy, your ability to sweep a girl off her feet is unmatched. Tell me more about your superpower."

"Lola can spend Saturday night at my mom's house, and her other grandparents will visit their son when Lola's at my mom's. You're invited to stay the night with me after you get off work on Saturday. Clothing is optional. And if I'm being frank, it's downright frowned upon."

She laughs. "Something will happen. You're getting my hopes up, but something will happen."

"Don't be a Negative Nellie. Could Lola get sick at the last minute? Absolutely. Could my house burn down before then? Of course. Might you find a guy who drives a car *and* has sex with you? For sure. But despite all those possibilities, I'm banking on everything going well. And I'm going to finally use that box of condoms that nearly landed me in jail."

Maren's laughter spreads along my skin, warm and sweet like honey. "Jail? We have so much to discuss. I know nothing about your parents. I'd love to see your whole house. And don't even get me started on all the questions I have about your box of condoms."

I hum. "Yes. So much to discuss."

"Ozzy, I feel like your dirty little secret."

"Don't be ridiculous," I say. "We haven't even done the dirty."

"Oswald."

I laugh because she's never met my mom, but she's mastered the tone in which my mother has always said my name.

"I miss you," I say.

"I miss you too. So, this weekend?"

"Yes. As long as Amos and Tia can get plane tickets. If not, we'll have to push it back a few weeks until your time off falls on a weekend again." I flop back onto my bed.

She sighs so hard I swear my phone feels heavier. "Do you wonder where we're going with this? Whatever *this* is? I feel guilty for inserting myself into your life, since you have a child and all the delicate complications that come with that role. Yet, simultaneously, I'm scouring real estate listings for a house because I want you and Lola to come see me and Bandit anytime. Speaking of Bandit, how is my furry friend?"

"You're never getting him back. You had to know this was going to happen."

She laughs. "Since you started this call with such honesty, I'll tell you how far I went for Lola's cat. You know that shed he lives in?"

I adjust myself because my dick has a perfect memory. "Yes," I say.

"Will is charging me double rent for Bandit to live in the shed."

"You're not serious." I run a hand through my hair, staring up at the ceiling.

"I'm dead serious."

I'm speechless for ten seconds before I fumble my first minimally coherent thought. "We'll keep the cat."

"Nope," she says with a pop to her lips. "Fitz and Jamie found a different house. The one with the tree house is still for sale. I'm thinking of making an offer on it."

"That's exciting *unless* you're buying it just for the cat. Then it's a little messed up." And by the cat, I mean Lola. But suggesting she's buying a house, in a roundabout way, for my daughter seems serious. I can't allow myself to be that level of serious with someone I have to sneak into the house through a window.

Jesus. Maybe she is *my dirty little secret.*

"I used to have a tree house, minus a roof," she says. "It was a platform with a railing. I'd lie on my back, staring at the sky, and that's when I fell in love with flying. I'd see planes and birds in the sky and wanted to spend my days in the clouds too."

I can't help but grin, imagining young Maren in a tree, staring up at the blue sky and dreaming of flying. "Buy the house," I say.

"You think?"

"I do. Real estate is always a great investment. Interest rates are pretty good. Go for it."

"Okay. I have to message my Realtor," she says in a rush.

"It's late."

"I know, Ozzy. But I don't want someone else scooping it up."

I laugh at her excitement. Joy is timeless. It doesn't matter if someone is five or fifty. It sounds the same, and it's unavoidably contagious.

"Go message your Realtor. Good night."

"EEK! Sorry, I let that slip. Okay, good night."

I drop my phone to the side and continue staring at the ceiling. I think of Brynn, and I wonder if she would have liked Maren. Or would she say I'm letting Lola get attached to someone who could die because she has a high-risk job? Can I live the rest of my life wondering what Brynn would think?

Chapter Twenty

MAREN

I haven't told anyone.

Not my parents. Not Will. Not Fitz or Jamie.

For some reason, I want to tell Ozzy first.

Thursday night, when I pull into his driveway to pick up Bandit, I can barely keep my hands and the rest of my body from shaking with excitement to see him. This is a foreign feeling to me and a little scary. I've liked other guys, maybe even loved one or two, but this is next level.

"Calm down," I whisper with a deep breath before knocking on the front door.

It's no surprise but no less disappointing when Tia opens the door. She offers me a polite smile that's just shy of believable.

"Hi. Hope I'm not interrupting dinner," I say.

She steps aside. "Dinner was over an hour ago."

I mirror her less-than-genuine smile. "Okay. Good to know," I say.

Her face wrinkles, and I ignore it because I don't care what it means or what she thinks of me; I just want to see Ozzy and Lola.

"Lola walked to the park with Amos, but they should be back soon because it's getting dark," she says, heading into the living room. "Your cat and Ozzy are downstairs."

"Thanks," I mumble, slipping off my shoes before making a beeline straight to the stairs just as Ozzy appears at the bottom.

I smile.

He smiles.

My heart tries to break through my chest as I descend the stairs. When I reach the bottom, Ozzy hooks my waist and swings me around the corner so we're out of sight. Before I can even gasp, he kisses me.

I claim his hair with my eager fingers, and he grips my ass. Absence makes everything grow fonder.

"That's not fair," I whisper, out of breath, when he releases my mouth.

Ozzy's expression morphs into something sexy and naughty while he presses his forehead to mine. He slides his hands up my back to my arms before softly cupping my neck. "You're not fair. I'm dying, and you have the audacity to show up with your hair all . . . *woven* like some goddess. And your skin smells like a flower garden. *And* all I want to do is remove your clothes, but we don't have time for that, so I'll be taking yet another cold shower after you and your feline friend head home."

I peck at his lips and giggle while my hands cover his. "Woven? Do you mean braided? And if I recall correctly, the last time I left here, I was the one who needed a cold shower."

Ozzy's face bleeds mischief.

I wrap my arms around his waist, resting my cheek against his chest. "Besides, it's only two more sleeps before we have all night together. And guess what?"

"Hmm?" He kisses the top of my head.

"I got the house." I lean away from him just enough to see his face.

"That is awesome, Maren. When do you move?"

I wrinkle my nose. "I don't know yet. My Realtor said she'd know more on Monday."

"Maren's here!" Lola calls two seconds before barreling down the stairs, wide eyed and out of breath.

Ozzy jumps away from me just in time.

"Bandit's probably under my bed. I'll get him." Lola runs straight to her room.

"Someday I'll teach her manners." Ozzy rolls his eyes.

Lola drags Bandit out from under her bed and cradles him like a baby, and for whatever weird reason, that kitten lets her hold him like that. "Maren, I really like your hair," she says.

I quickly glance at Ozzy because he called my pigtail braids a weave. "Thank you," I say.

Lola kisses Bandit on the head, and it will break my heart to take him from her. "My mom used to braid my hair," she says.

"I bet your beautiful curls look amazing in a loose braid." I smile.

She shrugs as Ozzy gathers the cat supplies. "I don't know. Dad can't braid and neither can Nana."

"I just haven't tried." Ozzy attempts to defend himself, dumping the cat litter into a trash bag.

"He says he needs to watch a video," Lola tries to whisper, but I know Ozzy hears her because he slowly shakes his head, tying the trash bag.

"I could teach him," I say.

Lola perks up. "Really?"

"Of course."

"Now?"

"Lola, it's late," Ozzy says.

She deflates. "It's the end-of-the-year track-and-field day tomorrow. A lot of my friends will have their hair braided."

"I'm excellent at ponytails," Ozzy says, setting the bag of cat supplies by the stairs.

"What time do you leave for school?" I ask.

Lola looks to Ozzy for an answer. He eyes her as if she should know, then says, "Seven thirty."

"I'll be here at six thirty to braid your hair before I go to work," I say, taking Bandit from her.

"For real?"

I chuckle. "For real."

"Oh my gosh! Did you hear that?"

Ozzy nods. "Yes. I'm not deaf. That's very nice of Maren."

"Well, I'd better go so you can get to bed." I reach for Bandit's bag, but Ozzy picks it up.

"Lola, I'm going to help Maren take things out to her car. I expect you to be in the shower by the time I get back inside."

"Good night, Lola," I say.

"Good night," she says, slapping her bare feet on the hard surface toward the bathroom.

When we reach the top of the stairs, her grandparents are nowhere in sight.

"You don't have to braid her hair tomorrow morning. She'll be fine in a ponytail," Ozzy says while I shove my feet into my sneakers.

"I was going to knock on your bedroom window around six and slide into bed with you." I glance over my shoulder at him.

Ozzy opens the front door. "I meant to say that if Lola doesn't have her hair in braids for track-and-field day, she will be devastated."

I step onto the porch with Bandit. "You're such a good dad. Thinking only of your daughter."

"What can I say? It's part of my laser focus. Give me one sec." Ozzy retreats to the kitchen and returns just as I reach the back of my RAV and put Bandit in his pet carrier.

"Hope is a slippery little bastard, but I'm trying to keep a grip on it," he says, glancing around the rear of the vehicle, making a quick inspection before ducking back around the corner with me.

"How so?" I ask.

"I know there's a lot stacked against us and whatever this is between us." He pulls me to him by sliding his hands into my back jeans pockets. "But thinking about you—the next time I can see you, how I can sneak a few minutes alone with you, and doing little things like moving Heaven and Earth—has resurrected something in my life that I didn't know I needed until you sent me on a scavenger hunt for tampons and toilet paper."

I press my hands to his chest and nuzzle my face in his neck. "The only thing stacked against us is your fear. Let it go."

He angles his head to find my lips, and we kiss. It's slow and easy. His mouth on mine has reached a point of familiarity. Everything fits.

Bandit meows, and we laugh, ending the kiss.

"I'll see you in the morning." He reaches behind himself and pulls spears of asparagus from his pocket—six, to be exact. Then he digs out a note from his front pocket. "You mentioned asparagus. Correct?"

I slowly shake my head in amazement and grin.

"Finding these feral little sproutings was harder than I thought it would be," he says.

I open the note.

> Asparagus has been cultivated in the US for 150 yrs, and it can give you stinky pee if you have the gene for that. Hope you love them!
>
> Ozzy x

"Ozzy . . ." I don't even know what to say.

He turns and heads up the walkway, glancing over his shoulder with a triumphant smile.

I climb into my RAV. "Enough with the smirk, Oswald," I mumble to myself. "I'm already falling for you. What more do you want?"

Chapter Twenty-One

OZZY

When I shut the front door, Tia steps out of her bedroom in her blue robe and moccasin slippers. "Is your *friend* gone?"

"Yes. *Maren* just left." I head into the kitchen, and Tia follows me. She's at least four feet away, but I still feel her breathing down my neck.

"I hope you're not giving Lola the wrong idea," she says, scooping her fiber powder into a glass of water while I grab an apple from the hanging basket by the fridge.

"The wrong idea about what?" I bite into the apple.

"I realize men and women can be friends, but Lola likes to let her mind wander. We need to keep reminding her that she is your only concern—your number one priority." Tia stirs her concoction, pinning me with a firm gaze.

I chew slowly for a few seconds before swallowing. "Lola is and always will be my number one priority. I don't think she's confused about that."

"She might get confused if she sees you giving attention to pretty women."

"Are you implying Lola is insecure?"

Tia takes several gulps of her fiber drink before rubbing her lips together. "I'm implying she doesn't live in the real world."

I chuckle. "How do you figure?"

"She can't get over Brynn's death. She won't get into a car. And everyone around her is allowing her to make up her own version of reality. So if she likes your friend and decides your friend should be more than a friend, I fear you'll let it happen. But it won't end well because raising that girl is a full-time job. Why do you think Amos and I are living with you?"

"How am I letting her make up her own version of reality?"

"By riding your goddamn bike everywhere. It's time for you to stand up to her. Get in a car like a man to prove that her world won't end." She lifts her glass to her lips.

"What if it does end? What if she loses me? How much is too much?"

Tia continues drinking. When the glass is empty, she sets it in the sink and stares at it with a focused gaze. "If you die, her world won't end."

"No?" I take another bite of the apple and chew it. "But will her world be a place she wants to live in? Will she be happy? Or will she live with even more debilitating isolation? Will she refuse to leave the house? Will she end up in a psych ward or be heavily medicated for the rest of her life? Everyone has a different breaking point. I don't want to find her breaking point. I want to empower her."

Tia scowls at me, but she doesn't speak.

"She'll get back to riding in a car," I say. "And when she does, she'll feel empowered. If you can't stay, then I'll figure something out. But I can't test her breaking point because as much as I'm her whole world, she is even more so mine." I stop short of saying the rest: Maren has become an important person in my life too. I need help, and Tia and Amos are the best help for now. So I'll continue to walk this thin line and deal with the future if and when it comes.

"You can't ask us to watch you pursue another woman. Brynn was our daughter and . . ." Tia swallows hard, eyes reddening. "You just can't ask that of us," she whispers before returning to her bedroom.

This is not just about Lola. It's been two years, and I've never looked for someone to date. Brynn continues to live in my mind. I think about her every single day.

I miss her every day.

But as sure as Tia can't help how she feels about me showing interest in another woman, I can't pretend I don't know Maren. I can't pretend that I don't have strong feelings for her.

My alarm makes a chiming sound at five on Friday morning. It's the least-annoying sound on my phone, but it's not how I used to wake up each morning.

Brynn was an early riser—up at five every morning for a long jog. She called it "getting her mind organized" for the day. She woke me by six—showered and filling the bedroom with the sweet rosewater scent of her conditioner.

This morning, I spent thirty minutes lifting weights, ten minutes showering and brushing my teeth, and two minutes changing my sheets on the hopeful chance that Maren wasn't lying about knocking on my window at six.

Do I wear a shirt or stick to my briefs since that's what I sleep in? Could I be more of a girl about this? Fussing over what to wear. *I'm an idiot.*

Proving that I *am* a girl, my heart skips when there's a tap at my window. I turn on the light beside my bed, pull the blinds, and slide open the window.

Maren bites her lip for a second. "I got to thinking that maybe you'd rather sleep in," she whispers while I help her inside and shut the window and blinds.

I slide my hands into her hair, gazing at her makeup-less face, which has a natural, beautiful glow. Her blue eyes are alight with life, and she makes it hard to breathe.

She furrows her brow. "Is your hair wet?" She touches the hair above my ear.

"I worked out and showered."

We keep our voices just above a whisper.

Her smile fades. "So much for me climbing in bed with you, since you're up and ready for the day."

I gesture to my nearly naked body. "Why would you say that? I'm simply showered and ready for whatever you have to offer."

Her fingers trace my tattoos. I'd like to say it doesn't immediately elicit an erection, but it does. "There might not be anything sexier than a man with his daughter's name tattooed on his body."

I tip my chin to watch her trace it. "When Brynn was in her final month of pregnancy with Lola, she thought I needed a tattoo. It was so random and spur of the moment. We passed a tattoo parlor, and she told me I needed one. Who was I to argue with a pregnant woman? It took three visits to complete it, but it was finished two days before she went into labor with Lola. She wanted an angel tattoo. A guardian angel to symbolize I was her protector. I wasn't feeling it, so I suggested a dragon, which she vetoed. Then, with the help of the tattoo artist, I talked her into my favorite tools spelling Lola's name. And yes, we had a moment, after the fact, where we worried that the ultrasound was wrong, and Lola might come out with a penis." I chuckle. "But I still think I need a dragon to symbolize protection, strength, power, and knowledge."

Maren lifts her gaze, keeping her warm hand on my stomach. "Some Christians believe dragons are monsters of death from the chaotic sea."

I chuckle. "You're not a fan of dragons either. Noted."

She shakes her head slowly. "I love dragons. Not the kind referenced in biblical times. More like *Game of Thrones*, *Harry Potter*, and

The Hobbit." She slides her hand past the tattoos to my ribs. "You have goose bumps."

Yes. And an erection that she *surely* notices.

"You're touching me," I say with a husky tone.

She kicks off her shoes. "What time do you wake Lola?"

"In thirty minutes, because that's when you said you'd be here," I murmur.

"And the upstairs tenants?"

"They'll be up in the next half hour as well."

"Is your door locked?" she whispers before pressing her lips to my chest.

"Yes." I close my eyes.

"And your *whole fucking box of condoms*?"

I softly chuckle, opening my eyes. "In the drawer."

She flits her gaze in that direction, and from her soft smile, I know she sees the six stems of yarrow.

"I gave you the note, but not the flowers."

"Ozzy?" She plants open-mouthed kisses up to my neck.

"Yeah?" I thread my fingers back into her hair.

"Take off my clothes."

I moved Heaven and Earth to schedule a weekend to have sex with her, and she's managed to show up thirty minutes early to a hair-braiding appointment with a solid plan to accomplish the same task.

But I'm not complaining.

I'm too busy removing her shirt and bra. Too busy sitting on the side of the bed while sliding her leggings and lacy underwear down her toned legs. And I'm way too busy palming her breasts and tweaking her nipples with my fingers until a half-suppressed moan vibrates her chest, and her back arches into my touch.

I lie back, legs hanging over the side of the bed, but before I can guide her to straddle my waist, she pulls down the front of my briefs. My next breath gets trapped in my chest, heavy with uncontrolled anticipation. A moan, with equal gravity, vibrates my whole body when she drags her tongue up the length of my erection.

"Maren," I murmur, closing my eyes for a few seconds. I don't know what I'm trying to say. Stop? Hell no. It feels too good, so I let her keep going. I'll stop her in a few more seconds.

Maybe in a few minutes.

And then . . .

A *fucking car alarm* blares.

Maren leaps off me and fights with her clothes to put them back on.

It has to be my stupid neighbor. He sets that goddamn car alarm off once a week, and it's always early in the morning. I sit up, sliding my briefs back into place and raking my hands through my hair while tugging it.

The alarm stops as Maren gets her leggings pulled to her waist. *Did that wake Lola?* she mouths.

I shrug, letting my hands flop to my sides, gripping the edge of the mattress. Sometimes the alarm wakes her, and sometimes it doesn't. When I hear nothing, I open the door and listen.

Still nothing. So I close and lock it again.

Maren gnaws her lower lip while hugging herself. I don't have to ask if the mood has been ruined; it's trenched in lines along her forehead.

"I'm . . ." I shake my head and sigh. "I don't know what to say."

She pauses her teeth and relaxes. A smile steals her lips. "Cuddle?"

Pussy or cuddling? How do I keep from appearing disappointed? I crawl in bed, and she slides in beside me, wiggling and adjusting herself until her ass is pressed to my dick. My briefs and her thin leggings don't hide much. This is torturous cuddling.

"If whatever this is between us doesn't last, you'll always remember me as the woman you almost had sex with but never succeeded," she says softly.

I groan, burying my face in her hair. "Don't say that."

Her body shakes with silent laughter. And instead of resting my eyes and feeling satisfied that she's in my arms, I snake my hand up her shirt and into the cup of her bra, stroking the pad of my thumb across her nipple. I'm shameless. Lola needs to wake up in fifteen minutes.

Maren arches her back into my touch, which presses her ass even harder against my cock. I tell myself to hold still. Be cool. Enjoy second base. Just because I've been to third and failed at getting to home plate doesn't mean I can't be satisfied with hitting a double. A double is pretty damn good for a Friday morning.

If only I listened to that voice of reason instead of my dick. If only Maren would stop grinding her ass against said dick.

I swallow hard, so fucking turned on I could die.

She reaches around and slides her hand into my briefs, stroking me.

We're not having sex this morning. It's too risky because of the time. It's too risky because of the stupid car alarm that may have brought Lola out of a deep sleep. We're *not* having sex.

We're just—touching each other.

Clothes on.

Ready for a fire should we need to evacuate.

Ready to answer the door should Lola knock.

I continue to caress her nipple with one hand while the other shimmies my briefs down my hips just a fraction so she can stroke the entire length of my cock.

Maren's breaths quicken and get a little louder.

This is enough.

I've made that my motto. We don't need to go any further. It's not a good idea. I can still hear that voice of reason, even if it's getting faint with the hammering of my heart.

But then Maren aims my cock toward her ass, and I accidentally jerk my hips, which shoves the head into her crack, restrained by the stretchy material of her leggings. Her heart pounds against my hand that's splayed across her chest.

"Maren," I whisper before kissing the back of her neck.

"God"—she pants—"I want you, Ozzy."

It bears repeating in my head. *We. Are. Not. Going. To. Have. Sex.*

With one hand, I shove her leggings and panties down far enough that just her ass is exposed.

That's it. That's all I'm doing.

However, *she's* the one who guides my dick between her cheeks, between her legs. Okay, I *may* rock my hips, but just a fraction, until the head of my cock reaches her clit.

She stutters my name between labored breaths. "O-Ozzy . . ."

My hand grips her hip, and we move together. It's not sex. Nope. We're basically dressed. We're just touching each other.

And it feels incredibly fucking good. Maren is warm and *so* wet. She's practically purring as I slide back and forth between her folds.

"God, Ozzy . . ." She rides my cock without penetration. "I'm . . . I'm going to come."

I know the feeling.

As she orgasms, I pull back and stretch my briefs over my erection. The moment I press it against her ass again, I release, jerking my hips several times.

Fuck! That feels good.

We've collectively shared four orgasms, but I still don't know what it feels like to be inside her. And that's a shame.

Chapter Twenty-Two

"Do you think she'll really come?" Lola pops her head into my room a short ten minutes later, after Maren made a quick escape. "Do you think Maren will really come here and braid my hair for track-and-field day?"

"I do," I say, pulling on my socks.

"You can't be sure."

"I'm pretty darn sure."

"What if she oversleeps?"

I stand and shut off the light, ushering her toward the stairs. "She'll be here."

Just as Lola reaches the top of the stairs, there's a knock at the door.

"She's here!"

I follow Lola to the front door, passing the dining room, where Amos and Tia are drinking coffee and eating breakfast.

"Who's here?" Tia asks.

"Maren's here to braid Lola's hair for track-and-field day," I reply.

"That seems unnecessary," Tia grumbles.

I ignore her because I wish she and Amos were *unnecessary* in my life.

"Good morning, Miss Lola," Maren says, stepping inside and removing her shoes.

"Come downstairs," Lola says with a quick pivot toward the stairs. "I'll get my hairbrush and ties."

Maren smiles at me. "Hi."

My fucking grin jumps off a cliff, entirely out of control. "Hi."

"Are you having a good morning?" she asks.

"As a matter of fact, I am. Coffee?"

"Sounds perfect." Maren takes two steps and glances into the dining room, pausing for a friendly greeting. "Good morning."

"Don't you have a job?" Tia asks, being her most charming self.

Maren laces her fingers behind her back. "I'm a tanker pilot—an aerial firefighter. I have ten days on and five days off."

"Cream or sugar?" I ask, attempting to save her from Tia.

"Black," Maren says, glancing over her shoulder with a smile.

"I bet Ozzy is envious," Amos says.

"Why is that?" Maren asks.

"Before our daughter died, Ozzy got his pilot's license."

Maren eyes me when I hand her a mug of coffee. "Really?"

I shrug. "It's nice to be able to fly the planes I work on."

She blows at the steam. "You're full of surprises."

"Am I?" I sip my coffee.

"Sounds like a dangerous job," Tia says.

Maren faces the dining room table again. "It's a necessary job."

"Are you married?" Tia takes a bite of her toast.

"I'm not."

"Kids?" Tia won't quit.

"Nope."

"Well, if you ever want a family, I imagine you'll have to find a new job," Tia says.

"Why is that?" Maren pushes back before I can jump in and save her. I don't think Maren Bernabe needs anyone to save her.

"When you have children, you must put their well-being first."

"By quitting my job?"

Tia frowns. "By not taking unnecessary risks."

Maren hums. "That's an interesting take on parenting. Well, I'd better get downstairs and braid Lola's hair. It was nice chatting with you." She heads to the stairs, and I follow her.

"I'm sorry about that," I murmur.

"Don't apologize. She lost her daughter." Several steps from the bottom of the stairs, Maren turns. "I'm not a parent, but I can imagine that losing a child would change you forever. And not for the better."

I let that sink in for a few seconds. If I lost Lola, like I almost did, I'd probably be a sad, grumpy, unbearable bastard.

"Here's my brush." Lola skips toward the stairs.

"Thanks." Maren takes the brush and sits on the sofa, setting her coffee mug on the end table. "What kind of braid do you want? Just the sides? Pigtails? Twist? French? Infinity?"

Lola's eyes pop out of her head as she sits on the floor between Maren's spread knees. "I don't know." She giggles.

"I'll do a French braid. It's quick and easy."

I stand with one arm over my chest and the other holding my coffee at my lips. It's early in this relationship, too early to think about a future with Maren, but it's hard not to when she does things like this.

When she rescues a kitten for my daughter.

When she stands up to Tia.

When she—*everything*.

"Does Bandit miss me?" Lola asks while Maren brushes her hair.

Maren winks at me. "Yes. He misses you already."

"I knew it," Lola says. "Dad, are you coming to watch my track-and-field day?"

"I am."

"Are Nana and Pa coming?"

"I'm not sure. Pa has a doctor's appointment, but I don't remember what time he said."

"Are you taking me to dinner, then?"

I laugh. "Lola, you sure know how to work me."

"I think dinner is the least your dad can do, since it's your big day," Maren says.

I toss her a fake scowl.

"Tacos," Lola says. "And dessert."

"Girl after my own heart," Maren adds.

"I'm outnumbered," I say. "Lola, do you want a smoothie or a breakfast sandwich?"

"Smoothie."

I nod, heading toward the stairs. "I'll go make it."

After I pull the fruit out of the freezer and add milk and yogurt to the blender, Tia brings her dirty dishes into the kitchen. I pray that she loads them into the dishwasher and ignores me.

No such luck.

"You're setting that little girl up for heartbreak again," Tia says after clearing her throat.

"I disagree."

"I don't know what you and that woman are doing, but Lola gets excited every time she sees her. What happens if the woman dies in a plane crash?"

I do my best to ignore her.

I add fruit and hemp seeds.

I blend.

I pour it into a glass.

But when I turn, Tia's resting her backside against the counter, arms crossed over her robe-covered body.

I sigh. "That woman's name is Maren. And you're banking on her dying. Yet you're so vocal about me overprotecting Lola when it comes to the car issue. You can't have it both ways. Pick a side. Otherwise, you just sound like a bitter old woman whose only goal in life is to see me suffer."

Tia parts her lips, jaw hanging open.

Of course, I feel instant regret. Maren is a better person than I am—times infinity. My ego can't see past Tia's accusations to recognize the mother who's still grieving the loss of her daughter.

I'm filled with nothing but frustration and flippant remarks when Tia voices her opinions about my life.

Maybe I need my own therapist.

"What's going on?" Amos asks while his gaze ping-pongs between us.

Tia closes her mouth, jaw clenched as she tips up her chin. "Nothing." She pivots and disappears down the hallway.

Amos narrows his eyes at me.

"Lola, breakfast is ready," I call, holding Amos's gaze, silently daring him to utter another word. My morning started with naked Maren. In less than an hour, my day has gone to shit.

"Your hair looks pretty." I kiss the top of Lola's head after she hops onto the barstool. "Where's Maren?"

"She's using the bathroom. But she can't come to my track-and-field day."

"That's life, pumpkin. Don't dillydally." I glance at the clock on the microwave. I can either make our lunches or find Maren and see if another stolen moment can compensate for my run-in with Tia. "Can you eat school lunch today?" I ask.

"I don't have to. They're ordering pizza for track-and-field day."

Perfect.

"I'm going to brush my teeth," I say, jogging down the stairs.

Maren's no longer in the bathroom; she's inspecting the photos on the wall behind the sofa.

I slide my arms around her waist, pressing my chest to her back and burying my face in her hair along her neck. "I bet I can make you come again before Lola finishes her smoothie."

Maren chuckles. "I don't doubt that at all. If you take off your shirt, I'll be halfway there before you even touch me."

I slide her hair away from her neck to kiss her warm skin.

She points to a picture of Brynn and Lola. "Where was this taken?"

I freeze for a few seconds before releasing her and scratching the back of my neck while gazing at the framed photo. "When Lola turned four, Brynn took her for afternoon tea. They enjoyed sandwiches, scones, and jams on those tiered stands and sipped tea while wearing pretty dresses. It was just the two of them. And it became a tradition on Lola's birthday."

Maren faces me. "I love that. But I bet she misses it."

I keep my gaze on the photo and nod slowly. "She misses everything about her mom, but I've tried to keep the tradition alive. I bought one of those tiered trays and a tea set. On her birthday, I make sandwiches and scones with jelly. We sip tea in the dining room, just the two of us. Lola wears a pretty dress, and I wear a suit and tie."

Maren wipes a tear from her cheek. "That's beautiful, Ozzy," she whispers.

I manage a sad smile. "If you saw my scones and sandwiches, you wouldn't say it's beautiful."

She laughs, blotting the corners of her eyes.

"We talked about one day taking Lola to London for her birthday tea." I sigh to release the emotion before it gets the best of me.

Maren's brows pinch together as she chews the inside of her cheek.

"Thank you for braiding her hair. It looks great. She'll have an extra bounce in her step today."

"You're welcome," she says, relaxing her face. "I'm going to go now." She glances toward the stairs before reaching for my neck and pulling me to her for a kiss.

She smiles against my lips when I palm her ass, bringing her flush to my body. "We're going to get caught," she says, tearing herself from my hold and running her fingers through her hair.

"Fine. You're no fun. Go home."

"I'm the definition of fun," she says, tossing me a flirty smile on her way to the stairs.

Chapter Twenty-Three

MAREN

Ozzy: See you tonight!

Maren: I'm headed to my plane. CU tonight!

Ozzy: Your properly inspected plane?

Maren: Check. Double check. Triple check. And then some

Ozzy: Be safe

Maren: That's the plan xo

After watching reports on fires, waiting for a call, playing cards, twiddling thumbs, and fine-tuning our equipment more times than I can count all day Friday, Saturday brings a spark of unknown origin, and we're headed to something new.

Thirty-five minutes later, I'm working the north flank. There are no ground crews on site yet, which makes things easier, and in my ear, I get the "line is clear to drop."

"Roger, 274 clear to drop," I say, releasing the retardant. It's the first of many on what could be a long day if the wind continues to pick up speed.

As hard as I try to stay entirely focused on the task at hand, the job I love, I can't help but think of Tia and her assumption that I wouldn't do this job if I had a family.

She's wrong.

I think.

◆ ◆ ◆

Maren: Do u want me to bring board games? I'm good at Scrabble

It takes Ozzy a few minutes to reply as I fill my water bottle and Will eats his dinner while scrolling on his phone.

Ozzy: I'm good at oral

My face flushes, so I angle my body away from Will.

Maren: I think the FedEx Cup is this weekend. Do you watch golf?

Ozzy: I'm good at driving things into a hole.

I snort, covering my mouth.

"Everything okay?" Will asks.

"Men are perverts." I screw on the lid to my bottle.

He finishes chewing his bite of steak. "Are you waiting for me to dispute your claim? Sorry. I can't."

"I didn't figure you could." I shake my head.

Will grins, and it's so familiar and comforting. I think of all the conversations we've had in this kitchen—the laughter, banter, and even a few tears.

"What will you do when all of your roommates move out?"

He shrugs. "I'm going to host more orgies."

I laugh. "More? Are you implying you've hosted any? Why was I not invited?"

He smirks while chewing another bite, but it fades as soon as he swallows. "I'm going to feel abandoned."

My heart suffocates beneath the weight of his confession. He'll feel abandoned, and I'll feel a little lost. Will and Fitz have felt like home more than the walls around me. Home is not a *where*; it's a *who*. I still see my brother napping on the sofa or gazing into the fridge at nothing in particular until I yell at him to save a little energy.

I clear my throat before my emotions reach the surface. "Are you getting new roommates?"

Will twists his lips. "I don't know. You guys are my friends. I don't remember the last time I thought of anyone as a roommate."

"Maybe it's time for you to take a wife and start a family."

Will chokes on his food, smacking his chest with a fist. "N-no."

"Jamie's not looking for another job outside Missoula, because she wants to start planning their wedding and thinking about babies. It made me think about my own life. I mean, did we ever imagine Calvin Fitzgerald getting married and having a family?"

Will shakes his head.

"Exactly," I say. "But it's happening. So now I'm starting to think there's hope for all of us."

"You're only saying this because some guy is sticking his dick in you on the regular."

I've had dick adjacent but not dick inside me, but I keep that to myself.

"It's not about the sex," I say. "It's about that life. He's a parent. And Jamie and Fitz will probably be parents. Don't you wonder what it would be like to have something in your life that matters more than your job?"

"I like my job," he says, pouring more steak sauce onto his plate.

"I like my job too. But it doesn't keep me warm at night. I don't get to braid its hair."

He squints. "Braid its hair?"

"I braided Lola's hair yesterday for her track-and-field day, and she was so excited to have her hair in a braid like her friends. And I had a moment. You know?"

"A moment? Like your uterus started aching, and you had a sudden urge to buy your own place with a tree house in the backyard? Oh, that's right. You *did* do that."

I stick my tongue out. "Stop being so grumpy. It's time for all of us to grow up. And the tree house is for Bandit, not my unborn children. I'm not saying I want to have my own kids. I'm just saying I got a glimpse of a different kind of life, and I didn't hate it."

My phone dings.

Ozzy: Are we using the condoms I bought?

Ozzy: Do we need to have the bc and std convo?

"What's that look?" Will asks.

I shake my head. "It's, uh, Ozzy's asking about . . ." I glance at Will. "Can I tell you something?"

A grimace slowly forms on his face. "I feel like I should say no. Nothing good comes after the words *can I tell you something*."

"I've never had sex without using a condom. I mean, I have an IUD, but—"

"No, Maren. Just no. I knew it. I *knew* you were going to overshare some shit that's only meant for Jamie's ears."

"Well, she's not here."

"Then you'd better wait until she gets home." He scoots back in his chair and takes his plate to the sink.

"I don't think Ozzy wants to use a condom. I think he bought them to be nice or something. I can't think of the right word."

"Chivalrous?" Will laughs. "Of course he doesn't want to use them. But just stop talking."

"Why do you say it like that? What does 'of course he doesn't' mean?" I lean against the counter and cross my arms.

"Maren, no guy likes wearing a condom."

"So it's just about pleasure, not like he's suggesting we should be in a committed relationship?"

He closes the dishwasher and sighs. "If he's a decent guy, then he's probably implying that he doesn't plan to screw anyone else right now."

I nod slowly.

"But he's mostly making a case for his dick feeling optimum pleasure."

"Why must you ruin a good thing?"

Will heads toward the stairs. "I believe you started this conversation with something along the lines of 'men are perverts,' so we should end it with the same sentiment."

I briefly stare at my phone's screen before sliding my thumbs across it.

Maren: I have an IUD. See you in an hour or so.

Chapter Twenty-Four

OZZY

"Let's go!" Lola says, speeding past me on her bike. "I can't believe I get to spend two days with Grandma and Aunt Ruth."

"Slow down, Speedy." I pedal after her.

"Aren't you going to be lonely while I'm gone, since Nana and Pa are gone too?"

"As much as I love you, it's sometimes nice to have time alone so I can get stuff done around the house."

"Are you going to paint my bedroom and put up the LED lights I got for Christmas?"

"I'm not sure I'll get to it."

"Pleeeease! You promised to do it last month, but you didn't."

"We'll see," I say.

"That's a no. You always say 'we'll see,' which means no."

"Lola, that's not true."

She makes a harrumph sound and gives me the silent treatment for a few minutes before changing the subject. "Why was Nana and Pa's car still in the driveway?"

"It didn't start for them this morning, so they got a cab. I took the afternoon off to work on it. That's why I'm covered in grease."

"Dad, you're always covered in grease." She glances back at me and smirks.

"You're always filled with sass." I speed up to ride alongside her.

Lola sticks out her tongue, but she can't hide her smile. "You'd better paint my room."

My plans for the weekend didn't involve paint, but I fear they might now, just like I wasn't supposed to spend my afternoon working on a broken car. I hope this isn't an omen for the whole weekend. I need to hurry home and finish fixing it before Maren shows up.

My plan fails.

After dropping off Lola and speeding home, the issue continues to give me grief. But I have to fix it before they get home, or they'll wonder what I did all weekend. Unfortunately, I'm not fast enough. A vehicle pulls into my driveway while I'm still under their car on my creeper. I speed up my motions, the wrench clicking in double time.

"How can I help?" Maren asks.

I tip my chin to see her light-gray jeans and cream ankle boots. "You can make yourself at home. There's a bottle of wine in the fridge. I'm about ready to call it for the day. Sorry. I didn't think their car wasn't going to start this morning. Gah! Fuck . . ." I wheel out from under the car.

Maren lifts her eyebrows into peaks as I stand and stomp into the garage for a different wrench.

"This isn't how I wanted to start the evening. I wanted to have it done before you got here so I could spend the rest of the weekend giving all of my attention to you," I grumble, flinging open the top drawer of my tool chest, trying to ignore Maren's hair in loose curls hanging over her chest, accentuated by her fitted blue V-neck shirt and the silver pendant necklace touching the swell of her breasts.

When I turn with a different wrench clenched in my fist, she's right in front of me.

"You should take a break and return to this when you're less stressed."

"Careful, I'm covered in grease," I warn, trying to step back, but I bump into the tool chest.

"It's sexy," she says while wetting her glossed lips. "When I arrived, you were on your cart, and your shirt was partway up your torso, exposing your tight abs and those tattoos." Her gaze sweeps from head to toe. "That was sexy too."

"Give me twenty minutes, and I'll shower quickly."

"I'll give you twenty seconds to shut the garage door."

I shake my head. "Your clothes will be ruined."

She shrugs off her shirt.

Clank!

I drop the wrench and shoulder past her to hit the button to close the garage door. As soon as I turn back toward her, I peel off my shirt and use it to wipe my hands.

Maren removes her bra, and I toss aside my shirt.

Fuck my dirty hands.

I grab her face, and we kiss. Her hard nipples brush my sweaty chest, and she releases a moan that makes my dick swell. Brynn never let me get within ten feet of her before showering and surgically scrubbing my dirty fingernails.

"Fuck, Ozzy," Maren whispers as my lips brush down the line of her neck. "I want to feel you everywhere."

I *hate* that my thoughts reach for every unfair comparison, but Brynn never said those words. In fact, Brynn never uttered a single swear word.

While I unbutton her jeans and pull down the zipper, she gazes at me with a seductive look that makes my whole goddamn body ache with need. The grease from my hands and face has painted her smooth flesh, but she's still beautiful—a beautiful mess.

On my knees, I discard her boots and peel her tight jeans down her legs along with her panties, but I only get one leg free before

I come undone with need. Hooking that leg over my shoulder, I devour her.

"Ozzy!" she cries, claiming my hair with both hands to keep her balance. "Oh god, yesss, Ozzy . . . yesss . . ."

I don't know if any part of me deserves any part of her, but I'm going to do my damnedest to pretend that every part of me does.

As I kiss my way up her body, more grease transfers from my hands and face to her stomach and all over her perfect tits. I guide her backward toward a stack of old tires wedged into the corner of the garage.

"You're so beautiful," I murmur over her shoulder and neck. "You make every goddamn day better."

She presses her hands to my cheeks, forcing me to look at her, and I know from the look in her eyes that she's trusting me with more than just her body. The tip of her tongue traces her bottom lip as she smiles, and I feel it—I feel her—in my fucking bones.

Our mouths collide, and I shove my jeans and briefs down a little farther to midthigh before lifting her leg with one hand and gripping the base of my cock with my other, lining it up with her wet entrance and driving into her.

Her deep moans make it hard to keep from coming, but I channel enough control to make this last longer than ten seconds.

Maren thrusts her tongue into my mouth as her hand grips my ass, digging into my muscles while I piston in and out of her.

This is, by far, the hottest fucking moment of my life.

She's warm, tight, and so goddamn wet. The garage fills with the rhythmic slapping of flesh and the scattered moans of pleasure. I don't feel like a dad. I feel like a seventeen-year-old who just discovered how incredible it is to bury my dick inside a woman. And for the foreseeable future (or at least the next twenty-four hours), this is all I want to do.

"God, I need this . . . so . . . much . . ." Maren's back arches, and I duck my head to suck her nipple into my mouth. I tug at it with my teeth, and she orgasms with my name echoing loudly from her lips, her insides clenching my dick.

I didn't realize how many emotions and physical needs I let die with my wife until now. Maren's bringing them—bringing me—back to life.

And that's all it takes for my hips to jerk faster, uncontrolled, until I spill into her. Mind-numbing bliss floods my body, racing and pulsing with my release.

The slapping stops.

The moans die.

Our bodies remain idle in a tangle of limbs.

And our labored breaths chase one another until they slow, welcoming a few seconds of silence.

It's been more than two years since I've had sex, and many, *many* years since I've had sex like this. Maybe I never have.

"Your neighbors might have heard me," she mumbles through a soft laugh.

I chuckle, easing out of her and lowering her leg to the floor.

How wrong is it that I'm semi-erect again just from a long look at her nearly naked body covered in grease graffiti, lips swollen, cheeks red, and hair mussed?

None of the above are all that wrong.

What's most wrong is how satisfied I feel seeing my cum running down her inner thigh.

I had no idea I was such an animal. But clearly I am.

Chapter Twenty-Five

MAREN

I don't believe it's possible to make up for lost time, but Ozzy's trying. If I look at him for longer than two seconds, it leads to sex.

By the end of our twenty-four hours together, I'll have had sex with Ozzy more times than all other men I've dated—combined. (Not really, but it feels that way.)

I'm *not* complaining. It's only an observation.

He smirks, buttoning his jeans after taking me from behind at the kitchen sink halfway through washing the dinner dishes Saturday evening. My pulse hasn't returned to normal yet, and my cheeks still feel flushed as I shuffle to the bathroom with my underwear bunched in my hand and wearing only his T-shirt. Ozzy doesn't even try to hide the satisfaction on his face. There are no shy glances. He likes to admire his work with confidence and a sexy grin.

After flushing the toilet and washing my hands, I stare at my reflection in the mirror and the permanent smile I've been wearing since I arrived a few hours earlier.

It's not just the sex; it's Ozzy and Lola. I've fallen in love with a single dad and his irresistible daughter. And I'm scared out of my mind of hurting them because I don't know if I can fit into their life with its shrunken borders.

Releasing a deep breath, I convince myself it doesn't matter this weekend. I have all day tomorrow with Ozzy, and I'm going to enjoy it, probably with his dick buried inside me.

"Is this the house you lived in with Brynn?" I ask, returning to the kitchen. Mentioning Brynn's name buys me some extra recovery time. It's the one subject that doesn't lead to sex.

Ozzy keeps his focus on the dishes, slowly scrubbing a pan. "Yes. When Tia and Amos decided to retire and move here to help with Lola, I finished the basement so we could sleep down there, and they could have the main level."

I dry the clean pan he hands to me. "Is this your first time without Lola overnight since Brynn died?"

"Yeah."

"Do you miss her?"

Ozzy doesn't answer for a few seconds. "Lola or Brynn?"

My stomach sinks. That was a stupid question. I'm sure he misses both of them. "Lola." I clear my throat. "Forget I asked. Of course you miss Brynn. And I'm sure you miss Lola. I'm just making small talk and doing a terrible job."

"Maren, you can ask me anything."

I feel his gaze on me when he hands me another dish, but I don't look at him.

"I saw several cardboard flats of seedlings in the garage. Are you planting a garden?" I ask.

"Yes, I was supposed to do that for Tia today. She nearly canceled their trip just to get her seedlings in the garden. But their car didn't start, so my day veered off course. And on top of that, Lola desperately hopes I'll paint her room and hang her colored LED strip lighting."

"Then let's do that. We can paint tonight. We'll hang the LED lights tomorrow morning and plant the garden." I set the last clean dish aside because I don't know where anything goes.

Ozzy drains the water with a familiar smirk. "I don't want to do any of that other stuff."

I throw the towel at him, and he catches it. "I know what you want to do, but I think we should take longer breaks from *that* and get these things done so Lola will want to spend more nights with her grandma. And Tia will trust you to do what she asks and, therefore, feel good about leaving you home alone again."

He prowls toward me, tossing the towel onto the counter.

I can't. Not yet. He's literally going to break my vagina. Or I'm going to die of orgasms. My voice is already a little hoarse from so much screaming.

"Thank you for coming," he whispers, brushing his lips along my cheek to my ear while caging me in with his hands on the counter behind me.

I chuckle. "I don't know if you're referencing my staying here with you or the other coming. But either way, it's my pleasure."

"So, painting?" He teases my earlobe with his teeth.

"Yes. Let's paint."

"Then we get naked again." He palms my ass, pulling me closer so I can feel his erection. "My face between your legs . . . ," he murmurs, dragging his tongue along my neck. "Sucking your pussy *and* your fingers while you touch yourself. God, I love that."

He's a machine.

I blush while angling my neck to let him kiss his way down to my shoulder. I never imagined this side of Ozzy Laster. He was my tampon-fetching knight. The endearing father riding his bike with his sweet daughter. Not a dirty-talking sex fiend.

I like—*I love*—every side of him.

"Yes," I say, a little breathy. "It will be your reward."

And mine.

He stands straight, lips corkscrewed for a few seconds, politely ignoring my hard nipples. "Then let's get to it."

◆ ◆ ◆

"Tell me about your family," Ozzy says while we cut in the purple paint in Lola's bedroom a little before nine. It's going to be a long night. "I know you lost your brother. Do you have other siblings?"

"I have no other siblings. My parents live in Nebraska. They're farmers. That's how I got started in flying and crop-dusting. Brandon couldn't wait to head west, so after he graduated, he moved to Missoula to pursue his career as a firefighter. I graduated two years after him. I worked on the farm for several years, then packed my bag to follow Brandon."

"How have your parents been since his death?" Ozzy asks.

I dip my brush into the bucket of paint. "My mom will never be the same, the way I'm sure Tia will never be the same. But my dad keeps chugging along. It's not that he doesn't miss Brandon; he's just better at suppressing his emotions. The harder he works, the less he thinks about Brandon. I was that way. After his death, all I wanted to do was get in my plane and do my job, but they forced me to take time off. So I sat at home thinking about him, and it was torture. My mom doesn't keep as busy as my dad, so she has more time—too much time—to miss him."

Ozzy doesn't respond right away. But after a few minutes, he releases a deep sigh. "I couldn't work after Brynn died. Cielo had just hired me, but I couldn't work because Lola needed me. I can't look at her and not see Brynn because Lola is a spitting image of her. And I can't not think of the accident because Lola wears it on her face. So last fall, when Tia and Amos suggested they sell their ranch and come live with us so I could return to work, I felt this huge weight lift from my chest. And it didn't matter that they had their issues with me. It didn't matter that I knew living with them would feel like I was less of a father and a man. I just *needed* something that didn't remind me of the tragedy."

He grunts while shaking his head and pouring paint into the roller pan. "How messed up is it that I needed time away from the most important person in my life? What does that say about me?"

"Ozzy—"

"No." He cuts me off with a painful laugh. "It was a rhetorical question. I know I deserve time alone. I know I need it. I had to have this conversation with Lola before this weekend. You get to this point where you know you can no longer swim, so you have two choices: drown or yell for help. I'm learning to yell for help because I don't want to drown. Lola needs me, and I want to believe that I have a lot of life left to live at thirty-six."

I hand him the roller. "Ozzy, I think you've been living your best life over the past five hours."

He barks a laugh before cupping the back of my neck and kissing me. Then he releases my lips but keeps a hold of me, gazing intently into my eyes. "I needed you so fucking long before I ever met you," he whispers. "You showed up out of nowhere, the way I bet your plane cuts through the smoke to deliver relief. *I* have felt so much relief since I met you."

We're going to finish painting this room before having sex again, but right now, I'm the one who wants to tear off our clothes and spend hours in bed with him because no man has ever made me feel this way.

So. In. Love.

◆ ◆ ◆

Sunday morning, Ozzy brings me breakfast in bed with six dandelions and a note.

> Please don't judge. These aren't yard weeds. Dandelions are edible and nutritious and a sign of healthy soil. They symbolize happiness, joy, resilience, and perseverance—and a bunch of other wonderful things. Hope you love them!
>
> Ozzy x

I glance up from the note. "I think the only flower you ever need to give me is the mighty dandelion."

Ozzy laughs.

"Where's our breakfast?" I ask.

"Under the sheets." He winks.

After my breakfast and his, we get to work around the house.

We install the LED strip lights in Lola's freshly painted room; then he finishes fixing the car. After lunch, we head to the backyard to plant Tia's seedlings.

"Can I ask you something?" I say.

He chuckles, running a box cutter through the top of the compost bag while I loosen last year's garden soil with a hoe. I'm sure Ozzy looks like sin in a suit, but I can't get enough of him in ripped, faded jeans, stained T-shirts, and dirty boots.

"It must be something heavy," he says. "I've noticed that you ask me if you *can* ask me something before you delve into a heavy subject. But you can ask me anything. No permission or preamble needed."

"Where were you when the accident happened?"

He pauses for a few seconds, eyebrows pinched. Then he sets the box cutter aside and spreads the compost. "Too fucking far away."

I work the compost into the soil with the hoe, but I don't look at him, because I know he's not looking at me. There are stages of confession.

Thinking it.

Saying it.

And looking someone in the eye. That's the hardest one.

I still avert my gaze when talking about my brother. Other people's sympathy unravels my emotions.

"I was in Las Vegas for a bachelor party. My mom called and . . ." He shakes his head slowly before tossing aside the empty bag and opening another one. "I don't remember how I made it home. My buddies somehow got me on a plane and then to the hospital. Lola was in surgery. Brynn and my dad were—"

I pause my motion. "Your dad?"

"Yeah." He scatters the compost and takes the hoe from me, keeping busy while I try to remember if he ever told me about his dad. Ozzy clears his throat while the lines etched along his forehead deepen. "He was in the car too."

"Was he driving?"

Ozzy shakes his head, and I wait for him to elaborate. He doesn't. I'm left with many new questions, but asking them would feel like forcing him to share more than he's ready to say.

Why was it just the three of them?

Where were they going?

Why do Brynn's parents blame Ozzy?

Was the accident her fault or that of another driver?

I start to speak. "You don't have to—"

"He needed a ride home from the bar," Ozzy says, stabbing a clump of dirt with the hoe. "He drank too much. He *always* drank too much. My mom used to pick him up, but when her vision deteriorated and she lost her license, I was the one who picked him up. But I was gone, so he should have called a cab. Instead, Brynn and Lola picked him up. At first, Lola didn't remember what happened. But eventually, she recalled my dad vomiting. So I think that distracted Brynn, and she veered into oncoming traffic. Luckily, nobody in the car they hit was killed."

"And Brynn's parents blame you for being gone?" I whisper.

He rests a hand on his hip and squints against the sunlight. "I'm sure that's part of it. They blame me for not getting help for my dad. But he didn't want help. He served in the military, worked forty years as an electrician, and felt he'd earned the right to drink as much as he wanted."

"It was nobody's fault," I say.

Ozzy tosses the hoe aside and kneels next to the garden, working one of the seedlings from its container. "It was . . ." He shakes his head. "I don't know. Maybe it was nobody's fault. Maybe everyone was a little at fault. What does it matter now? My father was a good man and an awful man. And that has left me feeling indifferent about him. But he's dead. Brynn is dead. And that's just the way life goes sometimes."

I kneel next to him. "Do you miss him when you think of him? I miss Brandon, but only when I think of him. Sometimes I can go a few days without thinking about him—without missing him. But as soon as he pops into my head, I feel a little ache in my heart. And I pause to listen, as if he's right here saying something to me. I think I'd feel this way even if someone had died on his watch. Does that make sense?"

Ozzy pauses his hands and whispers, "Yeah, I miss him. I miss the man he was before he fell in love with feeling numb." He stares at the seedling in his hand. "But if he had lived and she still died, the hatred would have eaten me alive. His death, while tragic, was necessary. It was closure."

I take the plant from Ozzy, and he sits back on his heels, head bowed, eyes closed. A moment later, he stands, kissing the top of my head before going inside to shower while I finish planting and watering them into the ground. When he comes upstairs in clean jeans and no shirt, running his fingers through his wet hair, I offer him a melancholy smile. His gaze slides to my bag by the front door.

"I'm going to head home before your family returns."

"I scared you off." His shoulders sag inward while he slides his fingers into his pockets.

"You didn't. You should take some time to yourself for a few hours, since I've done such a nice job ripping open old wounds."

"Maren, you didn't say or do anything wrong."

"I appreciate you saying that, but it doesn't change the fact that I put a damper on the afternoon with my curiosity. And I'm not saying I regret asking you about the accident, but I knew when I asked that it wouldn't be an easy subject." I stroll toward him, resting my hands on his bare chest. "But I want to really know you, so sometimes I have to ask the hard questions."

He cups my face, brushing the hair away from my eyes with his thumbs. "I'm going to make this work. I have no clue how I will make this work, but I will."

I can't help but smile before turning my head to kiss his palm.

"Do I get points for brutal honesty?" he asks.

"Oz, I'm giving you points for this weekend, but not for your brutal honesty."

"Orgasms." His eyes glimmer. "You're giving me points for orgasms."

"I was going to say your toaster waffles with peanut butter earned you the most points, but sure, the orgasms were fine."

"Fine?" He quirks a single brow.

"Decent. Acceptable. Good enough." I fight my grin.

His face falls flat, and just when I think I've won, a twinkle of mischief flashes in his eyes, and he says, "I did the best I could with what I had to work with."

I already love him, even if there's no way I'm saying it yet. But now he's just toying with me. How does he know I'd rather be with a man who keeps me on my toes than sweeps me off my feet?

Chapter Twenty-Six

OZZY

I didn't mean to screw the life out of Maren, but she started it in the garage. All the close calls, teasing, dreaming, and anticipating didn't disappoint. Did she leave thinking I couldn't keep my dick out of her? The answer has to be yes.

For the record, there were so many times when I did control my urges.

But now, sitting in Brynn's cream glider, alone in the living room with nothing but time and silence, a tsunami of guilt overtakes me, and I think of my wife.

Is it too soon? A decade after my uncle lost his wife, he still couldn't say her name without getting choked up, let alone think of another woman. It's taken me two years to feel ready again. But not just ready; I tried to screw someone else against every surface of the house my wife once lived in. What is wrong with me?

With my hands resting on the arms of the chair, fingers lightly drumming, I glide back and forth. The wind chime by the front door sings its gentle tune, and the kitchen still smells like burnt toaster waffles from the first one that got away from me.

When I close my eyes, I see Brynn moseying toward me in her short satin robe with tiny pink and yellow flowers.

"You're in my chair." With a grin, she gathered her curly blond hair and pulled it over one shoulder before sitting on my lap. She smelled like oranges and vanilla.

I wrapped my arms around her waist, buried my nose in her hair, and nuzzled my way to the back of her neck. When I playfully bit it, she jumped and giggled. My hand snaked between the gap in her robe, and she batted it away.

I made my case while my erection grew from sheer hope. "Lola's still asleep."

"I have to go grocery shopping." She guided my hand away from her inner thigh. "And it's morning. We're not morning-sex people."

I open my eyes, gaze affixing to the sofa where Maren straddled my lap, wearing nothing but my T-shirt. Reaching between us, I shoved down the front of my jogging shorts and briefs, and she happily sank onto me. That was after breakfast this *morning*.

It's not that I was unhappy in my marriage. I loved Brynn, and I loved our life. But she was regimented.

Sex three times a week between ten and ten thirty.

No oral.

No showering together.

Never outside the bedroom.

Missionary position.

When it was over, she'd kiss my cheek and smile, saying, "Thanks. That was nice."

While she was alive, I avoided comparing her to Tia. But in hindsight, I understand why Amos watches porn.

Pinching the bridge of my nose, I exhale a long breath as tears burn the back of my eyes. I fucking hate that my mind lets me remember anything but the good things about my marriage. I loved Brynn with my whole heart, and what made us great together had nothing to do with sex. Not once did I feel unhappy in my marriage. She made me smile for a million reasons that were deeper than physical intimacy.

There's no need to justify my feelings for Maren. There's no need for comparison. But this nagging guilt demands an explanation before it will let go.

Was Brynn not my soulmate, like my aunt was to my uncle? Am I a heartless failure of a husband for moving on so quickly? Is it cruel to let Brynn's parents help with Lola while I'm sneaking around with Maren?

This goddamn guilt is poison.

The silence isn't comforting, and neither are my thoughts, so I jump onto my bike and head to my mom's, even though they aren't expecting me for two more hours. Biking clears my mind, and with a clearer mind, I let go of the guilt. There's no need to compare Maren to Brynn. I don't need one to be better than the other to justify my feelings. There's no choice to make. One is not better than the other—just different.

"Oswald." Ruth drags out my name while inspecting me over her leopard-print-framed cat-eye glasses as I enter the house. She's buried under her usual pile of yarn on the sofa—always crocheting. The bangs of her black bob-cut wig hang a little lower today. She needs to adjust it back a quarter inch.

"Ruth," I say with a smile while closing the door behind me. "Where are Mom and Lola?"

"Gina's in the bathroom. And Lola's in the neighbor's backyard. She made friends with Don and Gwenneth's granddaughter."

"Aren't you early?" Mom says, making her way down the hall, running her fingertips along the wall, the sofa, and finally, her chair. I think her vision has gotten even worse, but she'll never admit it.

"What can I say? I miss my girl." I head into the kitchen to peer out the back window. Lola and the neighbor's granddaughter are playing with bubbles.

"Did you take your lady friend on a date?" Mom asks.

"Lady friend?" Ruth parrots her like Paxton, her actual parrot, would do.

"That was a secret, Mom." I return to the living room and sit on the arm of the sofa.

"Ruth won't tell Lola."

"Unless you don't reveal what I'm not supposed to tell." Ruth again gives me her owl-eyed inspection without stopping her hands from working the yarn and hook.

"Ozzy has a woman he likes. She's a pilot. And he said she's pretty," Mom says, turning down the volume on the TV.

"Tell us more. Did you spend the weekend with her?" Ruth asks.

I keep the details brief. "I saw her this weekend."

"When do we get to meet her?" Mom asks.

"Good question." I blow out a long breath. "I'm trying to sort through the pieces of my life to see where they fit. I don't bring a lot of normalcy to the table, so I don't know what's fair to ask of Maren."

"Maren," Ruth murmurs. "That's a lovely name. Is it Danish?"

I chuckle. "I have no clue."

Ruth's lips twist. "I believe it is."

"Did she stay the night?" Mom asks.

I don't want to answer the question. It's her polite way of asking if we had sex. Why else would she stay the night?

"Dad!" Lola saves me from answering the question as she runs toward me from the back door, then wraps her arms around my waist.

"Hey, pumpkin. Did you have a fun time?"

"Yes. Oh my gosh, I played with Paxton and Addie. Addie's grandparents live next door, but Addie lives in California. Can you believe that? I told her my mom used to live there. And when she asked about my face, I told her everything. She thinks my scars look kind of cool. She showed me her stomach. She had some operation, and she has a scar from it. So we're scar friends." Lola barely takes a breath.

I try to keep up by constantly nodding, even though her jumping from one thing to another makes it difficult. The biggest takeaway, and the only one that matters, is that she's happy and had a good time.

"Did you paint my room and put up my lights? Huh? Pretty please tell me that you did!" She makes prayer hands by her face.

"Go get your bag packed. You'll just have to see what I did or didn't do."

"That's a yes!" She runs down the hallway.

"Please tell me you painted that girl's room." Mom laughs.

"I did."

"You're a good dad, Oswald. Don't ever forget that."

"Thanks, Mom." I push off the sofa and bend over to hug her. "And thanks for letting her stay here."

"Anytime," Mom and Ruth say in unison.

"I'm ready," Lola singsongs, dumping her bag onto the floor to tie her shoes.

"If you're ever in my neighborhood with . . . anyone . . ." Mom clears her throat. "Stop by."

I roll my eyes. "Sure thing."

Ruth smirks just before Lola hugs my mom, and we head out the door. The whole way home, Lola gives me a play-by-play of her entire weekend. She's okay.

I don't know when or how, but she's going to let go of her trauma, get into a car, and be okay.

As soon as we reach our driveway, she parks her bike, and by park her bike, I mean she lets it fall onto its side in the grass. She abandons her bag on the porch and barrels through the door.

"Don't worry. I'll put the bikes away. I'll get your bag. I'll close the front door," I say to myself.

I hear her screams of joy as I reach the door. But before I reach the threshold, a taxi stops on the street. Tia and Amos climb out of it. So, after tossing Lola's bag into the entry, I head back outside to help them with their luggage.

"It's just one suitcase. I've got it," Amos says, closing the trunk.

"Did you fix our car?" Tia asks.

I plaster on my usual fake smile. "I did."

"Good," she says, and when her gaze meets mine, she pays me something resembling a sincere smile and murmurs, "Thank you."

I know those two words must taste bitter on her lips.

"I appreciate it, Oz." Amos does a better job of actually being sincere.

"No problem." I lead them into the house.

"What did you do all weekend?" Tia asks, hanging her rain jacket on the coat-tree.

"Aside from fixing your car, planting your seedlings, painting Lola's room, and installing her LED lights?" I lean my hip against the banister and cross my arms.

Tia's lips part into an O. I smirk, stopping short of gloating. Hopefully, that's enough for her to chew on, and she won't need to ask if I did anything else.

"Is Lola home?" She heads toward the bedroom where Amos took the suitcase.

"She's downstairs," I say.

"Did everything go okay at your mom's house?" Tia asks, stopping at her bedroom door.

"Yes. She had a great time. And my mom and Ruth loved having her there."

Tia nods slowly. "That's good."

"It is."

"Dad? How do I make the lights change color?" Lola calls.

I jog down the stairs and throw her over my shoulder.

"Dad!" She giggles and squeals.

It's been *the best* weekend.

Chapter Twenty-Seven

MAREN

Monday morning, Ozzy calls on my way home from the gym. "Hey!" I can't hide my enthusiasm.

"Good morning. I was going to text you, but seeing how my daughter manages to get into my phone, I thought a call would be better."

"What were you going to text me that you don't want Lola to see?"

He chuckles. "Nothing too inappropriate."

"A shame," I say.

Again, he laughs. "I wanted to say good morning but decided I needed to hear your voice too."

"Mm, good morning. Are you not working?"

"I just got to work, and I'm finishing my coffee before clocking in."

"Did Lola have a good time with your mom? And did she love her purple room?"

"Yes. And yes."

"That's good. Listen, I've been invited to a party. Fitz's smoke jumper buddy and his wife throw all the best parties. If I don't get called out of town this weekend, what are the chances of you being my plus-one on Saturday night?"

"I might be able to make something up."

Sneaking around was fun for a while. But now that my heart is invested, it's not as fun being Ozzy's dirty little secret. "Would Tia and Amos really have a major problem with you going to a party with me?"

"Yes. No." He sighs. "I don't know. Maybe. Probably. I don't know, but based on my experience, Tia will balk at anything involving me having fun with a woman who is not Brynn. She's just so angry."

I pull into my driveway and flip up the visor, staring at the back of Will's Bronco.

"Maren?" Ozzy says, breaking the silence.

"I wasn't going to get invested. That's my thing. I keep things casual. And you wanted to take things slow, so of course I was good with that. But, dammit!" I run my fingers through my hair. "I like Lola. I like you. And I like what we did over the weekend. I like it all so much that I've bought a house. And I don't need a house. Except I sort of do now, because I have a cat. And the only reason I have a cat is because of Lola. And now that I'm working, I see you less and less. And that's fine because I love my job, and I'm not the woman who clings to a man. Except I sort of do now, because I met this mechanic who has taken up permanent residence in my head, so much so that I bought a house so we could be alone together without sneaking in and out of windows."

I laugh at myself because it *is* ridiculous. "Ozzy, I bought a house for a cat and sex."

Again, we hold the line without speaking for eternal seconds.

"Message me the time and address of the party. I'll be there if you're there," he says.

I open my mouth to protest. That's what people do; they beg for something and then backtrack when it's offered to them. Mind games are the demise of many relationships. There's still so much more I want to say, but I'll take the win without throwing it back in his face like it no longer matters because I had to ask for it.

"Okay," I say.

More silence—the awkward kind.

"I have to work. I'll call you later," he says.

"Yeah. That's fine. Bye."

◆ ◆ ◆

We talk every day until Saturday, but Ozzy doesn't share his game plan for attending the party. I'm not sure he has one, but he said he'd be here. As I stare out the window of Gary and Evette's front room, my tummy feels wonky with anticipation.

"He's probably having trouble finding a parking spot," Fitz says from behind me.

I don't turn toward him. It's not funny, but for some reason I laugh. "I fly planes, and you jump out of them. Can you imagine going only as far as your bike can take you?"

He hums. "I'm not the one to ask. I've recently discovered how love can make you do just about anything."

I turn and smirk. "The world's least emotionally available bachelor is getting married and reversing his vasectomy." I sip my wine, and he chuckles.

Then he nods toward the window. "Looks like he found a spot."

I turn just as Ozzy secures his bike to a tree.

"Does he think someone is going to take his bike?" Fitz asks.

"If someone did, he'd be screwed." I hand Fitz my empty wineglass and head toward the front door.

Ozzy glances up just as I descend the porch steps. "Are you sure you want me to meet your friends? I have helmet head."

I giggle, moseying toward him until I can throw my arms around his neck. "I love your hair." I lift onto my toes and kiss him while combing my fingers through his thick hair.

As I start to fall back to my feet, he palms my face and kisses me again, but this time with an open mouth. If we were alone, we'd already be half-naked.

"Remind me when you're closing on your sex house," he murmurs over my lips, brushing his nose against mine.

I laugh. "Soon." I take his hand and lead him to the house. "Did you sneak or lie to come here tonight?"

He chuckles. "Let's call it a sneaky lie."

"I hate this." Before opening the front door, I turn toward him. "Being your dirty little secret isn't as much fun as I thought it would be."

"I didn't know you were planning on being dirty tonight." He waggles his eyebrows.

"I wasn't. Then I invited you, so there's no telling what could happen."

He holds his grin for a few seconds before it deflates. "If I tell Tia and Amos, I'll be fully accountable. And if they're fine with us by some chance, then life is great. But if they are not, I could feel forced to make a choice I don't want to make." He shrugs.

"And you need them to live with you."

He nods slowly. "It's not that I can't find someone to watch Lola after school. My aunt Ruth, who lives with my mom, would pick her up from school and watch her, but Lola won't get into a car. I don't know who would ride their bike or walk to Lola's school every day to escort her home, *even* in the winter, except Tia and Amos. They do it."

I search for a solution like a fly trying to escape from the inside of a car, but I don't have one. "Let's eat and drink." Taking Ozzy's hand again, I lead him into the house and toward the bar, where Evette's mixing drinks.

"Wine for you, Maren?" she asks, but she widens her eyes when she notices Ozzy. "Sexy mechanic!" she exclaims, quickly cupping a hand over her mouth. "Shit. I said that. I have to stop drinking."

Ozzy shifts his wide-eyed gaze between me and Evette.

"I take it Jamie told you about my friend Ozzy?"

Evette pours my wine, cheeks flushed while she shakes her head. "I'm, uh, Lola's math and science teacher." She risks another peek at Ozzy.

He points a finger at her. "I thought you looked familiar."

She hands me the wine. "I'm so embarrassed. But you have a reputation at the school. People talk. They shouldn't, but they do. And I can't believe I yelled that aloud. I need to mix more and drink less. What can I get you?"

Ozzy glances at me. "I'm used to kegs and red SOLO cups. This is impressive."

"Evette's a mixologist when she's not dementing—I mean *teaching* the next generation. The parties here are top notch."

Ozzy laughs. "Well, I'm easy to please. Any beer works."

"This is a local IPA. Gary's favorite." Evette twists off the top and hands him the beer. "And fair warning, some other teachers here will recognize you, stare, drool, and possibly embarrass themselves even worse than I have, so please don't judge us. When we're on the clock, we're all business."

I try to hide my grin, but I can't.

Ozzy eyes me with a lifted brow. "Did you know about this?"

I shake my head as we step away from the bar to let other people get drinks. "No. But I'm not disappointed, unless you start flirting with Evette's hungry-eyed friends."

He swigs his beer before smiling and glancing around the room. I follow his gaze, and sure enough, a group of Evette's teacher friends are huddled in a circle, gawking at Ozzy.

"Stiff competition for me tonight," I say.

"You *should* be worried. If you think they're hot for me now, wait until they see my sexy ride chained to the tree outside."

I snort, pressing my fist to my mouth. "I fear that only makes you sexier in their eyes. Single dad who escorts his daughter to school every day on a bike because she suffered an unimaginable trauma. You are their Everest of men."

"Who cares? The question is, am I your Everest?"

"If I'm your dirty little secret, you can be my Everest."

"We meet again," Jamie says to Ozzy while wrapping an arm around me.

"Hi. Yeah. This is quite the party. And a very cool house."

"Right?" Jamie draws out the word while releasing me.

The two-story Queen Anne–style house has small rooms and tall ceilings. It's filled with embellishments like elaborate dark woodwork, embossed botanical wallpaper in muted green-and-gold tones, and colorful stained glass windows. My favorite thing is the burgundy velvet drapes that Gary hates.

"Did you hear Fitz and I gave Maren the house with the tree house for her cat?" Jamie asks.

Ozzy nods with a slow hum. "Bandit is pretty spoiled, and so is my daughter for having her stray cat saved."

Jamie bats her eyelashes at me with an exaggerated smile. "I'd say Maren is pretty smitten with you and your daughter, but that might embarrass her, so I won't say it."

I roll my eyes. "Go find Fitz before you *accidentally* embarrass me any more."

Jamie giggles and offers us a wiggly-fingered wave while floating into the crowd, searching for Fitz.

"Are you smitten with me?" Ozzy asks, cocking his head to the side.

I'm in love with you.

"I'm shook. You've shooketh me. I *love* my job, but I'm dreading more inevitable trips out of town and not seeing you. I'm"—I shake my head and twist my lips—"not smitten. It's more of an addiction. What about you? How are you doing? I bet you're not even fazed, not one bit. I'm sure time flies in your busy life. You have Lola and her grandparents to keep your mind in the moment. And your mom. Your job. Gardening. Fixing people's cars on the side. There's no way you miss me when I'm gone."

Ozzy narrows his eyes and slowly wets his lips before rubbing them together. "Are you done?"

I clear my throat and nod once before sipping my wine.

He surveys the room, grabs my arm, and leads me to a less congested corner by the split staircase. "I go out of my fucking mind when you're out of town. If anything happens to you, I have nothing more than a bicycle to get to you. And I hate that you work in a male-dominated field, and you could close your eyes and randomly point to anyone else in any room who's more equipped for dating you than I am."

My heart doesn't know what to do. The butterflies in my belly devour his words like sweet nectar while my heart stumbles into an uneven rhythm because he feels inadequate.

I step closer, dragging my teeth along my lower lip several times before speaking. "Listen when I say, at the risk of sounding like I sleep around a lot—which I don't, but I'm in my thirties, so cut me some slack—you are *very well equipped* to date me and do plenty of other things to me."

The pain along his handsome face intensifies. "See, that's not helpful because this isn't my house or yours. And I have a bike with no back seat. And it's been almost a week since I've been alone with you—"

I slide my hand to the back of his neck, lift onto my toes, and press my lips to his. He tastes like beer and smells woodsy. And I quickly melt into the familiarity of his body touching mine. It's all a heady combination. "*I* have a car with a back seat," I murmur over his mouth.

"I just got here. Don't you think we should mingle or dance before we disappear?"

"Nobody's dancing." I laugh, releasing his neck.

Ozzy hooks his free hand around my waist, keeping me close to him. "Well, we need to rectify that." He moves his hips, swaying our bodies to Divinyls' "I Touch Myself."

He mouths the words to me, and I break into a fit of giggles. And of course, I can't help but wonder if he does think about me and touch himself.

"You're blushing," he says, ducking his head until his lips brush my ear. "I fucking *love* watching you touch yourself."

Now I'm having flashbacks of our weekend together, and my blush works its way across every inch of my skin. The wine doesn't help.

We dance in our little corner of the room. I turn so my back is to him, and he rests his big hand along my stomach, pulling me to him again. Closing my eyes, I lean my head against him and let him dance, sway, and seduce me to a four-minute song. When it ends, I finish my wine and welcome the buzz. I'll be catching a ride home with Jamie and Fitz.

"Okay, let's get out of here," Ozzy says, adjusting himself as I turn toward him.

"Come, you two. Badminton in the backyard. Gary just got the lights to work," Jamie says as Fitz pulls her toward the back door.

I wrinkle my nose at Ozzy. "Let's grab some food, play a game or two, then we can sneak out. Okay?"

Biting his lips together, eyes wide, he relinquishes a slow nod that's not overly enthusiastic.

"I'm worth the wait." I wink, taking his hand.

"I'm well aware, but it doesn't make the wait any easier."

I like his impatient, slightly grumpy side—my brooding guy.

"More wine?" Evette follows us outside with a bottle of red in her hand.

"I'm going to need a ride home," I say with a fake frown while holding out my empty glass for a refill.

"Can I get you another beer?" she asks Ozzy.

"I'm good. I can't get a ride home."

My grin dies, but he shakes off my reaction with a quick mumbled "Don't" and drops a kiss on my lips. "Never feel sorry for me," he whispers with his mouth brushing mine several times.

"I don't. You're getting laid in the back seat of a RAV4 in approximately forty-five minutes."

He chuckles. "Have you set a timer?"

"Yes. When you hear my phone chime, send your dick the memo to get ready."

Ozzy barks a laugh, tipping his head back. "Baby, I'm always ready for you." He rests his hand on my lower back and guides me down the deck stairs toward the yard, lit with string lights and lined with lawn chairs, with music flowing from several portable speakers synced to Hozier's "From Eden."

Forty-five minutes turns into two hours.

One last glass of wine turns into two. Four glasses are two past my limit. We lose badminton to three different couples—entirely my fault. My vision is too impaired to connect my racket to that stupid little birdie. Every miss triggers a fit of giggles.

"That was terrible, babe," Ozzy says, playfully swatting my ass with his racket after we lose for the last time.

Babe.

I've never had this. I've never been anyone's babe or baby. If I'm honest, I've never been in love, not like this.

While Jamie, Fitz, and a group of couples head toward the basement to play pool, I pull Ozzy around the side of the house to the front yard, trying to remember where I parked.

"Can you walk?" He laughs, grabbing my waist when I trip over a slightly uneven spot on the sidewalk.

I turn toward him, wrapping my arms around his neck and kissing him. My head spins. It's a great buzz. And he tastes so good. He feels even better than he tastes.

"Whoa . . ." He stops my hands from unzipping his jeans. "Let's find your RAV first."

"I want you," I murmur, kissing his neck and gripping his shirt to keep from losing my balance. "I want to *taste* you."

He groans, holding my face while rapidly scanning the area. "Some of Lola's teachers are still in the house. I can't have them witnessing this."

I giggle. "I don't think they would tell her."

He closes his eyes and shakes his head.

I sigh. "I love you."

There is nothing more sobering than a leaked declaration of love. Maybe he didn't hear me. I didn't mean it. Well, I did, but I didn't mean to say it now, or ever, for that matter. He's not some random guy. My heart is invested in him. I've told my parents about him. And maybe we haven't known each other long enough, but when you know, you know.

Ozzy's hands fall from my face like two bricks tossed out a second-story window. He parts his lips, but no words escape while he slowly blinks.

I swallow hard and squint. "I meant I love your humor."

Ozzy's expression intensifies. "I wasn't being funny."

I run my hands through my hair. "I'm drunk."

"Maren—"

"It's . . . it's nothing." I turn, taking a few steps away from him, trying to remember where I parked. "I love Jamie, Fitz, and Will. I even love my cat. Sunny days. Hiking. Carrot cake." I continue down the sidewalk as if I know where I'm going. "I *love* lots of things. It's such an arbitrary word. Don't you agree?"

After digging my key fob from my mini crossbody sling, I push the unlock button until my RAV beeps in the opposite direction. Spinning on my toes to follow the sound, I run into Ozzy. He grabs my arms to steady me without letting go, so I stare at his chest.

"It doesn't feel fair to love you," he says.

Given the wine I've had tonight, sweeping me off my feet should be easy, but that's not the right line. It doesn't feel fair to whom? Him? Me? Brynn? The universe?

"Whoa." I laugh. "You're blowing this way out of proportion. I *loved* you for fetching me toilet paper and a pad the day we met. I *love* these shoes." I kick a foot back. "I *love* a good bottle of merlot. But merlot isn't jealous of my shoes." I hold up my hands and pull away from his hold on me. "Don't read into anything. *Please.*" I brush past him toward my RAV. I sigh when I get there and grab the door handle to the driver's side. "I'm not driving home," I mumble.

My declaration of love has ruined the moment. This is supposed to be my subtle exit. But I need a driver, and it won't be him.

"Are we not getting into the back seat?" he asks, standing behind me.

I close my eyes and blow out a long breath. "I said the wrong thing because I'm not completely sober. Now I feel agitated that my thoughts are jumbled, and you're thinking that I meant something that I didn't, and—"

"Maren."

"It's late anyway. You should head home—"

"Maren."

"Because it's getting late. And—"

"MAREN!"

I startle and turn toward him, arms crossed over my chest. "What?"

"I said it didn't feel fair to love you. I didn't say that I don't love you."

Goddammit!

I'm not drunk enough—not numb enough.

Ozzy grins, brushing his knuckles along my cheek before tucking my hair behind my ear. "I didn't say it first, but I fell first."

Leaning into his touch, I whisper, "I didn't think you were going to sweep me off my feet tonight." I giggle because my mind is still swimming in merlot. "I was wrong."

Before I open my eyes, he kisses me.

Maybe it's not fair for him to love me. But nothing about my life has been fair.

So we climb into the back seat.

Love doesn't need anything more than a chance.

Chapter Twenty-Eight

OZZY

"Nice of you to find time for lil old me," my best friend, Diego, says, wiping his greasy hands on a rag as I park my bike just inside the detached garage he uses as a shop.

"You know where I live," I say, ogling the red Mustang on his lift.

"Where's your sidekick? Kai has been asking about her." Diego stuffs part of the rag into the back pocket of his sagging black cargo pants before adjusting the yellow bandanna tied around his head of messy black hair.

"Lola's at my mom's house. She's been spending more time there. I'm on my way to get her." I run my hand along the newly painted bumper.

"Driving yet?" he asks.

I shake my head. "I wish."

"I'm sure you do." He opens his garage fridge and offers me a beer, popping the top as if it's a foregone conclusion that I'm drinking.

I don't turn it down.

"Thanks." I take a swig.

"What's new?" he asks.

"I met someone."

"A woman?"

I nod.

"On your bike?"

"Well, I wasn't on my bike when I met her, but she's seen my sweet ride."

Diego chuckles. "Don't tell Cheyenne. I've led her to believe a man needs a muscle car beneath him to feel like a man. If she hears you've found someone, I'll have to trade in my Mustang for a fat-tire bicycle."

I shrug. "You don't need a car to feel like a man, but damn, I miss getting behind the wheel and driving up to Glacier. Four-wheeling in the winter. Windows down in the summer. But on the flip side, my legs are fucking fabulous."

Diego barks a laugh, shaking his whole body for a few seconds before he sighs. "Tell me about the woman."

I stare at the beer bottle for a few seconds. "She's a tanker pilot."

"Damn."

"Yeah, damn." I bite my lower lip for a beat.

"Hot?"

Shaking my head, I glance up at him. "That's your first question?"

"What?" He smirks. "Sorry. Is she beautiful on the inside?" He bleeds too much sarcasm to take him seriously.

"Her name is Maren. She's funny and confident."

"And hot?"

I ignore him by not looking at him. "She's a badass pilot. She adores Lola."

"Good in bed?"

I squint toward the street at nothing in particular. "She braided Lola's hair for track-and-field day."

"If you tell me she's given you head, I'm not returning your car. Cheyenne has the worst gag reflex. She won't even lick it."

"Diego . . ." I shake my head. "Dude, I'm talking about her braiding my daughter's hair. You can't mix that shit with giving head."

"Fine, fine, fine. She likes your daughter. I'm just looking out for you, Oz. You deserve to get a little something, you know what I mean?"

I grin before taking another swig of my beer. "I've known you my whole life. I'm pretty sure I know what you mean."

"So she's at least tickled your balls. Right?"

I spit out my beer and laugh, wiping the back of my hand across my mouth. "Yes, she's tickled my balls and licked my dick. She's fucking incredible in bed. Now, can we move on to more important things?"

Diego stills, unblinking, lips parted. When his shock wears off, his expression relaxes into something more serious. "Better than Brynn?" he asks.

Even though it makes me cringe, I'm not mad. He's trying to be serious, not disrespectful.

I can't look at him; all I can do is shrug. Sex and love are not interchangeable. Brynn was my wife. She was the mother of our child. It's not possible for me to love someone more than I loved her.

"Fuck, man," Diego whispers when my hesitation speaks the truth.

I shake my head, returning my attention to him. "No. I don't want to compare Maren to Brynn. It's not fair, and it's unnecessary."

Diego eyes me for a second before relinquishing a nod that's as tiny as his smile. "She flies a plane, and you ride a bike. You can't make this shit up. And let's not overlook the elephant in the room—you got your pilot's license. Seems almost torturous to date a pilot, don't you think?"

"I can see how you might think that, but Lola's alive. And Maren is amazing. I have a job I love. Although sometimes annoying, Brynn's parents have gone out of their way to help me. And Lola now spends time with my mom and my aunt Ruth."

Diego studies me. Of all the people I need to treat me like I'm not a lonely widower, it's him. So I give him what he wants.

"Lola stayed the weekend with my mom and Ruth three weeks ago, while Amos and Tia visited Brynn's brother. And Maren stayed the weekend. We had so much sex I lost count."

Diego beams. "I'm gonna need details."

"No."

"Come on, man. Give me something for my spank bank."

"Shut up." I chuckle while walking around his Mustang.

"I'm happy for you," he says with more sobriety.

"Me too. But now I must figure out how to tell Tia and Amos without rocking the boat. She'd love nothing more than for me to live a celibate life."

"She doesn't still blame you for the accident, does she?"

"Adjacent blame."

"That's messed up, Oz. What about Amos?"

I finish my beer and toss the empty bottle into the bin by the fridge. "Amos has his moments. I think he'd be fine with me moving on if Tia weren't breathing down his neck, telling him what to think and do."

"Play that angle. Get him on your side."

I hum. "Maybe. What about you? How's your family? What's Kai doing this summer?"

This feels good: a beer with my best friend, a woman I adore, and a spark of hope that Lola and I will survive everything.

After Diego catches me up on his family, I sit in the driver's seat of my green Land Rover Defender for a few minutes. I can still see Brynn next to me, still feel her fingers teasing the nape of my neck, still hear her soft laughter while Lola sings all the wrong words to her favorite song on the radio. Brynn hated the hood-mounted tire and hard, boxy lines. She said it looked like we were going on safari. And for that very reason, I swore I'd never sell it. She was so cute when she was mad.

Eventually, the memories become unbearable, so I slide out of the seat and gently shut the door, giving it two firm pats with the heel of my hand.

"I'm taking off," I say to Diego.

"I drive her once a week. She's still amazing. If you want to sell it—"

"I don't," I say while climbing onto my bike. "Later."

I head to my mom's house. All it takes is one smile from Lola to remind me everything will be okay.

◆ ◆ ◆

"She's here!" Lola squeals, running to the door in her pajamas a little before eight thirty. Maren starts another shift tomorrow, so Lola gets Bandit for a while.

Amos doesn't move from the sofa; he's glued to the Weather Channel. Tia, however, rests her book of crossword puzzles next to her cup of chamomile tea and stands from the gliding chair.

"Breathe, child," I say while Lola shakes with excitement as I open the front door. If only I could take my own advice, because I'm dying to see Maren. We've had a few moments of sneaking since the party, but we've mostly texted or talked on the phone.

She smiles at Lola and hands her Bandit before entering the house. We've purchased food, toys, and a litter box, so Maren doesn't have to transport anything but the cat.

"Hi," I say, letting my gaze slide from her fitted white tee to her long legs and untied white sneakers peeking out beneath the flare of her faded jeans. "Come in." I hold open the door and step aside just as Tia appears in the entry, petting Bandit in Lola's arms.

"Hi, Tia," Maren says before returning her gaze to me. "Actually, I'm going to head home and finish some laundry in case I leave town."

I nod, fighting the need to touch her.

"You can kiss her, Dad. It's not a secret," Lola says.

I turn my head. Lola doesn't look at me, but she smirks before nuzzling her nose into Bandit's fur. However, Tia's gaze burns into my skull.

I force a tiny laugh. "Lola, I don't know what you're—"

"Dakota's mom takes a cycle class with my math teacher, who said she saw you at her house with Maren. They have a name for you, but I don't think I should repeat it." She slides her gaze to me with a gotcha expression. "My teacher called Maren your *girlfriend*." Her grin splits her face in two. "I knew it!"

Tia clears her throat, but I don't give her an ounce of my attention. When I turn back toward Maren, her blue eyes are saucers, and her lips are trapped between her teeth.

"Lola, go brush your teeth."

"I already did, Dad."

"Then go to bed."

"But I have twenty more minutes."

"Lola," Tia interjects. "Go to your room. I need to have a word with your dad and Maren."

"Fine," Lola huffs.

I glance over my shoulder, watching Lola descend the stairs before narrowing my eyes at Tia. "I'm walking Maren to her car. If you want to talk to *me*, you can do it later. But Maren needs to get her sleep, and she owes you no explanation."

"Ozzy, it's fine. If Tia wants to talk, we can talk."

"Tia doesn't want to talk; she wants to lecture. There's a difference," I say, keeping my back to Tia.

Maren eyes her over my shoulder. I step toward her onto the porch, closing the door behind me.

"Evette told my daughter's friend's nosy mom about us? Isn't there some confidentiality thing that prevents teachers from discussing their private lives with students?" I say.

"I didn't think to tell her to keep us a secret." Maren pivots and heads toward her RAV.

"She should have thought about it all on her own."

"Ozzy, I'm sure it never occurred to her that our relationship is a secret. We're not having an affair."

"We're not going to have anything if Tia decides this is a hill she's willing to die on."

Maren turns and crosses her arms, leaning into the driver's side door. "What would you do if Tia weren't here? You'd survive."

"I wouldn't be working, or at most, I'd be part time to take Lola to school *and* be there when school got out like I've done for the past two years. And when Brynn's life insurance ran out, I'd have to sell the house and rent something small. And Lola wouldn't be in therapy because I wouldn't have insurance or a good-paying job to cover it. And sure, we'd get by, but it wouldn't feel fair to Lola. So, despite my distaste for Tia, I'm not relishing their not being here to help."

"Well, it's summer break now. You have time to figure it out. What if I help you find someone to pick her up after school in the fall—on a bike? What if I help pay for it?"

I shake my head and laugh. "Sounds emasculating. And it's not a solution if she gets sick."

"You mean to tell me that Brynn didn't make more money than you? Pay for more things than you?"

"That's different. She was my wife and Lola's mom."

"And I'm the cat woman you screw."

"Jesus, Maren. No, I'm not saying that. But we've known each other for two seconds, and I think abandoning all reason at this point would be pretty irresponsible. You could decide that dating a guy who only rides a bike isn't all it's cracked up to be. Then what? Are you going to continue to pay for after-school transportation and childcare? Or will I be on my own? Which is exactly what I'm trying to avoid by not pissing off Tia."

"You make more out of the bike than I do."

"Because *it's* emasculating too!"

She flinches.

I feel instant regret and release a long sigh. "I'm sorry," I whisper, stabbing my fingers through my hair. "This is my life, and I hate that I have to remind myself how lucky I am despite the loss. Lola lived. Had she died, I don't think I would have had the strength or the will to go on. And if Brynn had lived and Lola had died, I think it would have destroyed our marriage because both of us would have been mere shells of ourselves."

Maren stares at her feet. "Maybe the timing is all wrong for us."

I grunt. "It's too late. I can't fall out of love with you."

Her gaze lifts to mine.

"What?" I ask when she doesn't speak.

"They're just words, Ozzy—three simple words. Yet I'm dying for you to say them together in order."

I squint. "What do you mean?"

"You told me you never said you didn't love me. And now you're telling me you can't fall out of love with me. And I know what those statements mean. But you haven't just said it."

The words sprint to the tip of my tongue, ready to take flight, but I grin instead. "I need something to keep you coming back for more."

"Even if the timing is wrong?"

"Even if."

She chews on the inside of her cheek for a few seconds. "Well, I have to go."

I slide my hands along her cheeks, burying my fingers in her hair. "Be safe." I kiss the top of her head without regard to Tia, who I know is glued to the window watching us.

"I will," she whispers. "I love you."

"Yeah, me too."

Her hands grip my shirt, tugging it harder than necessary. "Don't be an ass. Just say it."

"I did. You wanted it in three words. I gave it to you in three words."

"Speaking of giving people things. I know what you're not getting anytime soon," she murmurs as I duck my head and kiss her neck.

"If you end up leaving town, I'm well aware of what I won't be getting." I kiss my way up to her mouth.

She turns her head just as I reach her lips. "Say it."

"You're beautiful." I kiss her cheek.

"Say it."

"I'm going to miss you." I kiss her forehead.

"Say it." She jerks my shirt a little harder.

"We fell in love." I kiss her nose.

"Ozzy . . ." She sighs with defeat and lifts her chin to kiss me.

Chapter Twenty-Nine

To my surprise, Tia's not waiting to kill me the second I walk into the house.

However, as I pass the living room, Amos solves that mystery. "Tia wants you to meet her in the garage when you're done tucking Lola into bed."

I pause at the top of the stairs and close my eyes. "She's gone. My heart will always feel a little broken. But she's gone."

"I know," Amos says. "But what I know and you know doesn't matter. Maren seems to be a nice young woman, but it's not the right time."

I take a step back to look at him. "I didn't think it was the right time to explain pornography to my ten-year-old daughter, but I did. And I did it because I don't fault you for having needs. And you know you're not supposed to smoke around Lola, but I know you do. You could have my back but choose to cower in Tia's shadow."

"I don't encourage her," he says, staring at the television.

"Your silence—your complacency—is all the affirmation she needs."

Amos narrows his eyes, but he doesn't speak, so I head downstairs to Lola's room. She's in bed with Bandit curled up next to her.

"I knew you liked her." Lola beams.

I sit on the edge of her bed and adjust her covers. "I do like her. Is that okay?"

"Do you like her as much as you liked Mom?"

This girl knows how to chip away at my emotions. Is she parenting me? Is she asking me this because she wants an answer, or does she want me to think about my feelings?

"I haven't known Maren that long. I knew your mom for years, not weeks. It's too early to compare feelings. I'm just happy that my heart feels open enough to like Maren the way I do. It means I'm not totally broken."

"Like me?" She frowns.

"No." I rest a hand on her cheek.

"I am. I'm broken. I can't get into a car. That's messed up. That's what Dakota said."

"Dakota doesn't know what he's talking about," I say.

"He's not being mean. He said it's not my fault."

"You're not broken." I kiss her forehead. "Good night."

"Night," she says through a big yawn.

Amos is asleep on the sofa when I reach the top of the stairs.

Coward.

I head to the garage, where Tia is perched on the stool at my workbench, stacking washers like building blocks.

"I can't stay here and watch you forget about Brynn. Forget about your vows. Forget about the reason she died. Forget about everything Amos and I are giving up to be here for you. Was that woman here with you when we were gone? When Lola spent the weekend with your mom? Were you screwing around with another woman in the house you bought with your wife? Is still having your life *and* Lola's not enough for you?"

"Tia, how . . ." I shake my head. There's so much to unpack that I don't know what to address first. "How can you think that I have or ever will forget Brynn? If Lola gets into a car again, will that mean she's forgotten how her mom died? And what the hell do you mean

I've forgotten my vows? My wedding vows? Till death do us part? Do you think that means until both people die? Had I been the one who died, can you honestly say you wouldn't have wanted Brynn to find love again?"

"Brynn was disciplined. She would have thrown herself into raising Lola and doing her job. And maybe, just *maybe*, after Lola went to college or married, she might have considered finding love again. Women live without men much easier than men live without women. So maybe it's not entirely your fault. Maybe it's in your DNA. But for heaven's sake, Ozzy, it's only been *two years*. Lola is still a mess. You just started back to work. And you clearly need help, so why would you add one more thing to your plate?"

"I'm not adopting Maren. I'm dating her. I'm not supporting her. She's not one more thing on my plate. And Lola likes her."

Tia frowns. "Exactly. Lola likes her. Lola will get attached to her. Hell, she's already attached to her cat. What happens when it doesn't work out? I don't give two hoots if you get hurt in this mess, but Lola can't handle any more heartbreak. I'm *not* okay with you gambling with her emotions. And Brynn wouldn't be either."

Those are always the final words. Now that Brynn is gone, Tia is her spokesperson. Tia is the all-knowing supreme being who knows what Brynn would have wanted in every situation. It's as if I wasn't married to her for nearly a decade.

"You're wrong," I whisper.

"What?"

"You're wrong," I say after clearing my throat. "Do you really think we never talked about it? We did. Maybe not in a way that felt real, because you never want to imagine your spouse dying. But sometimes, you lie in bed in each other's arms, and the love you feel in that moment ignites a fear of losing them. So you have that talk. You tell each other that if something happens and one of you dies, the other person should love again. Love again for themselves. Love again, so Lola sees that the only life that should end when someone dies is the one who's no longer breathing."

Tia stares at the stack of washers and pulls one from the bottom, letting them scatter on the workbench and ping like coins onto the floor. Then she slides off the stool and heads toward the door, stopping when she's a foot past me. "It should have been you," she says.

"I know," I whisper.

Maren: Are you in trouble with Tia? I haven't heard from you.

I grin at my phone when Maren texts me three days later, just as I drift off to sleep during the ten o'clock news.

Ozzy: What are you wearing?

Maren: Lol your shirt

I murmur, "Liar" while replying.

Ozzy: That would make you a thief

She sends me a picture of her from the neck down in a hotel bed, wearing my white tee with a rip at the bottom where I snagged it on a nail.

Ozzy: What are you wearing under it?

Maren: All your favorite things

This woman is killing me.

Ozzy: Waiting for another picture

Maren: Ha! No way

Ozzy: Tia's giving me the silent treatment. I don't mind

Maren: What about Lola?

Ozzy: She adores you

Maren: She adores my cat

Ozzy: I like your pussy too

Maren: I swear to god if you don't delete this conversation and Lola sees it, I will end you

Ozzy: Have you been flying?

Maren: Every day

Ozzy: Any news on your house?

Maren: I close next Thursday

Ozzy: What do you want me to work on first?

Maren: Me

Ozzy: Ur such a perv

Maren sends a long line of laughing emojis, but they're nothing compared to the grin on my face.

Maren: Sweet dreams

Maren: Hug Lola for me. I didn't get to tell her goodbye

Ozzy: I will. Be safe <3

And I love you.

I almost type the words. But at this point, knowing how badly she wants to hear them, I feel like I need to make the moment memorable.

Chapter Thirty

MAREN

Four fires in ten days.

Countless texts with Ozzy.

A dozen or so rounds of poker at the base.

And I crocheted a cat toy from a kit for Bandit.

It's been a solid start to the fire season.

On my final day, I make eleven drops before sunset and return to Missoula for five days off.

As much as I want to head straight to Ozzy's, it's late, so I drive home. When I walk in the door, KC and the Sunshine Band's "Please Don't Go" plays from Will's Amazon Echo.

I chuckle while setting my bags by the stairs. Will pokes his head around the corner from the kitchen with a banana in his hand as a microphone while he sings the lyrics. Without interrupting his performance, I slide my arms around his neck. His free hand hooks my waist as we dance, and I fall into a fit of laughter until we nearly stumble to the floor, tripping over each other's feet.

"Don't gooo . . ." Will belts the tune, dropping to his knees.

I pluck the banana from his hand, peel it, and take a bite.

"Maren." He draws out my name while I turn down the volume. "If you leave, I'll be all alone."

I giggle, seeing a new side to Will since Jamie and Fitz moved out two weeks earlier. "Maybe you'll commit to love. There's a doctor who hasn't had sex since you took her v-card. She's waiting for you to bring her the glass shoe."

Will stands and grabs my hand to take a bite of the banana. "That's bullshit," he mumbles. "You're my backup. Don't get too cozy with that mechanic."

I relinquish the banana and pour a glass of wine. "I'm moving out *just* so I can get cozy with him without having to time things perfectly between your work schedule or climb in through his bedroom window."

Will pauses the bottle at his mouth. "Mare, you climb in through his bedroom window? Like, up a ladder?"

"He's in the basement." I sip my wine.

Will smirks and shakes his head. "Well, you'd better come see me."

"Why can't you come to see me?"

"Because you have a fucking cat."

I cringe. "You *never* mentioned it."

"Well, if that cat's still alive when we get married, you're getting rid of it."

I snort. "*If* our lives hit that sad, pathetic point where I'm willing to marry someone who feels like a brother to me because no other man will marry me, then I'll get rid of the cat."

"That's all I ask." He manages to smirk and drink his beer simultaneously.

"Have you heard from Fitz and Jamie?"

Will shakes his head. "It's like I no longer exist. See why I'm a little concerned?" He moseys to the sofa, plops down, and picks up his gaming controller.

"I think Fitz is in Idaho," I say as I finish my wine and set the glass in the sink. "Jamie is probably busy nesting, but she's loaning me Fitz's truck to move my things."

"If you wait until Saturday, I can help."

"Jamie and I can do it. But thanks."

"Maybe your boyfriend can borrow a bike trailer and pull some stuff for you."

"Don't be a dick, Will."

He chuckles. "I'm kidding. Can't you take a joke?"

"Yes." I grab my bag and hike the strap onto my shoulder. "But I'm afraid you or Fitz will open your stupid mouth and *joke* to Ozzy's face before you've developed enough of a relationship with him to do so. And then he'll knock you on your ass, and I don't want to play referee."

"You can't possibly think he'd knock me on my ass."

"Well, he's not a black belt in tai chi, but I think he'd make you bleed."

"Now who's being a dick? And for the record, if there were a belt system in tai chi, I'd be a black belt."

I giggle the rest of the way up the stairs while a fight between Will and Ozzy, which will never happen, plays in my head. I honestly don't know who would win that fight, but I love ruffling Will's feathers.

◆ ◆ ◆

The following day, I close on my house and send Ozzy a picture of my keys.

Maren: MINE!

Ozzy: Congratulations! Can't wait to see you

When I pull into the driveway at what is now just Will's house, Fitz's black truck is backed into his old spot, and Jamie's carrying my folded metal bed frame out the front door.

"Is Fitz in Idaho?" I hop out of my car and help her slide it into the truck bed.

"Yep. It's just me," she says. "Fitz wanted me to wait for him to get home tomorrow, but I know firsthand how freaking excited you are, so let's do this. We are two very capable women." She hugs me, and we jump up and down together, squealing.

"I'm a homeowner!"

She giggles. "Me too!"

"Okay, let's get the rest." I link my arm with hers and pull her toward the house. "If everything is moved now, I can go furniture shopping this afternoon."

We load all my belongings into the back of Fitz's pickup and my RAV. I also thought I'd need Will's Bronco, but I overestimated my possessions. It's kind of depressing that I'm in my thirties with so few belongings.

"Ready?" Jamie asks as I stand in the middle of my empty bedroom.

"Did you feel like this when you packed up your things? Did you feel like everything ugly and everything beautiful happened within the walls of this house?" Tears burn my eyes.

Jamie reaches for my hand, squeezing it. "Close your eyes."

Tears break free when I do.

"See? Brandon's still there. This house doesn't hold memories. You hold them. No matter where you are, he'll be with you as you make new ones."

Sniffling, I nod.

Less than two hours later, I'm moved into my three-bedroom house with a weathered front porch and weed-infested yard. But who cares? I bought it for the tree house in the backyard.

"You have nothing," Jamie says before laughing at my empty main floor.

"I have beautiful hardwood floors." I narrow my eyes at the heavily scratched and moderately faded oak planks. "I have hardwood floors that can potentially be beautiful."

Jamie laughs. "I think you should hold off buying furniture until you do some renovating. Like, maybe just get one thing. Maybe a sofa. Then you'll have less to move and clean when it's all done."

"You're probably right." I wipe my hand along the worn laminate kitchen counter. "I guess that leaves more time for lunch."

"My treat," Jamie says. "And we can text the testosterone machines and let them know we did everything already."

I nod slowly. It's not a fancy house. I have *a lot* of work to do, but it's mine. And it takes only a second to imagine it filled with a life.

A handsome mechanic.

A young, curly-haired girl.

And a cat.

After lunch, I fall in love with a cerulean blue velvet sofa on clearance. So we muscle it into the back of Fitz's truck and head home.

"It's perfect," Jamie says when we plop onto it and stare at the brick hearth.

"I own a home," I whisper at the tail end of a long sigh.

"And a tree house."

I giggle. "Speaking of my cat's house, I must get him." I glance at my watch and text Ozzy.

Maren: Is it okay if I pick up my cat now?

"Is Ozzy the one?" Jamie asks.

I stare at my phone while waiting for Ozzy to reply. "In theory, yes."

"In reality?"

I read Ozzy's message.

Ozzy: Sure. I'll call and have Lola watch for you so you don't have to go inside.

"In reality, I feel like I have to make myself small to fit into his world. And if you tell anyone I said that, I'll kill you." I toss my phone onto the cushion between us and adjust my ponytail.

"That's sad, Maren."

"I know." I shrug a shoulder. "It feels like bad timing, but how many things in life happen at the perfect time, or what we perceive to be the perfect time? Do you think you met Fitz at the perfect time?"

"Yes." She twists her lips. "No. I don't know. I get what you're saying. It's a good time for you but not for Ozzy. But in a few years, if Lola gets better and the timing is right for Ozzy, you could be with someone else."

"Exactly." I wrinkle my nose. "And I feel like I need to be *all* in or get out. I need to completely walk away because I don't want to be another source of pain or loss in Lola's life by thinking I can hold out until she's better and their lives are somewhat normal again, only to have that never happen."

"So play this game with me," Jamie says. "Let's say she never gets into a car again, and therefore, neither does Ozzy. Missoula is the boundary of their world forever. Can you be part of that *small* world?"

I rub my hands over my face and mumble, "I don't know. Does that make me an awful person?"

"Of course not."

"But if I love him—"

"Do you? Do you truly love him?" Jamie asks.

"Yes."

She lifts her eyebrows. "You didn't even hesitate."

I grin because I always feel joy and uncontrolled giddiness when I think of Ozzy and Lola. "You know what I don't know?"

"What's that?"

I hesitate for a few seconds. "Had I met Ozzy, a single guy with no child, never been married, I know I would have been attracted to him. But I've been attracted to other guys. Good guys. You know? To me, Ozzy isn't just a sexy mechanic at Cielo. He's Lola's father. And a widower. And he's grounded, but not just in the literal sense. Is it weird that I feel like I'm attracted to the man he is *because* of the tragedy he's faced? Because he's a dad?"

"No. Tragedies change people. Think about it. Lola will never look at another person with scars the way she might have had she not gone through this experience in her life. People need silver linings. I bet you love Ozzy because these tragedies have made him a better man. And it sucks that his wife died, but I bet he is a different, perhaps better, person for having survived it."

I let her words settle for a few seconds before glancing at my watch again. "I have to get Bandit. Want to come with me?"

"To guard you from the grandma?"

I laugh and hold up my phone so she can see Ozzy's message about me not going inside.

"Yikes."

I stand. "Yikes indeed. I wish I could get her to like me."

"I'm sure it's not personal. You have to know that, right?"

"I know." I grab my purse from the bottom step.

"I'll stay here and clean a few things." Miss Clean Queen grins.

I open the front door. "Clean away. Wish me luck."

Chapter Thirty-One

"What took you so long?" Lola asks when I climb out of my RAV. Her blond hair blows in her face while she totes Bandit toward me.

I laugh. "Sorry. I was talking with a friend."

"My dad? I know he's not *just* a friend."

I take Bandit from her and open the back of my vehicle to put him in his carrier. "My friend Jamie. You met her and her fiancé, Fitz. They just bought a house, and they're getting married."

"I almost went to a wedding," Lola says.

"Oh?" I close the back door and lean against it, arms crossed over my chest.

Lola kicks a rock in the driveway. "Yeah, my aunt Jenny asked me to be her flower girl, but then the accident happened. Dad said it had nothing to do with my face, but I don't believe them. So Aunt Jenny and Uncle Darin anteloped."

"They eloped."

"Yeah." She giggles, and her nose wrinkles. "That's it."

"What's your middle name?"

"Winnie. Why?"

I gently frame her face, and her big blue eyes gaze up at me while my thumb traces one of her scars. "Because I need to use your full name when I say this to you so you know I'm serious. Okay?"

Lola blinks and whispers, "Okay."

"Lola Winnie Laster, I promise you that your aunt and uncle wanted you to be their flower girl even after your accident. There's a reason people say true love is blind. It's because the people who really love you see your beauty in all its glorious forms. They saw it before the accident. You radiated a bright innocence. And now, your scars"—again, I brush my thumb under her eye—"they are reminders of your strength. When people look at you, they see everything they hope to be themselves. Strong. Brave. And beautiful."

She swallows hard.

I lean down and press my lips to her forehead before whispering, "You're alive, sweet girl. And *life* is beautiful."

"My mom is dead," she murmurs.

I run my fingers through her hair to the back of her head and pull her into my embrace. "I know. And that is your ugly truth. My brother died. And that is my ugly truth."

She wraps her arms around my waist. "Thanks for loving my dad *and* me."

Tears burn my eyes just as something in the window moves. Tia folds her arms over her chest, eyeing me with displeasure, and I know I have to get out or go all in.

Lola is Ozzy's world. Maybe they can be mine. And perhaps that's all I'll ever need.

"I think your dad is bringing you to my house later." I release Lola.

"Yeah." Lola tips her head back, surveying the sky. "But Nana said it's supposed to rain."

"Hopefully not." I open my car door, and Lola glances inside my RAV. "Do you want to sit in the driver's seat? I used to sit in the driver's seat of my dad's car and pretend I was driving."

With an unreadable expression, Lola slowly shakes her head and whispers, "No."

It's the first time I've seen actual fear in her demeanor, tiny lines forming along her forehead while she chews on the inside of her cheek and wrings her hands together.

"If it rains, I'll send pictures. And you can come tomorrow. Did I mention I bought a soft, blue velvet sofa?"

It takes Lola a few seconds to recover. Where is her mind? Back with the accident? Does she remember much from that day? I regret suggesting she sit in my driver's seat. I'm sure more intelligent, more convincing people than me have tried to get her into a car.

She mumbles something, bringing her gaze to mine.

"What?" I ask.

"You should have bought leather."

"A leather sofa?"

She nods. "Nana said something about a six and a dozen something. Like cats scratch leather but shed on fabric."

Again, this girl makes me smile. My face cracks with a huge smile, or my heart breaks with her. "Six of one, half dozen of the other?"

Lola nods. "Yeah, I think that was it."

I glance toward the window again, and Tia's still keeping a watchful eye on us.

"She's right. I'm going with a sticky roller for the fur instead of the scratched sofa."

"Bandit's worth it," Lola says.

I climb into the driver's seat. "He is," I say. Bandit's worth it because he makes Lola deliriously happy, which makes me happy. I hope she knows that her father thinks she's worth every mile he's put on his bike.

Every missed opportunity.

Every scowl and snide word from Tia.

I hope she feels worthy of happiness and all the love from everyone around her.

"Be careful," Lola says with a sad smile. "Ignore Bandit if he meows."

Oh, Lola . . .

"I will," I say.

"And be careful when you're flying." She keeps tugging at my heartstrings.

"I will. I'll see you later if it doesn't rain, or tomorrow if it does."

"Okay." Lola waves when I close my door.

I'm in. I'm all in.

I love this little girl.

I love her dad.

I love this version of myself with them in my life.

It rains.

I finish cleaning what little Jamie left for me. Then I sit on my one piece of furniture.

It's quiet. Too quiet.

I don't have a TV yet, and my internet won't be connected until Monday. While I stare at the popcorn-textured ceiling from my velvet sofa with Bandit purring on my lap, someone knocks at my door.

A soaked Ozzy grins when I open it.

"What are you doing?" My jaw drops.

He shakes like a dog, and I wrinkle my nose when the water hits me.

"I snuck out," he says, removing his boots and stepping inside. He digs his hand into the pocket of his rain jacket and pulls out six dandelions.

We both stare at the sad, wet, and wilted little flowers.

"It's the thought that counts, right?"

I bite back my grin and nod while peeling them from his open palm. He has no idea how much his thoughts count, how much they matter to me and my sappy heart.

"Where can I put this so your wood floor doesn't get wet?" He holds out his jacket.

"Uh." I look around. "Maybe the bathroom. It has vinyl flooring."

Ozzy tosses his jacket into the half bath and lifts his T-shirt to dry his face.

I set the dandelions on the counter and turn, staring at his abs and tattoos.

"I assumed you and Lola would come tomorrow. It's almost ten, *and it's raining*," I say.

"I heard you got a new sofa."

I flip out my hip and cross my arms over my chest. "You heard I got a new sofa? That's why you're here? You couldn't wait until tomorrow to see it."

Ozzy cants his head, gaze shooting over my shoulder. "It's a bold color."

"I'm a bold woman. And you have blue appliances in your kitchen."

He smirks.

"I've missed you," I whisper.

Ozzy's attention shifts back to me. "I figured. That's why I'm here."

"You're so arrogant." I narrow my eyes.

"You mean *thoughtful*."

"Thoughtful?" I twist my lips.

"I knew you were missing me, so I rode in the rain to be here for you, *and* I remembered flowers this time."

God, I love him. But I won't submit so easily.

"And Lola said you talked about beautiful and ugly things today."

"I overstepped." I frown. "I'm sorry."

"No." Ozzy steps toward me, lifting my chin with his finger. "She said you offered to let her sit in your RAV, and for the first time since her mom died, she wanted to because she looks up to you. But she couldn't, and I could tell that bothered her."

I frown.

"Don't do that." He grins before pecking my lips. "Today was also the first time she seemed bothered by *not* getting into a car. That's progress." Ozzy kisses me again. "You're the reason she made progress today." He slides his fingers into my hair and kisses me deeper. As he releases my mouth and drags his lips along my jaw to my ear, he whispers, "I fucking missed you so much."

"Let's go upstairs," I murmur, clenching his T-shirt while my eyelids leaden from his hot mouth on my neck, licking my flesh and teasing it with his teeth.

We slow-dance our way to the stairs between kisses. I turn, gripping the railing and making it halfway up before he curls his fingers into the waistband of my jogging shorts, pulling them down my legs along with my underwear.

"Ozzy . . ." I make a weak protest while he playfully bites my ass.

With my shorts and underwear shackling my legs, I have nowhere to go but on my knees.

"I can't take you to the beach," he murmurs, "but *this* I can do."

My fingers curl into the worn carpeted stairs and my head drops between my outstretched arms while he unbuttons his jeans. In the next breath, he drives into me, and I moan.

The dichotomy of Ozzy, father to Lola, and Ozzy, caveman screwing the life out of me, blows my mind.

I don't care what he says. He missed me too.

My body starts to collapse with my release, so Ozzy lifts me to the top of the stairs until I'm lying on my back with him moving between my spread knees. When he orgasms, the tendons in his neck stretch tight as his head rears backward. He smiles while opening his eyes and catching his breath.

"I found a penny in the parking lot this morning. I knew it was good luck," he says, dipping his head and sucking my nipple between his lips. Then he releases it with a chuckle. "And when I walked into the hangar, there was music playing—James Brown's 'I Got You.'"

I giggle as he kisses his way to my other breast. "Do you want to hear my condom story?"

"Absolutely," he says.

I free my arms so my fingers can play in his hair while he gives my breasts the attention they deserve. "I don't remember how old I was, but I was too young to know anything about condoms. I found my dad's stash in his closet when my grandma was babysitting me and my brother. So I showed her the box, and she told me to put them back. When I asked her what they were, she told me they were what my dad used on lucky days."

Ozzy rolls us so we're facing each other on our sides, heads propped up on our arms, legs tangled in our partially removed clothes.

"So the next day, I took one of his condoms to school with me because my teacher was choosing a new helper for that week. And guess what?"

Ozzy beams. "What?"

"She chose me. So I told her I knew it was my lucky day, and I pulled the lucky condom out of my pocket and showed it to her."

Ozzy barks a laugh that settles into silent snickering, which shakes his body, and he covers his mouth with a fist.

I grin. "Let's just say it was an interesting meeting with my parents in the principal's office. I'm sure I should have been embarrassed, but all I remember is my dad sweating through his shirt, and my mom's cheeks looked like two shiny red apples."

Ozzy rolls onto his back and throws an arm over his face while he continues to laugh.

"You're welcome," I say, gathering my shorts and underwear before disappearing into my bathroom.

When I emerge with the girl parts all cleaned up and my clothes in place, I find Ozzy in the kitchen with the fridge door open.

So much for making it to the bedroom.

"Maren, you have no food. How am I supposed to refuel for round two?"

"I'll get groceries tomorrow. It might just be a one-round night. I assume you're going home before Lola or her grandparents wake."

Ozzy shuts the fridge door and leans his back against it. "Yes. I might have one of Lola's ZBARs in the inner pocket of my rain jacket to get me by."

"Since I'm sharing embarrassing things, I might as well let you in on another secret," I say.

He lifts his eyebrows.

I get a glass of water. "After our weekend sexcapade at your house, I had a killer UTI the following week. I think you deposited six gallons of sperm into me."

While narrowing his eyes, he corkscrews his lips. "You didn't hydrate enough."

I pause my glass of *hydration* at my lips. "Uh." I cough. "Okay. Sure. It was all on me."

Ozzy tries to offer a guilty grin, but it looks far more cocky than regretful or apologetic. "You want me to wear lucky condoms." He nods several times.

"*Or* we could space things out a little more."

"So lots of sex with condoms, or less sex but no condoms?" He scratches his chin.

"I feel like I'm talking to a sixteen-year-old boy, not a grown man." I laugh.

"Maren." He steals my glass and refills it with water, taking a few gulps before handing me the rest. "When it comes to sex, all men are boys. When we're not having it, we're thinking about it."

"Can I ask you a question about Lola?"

He buckles over, stumbling back a few steps. "No, no, no. You can't say my daughter's name directly after I tell you I think about sex a lot."

I finish the glass of water like a good girl and smile.

"And what have I said about you asking me if you can ask me a question?" Ozzy stands straight and rolls his shoulders back with a hard sigh.

"What do you do when Lola gets sick, and you have to take her to the doctor, or she gets sick at school and needs to come home early? Do you make her ride her bike?"

"I've walked to her school and carried her home. A friend picks up her bike and brings it home. And I have a family doctor who makes house calls, but thankfully, Lola rarely gets sick."

"A family doctor who makes house calls?" I ask.

"For Lola, yes."

"You've carried her home from school?"

He nods.

It seems silly to say you can fall in love with someone over and over without falling out of love first, but I fall in love with Ozzy every time we're together. Or maybe I just fall deeper. I'm starting to think there's an infinite depth to which I can fall for this man.

"What?" he asks with a funny grin.

I slowly shake my head. "You're the man, Ozzy."

"Thanks. That's reassuring, since I've always considered myself a man."

"No. Not *a* man. You're *the* man. There's a difference."

He narrows his eyes and parts his lips like he's going to say something, but then he wets them and saunters toward my sofa. As soon as he plops down, Bandit jumps onto his lap.

"My backup fiancé will never see the inside of this house because I rescued that cat for your daughter."

"Whoa, what?" Ozzy eyes me. "Backup fiancé?"

"Yes," I say, nestling into the corner of the sofa, hugging my knees. "Will's my backup husband if we're both still single in two more years."

"*Still* single? Are you single now?"

My heart soars when it detects frustration, or maybe even jealousy, in Ozzy's voice. "I'm single until I find a man who says he loves me," I say, inspecting my nails.

"What do I have to do to prove myself?"

I shift my gaze to his. "You have to say it."

"Pfft. Actions speak louder than words."

"They don't. It's just a cliché. There are a lot of silent actions. But words can be very loud."

"Unless you're deaf," he counters.

"But I'm not."

He moves his lips without speaking.

"You're such an ass." I smack him with one of the throw pillows, and Bandit flies off the sofa and runs upstairs.

Ozzy grabs my wrists and pulls me onto his lap. "But am I *the* ass?" He guides my arms around his neck and kisses me before I answer.

I pull back and smile while brushing my nose against his. "I don't even want you to say it now. I know you're saving it. So it better be epic when you do say it."

"That's a lot of pressure." He leans forward and kisses my neck.

"Can you help me refinish my wood floors?"

I feel his lips bend into a smile against my skin. "I can."

"New kitchen cabinets and countertops."

"Mmm-hmm." He slides his hands up the back of my shirt, unhooking my bra, and I can no longer think about renovations.

I close my eyes as my head lolls to the side. "Ozzy, are we in love?" I whisper.

He presses his hand to the side of my head, lifting it while the pad of his thumb brushes my bottom lip. "We're *so* in love," he says before kissing me.

Chapter Thirty-Two

The following day, I pick up groceries and Lola's favorite doughnuts. When I pull into my driveway, Ozzy and Lola are sitting on my front porch steps, laughing about something.

I put my RAV in *park* and watch them for a few seconds while slowly unfastening my seat belt. I would never steal another woman's husband or child. I would never steal another woman's life.

But I want Brynn's life that she tragically left behind. I want to pick up the tiny pieces and put them together with parts of my life to create something new.

While my thoughts hijack my attention, I don't register Ozzy and Lola walking toward my vehicle until I jump when he opens my door.

"Good morning," he says with a beaming smile.

Heat fills my cheeks like he can read my mind and see my dreams. "Hi," I whisper before swallowing hard and stepping out.

He leans toward me and stops, sliding his gaze to the side. Lola is waiting with wide eyes and an even wider smile. "Is this okay, Lola?" he says, asking for her permission to kiss me.

And it happens again.

It happens. Every. Single. Day.

I fall in love with Ozzy Laster.

Lola doesn't speak, but she nods slowly, lacing her hands behind her back while rocking back and forth on her feet.

Ozzy leans in the rest of the way, pressing his lips to the corner of my mouth in a kiss that feels intimate yet chaste at the same time.

Before my legs turn into limp spaghetti, I clear my throat and lean across the driver's seat to grab the box of doughnuts. "Have you had breakfast?"

"We had smoothies," Ozzy says.

"Good. Then I won't feel as guilty for getting doughnuts." I hand Lola the box, and she squeals.

"YES!"

Ozzy chuckles.

"The front door is open. Head inside while your dad helps me carry in the groceries," I say.

Lola pivots, lifting the lid of the box while going to the front door.

"I can't believe you took the day off," I say.

He shrugs. "More like playing hooky. Don't tell anyone."

"Move in with me," I say, completely changing the subject. Two seconds ago, I had no plans of saying those four words. My heart is louder than my common sense.

And from the shock on Ozzy's face, I'd say he didn't see it coming either.

"Not today," I reply with a nervous laugh as my brain hits reverse. But it's too late. I can't unsay it, and I don't want to. "After the renovations, of course. I want Lola to pick out whatever she wants for her room. And I want her to have Bandit with her every night. And I want that tree house in the backyard to be a place where she can stare at the sky and dream big like I did. And I don't want to crawl through any more windows. And I want you—"

Ozzy kisses me, sliding one hand to the back of my neck while his other grips my hip. This isn't a Lola-appropriate kiss.

This is how a man kisses a woman like she's his oxygen—like *I'm* his oxygen.

"Is that a yes?" I ask when he releases me.

"It's"—a hint of pain pulls at his brow—"a maybe. Some logistics need to be considered."

I nod several times. "Yeah. I know. O-of course," I stutter past a surge of panic. "I wasn't thinking when I said it." My words fall from my lips in a rush. "I pulled into the driveway and saw you and Lola laughing on my front porch steps. And my heart decided without running it past my mind first, and then you kissed me in front of her, and—"

Again, he kisses me. But this time, he holds my face with both hands, and it's a quick kiss—a kiss meant solely to shut me up. "Baby," he whispers over my lips, "I said there are things to consider. I didn't say it's impossible."

"Okay." I try to contain my grin, but it only lasts two seconds.

"Groceries?"

I nod.

Ozzy carries all four sacks of groceries, and I let him because I like having a part of my life where I'm not proving to the rest of the world that I can do anything a man does.

I can fight fires and fly planes.

I can be calm and keep a steady hand when it matters most.

I can be strong and brave.

But with Ozzy, I want to be the woman whose groceries he carries, whose wood floor he refinishes, whose bare ass he bites, and who he calls "baby."

"Can Bandit have a piece of my doughnut?" Lola asks, perched on the counter next to the cat.

Ozzy and I reply, "No" at the same time while unloading groceries.

"Why don't you have a kitchen table and chairs?" she asks.

"Because I'm going to remodel the kitchen and do a lot of things that are messy, so I'm waiting until that's done before getting any more furniture," I say, lining up cups of yogurt on the top shelf of my fridge while Ozzy picks out a doughnut.

"You should ask my dad to help you because he's really good at building and fixing things."

"What about you?" I ask, sipping the coffee I got at the doughnut shop. "Aren't you going to help me?"

"I can hold the tape measure like I did for my dad at our house. And I can watch Bandit."

"Perfect." I wink at her while hopping onto the counter next to her and picking a jelly-filled doughnut from the box.

Ozzy steals my coffee and takes a sip, eyeing Lola and me. His lips curl into a grin before he pulls the cup away from his mouth.

"Can I see the backyard?" Lola asks, licking her sticky fingers.

I widen my eyes. "You didn't show her the tree house?"

"Oh my gosh! You have a tree house?" Lola flies off the counter and runs toward the back door.

"Be careful," Ozzy warns just before she closes the door behind her. He rolls his eyes, but his satisfied smirk reemerges when his attention returns to me.

"What's that smirk about?" I ask.

He wedges himself between my dangling legs. "I could get used to this."

"What can I do to help make *this* happen?" I set the rest of my doughnut into the box and wrap my arms around his neck.

"You can be patient, because everything in my life requires so much patience."

"I can do that," I say, teasing the nape of his neck.

"She's a lot." He nods toward the back door.

"*I'm* a lot."

Ozzy hums. "Yes. But in a different way." His smile fades, replaced with worry lines stretching along his forehead as his gaze drops between us. "If you ever start to feel like you're in over your head—"

"I love her too," I say.

Ozzy's eyes find mine again.

I shrug. "I might have fallen for her before I fell for you. She's pretty adorable. And she likes to save abandoned animals."

His gaze washes over every inch of my face while he holds an unreadable expression.

I wait because it feels like he's trying to figure something out. Perhaps it's me.

I wait a little more.

The silence.

The slow inspection.

It's too much.

Did I say the wrong thing?

Then his gaze locks on mine, and a smile steals his lips while giving me a barely detectable headshake. "I love you," he says.

Tears burn my eyes in an instant. "It was supposed to be an epic moment."

"Maren," he whispers, trailing light kisses from my lips to my ear, "there's nothing more epic than falling in love with someone who loved my daughter first."

This is it.

This is everything.

I'm *all* in.

Chapter Thirty-Three

OZZY

Over the next month, Lola and I spend all our free time at Maren's, working on her remodel and cat-sitting. When she's out of town, we send her pictures and video updates of Bandit and the progress.

We haven't discussed Lola and me moving in with her since the day she suggested it. I can't sort things out in my head, so I don't know how to approach this with Lola and her grandparents.

"When Lola's better, are you still planning on moving to Florida?" I ask out of the blue. Tia and Amos are helping me clean the kitchen. Lola's staying with my mom tonight, and Maren is assisting with a massive fire in Canada.

"Why do you ask?" Tia answers all questions with a question. Brynn did the same thing.

"Has Lola changed her mind about riding in a car?" Amos asks.

"Not yet. But if you plan on staying in Missoula, which Lola would love, you should buy this house from me."

"Are you hurting for money?" Tia closes the dishwasher and leans against the counter.

I stay focused on washing the dishes in the sink while Amos dries them. "No. I'm thinking about moving in with Maren."

Tia scoffs. "Don't be ridiculous."

"Why is that so ridiculous?" I glance over at her as she cleans the stovetop.

"Because you've only known her for a few months, and it would be irresponsible of you to make such a drastic change in Lola's life right now. Never mind that you've already let that woman get too close to your daughter."

"That woman has a name. It's Maren. And Lola adores her."

"Of course she likes her. *Maren* got her a cat. *Maren* doesn't have to be more than Lola's fun adult friend. She's a stranger bribing a kid with candy."

"My god, she's not a stranger. And she's not bribing Lola." I rinse a saucepan and hand it to Amos.

"Where are you going with this?" Tia tosses the sponge into the dishwater and crosses her arms. "Are you planning on marrying her? And God forbid, if you are, you need to do it before you pack up your daughter and shack up with this woman. At the very least, you need to be a role model. If you don't want Lola making these kinds of rash decisions down the road, you need to set the right example now."

I pull the plug on the drain and dry my hands. "You still haven't answered my original question."

"You want us to buy your house so you can move in with another woman? No. If you don't need us, then we're leaving."

"I didn't say I don't need you."

"If you have time to fall in love and move in with someone, then I think that's a pretty clear indicator that you don't need us. Your mom can watch her."

"My mom can't get her from school in the fall," I say, tossing the towel aside while Amos slinks out of the kitchen like he always does when things get heated.

"Then ask *Maren* to do it." Tia narrows her eyes, tipping her chin up a fraction.

"Maren has a job."

"And that's my problem?"

I rub the back of my neck and sigh. "It's not. You're making this into a vendetta. I'm simply asking if you want to stay close to your granddaughter after she no longer needs you to help her home from school."

"Don't use her as a pawn, Ozzy."

"A pawn?" I cough a laugh. "How am *I* using her as a pawn? I'm asking you a hypothetical question. Period. You're the one putting conditions on helping out with her. As long as I stay single and submissive to your every request, you'll help with Lola, but if I want a life beyond the role of grieving widower, you're ready to pack up and leave. So if you're only here to control me, you might as well pack up and leave now. But if you're here for Lola and Brynn, stop making this about me."

This is why I've avoided the subject for a month. I knew it wouldn't go well. Tia is a stubborn woman with an eternal broken heart and a just-as-eternal grudge.

She draws in a long breath and holds it. On the exhale, she gives me a fake smile. "We'll start packing our stuff tonight. And tomorrow we'll tell Lola why we're leaving."

I'm fucked, but I can't bring myself to beg and submit any longer. "*We'll* tell her tomorrow so there's no confusion about why you're leaving."

"Grow up, Ozzy." She scowls before retreating to her bedroom.

Running my hands through my hair, I exhale a long breath as my phone vibrates in my pocket. "Hey," I answer, pinching the bridge of my nose.

"What's wrong?" Maren asks.

"Nothing. Sorry. How are you?"

"I'm eating crappy hotel food in my sketchy hotel bed after a boring day of waiting for the powers that be to get their heads out of their asses and send us where we're needed. Let's get back to you. Why do you sound so exhausted?"

"You're in Canada. Lola's at my mom's. And I just had dinner with Tia and Amos. And the postdinner conversation didn't go well, but it is what it is. I'm going to ride over to Diego's house. That should help."

"I'm sorry you had a bad evening. Who's Diego?"

"My best friend."

"Why am I just now hearing about this Diego guy? And I thought I was your only friend," she says.

I grin, heading downstairs. "Why have you never asked about my other friends? Also, you're so much more than a friend."

"A lover?"

"The best lover." I put her on speaker and toss the phone onto my bed while changing from jeans into shorts.

"A psychiatrist Jamie used to work with told her that there are some promising studies on VR use for symptoms of anxiety in people with phobias. As a side note, the doctor is obsessed with virtual reality—a gamer like Will. Coincidentally, Will took her virginity before she was eighteen because she was a prodigy in med school before she was old enough to vote. But Jamie said Dr. Reichart knows her stuff. It seems worth a try."

"How old was Will when he took this girl's virginity?"

Maren giggles. "*That's* what piqued your curiosity from everything I just told you?"

"Will's your backup husband, so I'm curious about the man you deem worthy of such an honor."

"You think it's an honor to be a backup husband?"

"Of course."

"It's like sloppy seconds," she says. "Can we get back to the VR therapy?"

"I'll ask Lola's therapist about it," I say, grabbing my phone and heading back upstairs.

"Okay. But if she's not receptive, you could do your own research or get a second opinion. And please don't think I'm telling you how to parent your daughter; I'm just—"

"You love her too," I say, shoving my feet into my sneakers. "So your opinion matters. Don't feel shy about making suggestions. Okay?"

Silence settles between us.

"Maren?"

"I'm here. It's just . . ."

"What?"

"Every day."

I open the garage door to get my bike. "Every day what?"

"Every day, you say or do something to make me fall a little deeper in love with you. How do you do that?"

I chuckle. "I guess I have great women in my life who make it easy to be a lovable guy. Or you feel sorry for me, and you've taken pity on me like you did with Bandit. That's the only explanation for why you would swallow."

She coughs a laugh. "Oh my god, you have sex on the brain all the time."

I latch my phone into the holder on my bike and fasten my helmet. "I take it that's not the lovable part of me?"

She laughs. I love her laughter and how it makes me feel alive and hopeful again. I wish it could erase my conversation with Tia, but that woman's words stain like a permanent marker.

"Your new kitchen sink comes in tomorrow. I'll have it set before you get home," I say, slipping in a Bluetooth earbud and heading down the street.

"My fridge is being delivered on Thursday. Jamie said she'd be there for the delivery if I'm not home. I feel like so much has happened in the week I've been gone."

"It's looking great. And Lola has a surprise for you."

"God, I miss her," she says with a sigh.

If I don't control my grin, I'll show up at Diego's with a dozen bugs between my teeth. Maren thinks she falls in love with me every day, but I fall deeper in love with her every second of every day.

"Be safe, baby. Okay?"

"I'll do my best. Hug Lola and Bandit for me."

"Bandit doesn't like hugs."

"He doesn't like hugs from you because you abandoned him. But if you tell him the hug is from me, he'll keep his claws in check."

I chuckle. "You're such a liar, but I love you anyway."

Maren hums. "Say it again."

"You're a liar."

"Ozzy."

I glance behind me before turning the corner. "I love you."

"Now I can sleep. It's like a warm blanket and a kiss on my forehead."

"If I were with you, I'd kiss you good night in far more intimate places than your forehead."

"When you press your lips to my forehead, it's very intimate. In fact, I don't think a guy kisses a girl on the forehead until he loves her. It's like a parent kissing a child on the forehead to see if they have a fever. It's a *loving* gesture."

Brynn used to kiss Lola on the forehead all the time. And last winter, when I wasn't feeling well, Lola tucked me into my bed and gave me her favorite stuffed animal while kissing me on the forehead.

"We're both right," I say. "If I were with you, I would kiss you in so many places, but before you fell asleep in my arms, I would kiss your forehead."

"I know. Good night. And I love you too," she says before ending the call.

◆ ◆ ◆

"It's Lola's dad!" Kai yells before opening the screen door.

"Hey, Kai," I say.

"Where's Lola?" She cranes her neck to look past me. "I haven't seen her in forever."

"She's at her grandma's house for the night."

Kai frowns as Diego comes around the corner, wiping his hands on a dish towel.

"Sorry. Dinner's over," he says.

"I ate."

Kai spins on her bare feet and heads up the stairs without another word.

"Ozzy." Cheyenne steps around the corner with her hand on her pregnant belly. "Good to see you." She hugs me.

"You too. And you look amazing."

She takes a step back and rolls her eyes. "I'm a mammoth."

Diego hands her the towel and kisses her cheek. "You're carrying our baby. That makes you a goddess. I'll be out in the garage with Oz."

"Then you're rubbing my feet." Cheyenne tosses her long black hair over her shoulder. "And my back."

He nods toward the door. "I'll rub everything."

I step back outside, and he follows me to the garage.

"I've gotten myself into a pickle," I say.

"A pickle, huh? Well, who doesn't love a good pickle?"

"Tia and Amos are leaving if I don't drop to my knees, beg for forgiveness, and vow to stay single for eternity. And while not having help might be fine this summer, I'm screwed when school starts."

Diego retrieves two beers from his fridge and hands one to me.

"Is this about the blow job woman?" He takes a swig of his beer.

"Let's call her Maren."

He smirks. "Is this about Maren?"

I nod. "She asked me and Lola to move in with her."

"Why don't they like her?"

"Because she's not Brynn."

Diego shakes his head. "That's messed up. It's been more than two years."

"It's not like I was searching for her. She kind of appeared from nowhere. I'm not on dating apps. I rarely go out to bars or put myself in situations to meet women. And now I . . ."

Diego eyes me, waiting for me to finish.

I don't. Instead, I drink my beer and admire the new rims on his Mustang.

"You love her," he says.

"Yep," I say, like I don't want to love her. But I do. I want to love her. I want to move in with her. And if I don't scare her away, I want to be the reason she doesn't need a backup husband in two years.

"And Lola?"

"She adores her. And I haven't told her that Maren asked us to move in with her, because when I explain why it's not an easy decision, it will fall on her shoulders because she won't get into a car or ride the school bus."

"What if she did online schooling until she got past this? It's something she could do at your mom's house."

I take another big gulp of beer and shake my head. "That's been brought up in the past by Tia. Lola loves school. Despite a few asshole kids who make fun of her scars, she loves it. And taking that from her would feel like ten steps backward. She'd hate me for it. That girl is a social butterfly."

Diego bows his head and stares at his beer bottle for several seconds. "What if you're overprotecting her?"

"What do you mean? She sees a therapist. Everything I do is at the suggestion of an expert. It's not like I'm making this up as I go. This isn't my pace; it's Lola's pace, which her therapist says I need to respect."

Diego shakes his head. "I'm not suggesting you push her into anything or that you make her feel guilty. But you can be honest with her in a loving way. You should tell her that Maren asked you to move in with her. And if that happens, Tia and Amos will leave. Then you can tell her about your predicament in the fall. Let her help figure out a solution."

"She'll feel guilty," I say.

"Or empowered. Maybe she'll feel a sense of responsibility to help find a solution."

I lean against his tool chest and cross one ankle over the other. "It could backfire on me."

Diego nods several times. "It could. But you said it yourself. You're in a pickle. I don't think you have a choice to keep this from Lola."

"Unless I tell Maren now is not a good time. And I make nice with Tia and Amos. Keep the status quo while we wait for Lola to get better."

Again, Diego nods. "You can do that. But is that what you want to do?"

I shrug a shoulder. "Want? Fuck, man, I can't realistically think about what I want because my wants feel selfish and irresponsible."

"That's just your shrunken testicles talking."

I finish my beer and toss the bottle into his bin. "You're right. I need to tell Lola."

"I think that's the best solution," Diego says.

Chapter Thirty-Four

"Is this about the neighbor's rosebush?" Lola asks while her grandparents and I stare at her over dinner.

During my lunch break, I called my mom to talk to Lola and told her we had something to discuss with her tonight over dinner.

But instead of a discussion, it's turned into a game of chicken. Nobody wants to be the instigator or the bad guy in this scenario. So we look ridiculous watching Lola eat while we keep quiet.

The good news (I think) is that Tia and Amos haven't started packing anything, so I suspect she was bluffing. But that could change at any moment.

"What are you talking about?" I set my fork on my plate and blot my mouth with a napkin.

"Addie and I were playing basketball, and the ball kept landing in the rosebushes, breaking some branches."

"Well, that's not good," I say. "But that's not what we want to talk about."

"Then what?" Lola shifts her wide-eyed gaze to Tia and Amos.

"Maren wants us to move in with her," I say just as Tia opens her mouth to speak.

Lola gasps. "Really? You're getting married?" She practically falls out of her chair with excitement.

Tia pins me with an I-told-you-so gaze. Someone, somewhere along the way, instilled it into my daughter that men and women don't live together until they're married. And maybe that should be every father's dream, but it's not every boyfriend's dream.

Boyfriend.

There's something about adults calling themselves boyfriends and girlfriends that sounds juvenile and just wrong.

Partner?

That conjures up other things that don't fit either.

"Lola, no. We're . . ." I shake my head, fighting frustration. "Sometimes people live together—*adults* live together even if they're not married."

"Living in sin?" Lola narrows her eyes. "That's what Nana said about Uncle Leroy living with his girlfriend."

Eyeing Tia, I give her my best *grateful* smile. Sure, it might look murderous to someone else, but it's not. I'm incredibly thankful that she's taken the time to pass along her standards of morality to *my* daughter.

Tia sits up a little straighter with an air of smugness. She hasn't had to say a word because she's already brainwashed my daughter, molding her into a judgmental disciple spewing Tia's doctrine.

"Lola, Nana thinks Leroy is living in sin because some book she read—"

"It's not *some book*," Tia interrupts. "It's *the Bible*. And I know your mother raised you better than to disrespect God's word this way. Just because you don't take Lola to church anymore doesn't mean you have the right to raise her as a heathen."

"Tia, for the love of—"

"What's a heathen?" Lola asks, cutting me off just as I raise my voice.

As a rule, we don't argue in front of Lola, but I feel attacked as a father and role model. I don't appreciate her making me look bad in front of my daughter.

"Lola," I say before taking a deep breath. "If Nana and Pa weren't here, would we figure out how to make things work?"

Tears instantly fill her eyes. "Are you sick?" She looks to them for answers.

"No, honey. We're not sick," Amos reassures her while Tia frowns at me.

I can't win.

"If they moved away from here, would we be okay?" I rephrase.

"Ozzy, that's a lot of pressure to put on a ten-year-old," Tia says. "How is she supposed to know if you'll be okay? She's ten. Who's the adult?"

"Why are you leaving?" Lola asks, rubbing the unshed tears from her eyes.

Amos and Tia look to me for that answer.

I'm the bad guy—a lousy guy who wants to sacrifice them to save myself. That's what Tia did to me.

Despite what she thinks, I won't use Lola as a pawn.

"Pumpkin," I say in a calmer tone. "Forget I mentioned anything about Maren. *You* are my number one priority. And it's incredibly *loving* of Nana and Pa to be here for you." Words have never tasted so bitter. I don't want to bend the knee, but I don't see any other choice.

Lola's too young.

Too traumatized.

Too everything.

I told Maren to be patient, but I'm the one showing a lack of patience.

"When the day comes that you overcome your fears from the accident, and I *know* that day will come, then we will look into life changes for the both of us. But for now, I think it's best to continue doing what we're doing. And"—I raise a finger—"Maren suggested we look into using virtual reality gaming to help you. Doesn't that sound like fun?"

"Pffft." Tia rolls her eyes. "Just what a ten-year-old needs—video games that take them away from reality."

"Well, when her reality is—" I bite my tongue. We can't do this in front of Lola.

I smile at Lola while digging my phone out of my pocket because it's vibrating with a call. "It's just something I will ask your therapist about," I say, standing and heading toward the kitchen. The number isn't familiar. "This is Ozzy." I hold the phone to my ear.

"Hey, Ozzy. It's Ira from work. Taylor gave me your number."

"Oh. Okay. What's up?" I can't imagine why Ira is calling me.

"Did you hear about Maren? Taylor didn't realize you and Maren were a thing. And maybe you're not still a thing, but—"

"Ira!"

Silence.

"What about Maren?"

"Ozzy," she says in a softer tone. "Maren's plane went down."

I take a step back. "Wh-what did you say?" My legs want to give out until the wall of floating shelves catches me with a *thud*, followed by dishes shattering.

"Ozzy?"

"Where is she?" The words rip from my chest. This can't be happening. This *can't* happen to me twice. No god is that cruel.

"Dad!" Lola yells my name as she, Tia, and Amos enter the kitchen. "What happened?"

"Search and rescue are on their way. That's all I know. I'm sorry. We're all praying for her. A lot of people are," Ira says.

"Was it in the drop zone? Were there other aircraft involved? Did anyone—" My mouth can barely keep up with my thoughts and a million questions.

"Ozzy, what's going on? Who are you talking to?" Tia asks.

"Lola, stay back. There's glass everywhere," Amos says with his hands on her shoulders.

"Ozzy, that's all I know," Ira says. "I heard about it from my friend who works at the base. She said she'll let me know when she hears more."

With my phone clutched in my hand, my arm flops to my side, glass scattered all around me and my bare feet.

"Don't move, Oz. Let me grab a broom and shoes for you," Amos says.

"Dad, what happened? Your eyes are red. Are you crying?" Lola's words become as desperate as mine were with Ira.

"Lola, you're going to get glass in your feet. Wait in the living room until we get this cleaned up, and then you can ask your dad whatever you want." Tia ushers her out of the kitchen.

Amos returns from the garage with a broom and a dustpan. "Oz, did something bad happen?" he asks in a slow, steady voice while clearing a path with the broom to get to me.

I can't fucking move.

Clank.

My phone slips out of my hand.

I still don't move.

"Ozzy, you need to tell us what happened," Tia huffs.

"Stay in the living room with Lola," Amos says.

"I want to know what—"

"For God's sake, woman!" Amos snaps. And he never snaps. "For once in your stubborn life, do what I asked you to do."

She stands her ground for a few seconds before exiting the kitchen.

All this talking, yelling, and questioning. For what?

My wife is dead.

My father is dead.

My daughter can't get into a car.

My ex-mother-in-law hates me.

And Maren and her plane are who knows where in Canada—shattered into a million blazing pieces of rubble?

I no longer believe there is a purpose to life.

Life is a joke. A cruel, fucking joke.

I blink when Amos touches my leg, squatting before me and guiding my feet into my work boots. As he stands, my gaze locks with his.

I've never hated him. He's always tried to see things through my eyes, even if doing so has been challenging with a wife who refuses to walk a single step in anyone else's shoes.

"Son, did something happen to Maren?"

I stare at him for long seconds, letting his words bounce and echo in my head. When the real possibility of never seeing someone again cuts through the surface of denial, it feels like an out-of-body experience. I felt it with Brynn and my father. It's as if we're forced to choose to stay or go.

I haven't loved Maren for long. My brain knows that. It's good at math and reason. But my heart doesn't have filters. It doesn't do equations. It doesn't acknowledge the existence of time. The heart is unreasonable and completely illogical.

Childlike. Innocent, like Lola.

"Yes," I whisper. And it's no longer an echo. I'm acknowledging my willingness to go on no matter where Maren is on this earth or the world beyond this life.

"Her plane?" Amos asks.

Brynn was a daddy's girl. Maybe it's because she was too much like her mom and they butted heads. Amos was protective like a good father, but he always awaited her with open arms—a safe haven.

"Yes," I whisper, averting my gaze to the glass he's swept into a pile by the fridge. "Search and rescue are looking for her now. That's all I know."

"You can't tell Lola."

I return my attention to him and swallow hard with a slow nod. "I know."

"One of the pilots who works for Cielo had trouble with a mission." Amos grabs my shoulders to ensure I'm listening. "You don't know the details yet. But you're concerned about them. And when your friend told you, you took a step backward and accidentally tripped. She will assume that you would tell her if it were Maren. Okay?"

"I can't lie." I shake my head.

"You can do whatever it takes to keep her from worrying about something you don't know with certainty. Okay?"

I laugh.

Amos squints, drawing together his bushy gray eyebrows.

I laugh some more.

Lola and I will pull up to Maren's funeral on bicycles. We can set our handlebar lights to flash mode to fit in with the procession. Maybe we'll bring Bandit with us. I should get Lola one of those backpacks for cats with the domed window.

"Dad?" Lola peeks her head around the corner.

My laughter simmers into a light chuckle. "Sorry, Lola. I didn't mean to scare you. Someone from work called me with some concerning news, and when I took a step backward, I tripped." I take the broom that Amos leaned against the counter and continue to clean up the mess. "Go get ready for bed. I'll be down after I clean this up."

I feel everyone's gazes on me, heavy and suffocating, but I don't look at them. My composure and survival hinge on my ability to believe my own lies and imagine bicycles and cats in backpacks for funeral processions.

"Okay," Lola says.

Amos, once again, steps up and shows me some compassion. "Come on, Tia, let's get out of Ozzy's way while he finishes cleaning this up."

I will cover for his late-night pastime until the day I die because he's throwing me a lifeline when I need it the most.

After sweeping the glass into a bag, I use the vacuum and a wet microfiber mop to remove any remaining shards so nothing ends up in Lola's feet. I have to keep moving. Idleness is the enemy.

I go over things I need to do.

Take the trash bags to the garbage.

Check the air in the bike tires.

Make a grocery list.

Pay bills.

Throw in a load of laundry.

Tuck Lola into bed.

Then I robotically follow them.

"Did you feed Bandit on your way home from work?" Lola asks when I step into her room.

"I did. You have an appointment with your therapist tomorrow. Nana or Pa might ride with you there, and I'll come straight from work and meet you."

Apples.

Bread.

Yogurt.

I go over my grocery list. We might stop by the store after her therapy appointment.

"Okay. Is Nana upset about the broken dishes?"

"She shouldn't be. They're our dishes. I'll replace them. They're just broken dishes." I straighten her blankets and the pile of stuffed animals around her. "Good night, my girl." I press my lips to her forehead.

I don't think a guy kisses a girl on the forehead until he loves her. It's like a parent kissing a child on the forehead to see if they have a fever. It's a loving gesture.

My heart surges into my throat, a noose cutting off all the oxygen.

"Love you," Lola says.

I keep my lips on her forehead because I can't speak. All I can do is nod.

As I lift my head and exit her room, I scratch my forehead to hide my face. Then I shut off her lights and pull the door 90 percent shut.

Mow the yard.

Grease the squeaky back door.

Trim the low-hanging branch on the maple tree.

The problem is I can't make mental lists and keep going forever. After I close my bedroom door behind me and take two steps, my legs give out, and I fall to my knees, fisting my hair while shaking with silent sobs.

But they don't stay silent for long; the pain is too great. So I reach for my comforter, pull it off the bed, and wad part of it into a ball to bury my face and muffle my cries.

Angry, hate-filled, soul-snatching cries.

"Nooo . . . God . . . p-please . . . n-nooo . . ."

It's been two years since I've felt my insides ripping to pieces.

Two years since I've hated God, the world, and life in general this much.

Two years since I had to pretend that I wasn't slowly dying, all in the name of a brave face for everyone around me.

When I've let out enough emotion to put the lid back on my feelings, I drop the comforter and stare at the window through dead eyes. I can still see her climbing into my bedroom.

Her giggles.

That unstoppable smile.

And a light in her eyes so bright that I felt it in my chest.

Maren was my second chance.

My last chance.

I'll never let myself feel this way again. Everything is for Lola. Perhaps Tia wasn't trying to punish me. Maybe she was trying to protect Lola and me from this. Why risk everything again if we were lucky enough to survive it once?

But that's what I did. And I don't regret it.

Still, I'm done.

I can't find my phone; maybe I left it upstairs. When I turn the corner into the kitchen, Tia's sorting her pills into their respective slots for the week.

I reach for my phone on the counter next to her. Before I can slide it off the edge, Tia rests her hand on mine and squeezes it.

"You don't deserve this," she whispers. "No one deserves this." She turns her head to look at me, but I can't move my gaze from our hands.

Not her.

I can't cry in front of the woman who has been the bane of my existence for years. In fact, I hate that she's being kind. It feels rather cruel after everything she's put me through. I'd find it easier to deal with her lecturing me on my poor choices, bad parenting, and a litany of other grievances about me.

"I hope they find her and she's okay." Tia lifts her hand and moves it to my shoulder.

I curl my fingers around the phone and turn, escaping her touch and her pity.

When I return to my room, I sit on the end of the bed and text Taylor.

Ozzy: Have you heard anything about Maren?

Taylor: Not yet. I can check again

Ozzy: Please do

Taylor: Is there something going on between you two?

I stare at his text.

Ozzy: Yes

I wait five minutes, pacing my room.

Ten minutes.

Just as I start to type another text, my phone pings.

Taylor: They've found her location. Crews are en route

Ozzy: Any word on her condition?

I swallow hard while my eyes burn with more emotions.

Taylor: No. But you need to prepare yourself

I ever so slowly type two words—five letters and a space.

Ozzy: I know

Aircraft accidents are unforgiving. *Life* is unforgiving.

Chapter Thirty-Five

After five hours of staring at shadows on my ceiling, I get a text. It's just after three in the morning.

Taylor: Maren's alive

He starts with the good part, and I take my first full breath since Ira called me last night.

Taylor: She's been transported to the nearest level 1 trauma center

Taylor: She's in surgery. I'll update you as soon as I can

I call him.

"Hey, it's all I know for now," he says.

"Did I work on that plane?"

"Yes, but it wasn't—"

"Jesus. I worked on that plane. I worked. On. That. Fucking. Plane."

"Oz—"

"Don't say it. You don't know yet. What if I missed something? What if she—" I choke on my words as emotion burns my eyes.

"One day at a time. Okay? It could be weeks or months before we know anything for sure. Today she's alive. You are a damn good mechanic. Meticulous and thorough. Don't take the blame for this. It's way too soon. Okay?"

"Yeah," I whisper.

"Get some sleep."

I slide my phone onto my nightstand and curl into a ball on my side. She's alive. Hundreds of miles from Missoula, but alive.

Eventually, I steal an hour of sleep before jumping into the shower. When I get upstairs, dressed for work and tired as fuck, Tia and Amos greet me from the kitchen table with matching melancholic expressions. I'm sure I look just as sad to them.

"You're going to work?" Tia squints.

"Maren's alive—for now. So yeah, I'm going to work because I need to stay busy, and the people there will get the most current updates on her condition."

"Are you going to see her?" Tia asks.

I grunt, pouring coffee into my thermos. "She's in Canada."

"Is her family from here?" Suddenly, Tia seems interested in Maren, *that woman*, whose name she refused to say when she didn't want me having anything to do with her.

"No. Nebraska. I'm sure they're either there or on their way." I take a sip of my coffee before screwing the lid onto the thermos.

She continues to prod. "Have you met them?"

"No. Nebraska is a ways away. I'm not sure biking there is a good idea."

Tia frowns. "You know what I mean. They could visit her here."

"I haven't met them. Just her roommates and a few other friends. I gotta go so I can check on her cat before work."

Amos finally breaks his silence. "When are you going to tell Lola about the accident?"

"When I'm ready."

Tia frowns as I open the back door. "We'll pray for her."

I pause for a few seconds, judging her sincerity. But it doesn't matter. I don't have the emotional capacity to worry about her thoughts or opinions. "Thanks," I mumble.

When I get to work, some of my coworkers offer sympathetic smiles. I've never tried to keep my relationship with Maren a secret, but I also don't talk much about my personal life. Since the car accident, I've thrived on keeping to myself. But now I know Ira has been busy sharing my relationship status. Knowing her, these people are part of a prayer chain. She's organized them for other people.

After stuffing my backpack into my locker, I bypass the break room and get to work. By midmorning, Taylor finds me.

"Maren's out of surgery," he says.

I climb down the ladder and wipe my forehead with my sleeve. "That's good."

"She's in a coma on a ventilator."

That's not as good, but yesterday I assumed she was dead. "What happened?"

"I haven't heard much. Of course, it's under investigation, but it could take a while to come to any conclusions, especially if Maren's in a coma and unable to give us any information. However, I've heard speculation that it might have just been extreme turbulence. Other pilots reported rotor-cloud activity. Maren had just finished her last drop. It will get sorted out eventually. She's alive for now; we both know that's pretty miraculous. So let's focus on that."

I nod several times.

Alive for now.

"When were you going to tell me about you two?" he asks.

"My wife died," I say.

Taylor's brow tightens. "Yeah, I know."

"I have a daughter."

He nods.

"She was in the car accident that killed my wife and my father. That was over two years ago. And my daughter still won't get in a vehicle. And she doesn't want me to be in one either. So I'm not the tree hugger you think I am. I'm just a guy with a daughter who is struggling. I'm a private person unless you ask me about my life. So that's why you didn't know about my relationship with Maren."

Taylor continues to nod slowly. "Ozzy, I don't know what to say. I'm sorry. I feel like an asshole for not knowing this."

"Don't. It's fine," I say.

"Well, we're all concerned about Maren. Everyone at Cielo is family. I'll let you know what I know when I get any updates. Henry, Cielo's CEO, is headed to the hospital this morning to be with Maren and help her and her family in any way possible. If you need time off to go—" Taylor catches himself, pressing his lips together.

"I won't be going anywhere to see her. It would be quite the journey on a bicycle."

"I'm sorry," he whispers.

"Oz, someone at the front office is asking for you," Brady yells.

I nod and grab a rag to wipe my hands.

"If you just need time off to process—"

"I don't," I tell Taylor, brushing past him.

When I reach the main office, a dark-haired woman in a green-and-white floral sundress faces me. It's Jamie. She draws in a shaky breath and finds a sad smile. "I didn't know if you knew about Maren."

I nod. She swallows hard and blinks away the tears welling in her eyes. "Fitz is in Canada, too, working the same fire. But he hasn't been able to see her yet. Will and I have a flight there this afternoon, and her parents arrived this morning." She hands me her phone. "Give me your number. I'll keep you informed. And if you could continue looking after her place and cat, we'd be so grateful."

I should be on that plane.

I'm angry and frustrated, but I don't know who to blame.

Nobody, I suppose.

"Thank you," I murmur, entering my contact information into Jamie's phone.

"How's Lola doing with the news?"

I shake my head. "I haven't told her. I don't know what to say. So until I truly know something concrete, I think it's best not to say anything."

Jamie takes her phone and slips it into her purse. "I think that's smart. One day at a time. And today"—she glances up at me with red eyes—"our girl is alive."

"Yeah," I whisper.

Jamie steps forward and hugs me before she ducks her head, sniffles, and exits the office.

Hillary glances up from her desk. "We're all praying for her."

"Thank you."

I make it through the day. Work has lots of lists and things to focus on, as long as no one says anything to me about Maren.

After aimlessly walking around the grocery store and grabbing random items, I head to Lola's therapy appointment. Taylor texts me while I wait for her to finish.

Taylor: Maren's having another surgery after some unexpected complications. We'll know more later tonight. Hang in there

I set my phone on my thigh and rub my hands over my face.

"All done. Let's get groceries," Lola chirps on her way out of the office.

"I already picked up groceries. We can head straight home." I hold the door open for her.

"Let's go to Maren's house. When will she be home?"

"We need to get the perishable items home. Maybe another night. How was therapy? Oh!" I stop. "I was going to talk to Victoria about VR."

"I talked to her." Lola climbs onto her bike and takes off without me.

"What did she say?" I follow her.

"She said she'd look into it, but I could try it if I have a VR, which I don't."

"I bet Amazon could have one here by tomorrow," I say.

"She said I could be triggered by a game with cars crashing. I told her I knew the difference between real life and a game. She said that could be a reason VR might not work for me. But I think we should try it anyway because it sounds fun. Dakota will freak out because he's been wanting a VR headset. Do you think he could come over and play it with me?"

"We'll see."

I follow Lola into the house with the two bags of groceries. Tia is chopping lettuce and tomatoes for a salad, and Amos is grilling on the deck.

Tia stills her hand on the knife and eyes me. "Any updates on Maren?" she asks after Lola's on the deck with Amos.

"She's in surgery again. There were complications."

Tia frowns. "That's too bad."

"Yeah," I mumble, putting away the groceries.

"I think you should tell Lola."

I close the fridge. "Why?"

Tia shrugs, keeping her focus on the cutting board. "I've been thinking about it. And what if it could change everything?"

"What do you mean?"

"It could force her to let you get on a plane and fly to Canada. I don't know what the outcome will be for your friend, but wouldn't it be nice if *something* good could come from this?"

"I don't know."

Tia scrapes the pile of cut tomatoes into the salad bowl. "She's going to find out. That's just a fact. Either she's going to hear the tragic news that Maren has died, or she's going to hear that she was in an accident, but she's going to live. Let her go through this. Let Lola feel the emotions while there's still hope. She didn't get hope when Brynn died."

She's not Lola's therapist, but I can't say that I disagree with her either.

◆ ◆ ◆

After dinner, I join Lola in the backyard, where she's playing both sides of the cornhole board.

"I have something important to tell you." I pick up the red bags while she retrieves the blue ones.

"What?" She tosses one of the bags, and it slides into the hole.

"Maren's in the hospital. In Canada."

Lola spins to face me. "What happened? Is she sick?"

"She had to make an emergency landing in her plane, and she was injured."

"Is she okay?"

"She's in surgery right now. I'll know more later."

Lola's shoulders sag. "Is she going to die?"

This is where I lie? Right? I tell her no. Right?

"I don't know, Lola. I think her injuries are serious. But I'm sure they're doing their best to fix her the way the doctors fixed you after your accident."

"Will she have scars on her face like mine?"

Oh, baby girl . . . "I don't know."

"When will she be home?"

I shrug. Lola frowns.

"I would like to go see her," I say. Victoria told me to be direct with Lola as much as possible and to express my feelings so that Lola would feel free to express hers.

Lola blinks several times before shaking her head. "You can't do that. She'll be home. You'll see her when she comes home." The words and a heavy dose of panic fly out of her mouth.

I don't jump in and save her, not yet.

"You'd have to be in a car. Mom died in a car. And then you'd have to be on a plane. Maren is in the hospital because of a plane. Why would you do that? No. Maren wouldn't want you to risk your life to see her. She'll be home. We just have to be patient. Maren is going to be okay." She nods a half dozen times, wringing her dainty hands.

"What if she's not?" I might be crossing a line, but I have to know. If Maren doesn't make it, and I didn't do everything I could to get to her, I would never forgive myself.

Lola's blue eyes fill with tears, but she doesn't do the grown-up thing of hiding them. With one blink, the big drops of emotion fall down her face.

"Lola." I squat in front of her, taking her hands in mine. "If something happened to me at work, and I got hurt really badly, would you want the ambulance to take me to the hospital to save my life?"

She sniffles, blinking out a new round of tears. Her lack of an immediate answer shows me how underdeveloped her ten-year-old brain is, even if she's smart for her age. Lola can't reason this properly. My question shouldn't require much thought, but it does for her.

"The answer is yes, Lola. Of course you'd want me to go to the hospital. The same way I'd want you to go to the hospital in an ambulance if you were hurt. And if I were at the hospital, and you knew there was a chance I could die, wouldn't you want to come tell me goodbye?"

"I'd ride my bike." She pulls her hands from mine and wipes her tears, but her lower lip quivers.

"What if you couldn't? What if the hospital were too far away?"

"It . . ." She shakes her head while tugging at her hair. "It doesn't matter because it's not real. Stop making me feel bad. You promised you would never make me feel bad. You promised you would never make me get into a car. And you promised you would never get into one either."

"Lola, sometimes people have to break their promises."

She releases her hair and balls her hands at her side. "No. You don't have to break your promise. Maren's coming home. She's going to be f—"

"Lola, you don't know that!"

Lola jumps, eyes wide and refilling with tears.

I sigh, turning my back to her and lacing my fingers behind my neck as she releases tiny sobs behind me. "Lola." I turn back toward her, lowering my voice. "I love Maren. My feelings for her are like the feelings I had for your mom. It's not the way I love you. Nothing can compare to how a parent loves their child, but my love for Maren is strong. My heart hurts so much right now. And I'm not saying any of this to make you feel guilty or to pressure you into being okay with me flying to Canada to see her. If you can't handle this, if it's too much, then I won't go. And I'll never make you feel bad about it, no matter what happens to Maren. But I have to be honest by telling you I want to go, or I'll regret not having this conversation, not trying. And I've told you to live without regrets, so I must do the same."

Tears cover her red cheeks, and that adorable lip won't stop quivering. It's all very heartbreaking.

"I-is it o-okay if you d-don't go?" It's not just her lip; her whole body is shaking. "She'll b-be f-fine. I p-promise. If God w-wanted her now, H-He would have t-taken her."

I lower to my knees and wrap her tightly in my embrace. The world is big, but my world fits perfectly in my arms. She always will.

"I'll stay," I whisper in her ear.

Chapter Thirty-Six

MAREN

When I was thirteen, I got a remote-controlled airplane for Christmas. Brandon wanted to try it the following spring, and he crashed it. So my dad made him buy me another one. It took all his money and a two-hundred-dollar loan from my parents. My brother swore I'd eventually crash it too.

I didn't.

I was a natural. Dad said it was my delicate touch. Sometimes, the wind would get a hold of it as I tried to land it, and he'd say, *Gentle, Mare. Don't panic. If you panic, you'll crash. If you stay calm, you'll find a suitable place to land it. Easy. Stay calm. That's it. You've got this.*

Sometimes, that suitable place was a tree. Once, it was a pond. And more times than I could count, I landed it in a cornfield. Sure, there were a few scratches and the occasional repairs needed, but I never nose-dived the eight-hundred-dollar toy into the driveway, as Brandon had done.

Gentle, Mare.

Don't panic.

Easy. Stay calm.

You've got this.

Over my years of crop-dusting and fighting fires, I've repeatedly replayed my dad's words in my head, but now I hear his voice, and it's not in my head. I don't know where it's coming from.

"My sweet girl, you're it. You're all we have left. I know you've been hell bent on chasing Brandon, but now is not the time. This is not your time. I won't give you my blessing to leave us. Do you hear me?"

"Aaron, let her be. Let's get dinner," my mom says.

This is weird. Is it a dream? If so, why can't I see them?

"We'll be right back," Dad says.

I try to speak, but I can't. Why can't I talk?

"Hey, Maren. I have someone who wants to talk to you."

Jamie? Is that you?

"Maren, it's me, Lola. You should wake up for Bandit. He misses you. And you should come home and see your house. It's *so* beautiful. My dad and I have been working hard, and it's almost finished. Dad hung a wood swing on your front porch and a wind chime I picked out. It has butterflies. Tomorrow, we're going to replace some old boards on the tree house. I can't wait for you to see everything. So you just need to open your eyes. I know it's scary. I was scared after my accident, but it's okay. You've got this."

You've got this . . .

"Dad, say something," Lola says.

"Hey, beautiful. The swing was supposed to be a surprise." Ozzy chuckles. "But Lola's right, you need to open your eyes. The world is an infinitely better place with you in it." He sounds different. Nervous? Scared?

Don't they know I'm trying to open my eyes? I don't understand why I can't see or speak, but I can hear.

"Oh, Lola wanted me to tell you that we're making a carrot cake with pineapple, of course. But since we're in Missoula, we need you to come home to eat it. Okay? It's time to open your eyes and come—" Ozzy's voice cracks.

"It's okay, Dad," Lola whispers.

Ozzy clears his throat. "Come home. I love you."

Why am I not home?

Everything fades like I'm falling asleep, but when I wake up, I'm not really awake. I come in and out of this peculiar state without awareness of time or space. I feel people touching me, but I can't move. It's frustrating. I get angry, but then everything fades. It always fades.

"Get the doctor," my mom yells. "The shades. Get the shades, Aaron. It's too bright in here for her eyes. Maren, can you hear me?" She squeezes my hand. "Sweetie," she cries.

She's messing with me and being too loud. I can't talk, and when I move, more people touch me, people I don't recognize, shining light in my eyes and *messing with me!*

"Maren, I need you to calm down. Try to relax."

Who's that? Why? What's happening?

"Maren, you have a tube down your throat. Stay calm; I'm going to remove it," a dark-haired woman in blue scrubs and a white lab coat says to me while my parents cling to each other behind her. "I need you to take a deep breath and exhale or cough as I pull it out. Okay?"

I cough, pressing a hand to my throat. It. Hurts.

Leave me alone. Stop messing with me!

I repeatedly fade away as people come in and out of view, some with smiles, others with pinched brows and tiny frowns. After a few days and lots of tests, I'm more aware of my surroundings, calmer, and able to talk.

The doctor proceeds to explain my injuries and the surgeries to stop the internal bleeding. Aside from two broken ribs, a dislocated shoulder, and a slew of lacerations, I'm in one piece and expected to make a full recovery, as long as I remain stable over the next few days.

When she exits the room, my parents breathe a collective sigh and converge on me.

"I'm in Canada?" I ask with a scratchy voice, adjusting the oxygen tube in my nose with my right hand since my left arm is in a sling for my broken collarbone.

Dad chuckles, rubbing my hand. "Yes. You've been here for a couple weeks, and you've been pretty upset the past few days coming out of your coma."

"Where's Ozzy and Lola? They came to Canada?"

My mom shakes her head, eyes narrowed.

"I heard them."

"You heard them? In your coma?" Dad asks.

I nod.

"Jamie called them and put them on speakerphone," Mom says, sitting on the edge of my bed.

"They must be worried," I whisper.

"We all were." My mom touches my cheek.

"But Lola lost her mom. Ozzy lost his wife." I touch my neck and clear my throat.

Mom frowns. "We lost Brandon."

My heart feels like it's being squeezed. I'm so insensitive. It's not that I forgot about Brandon. I just can't think straight. "I know," I murmur. "I'm sorry."

Mom wipes her eyes. "Please don't apologize. You're alive. That's all that matters. That's all that will ever matter."

"Did Jamie go home?" I ask.

Dad nods. "She stayed a week. Will was here for several days. And Fitz has been by twice. Your boss was here for the first two days. He's paying for our hotel, but one of us is always here."

"Jamie started a group text, so I have Ozzy's number if you want to call him." Mom holds out her phone.

I stare at it before nodding and taking it from her.

"We'll take a walk and give you some privacy." She pats my arm and nods toward the door while eyeing my dad.

"Be right back, sweetie," he says, following her out of the room.

I press the green button and put it on speaker.

"Hey, Colleen," Ozzy says.

"It's me," I say with a weak voice. "Maren."

"Jesus," he whispers.

"I, uh, woke up."

Nothing.

"Ozzy?"

The call ends.

I stare at the screen for a few seconds before calling him back. It goes straight to his voicemail. He's probably trying to call me at the same time that I'm trying to call him, so I just hold the phone, gazing at the screen, waiting for him to call.

Nothing.

I give up and call him again. And again, it goes to his voicemail. "Hey, it's Maren. I don't know why we got cut off. Call me."

I need to call Jamie, Fitz, and Will, but I don't want to be on the phone when Ozzy calls back. So I wait.

And wait.

Eventually, my parents return.

"How'd it go? Was he shocked?" Mom asks before taking a sip of her bottled water.

"We got cut off. I don't know if it's an international calling issue or what."

"But you talked to him?" Dad asks.

"Yes. I mean, he answered. I said it was me. He whispered 'Jesus,' and then it ended. And I haven't been able to reach him since then, and when I call him, it goes straight to his voicemail."

My parents exchange confused looks before returning their attention to me.

"Well, I have a list of people I've been sending updates to, including Taylor Reynolds. He works with Ozzy, right?" Mom asks.

I nod, scrolling through her texts with my good hand until I find Taylor.

Colleen: Maren is awake. She's having trouble reaching Ozzy. Can you have him call her?

For now, I avoid the "Hey, it's me, not Colleen" part. I just want Ozzy to call me back before I call anyone else.

Taylor: That's amazing! Give her a hug from me. I'll find Ozzy

I give his reply a heart.

"We talked with your doctor on our way out to take a walk," Dad says. "Dr. Haze said if you don't have any setbacks, you could go home in a week or less."

I try to show my excitement, but I can't focus on anything but Ozzy right now.

Taylor: Ozzy wasn't feeling well. He went home. I think it hit him hard. He might need some time. Let her know he's just really overwhelmed. I'm sure he'll contact her soon. Everyone is elated and grateful that she's awake. Thanks for the update

Mom glances at the screen. "Oh, Maren." She kisses my forehead. "It's okay. I know it's hard for you to see things through his eyes right now, but I'm sure he's been running on adrenaline. Every time Jamie put you on speaker for him and Lola to talk to you, my heart broke. He had the saddest voice. Give him a minute to process."

I stare at the message from Taylor, rereading it. "Process me being alive?" I whisper.

She lifts my chin with her finger until I look at her. "Process you not dying."

"Same thing," I mumble.

Mom furrows her brow. "No. It's not the same. And I know this because *I'm* still running on adrenaline fumes, but I know when it's my turn to go back to the hotel for the first time since knowing you're going to live, I will completely fall apart." She fights the emotion pooling in her eyes as she swallows hard, keeping her jaw locked while putting on her best smile.

"Mom—"

She quickly shakes her head and steps back, holding up a finger like she used to do when I got a warning for doing something wrong. "Not yet. You need to let me walk out of here without my eyes swollen shut. So we're going to talk about your dad's upcoming colonoscopy appointment or your uncle Jeff's grumbling over watching the farm for us while we're here. We can even talk about the election or the new manager of Quick Fuel, who likes to ruffle your dad's feathers by flirting with me. Pick your non-coma topic."

I open my mouth to speak but stop before my words come to life. My friends and family were preparing to say their final goodbyes. There's nothing I can say other than that must have been awful.

"I'd like to know more about the new manager at Quick Fuel," I say with a smile.

Dad rolls his eyes, and the tension melts from my mom's shoulders. I'm going to let her leave here without swollen eyes. We don't have to celebrate my recovery until everyone is done mourning the trauma. My scars will be superficial. Theirs are much deeper and may never fully fade.

My parents each share very different accounts of the flirtatious manager. Then I use Mom's phone to notify everyone else that I'm awake while Dad gets dinner for us. I don't eat much, but I'm sure that will change in the coming days.

"Go. Both of you," I say through a yawn.

"I'll stay," Dad says.

"No. I'm fine. Go. Please."

They look at each other and then at me. I make a shooing motion with my hand.

"If you're sure," Mom says.

"I'm sure. But before you go, can I see your phone again?"

She hands it to me, and I text Ozzy.

Colleen: It's me. Maren. Before my mom leaves with her phone, I want you to know I love you. And I'm SO sorry I put you and Lola through this kind of hell. I might go home next week. Take all the time you need and hug Lola for me. x Maren

I wait for a minute until the message changes from *delivered* to *read.*

He doesn't reply. I know it should be okay. Yes, he needs time to process. But that doesn't make it *feel* okay. That doesn't make it hurt any less.

Chapter Thirty-Seven

OZZY

"I'm an asshole," I say to Diego while we sit in lawn chairs, drinking beer and watching Kai and Lola ride scooters up and down the sidewalk.

It's been five days since Maren came out of her coma.

"You're human," he says.

"Humans are assholes."

Diego chuckles. "Undoubtedly."

"Tia thinks I need therapy, which is odd coming from her because she's not a fan of it. So I must be really messed up for her to suggest it."

"Let me save you some money," he says. "How did you feel when Maren called you?"

I laugh, shaking my head. "We're not doing this."

"Come on, humor me."

I roll the bottom of the beer bottle on my leg, eyeing Kai's black hair, blowing like ribbons in the air, just like Lola's. "I couldn't breathe."

"Why?"

I shake my head. Diego is not a therapist. This is stupid. Yet I keep answering him. "Because I felt guilty for putting Lola in a position to get hurt like that again. And I swore I would never do it again once we let Maren go because she wasn't going to wake up. She'd lost so much blood. They restarted her heart multiple times. She was in a coma for three weeks. We were going to say our goodbyes. End of story."

"But she didn't die," Diego says.

I nod slowly.

"Are you upset that she didn't die?" he asks in an incredulous tone.

"Of course not," I mumble. "But how can I risk Lola going through this again?"

"So what are you going to do? Dump her when she gets home? Now *that* would make you an asshole."

"Or a good father."

Diego grunts. "You've said it yourself. Lola adores her. How do you think she'll react to you walking away after all that Maren's been through?"

"How do you think Maren will react when Lola never wants her to fly again?"

Diego sets his bottle on the ground and laces his hands behind his head. "What makes you think Maren will ever want to get into a plane again?"

"Because it's in her blood. Like cops who take a bullet or firefighters who get burned, Maren will recover and go back to work."

"But *if* she didn't fly again, would that make a difference for you?"

"Yes. I'd have to deal with two traumatized women instead of one." I smirk because humor is my escape.

"I know you won't walk away."

I glance at him. "How do you *know* that?"

"It's the blow job."

"Fuck you," I mumble, shoving him until his chair begins to tip over. Diego catches himself while cackling.

When his laughter settles and my grin fades, I blow out a long breath. "I worked on her plane."

Diego doesn't look at me; he just slowly shakes his head. "Fuck."

I nod.

"You know there's a good chance it had nothing to do with the plane."

Again, I nod, but I don't know if I've truly convinced myself that it might not be my fault.

I check my watch. "I need to go feed the cat. And Lola wants to make Maren a welcome home cake before she arrives tomorrow."

"That should be a fun reunion. I can't imagine anything feeling at all awkward just because you've ghosted her since she woke up from a coma."

"The awkwardness will be short lived. We won't stay long. Jamie said Maren's parents will be with her. They're staying until she's fully recovered, or at least her mom is." I wish my confidence matched my words. I am scared out of my mind that everything is my fault. What if the reality is that I'm a bad dad, a shitty boyfriend, and an unreliable mechanic?

"So you're meeting her parents for the first time after coma ghosting."

I stand. "Shut up, man." I chuckle. "And I've talked with them on video calls, so it's not really a first-time introduction."

"Yeah, but they liked you then. Now they'll find you unworthy of their daughter. Awkward."

"Lola will be a good buffer. Everyone loves her." I toss my empty beer bottle and put on my helmet. "Lola, let's go."

"Five more minutes," she yells, zooming past the driveway with Kai behind her.

"Five seconds," I counter. "Later," I say to Diego.

"Let me know how it goes."

I head down the sidewalk. "I will."

"Dad! Wait!" Lola ditches the scooter in the yard and flies onto her bike to chase after me. "Bye, Kai!"

Maren's plane arrives Sunday afternoon. Lola insists we make a cake instead of buying one. Given the ninety-degree weather, I agree. Transporting a cake in this heat wouldn't end well.

So carrot cake with pineapple it is.

"*Welcome home* is too long to fit on the cake." Lola frowns while assessing the round cake as I fill the plastic bag to pipe the message in cream cheese frosting.

"It is if I let you do it."

"But I want her to know that I did it. So it has to be something I can do."

I shrug. "Then what do you think it should say?"

Lola cocks her head, eyeing the cake. "Hmm, it should be something nice. Maybe 'We love you.' It's short and sweet."

"You think it should say that?"

Lola nods a half dozen times. "Yeah. I mean, we love her. Right?"

Here I am, in another pickle.

After a few seconds, I nod and hand her the bag with a small hole in the corner. "You must keep pressure on it the whole time, or you'll have choppy letters."

"I know. I've done this with Nana on cupcakes."

"You weren't trying to spell anything on those cupcakes."

I don't know why I'm surprised, but I am, as Lola perfectly writes *We Love You* on the cake.

"Do you think she'll like everything?" Lola hands me the bag and licks her fingers while gazing at the room.

We have a **Welcome Home** sign, fresh-picked wildflowers in sets of six, balloons, and a stuffed teddy bear.

"I think she'll love it," I say, even if she's not going to love me so much because I'm a human asshole afraid of fucking up my daughter, my future, and my whole life.

Forty-five minutes later, two vehicles pull into the driveway. Fitz, Jamie, Will, Maren, and her parents climb out and make their way to the front door. My heart tries to break through my chest, one pounding beat at a time.

Emotions burn my eyes, but I fight like hell to keep my composure. I'm seeing the woman I never thought I'd see again. It's as emotionally unsettling as it would be if Brynn stepped out of a car in the driveway.

Lola can't wait. We planned to yell surprise when they entered the door, but she bolts into the yard.

"Lola!" I rush toward the door. I don't want her tackling Maren with her uncontrolled excitement.

Jamie must have the same thought because she steps in front of Maren and holds up her hands to Lola. "Be very gentle, okay? She has some broken bones."

Lola nods as Jamie steps aside and lets Lola wrap her arms around Maren, being careful of her sling. Maren runs her hands lovingly through Lola's hair.

"Fuck," I mumble, stepping back and hiding behind the door while I wipe my pathetic teary eyes. "Get your shit together." I give myself a quick pep talk and come out of hiding just as everyone makes their way up the porch stairs.

Maren has scabs on her face and moves slower than usual.

"Look at the swing," she says.

"It's so fun! Do you want to sit on it with me?" Lola asks.

"Maybe later," I say, stepping into view with my brave face. "Lola, let's let Maren get settled. I'm sure it's been a long travel day."

Maren shifts her blue-eyed gaze to me. It's a soft look and an easy smile, yet it pierces my chest.

Drawing in a long breath, I smile. "Welcome home."

She doesn't speak. She doesn't move.

"Nice to meet you in person," her dad says, offering his hand. I shake it.

Then her mom smiles and walks right into me for a hug. "Good to see you, Ozzy," she says, as if we've hugged before.

"Come see what's inside!" Lola leads the way.

Maren's parents, Jamie, Will, and Fitz step past me into the house with slight nods and smiles. They're leaving us alone. I don't know if it's by plan or by chance.

Foolish words line up on the tip of my tongue because this isn't a moment for which one can rehearse.

Glad you're alive.

Thanks for not dying.

I should have known better than to fall in love with you.

I didn't call you back, because I've been busy.

What's up?

Did you have a good flight?

Maren takes two slow steps toward me and leans forward, resting her good hand and cheek on my chest.

Not one word.

I close my eyes and slide one hand along her back while my other cradles the side of her head.

She's warm.

She's slowly breathing.

She's here.

She's alive.

"Are you coming inside?" she finally says in a soft voice, taking a step back as I angle my body away from her and pinch the bridge of my nose, but the fucking tears won't retreat.

"Yeah. Uh, just give me a minute."

Her fingers brush my other hand as she steps past me to the door. "I'll give you all the time you need."

I swallow past the lump in my throat and get it together. My experience with love has been extreme. The bigger the love, the greater the pain. And I don't know if it's worth it, because it fucking hurts to love someone this much.

When I reenter the house, Lola shows Maren the cake and the gifts. Maren gives Lola a one-armed hug, and I think she might cry after reading the *We Love You*. But then she lets her gaze drift to other things, all the things I did to her house while she was working and trying to die on me.

The newly remodeled kitchen.

The refinished wood floors.

The fresh paint.

We make eye contact, and she mouths, *Thank you.*

"Sit down, Maren." Her mom guides her to the sofa while her dad inspects my workmanship.

The next hour is a blur of echoey conversations and occasional glances from Maren as she eats cake and listens to Lola talk her ear off. Will has to leave before his cat allergy kills him, and Fitz and Jamie head to dinner.

"We're ordering pizza. Are you and Lola staying?" Colleen asks. "We'd love it if you would."

"I have work in the morning. And Maren won't get any rest if I don't get my daughter out of here."

"Dad!" Lola rolls her eyes. Of course she's listening when I don't need her to hear me.

"It's true. Maren needs rest to continue healing." I playfully tug her long hair.

Lola huffs a long sigh. "Fine. Bye, Maren. We'll be back tomorrow. Right, Dad?" She kneels on the sofa next to Maren and hugs her.

I avert my gaze when Maren eyes me over Lola's shoulder. "We'll see," I murmur.

"We can't thank you enough for everything you and Lola have done around here," Aaron says, shaking my hand again.

"No thank-you necessary." I smile.

"I hear you ride a bike," Colleen says to Lola. "Can you show Aaron and me your bike?" Again, I feel like her mom wants to give us time alone.

I'm not ready to be alone with her. Just a few minutes on the porch were plenty awkward. The guilt and shame are eating me alive, and I'm not emotionally ready or equipped to deal with it tonight.

"It's just a bike," Lola says with a shrug that makes Aaron and Colleen chuckle. "But sure. I'll show you my bike."

When they're out the door, I face the sofa and stuff my hands into my front jeans pockets. "I have some explaining to do, but I don't think tonight is the right time."

Maren slowly shakes her head. "You don't owe me an explanation. Has your silence hurt? Yes. But my feelings are not your problem," she says so calmly, so full of unspoken understanding, I can't help but feel unworthy of being part of her life. "And I *love* how everything looks. It's beautiful. The flowers, Ozzy." She blinks the emotion from her eyes. "The fucking flowers." Shaking her head, she sniffles and swallows hard. "Thank you." She tries to change the subject with flowers.

And maybe that's for the best, but it feels wrong. I don't deserve an out.

"What I did was unforgivable," I say.

She winces. "No, Ozzy. Something terrible happened, and you were just trying to survive. And that's all I was trying to do. It doesn't have to be pretty. The anger I felt has faded. And when I saw you step out onto the porch, it no longer mattered."

"I was weak," I whisper.

"You're anything but weak."

I stare at the ceiling and exhale a slow breath. "I have never felt so helpless in my life. Hundreds of miles away with nothing but a bike, the memories of Brynn's death, and a child who broke down when I begged her to let me go see you." I drop my gaze as tears trail down Maren's cheeks.

She doesn't try to hide them or wipe them away as Bandit jumps onto her lap.

"I have . . ." I shake my head, pressing my lips together while I find the words. "I have so many emotions that don't all fit together and make sense."

Maren nods, sliding her fingertips along her tearstained cheeks as she sniffles. "I'll be here ready to listen. And I don't care if your emotions make sense. I don't think a lot of things in life make sense. Maybe our love doesn't make sense, but I love you nonetheless."

Why does she have to be so kind?

I glance out the front window at Lola.

"Thank you for everything you've done to my house. It's more beautiful than I imagined." She repeats her gratitude as if working on her house makes up for ignoring her.

"I worked on that plane."

Maren's smile deflates, eyes narrowed as if she's not following my sudden shift in topic. "Ozzy, I don't think it was the plane. From what I've been told, there was rotor turbulence. And I was on my way back. They were grounding everyone. And I don't remember everything, but I do remember turbulence."

"Taylor said they don't know the cause and might not know for weeks. And Jamie said you didn't remember much when you came out of your coma. So how can you say it wasn't the plane when everyone knows you're a very skilled pilot?"

"You're a very skilled mechanic. *And* you don't travel with me, so you're not the last person to inspect the plane before I fly."

I know what she's saying is true, but I hate feeling so helpless.

"Lola's not going to want you to fly again," I say.

Maren keeps her gaze on Bandit as he purrs on her lap. "I know," she murmurs.

"But you're going to do it anyway, aren't you?"

She lifts her gaze to mine and nods. "I'm going to do it for myself. I'm going to do it for all the other pilots I work with. And I'm going to do it so Lola can see that not all tragedy ends in death. This accident wasn't an epiphany. It was a risk I take with my job."

I understand, but Lola will not. And that will put me in the middle of an impossible situation. "I'd better go," I whisper, but I don't know whether to step toward her or the door.

Maren gives me a sad smile as if she can read my mind. "Whatever you're feeling is okay. Maybe I'm not the only one who still needs to heal."

"I love you," I say because I don't think I can ever leave her again without saying it.

She frowns. "But?"

I shake my head while deciding I need my next step to be toward her. "No buts." Kneeling before her, I rest my hands on her legs, forcing Bandit to jump off the sofa. "I love you, even if it scares me to death. The only thing that scares me more is trying not to love you. But I have to come to terms with the fear that kept me from being there for you. I feel ashamed, guilty, and embarrassed."

"Ozzy," she says, pressing her hand to my cheek while her head tilts.

Closing my eyes, I lean into her touch and turn my head so my lips press to her wrist. "You have to let me work through this without feeling the need to make it better for me." I open my eyes and lean forward until our mouths are a breath apart.

She traces my bottom lip with the pad of her thumb.

"You just need to get better. Okay? And I'm here for you. I'm not abandoning you," I say with a smile. "Lola wouldn't let me."

Maren smiles, and my willpower dissolves as I kiss her. I want nothing more than something easy again. Life was easy before Brynn died.

Normal was easy.

Everything since she died seems to come with a warning or an asterisk.

Lola's alive, *but* . . .

I can go back to work, *but* . . .

An amazing woman has come into my life, *but* . . .

"I'm sorry that nothing about my life is easy. I'm sorry that I'm struggling at the worst possible time." I brush my lips against hers. "But make no mistake about it, I'm so fucking grateful that you're sitting here with me."

I have to make things right. She deserves better than the man I've been these past few weeks. I don't know how I'm going to do it, but I *have* to be a better man for her.

Chapter Thirty-Eight

"I'm going to ask Victoria to discuss Maren with you this week," I tell Lola when I tuck her into bed.

It's been a week since I've seen Maren. I've texted her daily to see how she's feeling, but I've let her spend time alone with her parents.

Who am I kidding?

I've been a coward, making up excuses to Lola for why we can't visit her. I know her friends have visited. That's what good people do.

I'm an asshole.

"Why do I need to talk to her about Maren?" Lola adjusts her pillow.

"Because you should discuss how it will make you feel when Maren returns to work."

"What do you mean?" She narrows her eyes.

"Maren's a pilot. When she's better, she'll get back in a plane and fight fires because that's her job."

Lola rolls her eyes. "No, she won't."

I brush her hair away from her face. "Why do you think that?" I know the answer, and that's why I need her to discuss it with Victoria.

"Because she almost died in a plane. Why would she do it again?"

I keep my hand on the side of her head. "Because people with risky jobs know that their job doesn't end just because something goes wrong."

"I'm going to talk to her."

I shake my head. "Maren is not your mom. We care about her—"

"We love her." Lola lifts her chin.

I sigh. "We love her but can't tell her what to do with her life. I *need* you to understand this. The whole reason you're in therapy is because fearing something to the point that it disrupts your life is no way to live. If Maren were scared to get back in a plane, she'd probably see a therapist too. And she may see one before she flies again just to ensure she's ready to be in the air once more. But that's her life. Not ours."

Lola's frown deepens. "Do *you* want her to fly again?"

This girl keeps me in check—too much. She's the living, breathing definition of accountability.

Cheyenne once said Lola is an indigo child with high intelligence, intuition, and empathy that can heal humanity.

I need to believe that she's right.

"No. The selfish part of me wants to hold her in my arms and never let her leave the ground again. But I'm a grown-up, and I must love her how she deserves to be loved."

"How does she deserve to be loved?"

I smile. "Like I want nothing more than to watch her soar."

"Like a bird?"

I nod.

Lola twists her lips, and lines of concentration etch her forehead. "When I'm a grown-up, I won't be as scared."

I kiss her head and stand. "You will be; you'll just learn to let love burn through those thick clouds of fear."

She grins. "And every day will be sunny."

I chuckle, shaking my head. "You're so smart. Too smart, just like your mom was."

I take my own advice on love and sneak out after everyone's in bed.

When I get to Maren's house, all the lights are off. So I retrieve the ladder (my ladder) from her garage and position it beneath Maren's bedroom on the second floor. And I do this with six dandelions held between my teeth.

A dim light shines when I get to the top of the ladder. I think it's the TV, but I can't tell, because the blinds are closed.

Sliding my phone from my pocket, I carefully type a text without dropping it.

Ozzy: Are you asleep?

Maren: I'm watching Jimmy Fallon

Maren: What are you doing?

Ozzy: I'm outside your window, trying not to fall off the ladder

Seconds later, Maren opens the blinds, eyes wide. "What are you doing?" she says, sliding up the window with her good arm.

"Sneaking around," I mumble over the dandelions while climbing into her bedroom.

Something between satisfaction and pride swells in my chest when I notice her wearing my T-shirt.

"My parents are across the hallway." She nods toward her door and suppresses a giggle while I hand her the flowers.

"I figured. That's why I said I'm *sneaking* around."

Her hair is messy and damp, as if she showered before bed. She sets the flowers on the nightstand and turns. "What are you doing?" she asks while I slide my finger along my phone's screen.

"Setting an alarm for four in the morning, so I'm out of here before your parents wake up, and I can get home before anyone at my house wakes."

Her smile doubles. "You're here to spend the night with me?"

I shrug off my T-shirt and remove my shorts. "I am." I gesture toward the bed with my chin.

Maren eases into bed, reclining onto the pillows stacked for her injured collarbone. She winces a bit, and I know it's her broken ribs.

"Close your eyes," I say, lying on my side next to her.

She narrows them. "Why?"

"Because I want to say some things, and it won't go well if you're looking at me."

Her gaze sweeps across my face before she turns toward the ceiling, closes her eyes, and whispers, "Okay."

I rest my hand low on her stomach, fingers splayed across her soft flesh. And I relish the feel of her warm body and the floral scent of her hair. "I prepared myself to lose you," I say. "To grieve you. To help Lola deal with another awful blow."

Maren rests her hand over mine, squeezing it.

"But you didn't die. And those feelings didn't vanish when you came out of your coma. Even if your death wasn't real, my feelings over losing you were. So I've needed to mourn your near death for my heart to reconcile all of those emotions and recalibrate to the reality that you're still alive and hopefully not dying anytime soon. I've had to find a way to navigate my feelings about love and loss while somehow leading Lola through another tragedy, even if the outcome has been different. Everything about Brynn's death came rushing back when I heard your plane went down. So my feelings have been . . ."

"Messy," she whispers.

"Yeah." I lift onto my elbow and kiss the corner of her mouth. "And now, the only messy feeling I have is regret about my messy feelings because tonight, I had a long talk with Lola about *grown-up* love. And in the middle of my speech, I knew it wasn't for her. It was for me. And for the past two weeks, I've let fear dictate how I love you. And I don't ever want to do that again."

Silence settles between us, and a few tears stain her cheeks. "If you asked me to stop flying, I would," she whispers. "I'd do it to be with you and Lola because I don't think I'll look back on the most memorable moments in life and see the sky. I think I'll see you and Lola."

Well, fuck. I'm not going to get emotional, even if she's bringing me to my proverbial knees. However, I need a few seconds to catch my breath. "I would never ask you to stop flying."

She slides her fingers between mine. "I know," she whispers. "But you need to know that I would."

With Maren in my life, it never feels like the right time to think of Brynn. But right now, I hope she knows that I've found someone special. Someone who loves our daughter.

Maren's body relaxes as she falls asleep beside me. And I blink, releasing the tears I've held since she arrived home from Canada. I still don't know how everything will work out, but I have to believe it will.

It has to.

Chapter Thirty-Nine

MAREN

Good morning.
Take it easy today.
The coolest biker in the world loves you.
Ozzy x

I grin at the note Ozzy scrawled on the inside of my bedroom door with a permanent marker. He knows stage two of the renovation will be upstairs, including new doors. However, now I will have to keep this door because it's where he's written his first official love note to me.

"There's our favorite girl," Dad says after I gingerly make my way to the kitchen, where my parents are making breakfast and coffee.

"The bar has been set low," I say as my mom kisses me on the cheek.

"Speaking of setting the bar low," she says. "Did a boy crawl in through your window last night?" She smirks, handing me a cup of coffee to carry to my sofa.

"A *boy*? What am I? Fourteen?"

"Well, only teenagers would crawl in and out of windows," she says, cracking eggs into a bowl. If she only knew that sneaking around and crawling in and out of windows are our thing—a Maren-and-Ozzy thing.

"He was so quiet. How did you know?"

My parents laugh. "We are all knowing," Mom says. "If you're ever a parent, you'll have this superpower too."

I hum and nod.

"Speaking of parents and kids, Lola seems pretty taken with you." My mom eyes me over her shoulder while whisking the eggs.

"I love Lola."

"Like you love carrot cake?" she asks, returning her attention to the stove.

"Like I'd love my own child."

Both my parents whip their heads in my direction.

"Are you ready for this?" Mom asks.

I laugh. "Loving Lola?"

"You nearly died because of your job. Is it fair to that young girl for you to be the woman in her life who loves her like a mother after her mother died in a car accident?"

"It will make her more resilient," Dad says, cubing the last mango.

"Aaron!" Mom punches his arm. "That's a terrible thing to say. When children lose their parents, it doesn't toughen them up like letting them fall off their bikes and scrape their knees."

"What if I don't die?" I say, bringing their attention back to me. "What if I do my job, and it doesn't kill me? What if I live for a century and die of old age? Because that's a possibility, too, right?"

Mom focuses on the eggs in the frying pan, slowly stirring them. "You're right."

I cup my hand at my ear. "I'm sorry, what did you say?"

"If you didn't hear it the first time, too bad. I'm not repeating it."

I laugh. "You said I'm right. Has hell frozen over? Are pigs flying?"

"Have you shown Ozzy this charming side of you?" Mom carries a plate of eggs and fruit to me.

"Ozzy has seen all of my sides," I say with an ornery grin.

"That is an example of something your parents don't want to know." She frowns, setting the plate on my wooden lap desk.

"Thank you," I say just as the doorbell rings. "Jamie's early."

"She is. I'll make more eggs," Mom says on her way to the door.

"Trust me, Jamie's already been up for three hours baking muffins, hiking, and cleaning her house." I laugh.

"It's not Jamie," Mom murmurs while unlocking the storm door.

"Who is—" I start to speak when Lola steps into the entry and removes her bike helmet and shoes.

"Good morning." She shrugs off her backpack and pulls out a white sack. "I brought doughnuts."

I peek over my shoulder out the front window. "Hey, Lola. Did your dad take the day off?" I search for him, but I only see her bike.

"No. He's working."

"We have eggs and fruit. Would you like some?" Mom asks Lola.

"Lola, who came here with you?" I inspect her as she roams to the kitchen.

"Uh, I came by myself. It's fine." She sets the bag on the counter as my mom spoons eggs and fruit onto a plate. "My dad's at work, and my grandparents think I'm playing the new VR I got. So I can't stay long, but I wanted to bring you doughnuts." She hands me a jelly-filled one.

I set it on my plate, returning a nervous smile. "This is nice of you, but nobody knows where you are, and you don't have permission to ride to my house. If your grandparents look for you and can't find you, they'll be worried sick."

"Trust me. It's fine." She climbs onto the stool at the counter where my mom sets her plate of food.

Mom smiles at Lola before padding toward me with wide eyes and a stiff smile. "Do you need me to get your phone so you can text someone?" she asks under her breath.

"Yes. Thanks. It's on my dresser."

"What grade will you be in, Lola?" Dad asks.

"Fifth," Lola mumbles after taking a bite of her doughnut.

"What's VR?" He narrows his eyes at her.

Lola giggles at my dad's question. "It's virtual reality. It's a headset I wear, and things look real. It's so cool. It was Maren's idea."

Dad shoots me a look.

"It's to simulate being in a car again. How's that working for you, Lola?"

"It's fun. But I know it's not real."

Mom returns with my phone.

"You're not calling my dad, are you?" Lola doesn't miss a thing.

"Lola, I need to let him know where you are."

"You can't. He'll be mad. And I'm fine. I wore my helmet. I looked both ways when crossing streets. And I didn't talk to strangers."

"You stopped for doughnuts," I say with a frown.

"That's different. The people who work there have seen me a lot, so they're not real strangers."

"What if I let your dad know you're here and ask him if it's okay for you to stay until he gets off work?"

She licks the frosting off her lips before twisting them. "Hmm, then he'll know I rode my bike here. But I think it would be fun to stay today." She shakes her head. "No. I can't risk him finding out."

My parents eye me while standing at the counter, eating their breakfast.

Maren: Thank you for the love note. I'm never replacing the door

It takes a few minutes for Ozzy to reply.

Ozzy: How are you feeling?

Maren: Conflicted

Ozzy: ?

Maren: Someone rode her bike to my house but she doesn't want me to tell on her. So I'm conflicted

Ozzy: WTF? Why would they let her do that? I have to call them

Maren: If you're talking about her grandparents, they don't know

Ozzy: I'm going to kill her

Maren: What if you don't? What if you let her stay here for the day and stop by to get her after work?

Ozzy: I'm so sorry

Maren: Don't be. I'm looking forward to spending the day with her

Ozzy sends me the unamused emoji.

I send him the kiss emoji.

"You need groceries. Will you be okay if your dad and I go shopping for you?" Mom asks.

"I can watch her," Lola says like such a grown-up.

My parents have to suppress their snickering.

"That would be great," I say. It would give me some time alone with Lola.

Maren: Don't forget to tell her grandparents

Ozzy: I just did. Thx

When my parents leave, Lola sits beside me on the sofa, playing with Bandit. "I should get home."

"Actually, you're spending the day with me," I say.

Lola freezes, except for her eyes, which shift her gaze to me. "You told him?"

"I had to, because it's more important that he and your grandparents know you're safe than it is for you not to get into trouble."

"Did you at least tell him not to ground me?"

"I didn't, but if you help out today, I'll put in a good word for you when he gets here after work."

"Are you going to fly again?" She changes the subject so quickly that it takes my brain a few seconds to catch up.

"I'm planning on it."

Lola drops her chin and traces the stripes on Bandit's back. "Aren't you afraid of crashing again?"

"Sure. I always have a tiny fear, but I love my job. I love flying."

"Aren't you afraid of dying?" she murmurs.

"I don't want to die. Not yet, anyway. But I'm not afraid of it. However, there is nothing wrong with being afraid of dying. It's a normal human fear. And honestly, there are a lot of pilots who don't get back in a plane if it goes down, and they live to tell about it."

"Like me not riding in cars anymore?"

"Yes. Like that." I put my good arm around her. "But I think you will ride in cars again."

"You do?"

I rest the side of my head on top of hers. "Yes. The car accident sent you on a detour. And that's okay. I can only imagine losing your mom at such a young age has left you feeling scared. But I see who you really are—a brave and strong girl. And I *know*, without a doubt, that one day you will be too big for Missoula. Your wings will spread, and your heart will need to soar. And this fear you have now will be too weak for your need to really live life."

Lola lifts her gaze with a glimmer of hope in her eyes. "Do you think I'll be able to fly like you?"

If there was any doubt that I'd fly again, it's officially gone. Lola's looking at me like I'm a prophet of her future. I want to fill every inch of her with hope. If I can inspire her to dream without limits, I'll happily take any risk to make that happen.

"You know what would be cool?"

"What?" Her eyes get nearly as big as her smile.

"If someday, you, me, and your dad flew somewhere special. Just the three of us."

She bites her lower lip, and I see the worry winning. It's heartbreaking.

"Not today. When you're ready, and you will be. We need to decide where we're going to celebrate when that day comes because you, my dear"—I playfully grab her chin—"are a caterpillar shedding your skin, growing and growing, and one day you're going to be—"

"A butterfly." Her whole face lights up.

I fight the burning emotion in my eyes. "A *beautiful* butterfly."

Chapter Forty

OZZY

Yet again, I'm in a pickle.

I'm mad that Lola rode her bike to Maren's house, but I'm grateful to Maren for suggesting Lola spend the day with her.

"Your daughter is such a joy."

I glance up while removing my helmet. When I pulled into the driveway, I missed Aaron sitting on the porch swing with reading glasses low on his nose and a book on his lap.

"Yes. She's quite joyous when she's not sneaking out of the house." I chuckle.

Aaron nods, removing his glasses. "She reminds me so much of Maren."

"Yeah?" I climb the porch stairs and lean my shoulder against the post.

"Maren used to push all the limits. Question everything. And she tried to grow up too quickly. And the eye-rolling . . ."

I laugh. "I swear Lola's eyes will roll right out of her head someday. Everything warrants the utmost drama."

"Maren used to stick her tongue out and razz me so much, I threatened to cut the thing out of her mouth." Aaron shakes his head.

I smile because I like imagining young Maren.

"She and her brother were thick as thieves. And when we lost him, I worried that we'd lose her too. Maybe not physically, but emotionally. For a while, her light was gone. And we got used to her not being fully herself. After all, we've never been the same since losing Brandon. Looking in the mirror, you see a different version of yourself without that person. And it can take a long time to feel like life has given you enough joy to fill that void.

"But you and Lola have done that for Maren. And despite her nearly losing her life a month ago, I haven't seen my daughter look this alive since before Brandon died. So I want to thank you for taking a chance on my daughter. I know you're protective of Lola, so your decision to let Maren into your life could not have come easily."

I drop my head, staring at my dirty boots, one crossed over the other. "Loving your daughter has been effortless. Frighteningly so." I shake my head. "And she has breathed life back into Lola and me. But I feel like I'm asking too much of Maren to patiently wait while I help Lola work through her issues from her mother dying."

"I think you're underestimating both of our daughters."

I lift my gaze to Aaron's crooked grin.

"Lola brings the really good stuff out of Maren, and I think Maren does the same to Lola. I advise you to step aside and let the women in your life work through things together. You're spending too much time worrying that Maren will die and break Lola's heart or that Lola's slow recovery will hold Maren back from living her dreams. I promise you, those girls aren't half as worried as you are."

I think about his wise words and return a slow nod. "You could be right."

"I am." He slides on his reading glasses. "They were picking out paint colors because they decided on their own that Lola needs a room in this house."

I smile, and it feels incredible. "Thank you," I say.

Aaron glances up at me over his glasses. "For what?"

"For helping bring Maren into this world."

Aaron returns his attention to the book, but not without a content smile settling on his face.

I open the front door, and Lola's gaze shoots to mine. She's playing a card game on the floor with Maren's mom.

Lola taps her finger to her lips. "Shh. Maren's upstairs sleeping."

Colleen glances over her shoulder and smiles. "She should probably wake up soon, so she'll sleep tonight. Unless she has a late-night visitor." She smirks. Luckily, it goes over Lola's head.

I remove my boots and head toward the stairs. "I have no idea what you're talking about."

Colleen returns a drawn-out "Mm-hmm."

Maren's on her side, hugging a pillow, hair fanned out over the other pillow and lips parted as she softly snores.

I crawl sideways onto the bed and rest my cheek on Maren's legs.

She exhales a long breath and soft hum, teasing her fingers through my hair. "She redeemed herself, so you don't have to ground her."

I grin. "Is that so?"

"Yes."

"It's getting ready to rain. I have to go. But I'll consider your recommendation."

"Stay," she mumbles. "It's your job to woo me, but your plate is full, so I'll make an exception and woo you instead. Now get up here and kiss me."

I have a few things to say about her wooing, but they'll have to wait until I'm done kissing her. She snakes her hand up the inside of my shirt.

"You and Lola have no patience. She wants to roam the entire city on her bike like she's twenty, not ten. And you don't see that I've been wooing you since we met because you're too twitchy to see that I have my own wooing style."

Maren's gaze sweeps in all directions along my face as she nibbles on her lower lip. "Twitchy? I'm not twitchy or impatient."

I chuckle. "You are, and so is Lola."

"She stopped for doughnuts this morning."

"Gah!" I roll to my back and throw my arm over my head. "Don't tell me that. I have enough worries."

Maren laughs.

"Yet another thing that her therapist needs to discuss with her," I say.

"Move in with me." Maren reaches for my hand and kisses the back of it.

"We talked about this." I roll to my side and stroke her hair. "I think I need to wait until Lola's making more progress before I let Tia and Amos abandon us. Because that's what they'll do: move to Florida."

"Let them move. We've got this."

I narrow my eyes.

Maren grins.

"We?"

"Give her room to spread her wings, Ozzy. She wants it. Why do you think she rode her bike here? Maybe living with you *and* her grandparents is too much. Too restrictive. Maybe she needs a change. A new home. A tree house. A cat. And a badass female."

I love this woman. I just *love* her so damn much.

"I'm out for the season. I don't have to fly for Ted. By the time she returns to school, my bones will be healed. I can ride a bike. If I'm being honest, I'm not the best at baking cookies. Jamie made the cookies I brought to your work. But I love to kayak, hike, stargaze, and I've recently discovered I can crochet cat toys. And don't forget, I'm good at braiding hair."

"Dad? I'm hungry."

We startle at Lola in the doorway. She's sneaky in her own right. I should put a bell on her.

I sit up, and Lola smirks, clearly pleased to see me lying in bed with Maren. "Let's head home for dinner."

"I had fun with you today, Lola. Thanks for cleaning Bandit's litter box and helping my mom with my laundry," Maren says.

Lola bites her bottom lip to control her grin as she nods her reply.

"We have to talk about your rebellious adventure." I start to guide Lola out of the bedroom.

"Let me hug Maren before we go." Lola slides past to give Maren a gentle hug. "Did you tell him to go easy on me?" She attempts a whisper, but I hear every word.

Maren winks. "You'll be fine."

Lola turns and takes two steps before craning her neck to the side, eyes squinted. She pushes the door until it hits my foot. "Oh. My. Gosh." She covers her mouth. "Did you write on her door?"

"It's getting replaced," I say. "Let's go."

"It's not." Maren smirks.

Lola's gaze ping-pongs between us. "I can't believe you wrote her a note on her door."

"Go get your stuff together." I grab her shoulders and give her a nudge.

Lola giggles, bouncing down the stairs.

"You've set the bar high for any man who tries to steal her heart. They'll have a terrible time living up to her daddy." Maren slowly sits up, adjusting her sling.

"For sure." I roll my eyes. "If my daughter gets in a life-threatening accident, she needs a guy who will completely ghost her."

Maren frowns while standing. "Stop. We're done with that. I had a full thirty seconds of feeling let down when you hung up on me. Then my mom made me look at it from your point of view—her point of view. And that was it. I wasn't angry or disappointed. Okay, that's a lie. I'm human, but I'm not superhuman. But I've let it go, and you need to do the same. Okay?" She strolls to me, rests her forehead on my chest, and my arms instinctively go around her.

"Okay," I whisper.

"Are you moving in with me?"

I kiss the crown of her head. "I have to go. I'll check on you tomorrow. I love you."

"You're torturing me, Oswald. Why? Why do that?"

Chapter Forty-One

Lola pedals her ass off all the way home so that I can't have a conversation with her. Then she flies off her bike and runs into the house like I've removed my belt and threatened to redden her behind (which I have never done).

"I take it you had a long talk with her?" Tia asks, peeking at the lasagna in the oven as the magical garlic aroma makes me drool. "She didn't even look at me before running to her room."

I deposit my backpack on the hook by the back door and remove my boots. "She sped home. I didn't have the chance yet. And I wasn't going to have the conversation at Maren's house."

"Now that you're done working over there and she's doing better, it might be a good idea to put some distance between Lola and Maren. She's way too attached and comfortable."

"Distance?" I chuckle, stealing a cherry tomato from the big salad bowl and popping it into my mouth. "I'm thinking just the opposite."

"What's the opposite?" Tia asks, pointing to the knife in the sink. Amos rinses it off and hands it to her.

"I think Lola and I are going to move in with Maren."

Amos coughs and exits the kitchen with his tail between his legs while Tia slowly sets the knife on the counter and lifts her gaze from the cutting board. "This again? It's a huge mistake."

I nod several times. "Maybe. But you've been itching for me to push Lola to move forward and face her fears. I think this change could be a step in the right direction."

"A change? Shacking up with your girlfriend is a good change? Is she going to quit her job and be there for Lola like we are?"

"Well, it's summer. She's still recovering from the accident and therefore not flying until next spring, so yeah, she can be there for Lola when I'm working."

"And next spring? Then what? Is she retiring?"

"No. We'll figure that out when we get there," I say with pride because I no longer want to live in fear of the "what if" moments. That's not living at all.

Tia shakes her head. "Let me be very clear, Ozzy. We're not buying this house to be your safety net. If you do this, we are moving to Florida. And if it doesn't work out between the two of you or if next spring you're in a bind, it's on you. We're not swooping in to save you again. So if I were you, I'd think long and hard before making this your final decision."

"I feel bad for Lola that you make so much of this about me. All the conditions you put on our situation or arrangement that's supposed to be about her. But every single time, you make it about me. My lesson to learn. My punishment for an accident I didn't cause. I've never tried to be ungrateful. And the times that I've felt guilty for letting you help us, I've always tried to look at it like this is where you want to be—in Missoula with your only granddaughter. Is none of it for you? For Lola? Is it really *all* about me? A favor to me? A way to control me?"

"You knew, and you did nothing." She seethes, eyes reddening.

I narrow my eyes.

"You knew your father had a problem. Your poor mother is legally blind. You have a child you let see him at his worst. It wasn't an isolated incident. He habitually got drunk. He was an alcoholic, and *you knew it*. Yet you did nothing. Had you not been such a coward and so complacent, and if you'd have gotten him the help he needed, then he wouldn't have called Brynn. And she wouldn't have loaded Lola into the car to get his drunk ass that night. She would be here. Alive. And Lola wouldn't have those scars on her face. And she wouldn't be afraid to get into a car. A. Car! Ozzy, do you get it? Do you get how messed up this is that your daughter won't ride in a car? You've physically and emotionally disabled her. You've had the biggest hand in ruining her life. And you think screwing some other woman and playing house with her and her cat is going to fix it. Fix Lola? Are you delusional?"

"Jesus Christ, Tia!" I throw my water glass across the kitchen, and it shatters against the fridge.

She flinches.

"Brynn is dead, but I didn't kill her. And no matter what you do to try and punish me, it won't bring her back. If this is about misery loving company, then I don't know what to tell you because my misery only makes Lola's life worse. Maren isn't some woman I want to 'shack up with.' I love her. And I'm sorry if that hurts you, but I'm not sorry for loving her. And I'm not sorry that Lola loves her too. And Maren is a good person who *adores* Lola beyond words. What is so fucking wrong with that?"

"Watch your mouth!"

Amos returns, holding up his hands. "Let's take this down a notch."

"You're a miserable human being," I say to Tia, narrowing my eyes.

Tia lunges for me as if she has a prayer at doing physical harm, but Amos holds her back.

"Go," he says to me.

MAREN

Ozzy: It's Lola. I'm using my dad's phone. Can u pick me up?

It's my first night out since I've been home. After Ozzy and Lola left, my parents decided to take me to dinner. As we finish our steaks, I stare at my phone.

Maren: Where are you?

Ozzy: Home

Ozzy: Dad and Nana are fighting about me

Maren: What do you mean by pick you up?

Ozzy: Take me to your house

Maren: I can't ride a bike yet. Do you want me to come over? I can sneak around the back of the house.

Ozzy: No. Just come get me. I don't want to be here

"Who are you texting?" Mom asks.

"Lola. She wants me to come get her, but I told her I can't ride my bike yet. Apparently, Ozzy and her grandma Tia are arguing."

"I could ride your bike over there," Dad offers.

"It's getting dark. I don't have a light on my bike." I frown, staring at my phone screen, trying to figure out how to help her.

Ozzy: Come get me in your car

I read her message over and over.

"How far is Ozzy's from your place? Could I drive your car, and your dad and Lola ride behind us?" Mom suggests.

"She wants to ride in my vehicle," I murmur slowly, just above a whisper.

"Are you sure?" Mom asks.

I show them the message.

They return wide-eyed gazes.

"Aaron, get the check," Mom says.

Minutes later, we're on our way to Ozzy's. I don't want to take off with Lola without Ozzy's permission, but I also don't want to pass up this opportunity if Lola's feeling extra brave tonight.

Maren: We're on our way. See you in five minutes. I'll pick you up on the street

As I give my dad directions from the back seat, I can't stop my knee from bouncing, my hands from fidgeting, or my heart from racing.

"There she is," I point to the sidewalk where she's waiting, closer to the neighbor's driveway, out of view from the front window of her house.

I open the door and slide over so she can step into my RAV. "Hey" is all I say as she nervously nibbles her bottom lip and wrings her hands in front of her, staring at the empty seat. I'm afraid to move another inch or say anything.

Lola glances behind her and back into my vehicle, and tears fill her eyes. "M-Mom said the middle is the m-most safe. But I-I wanted to sit behind her s-so I could see my grandpa."

"Do you want me to go inside the house with you?" I ask.

She slowly shakes her head. "If I do this"—her lower lip breaks free from her teeth and trembles like her voice—"they'll stop fighting."

I'm so conflicted. Do I let this happen? Do I encourage her to get into a car out of fear that they won't stop fighting? Will Ozzy be upset if I let this happen? What if we get into an accident? He'd never forgive me. I'd never forgive myself. I can't control other drivers like I couldn't control the weather in Canada. But my dad is an incredibly safe driver, and we don't have to go but a few miles and nothing over thirty-five. Still . . .

Just as my fear and self-doubt start to win, I open my mouth to tell Lola it's not the right time and this isn't the way to get anyone to stop fighting. But she climbs into the back seat, in the middle next to me, and fastens her seat belt. One of her hands grips the edge of the seat while her other reaches for my hand, holding on for dear life.

My parents angle their bodies, gazing back at us.

"Let's go home," I whisper, stroking my thumb against her hand.

No one says a word as my dad drives five under the speed limit back to my house. When we're parked in the garage, my parents climb out, but Lola doesn't move. Mom eyes me with her door still open. I give her a tiny grin, hoping she'll close the door and go inside the house.

They do.

Lola and I sit idle and silent for at least another five minutes. Then she eases her grip on my hand and exhales so profoundly that her relief also drains my lungs.

"I did it," she whispers.

And maybe it's not the best timing, but I don't have any control over the tears that spring from my eyes.

I need to text Ozzy and tell him the good news. I also need to let him know that I have Lola, and she hasn't gone missing or been kidnapped.

"Why are you crying?" Lola asks, unbuckling her seat belt.

I wipe my eyes. "Just . . ." I swallow past the lump in my throat, repeatedly shaking my head. "Happy." I try to laugh instead of sob while wiping my eyes. "I'm just happy." My complete sentence escapes as a whisper.

"I can't wait to tell Bandit I rode in a car." Lola climbs out the opposite side and runs into the house.

I stay in the back seat and take a few deep breaths before fishing my phone from my purse.

Chapter Forty-Two

OZZY

"Lola, dinner's ready," I call while towel drying my hair after a shower to cool my temper.

"Lola," I call again, knocking on her door two times before opening it. She's not in her room. I check the rest of the basement.

"Lola," I call again on my way up the stairs. "Is she up here?" I ask Amos when I round the corner into the dining room, because I'm not talking to Tia.

He shrugs and shakes his head. I frown while pivoting.

After checking the back and front yards, the garage for her bike, and calling her name a half dozen times outside, I return to the house with my fucking heart ready to explode.

Amos and Tia have started their own search in the house. She's not here. I checked everywhere.

"Did she go to one of the neighbors?" Amos asks when he reaches the top of the stairs. "Maybe she heard the arguing and decided to go to a friend's house."

I shake my head. "None of her friends live nearby, and her bike is still here."

Jesus. Where is my child?

My phone rings. I can barely hear it because it's downstairs. I fly in that direction, quickly answering Maren's call. "I have to call you back, sorry. Lola's missing, and I need to—"

"She's with me."

I shake my head. "What? No. Her bike is here. Are you here?" I turn in a circle. What am I missing? Is this a joke? Are they hiding?

Maren sniffles, and it's like a gut punch. Something is wrong. "What happened to her? Just tell me." I run a frustrated hand through my hair.

"She texted me and said you and Tia were fighting. She wanted me to come get her, but I told her I couldn't ride a bike yet. And—"

"Maren! Dammit! Is my daughter okay?" My voice cracks because this feeling in my gut is unbearably painful. It's the "Your wife is dead" or the "Your girlfriend's plane crashed" feeling.

"Yes, Ozzy. She's fine. We picked her up *in my RAV* and drove her back to my house because that's what she wanted."

I turn toward my bedroom door, where Tia and Amos are waiting. Tia has tears in her eyes, and her hand is cupped over her mouth. She knows something is wrong from my outburst, and she sees the panic on my face.

"What?" I whisper.

Maren laughs, or maybe she's crying. I can't tell. "Ozzy, Lola got into a vehicle, and I know she was scared but so damn brave too. And I didn't push her to do it. She decided all on her own. I wanted to call you but didn't want to jinx it or make her change her mind, so we just went with it. I wasn't driving, my dad was, but he's a very safe driver, and . . ." She trails off, out of breath, her words chasing one another like the world's longest run-on sentence.

She sniffles. "When we got here, I sat in the back seat with her for five minutes before she whispered, 'I did it,' unbuckled, and ran into my house to tell Bandit." Maren releases another laughing sob. "She wanted to tell the cat first. The *cat*, Ozzy." She laughs some more.

"What is it?" Tia steps into my room, blotting her eyes, face contorted with worry. "Tell us!"

I slowly shake my head and whisper, "She's fine."

Ghosts aren't my thing. I've never believed in them, and there's never been a day where I felt a dead person's presence. Sometimes, I've hoped Brynn was seeing something, like Lola striking out a batter in softball, but I've never *felt* her—until now.

"She's fine, Ozzy. You're both going to be just fine," Brynn whispers as if she were alive with her lips at my ear.

Over the next week, Tia and Amos pack their belongings. As much as I've looked forward to this day, it's bittersweet.

"She's what you need," Tia says while we watch from the porch as Lola follows Amos to the moving truck with the last box.

"I know. You've said this repeatedly." I sigh.

Tia rests her hand on my back. "I'm not talking about Lola. I'm talking about Maren."

I glance at Tia while she keeps her teary-eyed gaze on the moving truck.

She smiles, dropping her hand from my back to blot the corners of her eyes. "I hope you never lose a child. It changes you. Losing a child crushes your heart beyond repair. When the life you brought into this world leaves before you, happiness dies, and the emptiness in your chest fills with anger as you try to make sense of the incomprehensible."

She swallows hard and clears her throat. "Ozzy, I'm sorry. I hate the woman I am without my daughter. I hate that I can't stop blaming you for what wasn't your fault. It's like"—she shakes her head—"the burden to make it make sense is too much because it doesn't make sense. Unless . . ."

I do something I haven't done since Brynn died.

I turn toward Brynn's grief-stricken mother and hug her. "Unless you can put the blame on me."

Tia's body shakes with sobs while her fingers clench my shirt.

"It's okay," I whisper. "I can take it from you. I can't bring her back, but I can carry the burden."

She releases me, quickly wiping her face. Tia doesn't let herself fall apart for long. Her pride won't allow it.

"Maren will never be Lola's mom." She eyes me as if this is a fact that I need to acknowledge.

I slowly nod.

"But it's okay if Lola is her daughter. I want—I *need*—to believe that a strong, brave woman will walk beside Lola while she navigates some tough years ahead. And I believe Maren is that person. I see the way she looks at her."

I smile. "Maren fell in love with Lola before she fell in love with me."

Tia doesn't laugh, but her lips quirk into a grin.

"Pa said I can come visit anytime I want to," Lola says, skipping toward the porch.

She's free, and it's beautiful.

"I insist on it," Tia replies, giving Lola a big hug. "And we'll be back to visit. Lots of visits."

Amos rests a hand on my shoulder and gives me the everything-is-good smile.

"I can't . . ." I press my lips together for a few seconds and swallow past the emotion. There have been so many times over the past nine or so months that I've wanted to lose it with them. The guilt and feeling like a failure as a husband and father have created an unhinged version of myself I barely recognized at times. But it doesn't change the love they've given to Lola and to me by being here. I clear my throat. "I can't find the right words to thank you for putting your life on pause to help us through this."

"We didn't pause anything. Being with our granddaughter will always be a gift. And as much as it saddens us to leave, we know that you need time to write your next chapter. And you know what they say, absence makes the heart grow fonder." Tia reaches for my face and gives me a kiss on the cheek. "You're a good dad, Ozzy," she whispers in my ear. "And a good man."

Fuck. Not her. Tia is not allowed to make me cry. So I turn. "Let me give the house one more quick check to make sure you haven't forgotten anything."

I should have done more to help my father deal with his drinking problem. Brynn should be alive. Sometimes, life feels like nothing more than a repetition of would'ves, could'ves, and should'ves.

Instead of dwelling on everything I cannot change, I focus on today. Tia and Amos are leaving us for Florida.

And as soon as they pull out of the driveway, Maren will be here to take me to reclaim my Land Rover from Diego.

◆ ◆ ◆

The shock on Diego's face is priceless when we pull into his driveway with Lola in the center back seat of Maren's RAV. She's still not relaxed like a limp noodle, but she's improving. And music helps distract her. Today, we're listening to Taylor Swift's "Love Story," which she's been requesting a lot over the past few days. And every time I peek in the rearview mirror, she smirks and makes a laughable, although adorable, attempt at winking, especially during the "marry me" part of the lyrics.

She's anything but subtle.

Diego saunters toward us from the garage, wiping his hands on a rag. He has a blue Dodge Challenger on his lift.

"Am I seeing what I think I'm seeing?" he asks as we step out of the vehicle.

With a shit-eating grin, I nod. "Diego, this is Maren."

"It's great to meet you finally." He holds up his palms. "I'd shake your hand, but I'm a little greasy. I've heard so much about you." Diego gives me a look, and I know what he's specifically referencing because he's a guy.

"It's a pleasure to meet you too finally," she says.

"Is Kai inside?" Lola asks without hesitation, skipping straight toward the house.

"She is. Go on in," Diego says. "Cheyenne's at the store. She'll be so disappointed she missed you."

I shrug. "We'll be back. I'm just here to get my vehicle."

Diego's face nearly splits in half as he smiles. "I'm so fucking happy for you, man." He shifts his gaze to Maren and clears his throat. "Sorry. I'm so very happy for you."

She chuckles. "It's fine. I'm really fucking happy for him too."

Diego winks. "I like her, Oz. She's a keeper." He pivots.

I take Maren's hand, and we follow him into the garage, where he nabs my keys from a hook inside a cabinet.

"I'm going to miss Debbie," he says, handing me the keys.

"Debbie?" Maren narrows her eyes.

"Diego named my Land Rover Defender Debbie," I say, leading her behind the garage to *Debbie*.

"This is your vehicle?" Maren asks with a shocked expression. "It's . . ."

I offer her multiple choices. "A classic? Beautiful? Magnificent?"

She mumbles with a nervous laugh and a tiny headshake, "Unexpected."

"All the best things in life are." I kiss her forehead, which makes her blush before I open the front passenger door for her. "Tell Lola I'm leaving without her if she doesn't get her buns out here."

Diego laughs, glancing at his watch. "It's almost noon. I'm going to take a break for lunch. I'll make Lola something too. Why don't you take the afternoon for yourselves? It's a gorgeous day for a Sunday drive."

"She won't even know I'm gone," I say, shutting Maren's door and making my way to the other side. "I owe you one. Hell, I probably owe you a million."

Diego tucks his thumbs in the back pockets of his dirty jeans. "Oz?"

I start to open my door. "Yeah?"

His usual smart-ass expression vanishes, replaced with a sincere smile that guys rarely give to each other. "I'm happy for you."

I nod several times. "Thanks."

"A Sunday drive?" Maren says when I climb into my Rover.

I slip on my sunglasses. "Nothing beats a Sunday drive," I say as Debbie starts right up. "My parents used to take Sunday drives before my mom lost most of her sight and my dad traded the great outdoors for a barstool. I remember my mom rolling down the window, tipping her head back, eyes closed, and smiling as the wind hit her face and played in her hair." I pull out of the driveway.

"Let's pick up your mom."

I glance at Maren. "Seriously?"

She shrugs. "I haven't met her. She doesn't have to see well to feel the breeze on her face and hair."

"You want to meet my mom today? Now?"

"You said it: one day at a time. I want to meet your mom and tell her how in love I am with her son and how much I adore her granddaughter beyond words. Then I want to meet your sister Jenny and her husband. And we should take Lola to a tearoom in London for her birthday. I might even know a rich guy with a jet who'd happily loan it to us."

I focus on the vibration beneath me and the hum of the wind and tires. But I don't smile. "I feel like you're trying to outwoo me again. So impatient."

She bites her bottom lip when I shoot her a sidelong glance.

"For the next few hours, you're mine. All mine. I know a place where we can park and get naked in the back seat. Then I'll show you my secret spot to pick huckleberries. And then we'll pick up my mom and Lola for dinner. After that, we'll take a sunset drive before returning my mom to her place. Jenny's pregnant and due to have her first child in a few months, so we'll see her after the baby arrives. And as for London, well, you've left me speechless on that one."

Maren sighs. "I'm not done with physical therapy, but we can still get naked. Huckleberries sound pretty serious. I think they trump wildflowers." She narrows her eyes. "And when are you and Lola moving in with me?"

I shrug. "I think it will happen when you marry me."

She freezes. I don't turn my head, but through the corner of my eye, I can see her holding stone still. I take great pride in her reaction.

"You, uh, you're . . ." She clears her throat. "Are you asking me to marry you?"

"No." I pull off the road into a parking area at a trailhead. "I'm not asking you to marry me." I put my Rover in *park*, unbuckle, and angle my body to face hers. "But you are stealing all the moments. Saying I love you first. Asking me to move in with you. Suggesting you meet my mom and sister. London for Lola's birthday. You got the cat my daughter wanted. And you were the one to ride with her in a car for the first time in over two years."

Maren deflates with a tiny wince.

"So I'm calling dibs on this. Okay? Dibs on proposing. I'm not proposing today. It's not on tomorrow's agenda either. But *I* will be the one to propose. You have to give me something. So, for once, I need you to sit back, let me do the wooing, and let me decide when the epic moment will happen. Are you capable of that?"

Still, she keeps her gaze out the front window while slowly nodding and rolling her lips between her teeth. It does little to hide her amusement. So either she's silently mocking me or suppressing her excitement.

She grips the fixed door handle, squeezing it so tightly her knuckles are white. "We're getting married," she whispers, but it's tight, like air squeezing out of an innertube, shaking her whole body.

I pull a Lola and roll my eyes. "It's possible. Maybe. Someday. One never knows."

"Ozzy—"

"Shut up. Just shut up." I grin while grabbing her face and kissing her.

Epilogue

During October, Maren and I take short flights around Montana on the weekends, where I'm reminded flying will always be part of who she is.

And Lola finds a new passion.

"I'm going to be a pilot just like Maren," she says, taking both our hands while we walk to the hangar after a day trip to Bozeman.

"Why not a mechanic?" I ask.

"Ew, you have dirty fingernails. Maren wears pretty polish."

We laugh at Lola's strong reasoning.

"And when I have a baby brother or sister, I'm going to teach them how to fly."

I stiffen, waiting a few seconds to sneak a peek at Maren. Will Lola ever stop embarrassing me? Putting me on the spot? Planning out my future?

"Are you rescuing another cat?" I laugh it off.

Lola releases our hands and turns toward us, walking backward. "When you get married, Maren will have a baby. She's going to want her own, ya know. That's what Dakota's mom said."

"Dakota? Your friend from school?" Maren asks.

"Dakota, the bane of my existence," I mumble.

"Twins would be cool," Lola chirps, spinning in a circle. "Then I could have one to hold all the time, and you two could share the other one." She beams.

I'm so out of my depth, it's impossible to formulate a real reply. Maren and I haven't talked about kids other than Lola. And I haven't proposed, even though she's surely expecting it since I called dibs on proposing.

"Hi, Sean!" Lola runs toward the security guard she's befriended at the entrance to the building.

"Sorry. She has no filter." I take Maren's hand, but I can't look at her.

"It's refreshing," she says. "Some people think I don't have one either."

"You love your job, and—"

"I want whatever you'll give me, Ozzy." Maren steps in front of me, so I stop. "I want to fly planes and put out fires. I want to braid hair and go to softball games. I want to show Lola that she can do and be anything in life. That's what her mom did. Right?"

I nod.

"We have a home. A cat. A tree house. A curly-haired blond. We watch Disney movies and eat doughnuts on the weekends. Every week, I have a girls-only lunch with Lola, your mom, and Ruth. *Anything* you're willing to share with me, to give me, I'm in." She grabs my shirt and kisses me.

"Stop kissing. I'm hungry," Lola calls. "Gah! You're always kissing."

I don't stop kissing Maren, but we grin.

The next two months fly by with Lola turning eleven, Thanksgiving, and a wedding.

Fitz and Jamie have a holiday wedding, with ten inches of new snow and a very excited junior bridesmaid. They asked Lola to be the flower girl, but she thought junior bridesmaid sounded better—because Dakota's mom said eleven was too old for a flower girl.

Maren is the maid of honor. And I'm the guy tasked with keeping Will from getting drunk and sleeping with a doctor named Everleigh Reichart and breaking her heart for a second time.

Everything goes as planned, until the bouquet is tossed, and Lola catches it and gives it to Maren. "Now my dad has to marry you."

For the record, I have a ring in my pocket, but there's no way I'm letting the women in my life tell me when and where I'll propose.

"If you catch the bouquet and give it away, the person you give it to is cursed to a single life with cats and knitted toys for the rest of her life," I say.

Lola wrinkles her nose and opens her mouth while Maren laughs and hands the bouquet back to Lola. "You'd better keep it. I'm hoping to one day meet my Prince Charming."

Lola rolls her eyes. "Duh. He's right in front of you. And he even got a—"

I cover her mouth with my hand. She's the best, but also the worst. Lola can't keep a secret. I knew letting her pick out the ring was a mistake.

"Go find Will." I point across the dance floor. "He's talking to the dark-haired lady, but he owes you a dance."

Lola huffs. "Fine."

Maren bites back her grin.

"Don't give me that look," I say. "She's a pill and so are you. Both of you in your red tulip dresses are *pills*."

"I didn't do anything." She giggles before sipping her wine. "And it's a tulip-effect skirt in *mulberry* velvet, not red." She runs her hand over the *mulberry* dress that has a satin ribbon around the waist.

She's so beautiful I can barely breathe.

"You are handsome in this suit." She straightens my tie with one hand before feathering her fingertips down the length of it.

I might drop Lola off at my mom's later so I can have Maren in *all* the ways I want her.

"Jamie is a stunning bride. And Fitz has never looked happier," Maren says, watching her friends dance to Kacey Musgraves's "Space Cowboy."

I take her glass and set it on the table; then I lead her to the dance floor and pull her to me, slowly swaying in a circle. "I hadn't noticed Jamie. I'll take your word for it."

Maren gazes into my eyes. "I wonder if your mom would let Lola spend the night."

I chuckle and kiss her forehead. "Baby, I'm two steps ahead of you."

After the song ends, I call Ruth to make sure she and my mom are okay with us bringing Lola to the house so late. Then we stay until the end, seeing the happy couple off.

"You're going to Grandma's for the night. Ruth's getting you doughnuts in the morning," I announce when we climb into my Land Rover.

"Why?" Lola asks with a yawn.

Maren shoots me a wide-eyed gaze with her lips in a tight smile.

"It's late, so you need to sleep in tomorrow morning, but Maren and I are going to get up early to do some deep cleaning around the house."

"Oh." Lola yawns again. "I thought it was because you wanted to have sex without me there. Dakota's mom sends him to his dad's when she has a guy stay at their house."

Fucking Dakota's mom.

"Well, we're just cleaning house." I double down on my lie because I refuse to tell my eleven-year-old that I want to have kitchen sex, sofa sex, stairs sex, bathroom sex, and loud, headboard-banging bedroom sex with her new role model.

Lola mumbles an okay and falls asleep before we get to my mom's.

And by the time we pull into Maren's house (our house), she's asleep too.

I carry her inside and set her on her feet at the bottom of the stairs. Dropping Lola off was all for nothing. Maren looks so groggy.

"I'm going to check Bandit's water and shut off the lights. I'll be up in a bit," I say.

Maren nods and mumbles something I can't hear. I think it's "Okay."

After checking Bandit's water, I unknot my tie and start to slide my jacket off my shoulders while making my way to the stairs through the kitchen.

"Slow down," Maren says, standing next to the fridge, wearing nothing but a strapless dark-red bra and a black lace thong. "I like watching you undress." She scrapes her teeth along her lower lip. "Do you like watching me undress?"

I grin, *slowly* unbuttoning my white dress shirt. It's going to be a long night.

◆ ◆ ◆

I'm an idiot.

This is stupid.

I've managed to trick Maren into thinking dandelions are the world's best flower. What are the chances that she'll find this endearing and romantic? With Lola at my mom's and my brain fuzzy from practically no sleep, I let impulse drive my actions.

I slide the folded squares of toilet paper under the bathroom door. She's on the toilet. I can hear her peeing.

Yeah, this is already an epic failure, but I can't stop now.

"Ozzy," she laughs. "What are you doing? I'm going to the bathroom, and I'm so tired. I'm coming back to bed for actual sleep this time."

"I thought you might need toilet paper," I say.

She snorts. "I'm good. There are a half dozen rolls under the sink. Oh my god, you wrote on the toilet paper?" She laughs at my message.

Three words in the correct order: I love you

"I love you too," she says with a giggle before flushing the toilet.

I stare at the things in my hands and shake my head. Was I high when I thought of this? On a sex high? It's the only explanation, but I slide the sanitary napkin under the door anyway while Maren washes her hands.

It says: *Will you marry me?*

Then I quickly shove the diamond ring with a tampon in it under the door too.

The water stops running.

Everything's quiet.

Dammit!

What was I thinking?

I get down on one knee. Then I stand. Maybe I should have put on a T-shirt; I'm just in my underwear. As the door opens, I opt to take a knee again.

The tears in Maren's eyes make them appear a brighter shade of blue. I love all her emotions and how each one shows a different side of her beauty.

She pulls out the tampon and slides the ring onto her finger. Her hair is a mess, and she's naked under the blue throw blanket from the bed.

"Is that a yes?" I ask. "You put the ring on. No take-backs."

She nods a half dozen times and releases those tears.

"You have to say it." I smirk.

"You first." She presses her palm to my cheek, letting the blanket fall from her body.

"Will you marry me?"

"Yes," she whispers.

I'm in awe of this woman—her talent, love, patience, and perseverance. I will never stop thinking of myself as a fortunate man despite life's tragedies. It's never the things I see coming that take my breath away. It's the moments that come from nowhere.

A lost wallet.

A car accident.

And an empty toilet paper roll.

ACKNOWLEDGMENTS

There are so many technical parts to getting a manuscript into readers' hands that I often overlook the most important people in my life when writing my acknowledgments. Leslie and Dan, my loving parents and number one fans, thank you for guiding me through this messy life. Your love has inspired many of my characters, especially in books like this one, where I needed to convey a parent's love. I must equally acknowledge my husband and three beautiful boys for allowing me to be a mom and experience the greatest love imaginable.

During the book-writing process, I have random thoughts, mini breakdowns, brain fog, bouts of loneliness, and a frequent need to share things that make me laugh. Thank you to this special group of women for letting me share these vulnerable moments. Jyl, Jenn, Shauna, Nina, Kambra, and my lovely mom, you piece me together when I fall apart. You always listen and know the right things to say, and I know I take way more than I give. I love you.

Lauren Plude and Georgana Grinstead, thank you for working together to make my publishing dreams come true. Collaborating with kind souls who "get" my writing and want to see me succeed is a gift.

My editing team with Montlake has been phenomenal. I was initially apprehensive about having my words scrutinized by such an experienced group of experts. However, Mackenzie Walton and Katherine Kirk, you have not only edited my work but also mentored me through this process with kindness and professionalism. Your guidance has been instrumental in shaping this book, and I am grateful for the privilege of working with you.

The team at Montlake / Amazon Publishing, though too numerous to mention individually, has played a crucial role in bringing this book and this series to life. I am deeply grateful for your support and contributions, and I thank each and every one of you for your part in this journey.

Finally, I'm eternally grateful to my readers for taking a chance on my stories. Your love, enthusiasm, and generosity in posting reviews and recommending my books leave me speechless.

ABOUT THE AUTHOR

Jewel E. Ann is a *Wall Street Journal* and *USA Today* bestselling author. She's written over thirty novels, including *Look the Part*, a contemporary romance; the Jack & Jill trilogy, a romantic suspense series; and *Before Us*, an emotional women's fiction story.

Ann is a free-spirited romance junkie with a quirky sense of humor. After her best friend of nearly thirty years suggested a few books from the contemporary romance genre, she was hooked. With ten years of flossing lectures under her belt, she took an early retirement from her dental-hygiene career to stay home with her three awesome boys, manage the family business, and write mind-bending love stories. When she's not donning her cape to save the planet one tree at a time, Jewel enjoys yoga with friends, good food with family, rock climbing with her kids, and of course . . . heart-wrenching, tear-jerking, panty-scorching novels. She's living her best life in Iowa with her husband, three sons, and a goldendoodle.